Chronicles of the Clandestine Knights
HYACINTH BLUE

by Tony Nunes

Nunes Brothers Productions

Special thanks to Steve Nunes for his contributions to Cad's history, Christine Nunes for listening patiently to thousands of ideas, and Anna Nunes for heading up the sales department. Thanks also to the following: Gabriel & Susanah Ruhl, Skip Ronneberg, Brad Karhu, Andy Herzog, Brent Boyd, Alicia Hayes, Dave Venegas, and Craig Parker.

Questions & comments to
Tony Nunes
P.O. Box 5304
Chico, CA 95927
www.clandestineknights.com

NB
NUNES BROTHERS PRODUCTIONS
Chronicles of the Clandestine Knights
Hyacinth Blue
2nd Edition © 2005
© 2003 by Tony Nunes
All Rights Reserved
Printed in the U.S.A.

Maps & Illustrations by Michael Nunes
Cover by Renee Boyd

ISBN-13:   978-0-9773963-1-3
ISBN-10:   0-9773963-1-2
Library of Congress Control Number 2003102094

Nunes Brothers Productions

For Zephyr, Cad and Novak
"Pariter En Caelum Ego Precor"

In memory of Louis 'Bud' Boise
1918–2005

CONTENTS

Map of Astorian Realms

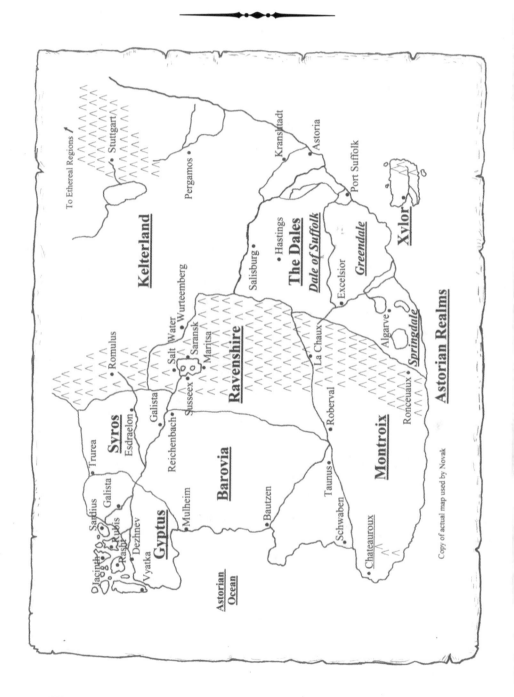

To Ethereal Regions

Stuttgart

Pergamos

Kranshtadt

Astoria

Port Suffolk

Kelterland

Hastings

Salisburg

The Dales

Dale of Suffolk

Greendale

Excelsior

Xylor

Salt Water

Wurteemberg

Saransk

Maritsa

Ravenshire

La Chaux

Algarve

Springdale

Romulus

Sussex

Roberval

Ronceuaux

Astorian Realms

Galista

Reichenbach

Barovia

Montroix

Trurea

Syros

Esdraelon

Taunus

Galista

Sardius

Mulheim

Bautzen

Schwaben

Djacinth

Kubis

Ragu

Dezhnev

Vyatka

Gyptus

Chateauroux

Astorian Ocean

Copy of actual map used by Novak

MAP OF XYLOR

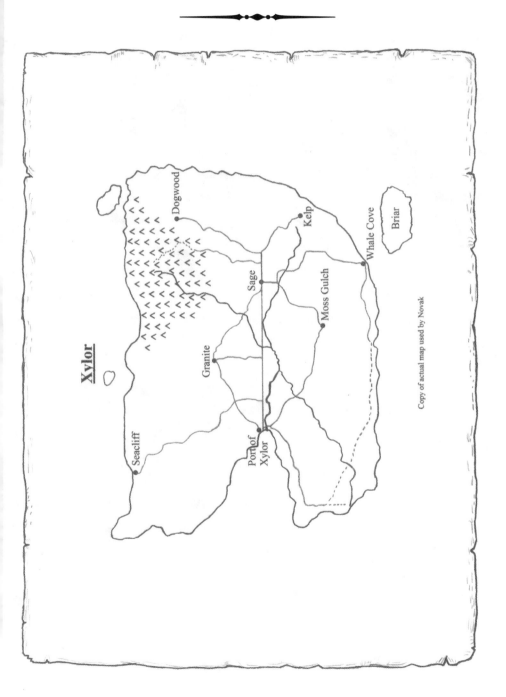

Xylor

Seacliff
Granite
Port of Xylor
Dogwood
Sage
Kelp
Moss Gulch
Whale Cove
Briar

Copy of actual map used by Novak

MAP OF RAVENSCLAW

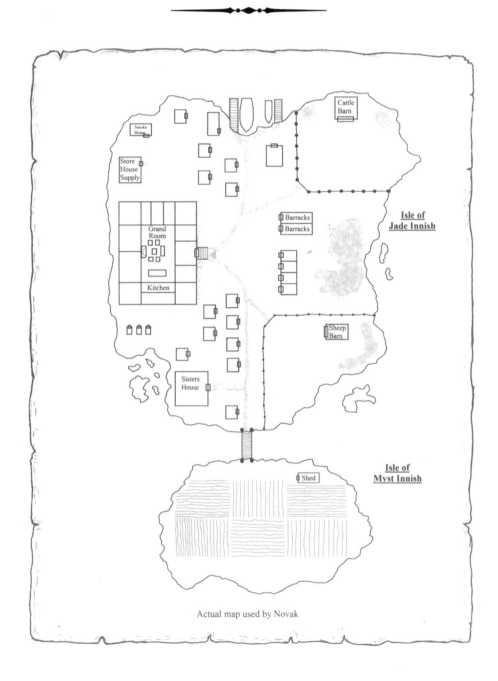

Smoke House

Store House Supply

Grand Room

Kitchen

Sisters House

Cattle Barn

Barracks
Barracks

Sheep Barn

Isle of Jade Innish

Isle of Myst Innish

Shed

Actual map used by Novak

PREFACE

WHAT DO YOU say when someone is willing to sacrifice their life to save yours? How could you ever repay them? When someone lays down all to liberate a people, no words, no reward, no honor bestowed could ever balance the account.

I've often thought about that in the years since the four strangers first appeared as unknowing deliverers. Obedient to a divine calling, they rescued a forlorn people. And history didn't care.

It's been said a true knight is born of nobility and is well educated in the social graces. I have to disagree. Knights are forged by fiery trials. They are ordinary people who respond courageously to extraordinary circumstances. They stand against tremendous opposition to do what is right. They are faithful and loyal when others have failed. How can you ever thank them?

All I can do is to tell their story….

PROLOGUE

———•◆•———

THUNDER RUMBLED OVER the small island and city of
Xylor and echoed off the mountains as the first spring storm
blew in from sea. Lightning sizzled across the sky and briefly
illuminated a shadowy figure in the alleyway. His burgundy
tabard whipped violently as he moved cat-like toward a darkened
window, his black hair tousled by the wind. He paused to glance
back as if he heard a noise somewhere in the black of night.
Another flash of lightning strobed over his chiseled, olive features.
Steel-gray eyes peered from beneath well-defined eyebrows,
carefully taking in their surroundings.

A thick, cloudy darkness swallowed the island and stifled its
usual bustle. Wind howled through tightly-closed shutters playing
mournful tunes for the hunkered-down townsfolk. Wooden
structures creaked and groaned under the storm's pressure. Leaves,
straw, and other debris tumbled down the streets. Few citizens of
Xylor would venture far from their warm fires on such a night, so
the mysterious movements of the figure in the alley were without
witness, save one.

Artois, as was his custom, had imbibed far too much ale
during the previous evening's card game. It was a routine oft

repeated. After losing all his money, he had angrily stomped off, vowing once again to exact revenge next payday. It was a threat his card mates counted on Artois trying to follow through with. Too drunk to make it home, he found a secluded alley where he collapsed near some empty, rickety crates. The moist dirt felt good under his weary frame; the wind cooled his flushed face. The alcohol made him oblivious to the cold, giving him a false sense of warmth.

Several three-storied wooden buildings towered on either side, looming over the narrow alley. Barrels sat below drainpipes waiting to be filled. A staircase rose skyward a short distance from Artois's feet, its wooden banister in need of repair. He stared catatonically into the starless sky. The surrounding buildings swayed to and fro. Artois shut his eyes tight in an attempt to quell his nausea. Being seasick on dry land had become a way of life and the fishy smell from a nearby warehouse did little to help his condition. Except for the stranger and Artois, this was a lonely alley. In the wee hours of the night in the tavern district, most alleys held little but solitude and despair. This one was no different.

A sudden gust of wind unlatched a shutter and slammed it against a wall. The noise startled Artois into a slightly higher state of alertness. It was then that he saw the strange figure breach an open alley window. Artois quickly tried to blink some of the stupor from his bloodshot eyes and raised his quivering head. Whoever it was moved fast. Looking hard, he tried to see the figure in the window, but like an apparition it was gone. Artois plopped his head back down, taxed by the effort to keep it raised.

A fragment of memory came to mind. Had the figure that slipped into the alley window been standing next to him a minute earlier? The man was wearing a burgundy tabard if Artois's foggy memory served him correctly. He vaguely recalled the figure bending down to look at him briefly. Yes, Artois could clearly see those dark eyes take him in with a piercing stare. He could remember the sound of boots walking away. He wondered if this was the same man he had seen climb into the alley window. They looked the same. But then again, maybe these events happened on different days. Artois couldn't be quite sure. There had been several nights where he awoke to find someone hunched over him, often times rifling through his pockets. That was how he had lost his shoes once. It hurt his head to try to analyze the incident. He wiggled his toes. His shoes were still there.

Artois drifted off again only to be awakened a few moments later by the sound of a scuffle. Something heavy scraped against wood and a chair creaked. The sounds came from the window the figure had crawled through. He heard a loud thump and what sounded like pottery shattering. A foot stomped, and then there was a loud cough. A muffled voice and another thump followed it. Then all was eerily quiet. For a moment there was peace in the alley again. It was short-lived.

A few minutes later an alley door opened. Artois wearily lifted his head and forced his eyes open. Everything was blurry and squinting didn't help. All he wanted was some sleep, and he couldn't get any as long as people were going to use his alley as a main thoroughfare. Another flash of lightning briefly revealed a man wearing the blue uniform of a Royal guard. He carried a burlap sack. Closing the door, the soldier walked out onto the street, likely on his way to stand late watch. The Royal guards were always up to something, little of it good as far as Artois was concerned. Why should this soldier be any different? He had already awakened Artois.

The wind still slapped that shutter against the wall, and now someone lit a candle and placed it near a window. What would be next? Artois was getting perturbed. The candlelight hurt his eyes, and made his head throb. A horse whinnied in the distance. People were coming and going at all hours of the night. Artois just wanted to be left alone. Usually people went out of their way to avoid him. He thought about moving to another alley but couldn't muster the motivation. He was too tired. Instead, he crawled wobbly-legged to a nearby crate. To make matters worse,

Artois cut his knee on a sharp rock as he crawled. He paused to finger his knee. It appeared to be minor and should stop bleeding on its own. Either way, the wound would have to wait till morning.

Artois turned a crate on its side and flopped down inside. He cursed this miserable alley and draped an arm over his eyes to block that blasted candle. The sky lit up like it was daytime. A loud burst of thunder rumbled through town. It would be a long night. He slipped in and out of sleep in his makeshift shelter. The crate was hard on his back but it helped block the wind. It would come in handy if it rained.

The mysterious figure never reappeared. Artois didn't know if the stranger was a burglar or had simply locked himself out. He didn't dwell on the peculiar behavior. Many seedy characters passed through the island port, and the docks attracted some of the most unsavory ones. Many strange things happened in Xylor. All sorts of illicit activities were conducted at all hours of the night, and it was often better not to know too much. Artois was good at not knowing too much. No one else emerged from the alley doors, but that candle burned all night long. Artois wrote the incident off as just another odd occurrence in an already eerie night.

I

—◆—

"I'LL FREEZE TO death before this night is through!" A sentry in the crow's nest grumbled and blew warm air into his hands trying to regain some feeling in his numb fingers. They ached when he moved them, but at least it wasn't raining. Standing watch in these conditions was not only boring, but downright miserable. The four-hour watch was taking an eternity to pass.

Lightning whipped across the dark sky as the sentry pulled his coat tighter. The chill fought its way in through his sleeves and collar. An explosive stampede of thunder rumbled across the waves and resonated in the sentry's chest. It was unusually cold for this time of year; and being in the crow's nest was to be in the center of the fury.

The wooden hull of the *Pegasus* creaked as it headed bow-first into swell upon swell. Its masts cut silently through the darkness. Very little moonlight seeped through the clouds' thick veil. Fog crept shoreward obscuring all traces of land from the sentry's view.

A young lieutenant stood at mast. He gazed out into vast darkness, distant and remote, his bright blue surcoat contrasting with the night when lightning flashed. In one arm he cradled his helmet. Chain mail sleeves and black knee-high boots extended from beneath the surcoat. A sword in an ornately decorated scabbard hung from his hip completing the uniform. Lieutenant Tiberious always looked sharp as was expected from every officer in the Royal Guard. In his late thirties, he looked distinguished with his trimmed beard and salt-and-pepper hair. Recently reassigned command of a squad of foot soldiers, he still sported a small paunch as a result of his absence.

Thirty minutes earlier the *Pegasus* had left Xylor, a small island in the kingdom of Kelterland. The island had been conquered years earlier after a long and bloody war that swept the region. It was now a prized possession in the hands of its captors.

The Royal Guard had commandeered the *Pegasus,* which was normally a transport ship for commercial goods, and Lieutenant Tiberious was placed in charge of a detachment whose mission was to take two prisoners to the mainland to stand trial. One prisoner, an impish vagabond, had been caught stealing food. The other, a stranger to Xylor, was charged with blasphemy against the sea goddess Tanuba. Many Xylorians were zealous of their mermaid goddess, and proud participants of the only legal religion sanctioned by the state. Those who were not followers of Tanuba kept their peace for fear of their life. All legal matters were tried on the mainland, and this was nothing more than a routine voyage. The *Pegasus* had been commandeered to ferry prisoners back and forth to the mainland more times then the crew cared to remember.

Lieutenant Tiberious, unconcerned with the bitter cold, studied the ship around him. Six sentries stood watch at various posts on deck. All probably wished they were someplace warmer. Looking up the mainsail to the crow's nest, he saw a seventh sentry trying vainly to bundle up against the wind. The lifeboats were on the port side of the ship and seemed to be secured firmly. Kegs of ale were roped down tightly, as was all deck-side cargo and equipment. Light from a stairwell leading below deck flickered with the rocking of the ship. A variety of catapults were strategically located on deck. From the catapults, the ship's crew could launch a fearsome bombardment.

Lieutenant Tiberious made his way slowly downstairs to his quarters as cedar steps groaned under his polished leather boots.

"Good evening, sir," a soldier snapped as the lieutenant passed him at the bottom of the stairwell. Lieutenant Tiberious turned slowly to meet his greeter.

"Good evening. I'm sorry, what is your name again?" The lieutenant replied hoarsely.

"Gunar," the soldier was slightly puzzled. "Johan Gunar."

"That's right," Lieutenant Tiberious said. "I need you to do me a favor, Johan. Have the steward meet me in my quarters as soon as he can."

"Yes, sir." The soldier about-faced and left to carry out his order as Lieutenant Tiberious crept down the corridor to his quarters.

After fumbling with the lock, the lieutenant entered a cramped cabin and sat on a rickety wooden chair in front of a cluttered desk. The ship's steward had left an oil lamp lit and ready for the lieutenant's arrival. While he waited, Tiberious sat still, meditating on the lamp as if trying to move it with his mind. The oil sloshed gently back and forth in time with the rocking ship. A thin wisp of black smoke rose from the burning wick. The pungent smell of hot oil mingled with the damp, musty odor of his quarters. He heard muffled voices chatting in a neighboring cabin. He turned his attention to the desk and sank further into his meditative state. A door creaked in the distance and footsteps moved away from his location. The faint smell of tobacco wafted under the door as voices in the next cabin grew louder. A card game was in progress; the conversation about hunting was punctuated with belches as ale steins clunked on the table.

Lieutenant Tiberious shook off his meditative state and leaned forward in his chair to get a closer look at his desk. He carefully placed his thumb on a discolored portion at the edge of the desk. Slowly sliding his thumb back and forth over this spot, he could feel that it was worn smoother than the rest of the surface. He smiled. With a little manipulation, the discolored spot slid down with a click, revealing a keyhole. He held the lamp to the hole. He reached into his boot, pulled out a small leather pouch, and removed a metal object. He worked the object into the keyhole until he heard a click. Now the whole desktop could be slid to the right unveiling a small drawer. Inside lay a golden, collapsible spyglass, and some papers. Two V's were etched onto the side of the spyglass. A shocked look broke the lieutenant's calm features. Ignoring the papers, he quickly shook off the shock and placed the spyglass in a leather pouch then hurriedly closed the desk as it was before.

A loud rap sounded at the door. "Steward here, sir!"

Lieutenant Tiberious slowly opened the door and peered out.

"You called for me, sir?" the steward inquired, wondering what was so important it couldn't wait till morning.

"Yes, I want you to go to the galley and pack some food." The lieutenant spoke with a hoarse, gravely voice.

"Yes, sir. What do you want?"

"I want rations for two days. Dried herring and fruit will do. I also want three full skins of water. Place them all in a sturdy cloth pack." Tiberious saw the quizzical look on the steward's face when he spoke. "I'm coming down with a sore throat. It's the cold air."

"You want three water skins, sir?" The steward nodded his understanding.

"Yes. I need the extra water to freshen up."

"Yes sir. When do you want it?"

"Now; go get the supplies now and bring them back to me as soon as you can." Tiberious swallowed hard, his throat obviously painful.

"Yes, sir." The steward thought the request odd, especially at this hour, but complied.

Lieutenant Tiberious closed the door and then sat on the edge of the bunk. He grabbed a whetstone from a nearby shelf and drew his sword. He set to touching up the edge of his blade while he waited for the steward's return. The card game next door was still going strong. One man was telling a boisterous story about his exploits with a priestess of Tanuba. Again belches added ambience to the chatter. Drunken laughter erupted in regular bursts. The *Pegasus* was sailing with a different contingent of guards today. Tiberious wondered if these riffraff were indicative of the new squad.

A short time later the steward returned with the requested supplies.

"Here you are, sir." The steward handed over the pack.

"Thank you. That will be all."

Lieutenant Tiberious closed the door then set about the task at hand. A quick search of the closet yielded little except fifty feet of rope. Taking the pack and rope, and grabbing his cap from a peg, he headed to the armory. He left his helmet behind.

Tiberious poked his head out the door and glanced down the hall. The corridor was empty. Swiftly he traversed the maze of corridors on his way across the ship, pausing a few times to get his bearings. The Pegasus was a four-deck, lengthy vessel with dimly lit corridors. After finding the main corridor, he was on the other side of the ship. The armory looked deserted. The lieutenant peeked over the counter but didn't see anyone. Tiberious banged on the counter. *Thump! Thump! Thump!*

"Hello! Is anyone working here?"

Startled awake by the ruckus, the armorer jumped to his feet and hit his head on a shelf. He rushed to the counter, rubbing his eyes as he came out of the back room.

"Yes, sir! Uh…can I, uh…help you? The armorer nervously wiped drool from his chin and widened his eyes trying to look wide-awake.

"We'll see." The lieutenant eyed the armorer with displeasure and left no doubt that he knew the armorer had been asleep. "I need a two-handed sword and a longbow with two dozen arrows."

"Uh…we don't have any two-handed swords, sir. None that ain't broke anyway."

"What? All of the two-handed swords are broken?"

"Yes, sir. We only have two on board; one has a piece of the blade broken off and the other has a loose handle. We never use them any…"

The lieutenant cut the young man off. "It sure looks like I'm using one today!" His raspy voice was unable to get the volume necessary to convey his anger. The armorer got the message regardless.

"Yes, sir." The young man fidgeted nervously. He was off to a bad start this evening.

"Well then, make it a long sword." Tiberious cooled down. He didn't have time to discuss the situation. "Do you have the other items?"

"Yes, sir!" The armorer quickly gathered the requested weapons and brought them to the counter.

"If you don't mind me asking, sir, but I've never known you to be much of an archer? In fact, I've never seen you with a bow before?" Not only had the armorer made this trip dozens of times with the lieutenant in the past months, he also assisted him on occasion in his previous assignment.

Lieutenant Tiberious paused for a second. "Oh, it's just something I've been thinking about for years. I've always admired the Royal archers for their marksmanship, and now, I guess is as good of a time as any to learn the skill. If I become half as good as the Royal archers I will consider myself successful."

"Where are you going to practice on board ship?" the armorer asked cautiously, not wanting to seem like he was interrogating a superior.

"Oh I'm going to wait until we get to port. You know, take a few days off after we deliver the prisoners, see where I stand with the weapon. *Is that all?*" Tiberious let it be known that he had no more time for chat.

The armorer jerked his head up and down, nodding his understanding. "Well, here you are. Sorry about the two-handed swords."

"Yes, have at least one two-handed sword available at all times in the future," Lieutenant Tiberious ordered as he turned and left with the supplies.

"Yes, sir!" The armorer stood rigidly as he watched the lieutenant disappear down the hall.

Lieutenant Tiberious pulled his cap down tighter in answer to the wind as he stepped onto deck. He quickly made his way to the port side, moving as silently as possible. He paused near a rowboat and glanced inside. In the dim light it looked empty. Feeling around, he realized two oars lay on the bottom of the boat. He looked around. The sentries walked their posts and paid him little attention. He wondered if they noticed him at all. When the ship was at sea, sentries were more for show than security.

He tossed the pack and rope into the lifeboat in one smooth motion, then more carefully placed the longbow and quiver of arrows inside as well. He knelt and studied the device fastening the boat to the deck rail. If the two ropes tying the boat to the rail were removed, the boat could be lowered to the water by a hand-cranked winch. A rope running through two pulleys, one on the bow and one on the stern, guided the boat to the sea below. In an emergency the boat could be launched in less than two minutes.

Still on one knee by the hand crank, Lieutenant Tiberious suddenly froze. The wind blowing from his back now carried a new scent. The foul stench of body odor stung his nostrils. It was the stench of someone who had gone a month without a bath.

"Where did they get this crew?" Lieutenant Tiberious quickly pulled a cigar from his surcoat.

"Sir, what are you doing?"

Pretending to be startled, he stood and turned to face the curious sentry.

"I'm trying to light my cigar, but this wind…" Lieutenant Tiberious noticed mold growing on the five teeth in the sentry's crooked smile.

"Yes, sir. I didn't realize it was you. I was just making sure one of the prisoners hadn't escaped." Spittle flew from the sentry's mouth as he spoke.

"You are to be commended for your diligence. I guess I can wait until morning to smoke this. It'll only irritate my sore throat further anyway." Lieutenant Tiberious held the cigar up with one hand while wiping spit from his cheek with the other.

"No need to, sir; here, let me light it for you."

"Thank you." *Now I'll have to smoke the nasty thing,* the lieutenant thought.

The sentry grabbed an oil lamp that was hanging at his post, and with cupped hands had the cigar lit in no time.

"Thanks again," Lieutenant Tiberious said as he walked off. He wondered why the sentry never asked him how he planned to light the cigar.

The lieutenant took his time. It was thirty yards from the rowboat to the door leading below deck. After closing the door and taking a brief look around, he threw his cigar down the stairwell. Then he made his way to the brig where the prisoners were held. The brig was down deep in the ship at the end of a long door-lined corridor. The air was stale and musty, and noticeably warmer. The floor, moist from seeping seawater, provided for a slippery journey to the brig. Pale green mildew grew on the planks. He paused outside the brig and placed the long sword in a corner.

Then the lieutenant closed his eyes and seemed to meditate. After a good minute he opened his eyes and pulled a small leather pouch from his pocket. Inside the pouch were a small metal vial and a brass ring. The ring looked like a typical wedding band with a unique twist—it had a quarter-inch needle-sharp spike on its outer edge where a gemstone would normally be. Lieutenant Tiberious removed the cap from the vial and dipped the spike into a thick, syrupy liquid. Then he slipped the ring onto his right index finger and replaced the pouch and vial in his pocket.

Two startled guards jumped to attention when Lieutenant Tiberious entered the brig.

"Good evening, sir. The prisoners are still secured," one guard eagerly reported.

"Good. I came to see how things are going." Tiberious replied with a cough.

Tiberious quickly surveyed the room. Inside a cell two prisoners sat on a worn and rickety cot. Three other cells remained empty. The lieutenant studied the men he was to transport to the mainland to stand trial, a task usually left for the morning and better weather. For some reason the count was in a hurry with these two.

The prisoners had wrist irons on as extra security. Both had been stripped of armor and weapons. One of the prisoners was a hulking brute dressed in a black cotton shirt and pants. Novak was quite an imposing figure with a six-foot-five-inch frame carrying a well-muscled two hundred and forty-five pounds. As if to dramatize his size, he also wore a black cloak. Novak glared at the lieutenant, eyes glowering beneath his single eyebrow, his dark brown hair askew. Clean-shaven, with deep blue eyes, he was sure to be popular with the ladies. Seated on the cot next to Novak was a considerably smaller man wearing a tattered brown robe and worn, brown leather shoes. At five-five and a hundred twenty-five pounds, he was dwarfed by Novak's incredible stature. Bartus looked as frail and weak as Novak looked strong and imposing. The small man's matted hair and gray scraggly beard compounded his dejected look. He peered at the lieutenant with watery, sunken eyes.

Bartus had done nothing more then steal bread because he was hungry. He didn't understand why the powers-that-be had to order a special trip just for two prisoners. He hadn't done anything that warranted the attention. Even a murderer was held until the morning. Something was suspicious. There was more to this then met the eye. It bothered Bartus that he couldn't figure it out.

Novak, on the other hand, had committed one of the worst offenses possible in Xylor, according to Drakar, the temple cleric of Tanuba. The count felt challenges to his authority were the worst offenses, but in order to appease the people, he also brought justice to those who offended influential citizens, especially ones like Drakar.

The offense happened in the town square where a statue of Tanuba, the sea goddess, stood. Novak was new to the island and unaware of the ramifications of insulting Tanuba. He was looking over the inscription, which read in part: *Faithful…Mighty…All Powerful…Tanuba,* when a party of Xylorians came to worship the idol.

"She's beautiful! Don't you think, sir?" An elderly man enthusiastically exclaimed to Novak. He noticed the gargantuan stranger was armed and wore a bronze helmet. When Novak turned, the old man saw his decorative cuirass and greaves. His cloak had previously hidden them from view. It was uncommon for such a heavily armed person to be in the town square. They usually stayed near the docks.

"I suppose as much as any other statue. Art is not an interest of mine," Novak stated flatly.

"What? Haven't you heard of the great goddess Tanuba?" The man was deeply shocked. "She reigns over this island, caring and providing for her people."

"You're wrong." Novak was a man of few words. When he spoke, he said what he felt no matter the outcome. It was a trait that frustrated his friends. He hoped that the old man was senile but knew he was serious. But Novak wasn't going to back down, especially to pagans. His moral code wouldn't allow that.

"This is not a god. It's a carved rock. There is only one God and *He*—" Novak stressed the "he" part. "—is not a mermaid."

A hush fell over the small group that had started to gather around Novak and the old man. The once joyous mood of the worshipers grew somber and tense.

"Recant your blasphemous words, sir, lest you bring the wrath of Tanuba on us all," the old man pleaded.

Novak was unafraid of Tanuba. He refused to mince words, and was blunt to a fault. "The only way this statue will hurt anyone is if it falls on them. And I don't foresee an earthquake anytime soon."

The elderly man's face grew red in anger. All eyes in the frantic crowd were fixed on the volatile discussion.

"Pray to Tanuba for forgiveness now!" An angry voice shouted.

"I will not!" Novak feared no man and did not ruffle easily, but once he was pushed to the point of raising his voice, he never backed down. When Novak got angry, he could erupt with a burst of energy that shook most men in their boots. "Should I pray to this bench? What about this flowerpot? They are both made out of the same stone as this statue." Novak stood firm, even taunting the crowd. The Tanuba worshipers were treading on thin ice.

A young man with a club rushed forward and waved it threateningly in Novak's face. "This is your last chance to beg forgiveness from Tanuba!"

Novak locked eyes with the young man, who was about eighty pounds lighter. Fear crept over the young man and replaced the blood that drained from his face. Novak was even bigger when you stood close to him.

Someone called for the Royal Guard, and a few others fled the scene. Novak knew he had little time left before the authorities arrived. The crowd started to press around him, bolstered by their numerical advantage. Novak snatched the club from the young man, and a gasp spewed from the growing mob. The crowd had him surrounded and left with few options. If he was going to go out, it was going to be in a flurry. Muscled arms raised the club and brought it down on the statue's head, sending an explosion of pebbles on all that stood nearby.

"DEATH TO TANUBA!" Novak roared.

The crowd rushed him, and bodies began to fly in every direction as Novak's knuckles met with more then a few chins.

There would be several gap-toothed grins come morning. Ribs cracked, and noses bled under the fist pounding Novak administered. He dealt punishing blows, tenderizing bodies like a butcher tenderizes a steak. Tanuba couldn't protect them all.

After a spirited and violent struggle, Novak was finally overwhelmed and taken prisoner by the angry mob. Soon the Royal Guard arrived and wended their way through the unconscious bodies. A sergeant asked a bystander what happened. The mob was all too happy to talk. They had been wronged. Many angry fingers pointed at Novak and the decapitated statue of Tanuba. Hysterical cries mixed with angry accusations. Their goddess had been insulted, her image disgraced. The mob demanded satisfaction. They all wanted to know what the Royal Guard intended to do about it.

Novak was arrested to quell the brewing riot. He was led away by the troops as lamenting citizens wept bitterly at the destruction of their stone idol. His fate was in the hands of the count now.

Lieutenant Tiberious studied the two prisoners he was transporting to trial.

"Have they been giving you any trouble?" the lieutenant croaked hoarsely to a guard with greasy hair.

"Everything's fine, sir; the big one gets irate and bangs on the bars now and then, but it's nothing we can't handle. Of course they both claim to be innocent, but don't they all." The guard cackled.

Lieutenant Tiberious eyed Novak carefully, "Innocent? Is that a fact?"

The guard walked closer to the cell door. "Yeah, this big ox thinks he's tough, too. He'll find out that everyone must answer to the royal justice system, especially blasphemers." This guard was a fervent Tanuba worshiper and took Novak's crime personally. Bartus stared at the floor hoping to remain invisible.

Novak shifted his gaze to the guard, trying to penetrate his skull with a stare. "You know what you can do with your royal justice system, you sickening coward."

"Do you see what I mean?" The guard pointed at Novak, shaking his finger; "You're lucky you're under arrest in that cage. Had we met at the docks I would have to teach you...." The guard stopped speaking with a deep gasp when Novak sprang to his feet.

In an eruption of rage, Novak ripped the cot from under Bartus and sent the slight man tumbling to the floor. He swung it several times at the cell door, reducing it to splinters. "Are you threatening me? Huh? Open this cell door! I'm unarmed! Maybe you'll end up like your statue. Come on! Open the door, you weasel!"

Novak's scathing outburst left the guard trembling, mouth agape. Silence filled the room as he slowly composed himself. The unruffled lieutenant waited to see how the guard would meet the challenge.

The guard brushed wood splinters off his uniform. Fear and embarrassment quickly turned to rage. "What you need is to feel the punishment you deserve, you infidel." A wad of snotty spit flew from the guard's mouth and hit Novak in the left eye.

Novak wiped his eye and looked the guard directly in the face. "You'll pay for that."

Novak turned to the lieutenant. "They've been harassing us like this all day without ceasing; not that you'll do anything about it. But I've had enough."

"Maybe I will," Lieutenant Tiberious interrupted, raising a hand. Deciding to play off the guard's extreme hatred for Novak, he continued. "A little discipline may be in order for this prisoner. Go to the armory and bring back a cat-o'-nine-tails. We'll flog some respect for Tanuba into him." Novak was unworried by the threat. Bartus on the other hand was quaking in his shoes. Why was the big man bringing all this attention on them? He moved to one side of the cell trying to distance himself from Novak. He prayed the guards wouldn't flog him also.

The guard snapped a salute and left for the armory feeling smug, relishing the thought of Novak's fate.

Lieutenant Tiberious called the other guard over. "Do you have the keys to the cell door?"

"Yes, sir!"

"Good, then open the door. Let's get the prisoner in position at the whipping post." Lieutenant Tiberious rotated his ring around on his finger so that the spike would now be palm down. He watched the guard open the door.

"Oh, and one more thing," he added placing his hand on the guards shoulder, pressing the spike through his shirt into his flesh. "Be careful. The big prisoner is very unpredictable."

The guard nodded his understanding and swung the cell door open. Immediately the prisoners knew something was wrong. The guard's eyes rolled up into his skull after a few faltering steps forward, and he collapsed in a heap on the floor.

Novak rushed to the fallen guard and felt for a pulse. "He just passed out." It didn't make any sense.

Novak would have rushed his last remaining captor immediately had this incident not been so bizarre. If this wasn't a trap, then why wasn't the lieutenant alarmed. Novak waited to analyze the situation further.

Lieutenant Tiberious stood expressionless at the cell door, apparently unworried that he was now alone with the two prisoners. His guard collapsed, possibly dying, and he didn't seem to care? An opportunity for escape had manifested itself, and the lieutenant in charge wasn't bothered in the least. The whole situation was surreal. A slow smile crept over the lieutenant's face. "Well what are you waiting for, Novak? We don't have much time." Tiberious's voice sounded different now. It resonated clearly, no longer raspy.

Novak studied the lieutenant carefully. "Scorpyus, is that you?"

"Well it sure isn't your sister." The lieutenant sported an uncharacteristic grin.

Novak smiled. "Well, Scorp, you've outdone yourself." Novak was impressed. "I didn't recognize you."

"That's the point, my frequently-imprisoned friend. But there's no time for that now. We'll have to hurry to make our escape. I have a weapon for you outside the door." Scorpyus motioned for Novak to hurry. "I have a lifeboat packed and ready. Let's move; the other guard could show up at any time."

Bartus stepped forward and clung to the lieutenant's sleeve, desperation in his eyes.

"Please take me with you," he pleaded. "They'll kill me if you don't."

The situation was grim for Bartus. If he stayed he would undoubtedly be blamed for aiding the escape. If he went, odds were he wouldn't be able to keep up. He would be a burden to the escape, but they didn't have the heart to leave him behind, knowing his fate.

"Do as you're told, stay close, be quiet, and we'll take you with us," Scorpyus ordered. Novak took the guard's keys and removed his and Bartus's wrist irons.

"This will be a risk. Before we left port a Royal Guard supply wagon was robbed. As a result there are extra patrols out tonight." Scorpyus lifted his surcoat and removed the padding that formed Lieutenant Tiberious's paunch. Then he removed the cumbersome chain mail. "I'll move a little faster without that stuff."

Scorpyus straightened his surcoat while Novak bound and gagged the fallen guard.

Novak asked, "How long before the real lieutenant misses his uniform? Or did you give him a dose of the stuff you gave this sap?" Novak proceeded to drag the guard into the cell.

Scorpyus smiled. "He'll be out for a few days just like the lieutenant. And he'll have a headache when he awakes, but other then that, he should be his same old self."

Scorpyus was quite knowledgeable in the art of herbal remedies and concoctions. It was a skill learned from his gypsy grandmother, a skill that had served him well on many occasions.

Bartus watched Novak remove seven gold coins from the guard's pocket and slip them into his own.

"He stole my money before locking me up," Novak explained and retrieved the sword Scorpyus had placed outside the guardroom door.

"Let's go. We're thirty minutes from shore so we have work ahead of us. Sorry about the long sword, Novak, but they didn't have any two-handed swords. And Bartus, I didn't expect you, so you'll have to make do with the guard's dagger. That's all I could get. No armor or shields, but there's food, water, and a longbow on the rowboat." Scorpyus gave last minute instructions while the others prepared for their escape. He knew Novak would be uncomfortable without armor since he usually wore it. Novak relied on brute force and was always in the thick of the fight. As a result, he found armor a necessity.

All three men moved quickly and headed for the jailhouse door. Before they could get there, the other guard returned with the flail.

"Here's the cat-o'-nine-tails, sir." The guard reported to Lieutenant Tiberious.

"Good work. Let me have it." Scorpyus pretended nothing was amiss.

The guard handed over the whip before he noticed that the prisoners were no longer in their wrist irons and that his fellow guard was bound and gagged. "Hey—what happened to?..."

Crack! Novak retracted a large-knuckled fist from the suddenly-silent guard's face as blood welled up from the sockets where two front teeth had been. Regaining his balance after his head bounced off the wall, the guard pulled his sword and charged Novak. Novak sidestepped the dazed guard who now had blood trickling down his chin. The guard turned for another attempt. He swung his sword wildly in a fit of rage.

BOOK 1 OF 3

"You're dumber then you look." Novak ducked as the guard's sword slammed into the wall. If he insisted on a fight, Novak was more then happy to oblige. And Scorpyus let his large friend have the guard all to himself.

The guard charged again. This time as Novak sidestepped he delivered a massive upper cut to the solar plexus, putting the full force of his weight behind it. He raised the guard a full foot off the ground with the blow. The guard cradled his stomach in agony, and collapsed to the floor.

"Throw him in the cell," Scorpyus said and went to the door to listen for the arrival of more guards. "Hurry, someone may have heard the commotion!"

Novak dragged the guard by the collar and locked him in the cell. "If that was your best, you should keep your mouth shut next time."

After securing the cell, Novak and Bartus followed Scorpyus to the door. He was already spying out the corridor.

"Lead the way, Scorpyus."

The trio moved cautiously down the hall and up the stairs to the door leading to the deck, careful to step lightly, but even so the wood flooring and stairs creaked underfoot. Scorpyus slowly opened the door and peered out.

"I don't see any nearby sentries, just a couple some way off, but as soon as they see us they'll come to investigate. They might even sound the alarm. No one is supposed to be on deck this late." Scorpyus waited for the sentries to turn away then gave the order to move out. "Stay close and take advantage of any available cover."

Novak and Bartus nodded. They snuck on deck and made their way toward the lifeboat Scorpyus had prepared. They stayed low and took advantage of barrels, masts, and other equipment as concealment. Novak made Bartus move when he should and duck when he should. Clouds hid the moon and stars, providing darkness for the escape. The clouds also obscured the hand signals Scorpyus and Novak had developed in their many adventures. Nevertheless, they covered the distance from the door to the lifeboat without a word. When they reached the lifeboat, Scorpyus untied the rope that secured it to the ship's railing. Bartus and Novak took cover behind a stack of cargo and waited for Scorpyus to launch the boat.

Then things took a turn for the worse. Novak's hand clamped down over Bartus's mouth before the small man had a chance to warn Scorpyus of the sentry's approach. He didn't need Bartus giving away their position yet.

The sentry was curious about Scorpyus's actions. "Sir, what's going on?"

Scorpyus's heart skipped a beat. The sentry took him by surprise, but he hadn't made it this far in life without the ability to think on his feet. Scorpyus saw that the sentry wasn't aware of Bartus and Novak.

"Oh, I just needed a little fresh air. Everything's fine. You can go back to your post now." Scorpyus replied hoarsely.

The sentry was still curious. "It looked like you were getting something out of the life boat."

"No, I was just leaning over the side because I feel a little sick. My dinner doesn't agree with me. I must be getting old." Scorpyus rubbed his belly and grimaced a little.

"Yes, sir, but I thought you were going to turn in for the night. He cut himself off mid-sentence when he saw Bartus out of the corner of his eye. The fellow was peering over a crate of cargo to get a better look at what was going on. "Halt! The prisoners have escaped! Sound the alarm!"

Novak grabbed Bartus by the collar and jerked him back down. "I told you to stay down!"

In an instant the sentry's face went expressionless, eyes opening wide, as a huge gasp escaped him. His lips started to quiver as if to speak, and a tiny drop of blood formed at the corner of his mouth. Scorpyus placed his foot on the sentry's chest, and shoved him off his sword. Bartus ran from cover to the rowboat and started frantically working the hand crank. Scorpyus and Novak covered his back, bracing to defend against the onslaught that was sure to come. Sentries scurried in the distance, surprised at the news of the prisoners' escape. Many were excited at the thought of finally seeing some action. Lamplight flickered across the deck as the crew readied itself for battle.

"This crank's rusted solid!" Bartus exclaimed. "I can't budge it!"

Novak moved into position at the crank. "Hold my sword while I try." He pulled up on the crank with a vengeance, teeth gritting from the strain. The metal handle bowed severely but the winch didn't turn.

An arrow slammed into the deck railing. Scorpyus clutched his right side; the arrow had grazed him. Another arrow ricocheted off the metal crank. More whizzed by overhead.

"That's a little too close. I've been grazed." Scorpyus glanced to see blood on his fingertips. "Where did it come from?"

"Up there." Bartus pointed. "In the crow's nest."

Novak crashed to the deck when the hand crank broke off from the winch. Two sentries ran towards their position, swords in hand.

"Bartus, give Novak back his sword!" Scorpyus said and pointed out the rapidly approaching sentries. "Inside the rowboat is a longbow and arrows. I need them for the man in the crow's nest."

"What are we going to do now? The hand crank broke!" Bartus yelled hysterically after reaching into the rowboat and retrieving the bow and arrows for Scorpyus. Seeing armed sentries charging towards him, Bartus trembled with fear.

Novak grabbed his sword from Bartus. "Don't freeze up. If you want to live, figure out a way to launch that boat. And hurry, we can't hold them off forever."

Another arrow whizzed past Scorpyus and struck the deck inches from his feet.

Yet another arrow struck the tip of Novak's upraised sword with a clank.

"This is not looking good!" Novak braced himself for the charging sentries.

Scorpyus drew back his bow and took careful aim at the sentry in the crow's nest. He heard swords clanging to his right as Novak met the sentries in combat. Scorpyus loosed his arrow only to see it miss his mark by a foot.

Concentrate, Scorpyus told himself and reached for another arrow.

Bartus cut the ropes to the winch and sent the boat crashing to the water below. "The boat's launched!" He looked toward the bow and saw other sentries ready with slings. Reinforcements were coming from below deck. "We're running out of time, hurry!"

Novak swung his sword and sparks flew as he blocked a barrage of incoming blows from the two sentries. One sentry lunged at Novak. Stepping to the side, Novak brought the hilt of his sword down on the back of the sentry's helmet, sending the man to his knees. Then Novak turned and squared off to face the second sentry. The second sentry was no match for Novak and had a hard time just holding onto his sword against Novak's barrage of blows. In a flurry Novak brought his sword down again and again, thrusting and swinging. The sentry could feel his joints rattle from the force of the blows he was blocking. Seeing an opening, Novak brought his sword down over the sentry's left shoulder. The sword crashed into a barrel, spilling ale onto the deck.

The sentry danced to the side then came up on Novak's left rear. His opponent's weapon was stuck! He had an opening! But Novak worked his sword out of the barrel, turned, and swung it in an upward motion to meet the sentry's flanking attack. His blade struck the sentry in the abdomen. With a loud groan, the sentry fell to his knees cradling his midsection.

Scorpyus loosed his second arrow, and this time the man in the crow's nest fell against the mast, no longer a threat. Squads with slings were almost ready to launch a barrage at the escapees. Scorpyus chose them as his new targets.

Two more sentries came at Novak. Together they were able to work him up against the deck rail. After Novak locked swords with one, the other came in for the kill, but when the sentry raised his sword to attack, he was met with a sidekick to the mid-section that sent him sprawling across the deck. Novak pushed the other sentry away and resumed the fight. The swords clashed and danced amid sparks, each man seeking an opening to a softer target. Novak worked his foe up against a crate. With a massive blow he knocked the sentry's sword from his hand and it skipped across the deck. Instead of retreating, the man pulled a dagger and came at Novak again with a loud bellow.

It was no use. The sentry ran into the deck rail when Novak sidestepped his attack. His momentum carried him up and over the side to the water below. With his armor on, the man sank like a stone.

The second sentry saw his chance to kill Novak while he was distracted. By the time Novak realized what was happening, it was too late for him to react. The sentry raised his sword for the kill, but before he could bring it down, an arrow struck him below the chin. He fell against Novak, clinging to him for support and gasping for air. Novak gave Scorpyus a quick nod of thanks and let the sentry drop to the deck.

By now the whole crew had been alerted, and several men with slings were ready to fire. Though time was running out, at least one thing was going in the trio's favor: fear of being hit by the slung stones kept the other sentries from attacking the escapees.

Novak turned to face the remaining sentry who decided Bartus would be an easier adversary. Apparently, he was oblivious to the fact his comrades were ready to launch an attack. Novak charged him, knowing he wouldn't make it to Bartus's rescue in time.

"Bartus, Look out!" Novak roared a warning.

Bartus had just finished tying excess rope from the winch to the railing of the ship to provide a way to climb down to the boat.

He turned in time to see the sentry, sword raised, ready to bring it down on him. Bartus jumped overboard. The sentry's sword smashed into the hand crank, freeing up the rusted winch. He rushed to the deck rail in time to see Bartus climbing out of the cold water into the rowboat. The sentry screamed when Novak skewered him.

The other crewmembers had loaded their slings with fifteen fist-sized stones. They launched them at Scorpyus and Novak as they prepared to climb down to the rowboat. Novak held up a dead sentry as a shield against the incoming stones while Scorpyus slipped over the side. Stones thudded down all around; two slammed into Novak's human shield. Another stone ricocheted off the deck and struck him on the shin. Another smashed into the deck rail near Scorpyus's hand.

Novak dropped the sentry and limped to the railing. He lowered himself into the rowboat where Scorpyus handed him one of the oars.

"Alright, Novak, ready…stroke…stroke…stroke…." Scorpyus counted out a rhythm so they could synchronize their rowing.

On deck, archers prepared to attack the fleeing rowboat. By now the crew started turning the Pegasus around in pursuit. Crewmembers scrambled over the deck and up the masts.

Scorpyus and Novak paddled rigorously, putting as much distance between them and the Pegasus as they could. The rowboat wouldn't move fast enough. They drove the oars into the water like they were stabbing pitchforks into dirt, frantically pulling them back through the sea. Bartus ducked down, practically getting under the wood-plank seat. Arrows darted all around, encouraging the rowing. It would take a while for the Pegasus crew to reverse course.

II

◆◈◆

A THICK FOG slowly enveloped the port city of Xylor, adding
a chilling dampness to an already spooky night, a night that
made the hair on the back of your neck stand up. Peculiarities
abounded. The first—a supply shipment ambushed by
highwaymen—brought the Royal Guard out in full force and had
tensions high. And now, the latest oddity only fueled the growing
unease.

A crowd of overwrought citizens gathered a few streets from
the docks near an abandoned, run-down warehouse. Most had
hurried into the streets with coats pulled over their bedclothes.
"Someone murdered Lieutenant Tiberious!" a voice announced to
the gathering.

A woman in front sobbed at the news. "Oh, great goddess
Tanuba, why? Why? Why?"

Most of the people were visibly grieved by the report, and
murmured voices could be heard talking about the lieutenant.

"A great neighbor…"

"Always there with a helping hand…"

"A loyal servant to Tanuba and the count…"

A very attractive woman stood some distance from the crowd.
She appeared unaffected by the commotion. Even those who

detested newcomers to Xylor would agree there was something about this stranger that was mysteriously irresistible. Zephyr was a sprite of a woman with locks of copper hair that flowed from under her cap and eyes as green as emeralds. With her hair pulled back in a ponytail, she gently chewed on her full lower lip as she watched the commotion attentively. Her sword and longbow gave a dangerous edge to her beauty. At five-feet-four and a shade over one hundred and fifteen pounds, Zephyr's size had misled many people about her ability. What she lacked in size, though, she made up for in speed and God-given instincts that would make any swordsman envious.

Zephyr was an accomplished tracker and looked the part, dressed in a forest green jerkin with brown trim, matching leggings, and soft leather knee-high boots. She watched the unfolding scene with curious interest, arms crossed under her short cape.

A teary-eyed woman walked up to Zephyr. "Who could have done such a horrible thing? I hope the poor man didn't suffer."

"So do I Madame." Zephyr was puzzled. Surely there must be some mistake. The lieutenant had to be alive. She carefully reviewed the growing mob of onlookers. All kinds of speculation and gossip ran rampant. The rumors ranged from murder, to robbery, to a ransomed kidnapping. Someone even suggested the lieutenant had been abducted to another dimension by evil spirits. Imaginations roiled and tongues wagged uncontrollably. A colonel in the Royal Guard stormed out of an open alley doorway. He dispatched a soldier to tell the count the news and ordered others to search the area. Then the colonel stood on an ox-drawn hay wagon to address the crowd.

"Calm down! Calm down! Lieutenant Tiberious is not dead. I repeat; he's *not* dead. He *is* unconscious, however, and that is the work of a traitor. The lieutenant should awaken within a few hours."

A sigh of relief escaped the gathered citizens, and the colonel continued. "If anyone has any information about this, or has seen anything suspicious, let a Royal Guard officer know. Even if you think the information is of little worth, it could help us. There will be a handsome reward for anyone who turns in the party guilty of this grievous crime. This act of treason will not be tolerated. The traitor will be caught and punished. Nobody gets away with dealing treacherously to an officer in the Royal Guard."

As the colonel continued addressing the people, an older gentleman with thinning, gray hair and well-defined wrinkles approached Zephyr. In his right hand he clutched a small parchment. He wore a bland brown cotton shirt and pants under a threadbare cloak. It looked as if he had slept in his clothes the night before. He had an air of urgency about him. He whispered to Zephyr.

"Excuse me, but are you with the party that's on the island searching for a rare medicine?"

Zephyr concealed her complete shock with a sweet smile. "Je regrette monsieur, but you must have me confused with someone else." She eyed the stranger carefully. He was unarmed and looked like a man of meager means. Zephyr noticed his shoes had dried mud on them.

The old man was persistent. "You *are* with the party of four that came to town two days ago to seek out a special medicine, are you not?"

"Monsieur, I do not know what you are speaking about." Zephyr looked the man in the eyes. They were tired and weary, but it didn't look like he was pulling a bluff. How could he possibly know her? She had no recollection of ever meeting him. She didn't like being at such a disadvantage.

"It's imperative that you talk to me. You're in danger. What you are here to do will touch countless lives," the old man said with a firm sincerity in his voice.

Zephyr glanced over the man's shoulder and saw two unsavory fellows across the street that seemed overly interested in her conversation with the older man. Once they realized Zephyr had spotted them, they quickly glanced away and pretended an interest in the commotion of the crowd. Zephyr scanned the crowd in case there were more people interested in what she was doing. The mob still congregated around Lieutenant Tiberious's room. Nothing else looked unusual. The Royal Guard escorted a vagabond they found near the scene. He had a blood-stained knee and was the focus of an intense interrogation.

Zephyr noticed that the two unsavory men were armed and dressed to blend in with the crowd. Nothing made them stand out from the rest of the people other then their occasional glances toward Zephyr and the old man. She didn't need to see any more.

"You are being followed! Quick Monsieur, come with me!" Zephyr said and grabbed the old man's sleeve and pulled him down an alley. The old man was startled by the move, but went with her anyway. It was as if he knew he was being followed. There was a certain peace about the older man, a certain resignation to whatever fate had in store. Zephyr led the way to a darkened doorway and they both pressed back into the darkness.

The two men shoved their way through the crowd and ran into the alley Zephyr disappeared into. She heard them running towards her location. Quickly she clasped her hand over the old man's mouth as their pursuers swept past.

The two men ran to the end of the alley, and shot a quick glance both ways. Both took off to the right. Zephyr knew she didn't have much time.

"Well, monsieur, what do you have to say? Hurry, they could be back any moment!"

The older man handed Zephyr a note that read:

> Hyssop Creek Oratory, Vespers
> Codeword: Orion
>
> *A legend runs deep in the forest of Xylor*
> *But few will there be who master their fears*
> *The mountains and thicket hold perils and danger*
> *Concealing the treasure of sapphire tears*
>
> Thadus (Sage)

"What is this?" Zephyr wondered aloud. This was no time to try to solve a riddle.

"The details will be explained later. More than a few good people have died to obtain this note and set up this meeting. But I warn you: you are in danger. Things are not how they appear at first glance. Be wary of who you trust." He spoke with absolute earnestness.

"Why should I trust you then?" Zephyr asked. "And if this note is so important, why are you trusting it to me; a complete stranger?"

"I work for the true kingdom. I fear my time of service is near its end. As you are well aware, I am hunted as we speak. Your party must help us save the true kingdom or leave Xylor. Many lives, including your own, are at stake."

Zephyr was confused. "How do you know me, monsieur? I do not understand what this is all about? You make no sense."

"You are a good person. I can see it in your eyes. I have been led to you near the end of my service. But beware; you must choose your destiny wisely lest you unknowingly serve the furtherance of evil." The old man placed a hand on Zephyr's shoulder and smiled warmly.

Zephyr stood momentarily speechless, a thousand things going through her mind.

The old man looked at Zephyr pleadingly. "Let the Spirit lead you."

The old man obviously meant what he was saying, and he really wanted her to understand, but this was all too much, too fast.

"What? What do you mean? I do not know what you are trying to say? We do not even know each other? There must be a mistake."

The man clasped Zephyr's arm. "Please listen. I know this is difficult to take in all at once, but you must—ackk…

An arrow struck the elder man in the back. Zephyr looked down the alley and saw an archer in a second story window.

"They're over there!" The archer yelled and pointed for his comrades.

The old man collapsed against Zephyr, clutching at her jerkin as he sank to the ground. He gurgled, spitting up blood. Zephyr knelt beside him holding his head. She leaned him against the doorway.

"And so…my time…has come." The older man coughed and tried to speak, taking shallow gasps of air between every few words. Zephyr knew he was wounded in a lung. What was happening? A man was dying and she didn't know who or why. What swept her into this nightmare?

She shook her head and took a deep breath. The difference between survival and death depended on how fast she recovered from this shock, formed a new course of action, and then moved ahead decisively. She had to react swiftly or suffer the same fate as the old man.

His breath was heavily labored and his lips were turning blue. "The…Lord has…set this before…chosen…you."

Zephyr's eyes grew wide. She didn't simply hear that! Her heart raced and she felt suddenly numb in her extremities. This wasn't happening! It was pure lunacy. Yet in her heart she believed everything happened for a reason.

"Remember…last thing," the man continued, "Beatus Es… Dominus Deus…In Aeternum."

"What?" Zephyr asked the old man, vainly trying to get him to repeat his words. "What does that mean?"

It was useless. She lowered his lifeless head to the ground. She didn't even know his name.

Zephyr saw three men round the corner of the alley and lope toward her. She had to move or follow the old man. Like a jackrabbit she was gone, ignoring their commands to halt. They chased her down several streets and alleyways but couldn't gain on her. Zephyr mazed her way through the early-morning merchants, boxes, horses, and barrels with practiced agility. The bigger, lumbering men took more time to clear these obstacles, knocking several people aside. The gap widened between the hunters and their prey. Rounding a corner Zephyr came upon a man walking beside his horse. She grabbed the reins with one hand, and brought her other elbow across the man's chin, knocking him back. Before he had time to shout a protest, Zephyr had mounted the horse.

"Forgive me, monsieur, he will be returned to you later." Zephyr spurred the horse into a full run, kicking up clouds of dust. Hooves beat their familiar pattern onto the street. The three men chasing her rounded the corner to see they were a little late.

"No! She's got a horse!" one of them cursed.

Two of them took the only two horses that were hitched in front of a dank, dirty tavern. A drunken patron was dipping his head into a horse trough, trying to reverse the effects of too many pints of ale.

"She can't be too far ahead of us. Let's go!" one exclaimed.

Though an accomplished rider, Zephyr realized her near nag of a horse wasn't going to outrun the other horses for long. The old horse was making a valiant effort, but it wouldn't be enough. She took an arrow from her quiver and tied the piece of paper the old man had given her to its shaft. Zephyr took the street that led past the stables. During the day there would be no way to gallop a horse down this street. There would be too many people about. But because of the early hour, few people strode the streets.

Looking back, Zephyr was relieved to see the men chasing her were a good distance behind. It wouldn't stay that way for long. Crouching low in the saddle, she loosed the arrow into the nearby livery stable as she passed.

Message delivered, Zephyr thought. *Now I've got to lose these men.* Zephyr raced for a wooded area just outside the city limits. She rode two miles into the dark woods and then abruptly reined her horse to a stop, stood in the saddle, and disappeared into the branches of an old pine tree. Then she pulled her sword and slapped the horse on the rump with the side of her blade. The old nag trotted off as Zephyr climbed higher into the tree. She hid motionless in the branches. A few moments later the two men rode by beneath her, unaware they were now chasing a riderless horse. She would be gone before they discovered their error.

———•◦•———

Scorpyus and Novak pulled furiously on the oars trying to distance themselves from the Pegasus. If they could make it to the fog near the coast, they would find a measure of concealment. Bartus, dripping wet, sat low in the boat shivering against the brisk wind.

"We won't make it out of arrow range in time," Novak stated flatly. An arrow struck the side of the boat as if on cue. "See, I told you."

Bartus started weeping, gently rubbing his forehead with his fingers. He kept his eyes clamped closed.

"Please, Lord, let us live," he prayed.

Scorpyus and Novak glanced at each other and nodded approvingly. They were relieved to realize that Bartus wasn't with the Tanuba cult. It was the last thing they wanted to deal with at a time like this.

"Now's the time for prayer," Scorpyus commented as a flaming arrow slammed into the seat next to him. "Whoa, that was close!" He jerked away from the flames.

Novak scooped handfuls of water onto the burning arrow, extinguishing it. Bartus watched in terror as more flaming arrows streaked overhead.

"We need fog," Novak cried. "The only way they'll be able to find us in there is if we make noise." *Or they hear Bartus's teeth chattering,* he thought

The Pegasus was still in the process of turning, so they were still putting distance between their boat and the archers on the ship. Bartus prayed in terror, flinching each time an arrow streaked by. Novak and Scorpyus concentrated on their rowing, and paid little attention to the flying projectiles. They handled the high danger with a coolness that amazed Bartus. What was out of their control was in God's control. They couldn't direct the trajectory of the arrows, only the speed of the boat.

Rowing because their lives depended on it, they soon found themselves enveloped in a thick, moist fog. When they felt they were adequately out of sight, they relaxed a bit, and proceeded to handle the oar work more quietly. Too much splashing would give them away.

After a few minutes, Scorpyus stopped rowing and set his oar down in the boat.

"Hey, Novak, hand me the pack."

Novak handed it to Scorpyus, then resumed paddling, gently placing the oar in the water to minimize splashing. Scorpyus removed some cloth and set to work bandaging his side. Though it was a minor wound, he now had a sizable bloodstain on his shirt and surcoat. He put an oily liquid on the wound, and then dressed it with cloth strips. After tending to the wound, he pulled a small vial from his pocket and poured a gel-like substance into his palm. He rubbed the gel onto his hair, face, and head and peeled off the false beard, leaving only his mustache. Holding his breath he leaned over the boat and dunked his head into the cold water. Scorpyus vigorously worked the gel over his head while under water. He surfaced with a deep gasp then slicked his wet hair back, revealing a leaner, darker, and more chiseled face.

Gone were the lieutenant's pasty skin and graying hair. His jet-black hair, obsidian eyes, and olive skin were proof of Scorpyus's Gypsy blood. Bartus was amazed at the transformation, at the bronze young man suddenly before him.

"One of your best disguises yet," Novak proclaimed as Scorpyus removed the blue Royal Guard uniform surcoat and tossed it into the ocean.

"It's nothing but a little bit of make-up, a little bit of luck, and a great deal of skill," Scorpyus smiled. "By the way, we should be close to shore here very soon. We were only half an hour away when we jumped boat."

"We'll never get there if we don't stop yapping and get to work," Novak chimed in, handing Scorpyus his oar.

Novak and Scorpyus changed their course as a precaution.

Back on the island of Xylor, Zephyr climbed down from the tree. She effortlessly ran the two miles back to town in less than twelve minutes. Zephyr headed straight for the livery stables she had fired her arrow into. Looking inside, she saw an imposing man.

He appeared to be in his late twenties with light brown hair and a neatly trimmed goatee.

He was dressed in a gray tunic and pants. The man was big, a good two hundred pounds, solid, and lean. He was a good-looking fellow. He wore a cuirass, greaves, and plated gauntlets, and was armed with a sword and battle-ax. In one hand he held a shield, and in the other, a piece of paper. The visor to his helmet was raised as he read.

Zephyr burst into the stables. "Thanks for all the help, Cad. Do not let me interrupt you."

Cad didn't look up. "The day you can't shake a few blokes in the woods won't arrive during our lifetime. I didn't want to get in the blooming way. What is this?" Cad inquired, holding up the note. "And it's a good thing I wasn't standing in the doorway when that bloody arrow came whizzing in."

"Je ne sais pas what it is. An old man gave it to me and said that we are in danger. It was eerie. Men were after him, and he knew he would be soon discovered. I tell you this; he knew too much about us. I am not kidding you, Cad; he even knew *why* we are here! He believed we have been chosen to continue his cause, something about a 'true kingdom'. The poor man was killed before I learned more. They shot him in the back from across the street! I think he wanted me to go to this oratory for more information? I cannot figure out the note. It is a riddle, or poem, or something? No? Oh yes, he also whispered something about a 'Beatus Esse Dominus Deus In Aeternum.' Whatever that means."

"This mission is getting a bit daft, growing more and more complicated." Cad was perplexed. "First Novak gets arrested, which is always a variable with him. Then Scorpyus has to impersonate some lieutenant to rescue him. And now this. What's next?"

Zephyr continued, worried. "The old man knew why we are here, Cad. If *he* knows, it is likely somebody else does too, someone powerful enough to hire people ruthless enough to kill that old man. I am telling you this Cad, people were appearing out of the woodwork. I do not know how many were tracking this old man, but they had an elaborate surveillance network."

Cad shook his head at the thought. "Sounds like it could get blooming fierce. They're obviously well organized and brazen, and evil enough to put an arrow in a blokes back. We're going to have to find a hideout and take our work underground, make this a clandestine mission." Cad looked to the note again. "Since it looks like we're going to Sage to find this Thadus, we may as well find a hideout there. The only question is how we get word to the others."

"I would not worry," Zephyr said confidently. "Scorpyus and Novak must have escaped by now. They will find a way to contact us, I just know it. We have to warn them about this though. And the soldiers already found the lieutenant. There was a crazy mob by the docks."

Cad shook his head. "We've never had this many bloody problems pop up so early in a mission before." Cad had a sixth sense about these things and didn't like the tone that had been set thus far. "Let's go to the inn, retrieve our belongings, and find a place to hide. Sage is a small village, I think of around two hundred. And if I remember right, it's maybe five miles away."

"Are you sure we should go to Sage? There are thirty thousand people in Xylor. We have a much better chance of blending in here."

"Yes, unless we need to run. If one of us gets into trouble where can we go? These blokes are more familiar with this city than we are. We can't hide here for long, especially if the walls have eyes as we suspect. Who else knows we are here? If we set up our hideout in Sage, we have a place to go when things get ugly. There are fewer eyes to hide from. Plus, we can lose them in the woods. There are seven or eight other villages besides Sage. They won't know which one we went to, or even if we stayed on the island."

"Okay," Zephyr agreed. "We will go to Sage. Let us hurry and get out of here. I do not like what is happening."

Cad pulled his battle-axe and gouged the east wall with several slash marks. They both saddled up their horses and set about their changed itinerary. It wasn't far to the inn. The pair made their way down the streets of Xylor amid a bustle of activity. Many citizens turned out to see what had gone on the night before and excitement filled the crowds as soldiers from the Royal Guard worked to solve Lieutenant Tiberious's abduction and to find out who had ambushed the supply wagon. Cad and Zephyr saw several search parties form, preparing to search the island for those responsible. If Zephyr was right, Scorpyus and Novak would be walking into an alerted army. Who boarded the ship with the prisoners if the lieutenant was tied up in his room? What was the imposter doing on the Pegasus? The commanders of the Royal Guard feared the worst. What would they tell the count? Worst of all, would the news of this night's insurrections embolden others to try similar schemes? The soldiers scampered about, carrying out the orders of frantic sergeants who in turn carried out the orders of stressed officers. All the while, Cad and Zephyr moved nonchalantly through their midst.

III

SCORPYUS AND NOVAK rowed quietly toward shore. They could hear surf break against the rocks ahead of them while behind excited shouts from frantic crewmen reached them through the fog. The ship's crew kept archers in place, and the catapults were armed and ready. First sight of the escapees would trigger a massive barrage of projectiles. A new sentry in the crow's nest strained to catch a glimpse of the escapees.

"The fog is thinning as we get closer to land. The Pegasus will probably see us about the time we beach. It'll be close," Scorpyus thought out loud. For the first time Bartus noticed that Scorpyus had a slight accent. He rolled his Rs now and again.

"Over there!" Novak pointed to the faint glow of torchlight in the distance. "It might be a search party."

Bartus went pale and started to tremble as the others paddled faster. "Oh no, this isn't good," he said.

Novak grimaced at Bartus's expression of fear; having him always jumping around like a deranged cat at every new danger was getting old. "Relax, that's the least of our worries. Make yourself useful; here, take the rope." Novak handed the rope to Bartus as Scorpyus slung the bow and quiver on his back.

"We'll run southeast across the beach towards the woods," Scorpyus advised while methodically scanning the beach with the spyglass.

"What do you see?" Novak inquired.

"There's a small entourage camped out on the beach. I don't think they're the Royal Guard. They seem to be asleep. Anyhow, we do not need witnesses, especially if there is a search party. I can't believe they found the lieutenant so soon."

"That means we'll have to scale those cliffs." Novak pointed to a thirty-foot high, rocky and jagged shoreline. Scorpyus nodded. The two of them paddled the boat southward along the shoreline away from the party camped on the beach.

Novak evaluated Bartus. "I hope all of us can climb," he said. He held little confidence in the scrawny man's abilities.

Bartus sat at the bow watching the others row. Suddenly his eyes grew wide.

"The ship's right behind us! Now what do we do?"

Scorpyus and Novak looked back to see the looming Pegasus emerge from the fog like the moon from behind a cloud. Shouts from the ship confirmed that the trio had been spotted.

"They're closer than I thought!" Scorpyus exclaimed. "Quick, put it aground here!"

They ran the boat aground and scrambled out, splashing into the cold surf. Shooop, shooop, thunk! Arrows whizzed overhead, one slamming into the lifeboat.

"Let's go! Move! Move!" Novak yelled.

They ran across the surf-swept beach, fear prodding them along. Toes and fingers frantically dove into nooks and crannies as they climbed the rocky crag. Arrows slammed into the rocks all around them, some splintering on impact. Whack! A large boulder catapulted into the cliffside near Novak, showering him with debris. The thud shook the cliff and dirt sprinkled the ascending party. Gritting his teeth, Novak pressed on, ramming bleeding fingers into any notch he could find. The thirty feet of cliff seemed endless under the onslaught of projectiles. Scorpyus beat Novak to the top and started arching arrows back at the ship. Bartus struggled, still only half way up. For him the climb would be difficult under the best of circumstances. An arrow struck Novak's backpack and burst a water skin before lodging in the pack's wooden frame.

"Being the biggest target has its disadvantages." Novak chided as the leaking water soaked his clothes.

A barrage of smaller rocks hammered the earth around the men. The thudding rocks sent shock waves through the escapees chests.

"Hit the deck!" Scorpyus yelled as rocks continued to rain down all around. He dove behind a few small boulders and took in a mouthful of sand in the process. An avalanche of cascading debris knocked Bartus loose and he fell to the wet sand below.

Another boulder slammed into a tree, severing a branch. Scorpyus looked up at the crashing sound of splintering wood just in time to see the branch before it landed on him, pinning him to the ground. Novak cast a concerned look toward Scorpyus as he swung himself onto the cliff's edge. Scorpyus struggled to free himself from the tangle of branches.

He's fine, Novak thought before shouting down to Bartus, "Tie the rope around your waist and throw the other end up."

Bartus frantically complied and Novak hauled him up, ignoring the rock that narrowly missed his head. Bartus was bleeding from a gash to the forehead. Novak muscled him up the cliff in two-foot bursts. At least Bartus was a lightweight.

Scorpyus managed to free himself, and then silenced one of the catapult crews. "Let's go, I'm almost out of arrows."

"Look! The Pegasus is on fire!" Novak exclaimed in his resonating voice.

"Hallelujah!" Scorpyus shouted. "It must have been the cigar."

Half the sentries were now busy trying to put out the shipboard fire. It was a fortunate break for the escaping trio. Still the Pegasus was close enough to shore so that the rest of the crew could safely launch its lifeboats. Armed sentries piled into the boats. It would take them a while to reach shore, but they weren't going to give up now. The sentries would face terrible repercussions for allowing the prisoners to escape.

The three fugitives took the nearest trail, running as fast as the darkness allowed. Novak plowed a path, and Scorpyus brought up the rear.

"We can't stay on the trail forever; it'll be too easy for them to track us in this soft dirt. We have to take our chances out there." Novak pointed into the thicket where a thick layer of pine needles covered the forest floor.

They left the trail and met an obstacle course of rocks, roots, and underbrush that slowed their run to a stumble. Weaving between trees and around bushes, they struggled for a half-mile until they came to a clearing.

"It'll be hard to track us through the woods at night but not impossible." Scorpyus said. "According to my map, on the other side of this meadow should be the river. The Royal Guard will expect us to follow the river to Xylor, so let's give them what they expect. We'll cut across this meadow, follow the river, and then go northwest towards Xylor as expected. But instead of going to Xylor, we'll find a place to hide along the river somewhere. Let them stumble past us in the dark."

Novak pondered the plan. "It's a gamble. What if they have dogs? "

"Then we're in trouble. But I didn't see any on the ship. At least we'll be rested up though." Scorpyus tried to make light of the situation. "The Royal Guard is well trained and has experienced troops. If we do the obvious, they will surely be prepared. Our best chance is to hide in the area. They won't expect anyone arrogant enough to stay and face them."

Novak agreed. "Ya, any leader worth his salt would have an ambush waiting downriver. Getting to Xylor is logical. They won't expect us to stay here, but a good leader would bring dogs just in case. Our choice is between the lesser of two evils."

"I know. Let's hope there wasn't time to round up dogs. And if there was, we'll fall from that bridge when we get to it." Scorpyus cracked a whimsical grin.

"I don't like either plan," Bartus said. They both were too dangerous. Surely there had to be a better way.

Novak glared at Bartus. "We didn't ask you."

Bartus curled away and fell silent. He didn't want to rile Novak.

Scorpyus took some time to explain. "It's like this, Bartus: they expect us to head to Xylor. The Royal Guard will send troops downriver to head us off. Staying here is risky, but they won't expect it. Even if they have dogs, we at least start from a position of surprise."

"And going away from Xylor takes us into the unknown and away from help." Novak added.

"And they can still track us either way." Scorpyus continued.

Bartus nodded, embarrassed to have questioned Scorpyus and Novak. What did he know about such matters? All he knew was that he felt exhausted and dazed by the day's events. He hadn't seen this much excitement in his life, and he hoped he never would again. He couldn't wait for this to be over, for the danger to pass. If this was an adventurous life, Bartus would rather have boredom. He cursed the day he stole the bread and started this nightmarish journey.

The trio set off across the clearing and forded a shallow spot on the river as planned. The frigid water numbed the pain in Bartus's feet as the three men slipped over moss-covered stones in the waist-deep water. They had to climb over a tree that had fallen near the opposite bank. Almost across, Bartus found a sinkhole and suddenly disappeared beneath the water. Novak shot in a hand and pulled him up choking and coughing. How much more of this could he take? He didn't even want to know what it was that was nuzzling his ankle under the water.

They headed toward Xylor along the opposite shore. The air chilled them in their wet clothes as they trudged along without a trail. Roots reached out to trip the men up, and branches fought to hold them back. Soon they came to a rocky bluff where a small waterfall trickled into the creek.

"Let's climb up there and hide at the top of this bluff." Scorpyus pointed to an outcropping of bushes on the bluff edge.

Their legs were so cold they were starting to ache, and everyone was anxious to rest. This bluff wasn't as steep as the one by the seashore, and they climbed the hundred feet to the top in a slower, more careful manner. They completed their ascent and nestled down in the brush behind a boulder where Bartus tried to catch his breath.

"Now we wait," Novak told Bartus who was immensely relieved to stop moving for a while. Bartus's head hurt, his muscles ached, and his lungs were on fire. He was panting like a hound dog, his face beet red. Even his teeth hurt from sucking in cold air. The pace the trio had been keeping was punishing for even the fit, and Bartus was not in shape by any stretch of the imagination. Novak removed his pack and handed out food to Scorpyus and Bartus. "Dried herring; one of my favorites!" Novak liked the salty fish, or anything salty for that matter. He was known to generously salt all foods he ate.

"You two do this a lot?" Bartus said as he removed the dried fish from its cheesecloth wrapping. "I mean, we narrowly escape with our lives and neither of you seem rattled by it."

"We've been doing this for a long time, since we were kids, "Scorpyus replied pensively. "Are we rattled? Sure we are, but you have two choices even when you're rattled: freeze up or move forward. The guys who freeze up don't survive for long. God helps those who give it their honest best." His Gypsy accent was more pronounced now that he was weary.

Bartus pondered the thought. "OK, but aren't you afraid that someday you'll be killed. You play a dangerous game."

"Well, nobody wants to die." Novak interjected. "But when it's your time to go, it's your time to go; and when it's not, it's not." Novak had seen people survive the apparently unsurvivable, and people die who should have lived. There was more at work in the universe than mere coincidence could account for.

"It's a matter of faith. We do the best we can and let God worry about the details. He's the only one who can control all the variables. Worrying about what we can't change will only add another problem to an already difficult situation." Scorpyus continued, expounding on his personal philosophy. "If God wants to call us back, no one can stop it. The best of plans won't stop it. If it's His will we live, no two-bit thug working for a dictator is going to circumvent Him and push us out of the world. We all have a purpose to fulfill in life, and choices to make. We live in an evil time, so choose wisely."

"Right," Novak's deep voice boomed. "There's a saying: If God be for us, who can be against us? But more importantly, choose God. Without that, everything else is pointless. We're lucky. We have an adventurous life. The difference between excitement and terror hinges on the choice you make."

"We also train and practice continually. We're not idiots. We don't brazenly walk into situations. God gave us some common sense and certain skills that He expects us to use." Scorpyus informed Bartus who sat eagerly taking it all in. "But you never know. Sometimes evil plots succeed. Sometimes bad things happen to good people. Nobody really knows why things happen the way they do except God."

"You can't tell people here that. They think a mermaid is god." Novak laughed. "I found *that* out."

"You two are right. Many Xylorians used to think like you before the count seized power ten years ago. He's the one who mandated Tanuba worship and largely implemented it by killing most of our religious leaders. He also silenced scores of citizens who criticized his mandate. A lot of people took the easy way out and abandoned previously-held beliefs and morals. The count *had* revived a faltering economy, after all. The people enjoyed, and continue to enjoy, tremendous prosperity. It was easy for most to go along with the new regime since it was a comfortable journey.

Of course, when the killing started everyone was shocked, but it became easier and easier to turn an apathetic eye the richer we grew. Most who saw the evil for what it was said nothing for fear of their lives. Thank God there are a few who are determined not to take it lying down, even if they have been forced underground. I used to own a farm. When I spoke out against the paganism, the merciless killings, and warned of the growing dictatorship, my land was seized under the pretense that I had not paid my taxes. I appealed the matter to the courts, but by then the count controlled the judges. But now, hearing you two, the way you talk, the passion and raw determination to stand up to evil—" Bartus released an angst-ridden sigh. "It reminds me of how much my people have deteriorated morally and socially in the short time Count Reddland has been in power. We turned our back on God and now suffer the consequences."

Scorpyus and Novak nodded. It wasn't all that long ago that their homeland of Ravenshire had suffered a hostile invasion also. Sitting with his back against a boulder, drawing lines in the dirt with a small twig, Scorpyus thought about a day in his youth....

...The war had stretched on for almost seven years, the bloodiest the region could remember. Everyone had lost a relative in the war, and most able-bodied men fought. Women and children played vital roles in the war also, acting as spies or tending the wounded; some were even soldiers. The mighty kingdom of Kelterland waged destruction against its neighbors, sending invading armies out to expand its territory. Scorpyus, as well as Novak, Cad, and Zephyr, were children at the time. They saw their land invaded, their friends and family killed, and their property taken. Scorpyus's village was hit harder than most because of the invading army's hatred for Gypsies. Gypsies were well acquainted with the tears of sorrow born of rejection. They suffered accordingly at the hands of the invaders. Ravenshire lost the war shortly after their elite knights were defeated at the battle of Saltwater Hill. Rumors circulated about a traitor betraying the knights, conspiring with the enemy against them. The knights were slaughtered in an ambush. Most felt that the experienced soldiers had to have been betrayed to be so soundly defeated. Nothing was ever proven, though, because there were no survivors among the knights to shed any light on the subject. Upon Ravenshire's defeat, Kelterland put a new tyrannical government into place. The Kelterlanders held it a non- priority to investigate the possibility of a traitor.

Weeks before the ambush that wiped out the Ravenshire Knights, the war came to Scorpyus's family on a gentle summer day, a day perfect for an attack on an unsuspecting village while the defending army launched an offensive forty miles to the north. Scorpyus, just eleven at the time, sat down to breakfast with his grandmother and older sister Isabella. The gentle old widow wasn't his blood relative. She had taken Scorpyus and Isabella in after finding them abandoned at a burial pit outside of town, discarded with unclaimed bodies. More than likely they had been abandoned by a mother who could no longer care for them after the loss of her husband in the war. It was easier to survive in these war-torn times without the burden of two extra mouths to feed. Whatever the reason, the old woman could not just leave the abandoned children.

Two-year-old Isabella was doing her best to console her screaming infant brother. Her frightened eyes peered from behind a dirty face at the passing stranger. The elder Gypsy woman had pity on them. It enraged her to think someone could be that callous. The children looked like they were less than full-blooded Gypsies. She suspected that had something to do with their abandonment. They were filthy and lice infested. Fortunately they hadn't been there too long. The old woman took them home and cleaned them up. Her only child was now grown and she had long wanted more.

The Gypsy woman never learned who abandoned the children, and quite frankly didn't care to meet them

Eleven years later the children's world was shattered once again.

"You better finish your food or you'll get hungry later," Scorpyus's grandmother warned. "You'll need your strength for chores."

"But, grandma, I don't like eggs," Scorpyus complained. Isabella stuck her tongue out to taunt him in his plight.

With a loud smash the front door to the cabin splintered into a dozen pieces, and in walked five armed men. Scorpyus's family went silent, frozen like statues, as the fat intruder started snorting down biscuits. Two others grabbed Scorpyus's grandmother and forced her into a chair.

"Well it looks like we've got ourselves a Gypsy wench and her two thieving half breeds!" The fat one spit while rubbing his belly.

The others cackled joyously while scavenging what was left of the food. Scorpyus didn't have to worry about eating his eggs anymore. Chewing with his mouth open, the fat man bent down so that his red, bulbous nose was inches from Isabella's face and added, "And this one here is mighty pretty."

Thirteen-year-old Isabella flinched at his alcohol-glazed eyes, at the bits of dried food encrusted in his beard. Her eyes started watering, partially out of fear, and partially because her nostrils stung from the stench of the fat man's breath. Isabella tried to stand to leave but was stopped by two hairy hands.

"Leave her alone!" Scorpyus shouted and jumped to his feet.

A gloved fist smashed into his right eye and sent him sprawling across the room and slamming into the wall. A flash of white light shot through the boy's brain; a dull ringing sounded in his ears. The fat man and his cohorts laughed raucously. Blood flowed freely into Scorpyus's eye.

"Tie the brat to a chair!" The fat man sputtered as he ate another biscuit. Isabella started to cry. "And you shut up before you get the same!"

The men quickly scarfed down the family's breakfast, snorting and grunting, pausing only occasionally to scratch their lice-ridden, matted-down hair, or wipe their hands on their soiled clothing. Their stink now filled the small home.

Scorpyus was tied tightly to a chair. His wrists throbbed in pain, rope digging into his flesh. After cinching his ankles to the legs of the chair, the men proceeded to ransack the house and destroy everything they didn't take for themselves.

"You better leave while you still can. My son will be back soon with his friends," Scorpyus's grandmother lied. Her son was a member of the Ravenshire Knights and had been like a father to the children. Unfortunately he was miles away.

Again laughter filled the room. The fat man stomped over to Scorpyus's grandma and backhanded her, splitting her lip.

"I said shut up!" What started as an angry outburst turned worse. Vile thoughts wriggled into the fat man's brain, thoughts that he readily entertained. His mind squirmed like a plate of worms, with the abominations slithering around inside, each fighting for a way out. The fat man was more than happy to release a few. He started to stroke Scorpyus's grandmother's graying hair.

"Hold her down for me boys," the fat man ordered, already out of breath. He licked his greasy lips in anticipation.

Scorpyus's grandmother's eyes grew wide with terror. A rush of nausea welled up from the pit of her stomach, almost causing her to vomit. She bit her lip and held back tears, refusing to give these pigs the satisfaction of breaking her in front of her children. The fat man dragged Scorpyus's chair closer to the action, forcing him to witness the sadistic act.

"Watch and learn about man's work, kid," he bellowed out an asthmatic laugh.

Scorpyus shut his eyes tight. He could hear his sister crying hysterically. He heard his grandmother scream when her dress was torn. Isabella's wailing shook him to his bones. Tears squeezed out of his closed eyelids and he sobbed. Grizzly hands grabbed him by the hair, forced his head back, and pried his eyes open. The men each took a turn with his grandmother, beating her repeatedly when she tried to resist. Scorpyus trembled and struggled in his chair.

"NOOO! STOP IT! QUIT!" He yelled, rage ripping through him.

"I thought I told you to shut up, you stinking Gypsy trash!" The fat man cursed when he was finished with the grandmother, then kicked the legs out from under the boy's chair.

Scorpyus's face bounced off the floor, and he tasted blood in his mouth. He struggled to free himself until his wrists bled, but the ropes were too tight. One of the men walked over and kicked him in the ribs again and again. Scorpyus stopped screaming when the wind was knocked out of him. The most he could do was gasp for air. Soon the other men followed suit, and Scorpyus became the object upon which the intruders vented their rage. He slipped in and out of consciousness as they beat him. The remaining events became a blur of half-conscious observations. Scorpyus remembered opening the eye that wasn't swollen shut when he heard his sister moaning and whimpering and seeing his sister being defiled also. It was a haunting sound he would never forget. After that he blacked out.

Scorpyus awoke some time later to his sister's mournful, howling cry. She sat in the fetal position, gently rocking back and forth by an overturned chair, pulling her torn and tattered dress around her shoulders. The invaders were gone. Scorpyus's grandmother's severed head was impaled on one of the legs of the chair.

"Izzy, can you hear me?" Scorpyus called gently to his sister; his split, swollen lips hurt when he talked. She didn't respond. For three days she just cried, rocking herself as she stared blankly at the floor. For three days she and Scorpyus had nothing to eat. The home grew fetid with the smell of their grandmother's corpse. Time crept slowly by. It took three full days before Isabella regained enough composure to untie Scorpyus from the chair. His joints were stiff, and every move hurt. His lungs burned like fire with each breath. His face hurt too much to eat. It took the rest of the day to clean things up. Scorpyus buried his grandmother while Isabella tidied up the small house.

Months would pass before Scorpyus and Isabella recovered physically from their ordeal. Mentally they would never fully recover. But this was the moment of truth in the young boy's life. A path forked before him, and the choice he made now would set his course for the rest of his life. He could have let the hate he felt rule his life—and he felt enough hatred to kill a thousand men—or he could turn from his wrath and become the young man his grandmother had dreamed he would become. Scorpyus's grandmother had been a godly woman. She taught her two children to follow the Lord. As a result, his grandmother's influence would shape his decision. It was on that day that Scorpyus vowed to do everything in his power to stop the spread of evil. He was not going to let this event, or any other event he suffered in the war, turn him into one of the men who did this to his family. God would see him through. Scorpyus and Isabella clung to God like a life raft for survival. Vengeance would be the Lord's. Scorpyus did not know it at the time, but there were others who felt the same way. A few would later join forces with him. This day, and this war, spawned the seed that would grow into a small band of friends whose mission would be to fight those who infected the world with the stench of wickedness and greed. This day saw the birth of the Clandestine Knights....

"Are you sick?" Novak noticed that Scorpyus was looking a little pale.

"Huh? What?" With a flinch Scorpyus came back from Ravenshire to see Bartus sitting asleep with his head bobbing on the end of his neck. "No, I'm fine."

Novak eyed his friend and took a large swig of water while wiping his brow with the back of his hand. "Take my advice, Scorp, don't dwell in the past. Take it from me; it only drives you mad." He pointed to the napping Bartus. "I'm going to bandage that gash on his head. It looks like you could use a fresh dressing on your side also."

Scorpyus saw that blood had soaked through his bandage. Novak cut the pack into strips of cloth and handed a few to Scorpyus. He then set to work on Bartus, waking him.

"Bartus, you need a few stitches. I don't have a needle or thread so you'll have to get it taken care of in town. In the meantime I'll throw a dressing on it. That should keep most of the blood out of your eyes.

"Thanks," Bartus grimaced when Novak pressed and tied a bandage to the wound.

Scorpyus had just finished putting a fresh bandage on his side when he caught the faint glow of a distant torch out of the corner of his eye. It looked like it was coming from somewhere up creek. "Novak!"

Novak pushed Bartus down and crawled into position next to Scorpyus who was looking through the spyglass at the edge of the outcropping.

"It looks like the same party we saw on the trail near the beach," Scorpyus whispered. "Wait! What's that?" He cocked his head as if he heard something.

The trio kept absolutely quiet and motionless, straining to hear what Scorpyus thought he heard. Novak and Scorpyus gave each other a look of dread. Dogs barked faintly in the distance. Bloodhounds were on their scent.

"What does that mean? What do we do now?" Bartus's voice trembled and stuttered.

"Now we have to make it to Xylor. What rotten luck!" Novak flared. "I suppose it's too much to hope for those dogs to come across a skunk. That would desensitize their noses for awhile."

Bartus's face contorted in horror. "You said they would be waiting for us if we went back to Xylor."

"Ya," Novak nodded. "Would you rather stay and get eaten by dogs?"

Scorpyus handed out the remaining food, thinking out loud as he did, more as a means of explaining the gravity of the situation to Bartus than anything else: "We each have a day's food left. Each man carries his own. Novak and I will take the two remaining water skins; Bartus, you take the rope. Let's see—I have four arrows left. Not good. My guess is we're three or so miles from Xylor. If they have someone waiting for us, maybe we can dodge them. It's going to be rough. The search party is on foot also, so we should be fine until they cut the dogs loose. If we don't make it to town—well, let's just say we can't let the dogs get us cornered. Being captured would be better than what could happen if the dogs find us first. Let's go, we don't have a lot of time."

"Just leave me here. I'll only slow you down. I'm exhausted, and I don't think I'll make it anyway." Bartus, resigned to defeat, sat holding his throbbing head.

"Get on your feet!" Novak ordered and gave Bartus a look that made him light-headed.

Suddenly Bartus felt more energetic, and he sprang to his feet. Facing Novak seemed worse then facing the dogs.

They started off at a fast pace, through brush, around trees, and over rocks. Faint barking was a constant prod to keep moving. Once the search party made it to the top of the bluff, the dogs would pick up a fresher scent and start closing in on the trio. Pushing hard, the men dripped with sweat despite the cool night air. Boots came down in mud; clothes snagged on thorns, bodies waded through stagnant ponds of scum. Up slope, down grade, across rotted logs—travel was brutal. They eventually came to a steep slope, paused, and then cautiously descended it.

Bartus tripped and tumbled down the embankment. Reaching out for support he pulled Scorpyus with him. Novak looked back just as he was bowled over by the other two. Collectively they cascaded down the slope, a human avalanche. Novak went down on his belly, leaving a rut in the pine needles as he slid, Scorpyus skidded down on his back, bouncing off several trees. Bartus tumbled like a jester. They all hit the bottom without any injuries worse than minor scratches.

After brushing the dirt off his face, Novak again led the way, and picked up the momentum. For twenty minutes they scurried at a frantic pace, the dogs yelping in the distance. Bartus, covered with pine needles, was ready to collapse under the punishment. Unlike the others who had hard-soled boots, he had soft leather shoes. His feet felt brutalized, his body ached, and he started to lag.

"Keep moving!" Scorpyus tried to persuade Bartus, but it was no use. He and Novak each took one of Bartus's arms and pulled him along, Bartus gasping for air like a man nearly drowned and just emerged from the water. Scorpyus and Novak's breathing was labored also, and pulling Bartus along wasn't helping matters. They weren't even close to Xylor yet and Bartus was being dragged like a piece of farm equipment.

The hounds got louder, their barks taking on that high-pitched yelp that meant they were excited about closing in on their prey. A few minutes later and Bartus was nothing but dead weight. Novak and Scorpyus might as well have been lugging his corpse. It became painfully obvious that Bartus could no longer continue. The three stopped and Bartus collapsed in a heap on the ground. He sucked wind fiercely and was pale and clammy. His face contorted with agony, and he clutched his side aching with muscle cramps. Scorpyus and Novak looked at each other with the same thought. Their best chance for survival was to leave Bartus behind. Both knew he would be executed if he were caught. That's if the dogs didn't chew him to pieces first. The barking grew louder and louder, and now the hounds could be heard rustling through the brush.

"They've cut the dogs loose; it's only a matter of time now," Scorpyus said, discouraged, holding up his hands in a gesture of futility. "Well, God, we need a miracle."

Novak paused a few seconds, looking down at Bartus crumpled form. The situation demanded that everyone pull his own weight. It was maddening. There was nothing more frustrating than when someone didn't do his share. Novak was accustomed to working with an efficient team of skilled professionals who complemented one another.

"Oh, God, I'm dying," Bartus panted. He was so taxed he vomited up his meal in a few convulsions.

Slowly Novak softened, relaxing his furrowed brow. It wasn't as if Bartus were being lazy; he was physically incapable of the rigorous demand, even to save his own life. Besides that, the guy was a lot older.

"I'll pack him first," Novak sighed as he threw Bartus over his broad shoulders like a sack of grain.

They trudged across a small clearing and into the woods on the other side where they came to a rocky embankment that sloped down into darkness. With Bartus on his shoulders the trek down for Novak was precarious. They made their way over large boulders and through a dense patch of brush until suddenly they found themselves on the banks of a swift-flowing river.

"What's this, the river that comes out at the port of Xylor?" Scorpyus wondered.

"Are there any other rivers on this island?" Novak asked.

Scorpyus was puzzled. What river had they been following earlier? "I don't know? I didn't expect to see this one. My map must be wrong."

Novak and Scorpyus looked at each other, realizing they were lost. Where this river led they didn't know.

Eight to ten snarling, snapping, yelping hounds erupted from some brush and were barreling down on them. The dogs were wild-eyed and crazed, foaming saliva dripping from gleaming steel-trap teeth that protruded from curled-back jowls. A few seconds from their prey, the hounds could barely contain themselves.

"Jump!" Novak yelled and leaped into the river, pulling the others with him. All three let out gasps upon hitting the icy water. Scorpyus and Novak emerged from the drink with pronounced exhales, but didn't see Bartus at first. Then they saw him, washed away downstream, facedown, drowning. He didn't even have the strength to flail his arms. Novak and Scorpyus swam over to him and held his head above water as all three were swept rapidly down the river. The swift water banged them into rocks in the darkness. Scorpyus looked back to see the dogs on the riverbank, angry at losing their prey. A few ran along the bank after the swimmers until they could no longer keep up. The water was much too swift. The three men entered turbulent rapids and in a few seconds vanished into the darkness.

IV

ZEPHYR AND CAD walked their horses through the streets of Xylor toward the inn. Royal Guards in their blue surcoats and chain mail were everywhere.

Zephyr and Cad arrived at the Shorebird Inn and used the side entrance. The inn was a rustic two-story wooden structure with rooms on the top floor and a restaurant with tavern on the lower floor. The place was decorated to the tastes of a hunter, with several mounted animal heads adding to the ambiance. Elegant tapestries depicting wildlife scenes hung on the walls. The smell of burning pine came from a crackling fire in a stone fireplace.

The tavern was full of patrons eating mounds of food from wooden plates. Maidens kept busy bringing thick steaks, lentils, and loaves of bread from the kitchen. There wasn't an empty table, and a few customers ate while standing, resting their plates on their steins of ale. Most ate and drank quickly and efficiently, using their hands. Those not eating stood at the bar. They wore armor with a full complement of weapons and drank ale from foamy steins. This group had been there a while. The ale was starting to affect their motion and showed in their eyes. The Shorebird Inn was near the docks and housed some of the many visitors that came to Xylor. Judging from the crowd, most had risen before the sun to get an early start on their day. Those at the bar hadn't called it a night yet.

As Zephyr and Cad made their way through the bar, they noticed a lone individual standing in the corner. He was not eating, and when he caught Cad's gaze on him he quickly looked away and sipped at his ale as if it were a hot herbal brew. Everyone else could care less about those that entered the Inn. Zephyr and Cad exchanged suspicious glances then headed upstairs. Zephyr took the steps soundlessly. Cad wasn't as fast or as successful at being quiet. The stairs called out the presence of his hefty frame a few times during his ascent. At the top he looked down the hall to see Zephyr near one of their party's rooms. She moved slowly to the next door, staying quiet. Cad stayed put. His instincts told him that Zephyr didn't want him too close while she investigated something.

Zephyr looked at the second door. It was just like the first. The pattern of scratches around the keyhole was obviously the work of an amateur. She listened at the door and tried to peer through the keyhole.

Cad heard a noise behind him in the stairwell and turned to look while flattening against a wall. No one emerged from the stairwell. He heard the unmistakable strain of someone stepping on a loose stair three times before signaling Zephyr of the company. Someone was trying to sneak up the stairs. Zephyr rushed for the back staircase with Cad following quickly. He stopped abruptly when Zephyr froze, peering down the back stairwell. When Zephyr spun around to meet Cad's gaze, he knew there was trouble.

"They're in the hall!" One of the guards alerted the others. The door to Cad and Zephyr's room clattered open and out poured several soldiers with drawn swords. Zephyr gripped her sword, ready for the onslaught. Cad rushed to another door across the hall and kicked it in. He startled a sleeping man who struggled to throw off his blankets and came to his feet revealing a very thin physique. He rushed Cad. Cad effortlessly shoved him back into bed, ran by, and threw open the window in one smooth motion. Zephyr sprang into the room and quickly shut the door. When she saw the thin man she pulled a dagger. The man decided to remain on his bed clutching his blankets around himself for comfort. He seemed embarrassed to be exposed in front of a female, and retreated against the headboard. Zephyr thrust her dagger under the door and kicked it into the floor with her foot, jamming the door shut for the moment. She joined Cad at the window. In the background, the sound of men battering a door down rattled the room. If the door was hefty enough, it would buy them some time.

"I don't see anyone," Cad said. He climbed out the window and hung from the casement. Then he dropped. Cad scanned the alley as Zephyr followed him. At the end of the alley, Cad peered around the corner at the front of the inn. Their horses were gone. A dozen archers for the Royal Guard stood in the street. Cad and Zephyr had blundered into an ambush. But why did the Royal Guard want them?

Cad leaned back and whispered, "What now?"

"Maybe we can hide on the roof?" Zephyr nodded at a trellis on the shop next door. "Then we could make our way to the stables."

He looked up the trellis then nodded to Zephyr. It was the only option. The banging upstairs indicated they still had a bit of time left.

Zephyr ran to the trellis and climbed it with the agility of a cat. Once on the roof she readied her bow to cover Cad who was about halfway up. She watched the window and wondered about the thin man. He obviously hadn't opened the door for the soldiers. Out of the corner of her eye, Zephyr saw an archer come from behind the inn to the side alley. He was interested in the steady banging and eyed the window of its origin. During a pause in the battering he heard the trellis rustle and looked directly at Cad. It was dark in the alley and he couldn't make out what caused the noise; but as Cad took his next step, the archer realized what had happened. Immediately he raised a hand to his quill for an arrow. He was about to yell an alarm when an arrow pierced his throat.

Cad heard the arrow leave Zephyr's bow. He looked down and saw the archer fall to his knees. The arrow hit a bit high, he thought, but was effective nonetheless. It was a great shot at that angle.

Zephyr waited for Cad, covering his ascent. The fallen archer clutched his throat in agony as he crawled a few feet towards his friends. She had her next arrow ready and thought about trying to put the archer out of his misery. But there was a slim chance she could end his suffering and a good chance she could make it worse. She watched the archer collapse as Cad climbed onto the roof.

Together they raced from roof to roof, jumping the small gaps between buildings until they came to a building that was twenty feet away. It was too far to jump. They shimmied down a drainpipe to the back door of a fabric shop. The door had a poor lock and Zephyr had it open quickly. Behind them they could hear shouting. Peering out of the store window, they saw a mob of citizens looking for the free show. It wasn't even daybreak yet. People were up early. It had been an exciting night of odd occurrences. Some things never change; thirst to see mayhem and gore never waned. That's why public executions were so popular. The citizens began engaging the archers with questions they didn't have answers to, mobbing them, and obstructing them in their duties. Zephyr and Cad took advantage of the chaos, and slipped out the door and dashed to the stables.

They ran the five blocks, keeping to the alleys, and reached an open, lighted door. Inside they saw a guard securing Zephyr's horse in a stall. Another guard stood nearby. The Royal Guard had confiscated their horses. If they were to escape, they had to get the horses back.

Cad rushed in clutching his sword and engaged the closer soldier who proved to be a better swordsman than expected. Blades slammed and thrust, seeking a soft target. The guard spat curses at Cad as he swung for the kill, but failed to realize the exact confines of the stables. Instead of striking Cad on the shoulder, his sword struck a rafter, a costly mistake. Cad drove the guard back into a ceiling post where he couldn't maneuver and lost his footing. Once on the ground he panicked, and Cad delivered a killing wound to the frantic guard's side.

Zephyr locked swords with the younger guard who wasn't much more than eighteen. She was faster and better with a blade.

The kid may have been stronger, but as long as he continued to swing wildly, it wouldn't be enough. He was striking the wall, floor, and stall gates, everything but Zephyr. He was overconfident, and Zephyr found it easy to dodge his blows. She knew this wouldn't take long. It would be a shame to have to kill this boy. Zephyr could have ended it anytime she wanted, but felt that if she could wear the boy down, he just might flee for his life once he knew it was hopeless. The boy momentarily retreated. Zephyr didn't pursue, and lowered her sword. A quizzical look crossed the young man's face. Was she giving up? This had to be some sort of a trick. He cautiously eyed the flighty woman and wondered what she was up to. Zephyr watched as Cad brought the hilt of his sword down on the boy's head. The boy grimaced in pain, his eyes rolled, and he lost consciousness. He'd have a headache when he awoke.

Zephyr tied the young guard up, and then hid him in the stall farthest from the door. The horses were ready for riding moments later. Cad tied a lead onto Novak and Scorpyus's horses.

"We'll take the other chaps horses as well. It's a good thing Novak and Scorpyus left their packs in the stables. If they had taken them to the room they would be lightened of their possessions." Cad eyed the slash marks on the wall, making sure they were still there.

Cad and Zephyr mounted up and rode out of town heading for Sage.

Zephyr yawned. It was near daybreak and she had been up all night. "I hope the others find us soon. In the meantime let us find a place to get some rest. I am exhausted."

Cad nodded his agreement. "Sounds good; I suppose we won't be checking out of the blooming inn."

—•◆•—

Sage was a farming community that supplied most of the Kingdom's medicinal herbs and remedies. Cad and Zephyr reached it after three miles on a trail about the width of a small wagon and bordered on both sides by a dense forest of oak, cedar, birch, and pine. Underbrush and ferns grew out of layers and layers needle-covered humus. Countless trickling rivulets turned into creeks, eventually making their way to a river. Moss-covered trees and the musty smell of mud reminded Zephyr of home. Warblers chirped overhead, and a few squirrels and chipmunks scurried about. Cad and Zephyr eventually came to a clearing where farmers plowed their fields. It was a sharp contrast to the trail from which they had come. The thin layer of fog was burning off in the crisp morning air. Cad and Zephyr enjoyed their ride to Sage, taking in the lush countryside around them. Xylor was a beautiful island. It was a shame that it had to be steeped in idolatry and under the rule of a tyrannical leader. Strangers in Sage were uncommon, but not so rare that they gained much more attention than a curious glance or two.

"This looks to be a peaceful little place," Cad observed, leather creaking as he shifted in the saddle. "This might not be a bad assignment after all, scenery-wise anyway. I definitely could get used to this. The village looks small enough that I bet it won't be too hard to find the stables either," he chuckled.

Zephyr nodded in agreement while eyeing a peach grove. "I just hope we can trust this Thadus. I mean, we really do not know what we are getting into. We have been ambushed once. I do not want it to happen again. And can we trust the old man who gave me the note? I tell you this, maybe using Sage as our staging point is not such a good idea after all."

"You're having second thoughts, I see. Don't worry too much; after all, the old bloke died for his cause. The Royal Guard ambushed us. I seriously doubt the old man was working for the Guard. In fact, I bet he was working against them." Cad was taking in the beautiful morning.

"I know, Cad, but he could have been a double agent. I would not want to unknowingly help the furtherance of the Xylorian government. From what I have seen so far, this government is as wicked as the one we have now in Ravenshire. Maybe it is worse."

"True." Cad thought for a moment. "But the chap did trust us with that coded message. If he wanted to help the government, wouldn't he have given the note to a Royal Guard? There are certainly a lot of them around. We don't know what the note means yet, but a number of chaps are willing to kill for it. They killed the old man for it, and would have killed you for it. I have a hunch that whoever is responsible for doing in the old bloke is the one we should worry about."

"If the old man was on the side of good," Zephyr replied sarcastically, "how come he did not want us to complete our mission? We are just bringing back some medicine to help out a sick and dying man."

Zephyr and her friends had been hired to come to Xylor and obtain Hyacinth Blue, a rare medicine, to save the life of a sick man. They agreed to the mission although they had never heard of Hyacinth Blue. After all, it seemed like a worthy cause. Besides, the pay was good, and they needed the money. They never met the sick man who needed the medicine, but they knew he was wealthy or had a wealthy benefactor. An extremely polite and well-dressed man who claimed to be the sick man's personal physician had hired them. Anyone with a personal physician had to have money. The physician told them that the medicine was scarce, and one of the few places they could find it was in Xylor. Until the arrest of Novak, the task seemed straight forward enough. Now it looked as though it would take a little longer than they had thought.

"The old bloke didn't exactly say he wanted us to abort our mission, did he?" Cad inquired. "I thought he said things aren't how they seem, and lives were in danger. Nothing is to say he even knew what our mission was. He only thought he did."

"Je ne sais pas, maybe you are right, Cad. Maybe I just read into the situation. I had the impression he did not want us to find the medicine, though." Zephyr relaxed and stretched in the saddle.

"It'll give us something to chat about. Like I said, we aren't even sure if the old chap really knew why we're here. He *claimed* to know, but he never came out and clarified it." Cad and Zephyr soon came to small building next to a corral.

Cad surveyed the livery stables carefully as he tied his mount to the hitching rail. Zephyr did likewise. She hitched Scorpyus and Novak's horses also. The animals drank eagerly from nearby troughs. Larek's stables were a relatively new wooden structure with a shingle roof. Its two wide entry doors were swung open and blocked in place by sacks of feed. Cad could see hay-lined walls inside. Livery equipment and a few lanterns hung from wooden pegs on the stall posts. To one side lay a small corral with a pair of horses in it. The smell of horse manure filled Cad's nostrils.

"I love the smell of horses," Zephyr sang. "It reminds me of home." Zephyr grew up on a horse ranch.

Zephyr practically skipped into the stables, anxious to see the animals. Cad shook his head, amused.

The stables had eighteen straw-lined stalls, three of them with horses. Tack and harnesses hung from the walls, and a few stall gates had saddles slung over them. Saddle blankets were stacked on a bench. A wooden ladder, nailed to a post between the fifth and sixth stalls, led to a loft piled with hay.

A rugged-looking man stepped out of a tiny office in the corner and asked, "Can I help you?" He watched Zephyr, who had squatted down to run her hand along the back of a horse's leg.

"Maybe. We're looking for a chap named Thadus. He's supposed to be at the stables here. Do you know him?" Cad inquired. Zephyr curiously peeked out from behind the horse.

"I might. Why are you looking for him?" The man replied hesitantly.

"We can't really say." Cad noticed that the man was unarmed. "Someone told us to contact him here."

"Who?" The man looked at his visitors with narrowed eyes.

Zephyr stood and joined the conversation. "We do not know his name, monsieur. He was an old man. I met him last night in Xylor near the area where they found that lieutenant from the Royal Guard. He told me to come to Sage and meet with Thadus.

By the way, that horse has a bruised ankle and you should let it rest a week or so."

"Do you make it a habit of doing what strangers tell you to do?" The man asked suspiciously.

"We do when that stranger knows too bloody much about our business," Cad said bluntly. "Especially if he gets killed telling us that."

The man's face went white with shock. Tears welled up in his eyes and he glanced around nervously as if he didn't know what to say next. He shut the doors to the stables and motioned for Cad and Zephyr to step into his office.

"Was this man wearing a light gray cloak, in his midseventies with gray hair and a beard?" The man asked. He sat down behind a cluttered desk. "Please have a seat."

"Yes, monsieur, that is the man," Zephyr said while shutting the office door. She and Cad took seats opposite the man.

The man wiped a tear from his cheek. "I had heard about the lieutenant, but I didn't know that anyone had been killed. That man's name was Isaac. He was a dear friend."

"Oh, monsieur, I am sorry," Zephyr said solemnly, and then pressed on. "He seemed to want us to meet this Thadus. If you know where he is, we will be trouble you no further."

The man sighed deeply, taking a moment to regain his composure. "I'm Thadus. If Isaac told you to contact me, it must mean you two are with the entourage sent here to find a rare medicine."

Does anybody not know why we are here? Cad wondered, totally amazed his mission seemed to be as well kept a secret as the discovery of fire. A full minute of silence passed as Cad and Zephyr sat speechless.

Thadus was in his late forties, blond, blue-eyed, and weather-beaten from long hours in the sun. He was burly, short, and stocky, with hairy forearms. He looked tough as leather and well acquainted with hard work. He wore a white shirt with sleeves rolled up and a buckskin vest and pants. He sat patiently with callused hands folded on the desk waiting for a response.

Zephyr spoke first. "Well, I am afraid you have us at a disadvantage. You know so much about us, and we know nothing about you."

Thadus eyed his guests, and then got to the point. "Look, we really don't know much about each other. You want to find out what and how I know about your mission in Xylor. I want to know what Isaac told you and what your true intentions are. Circumstance has forced us into a position where we'll have to trust each other somewhat. Let's start by my asking what you know about Xylor."

Cad bristled at Thadus's bluntness but restrained himself. After all, the poor guy just found out his friend had been killed.

"Fair enough, but if I get the impression that I'm being lied to, or being set up—well, let's just bloody well say there will be a significant amount of repercussions," Cad warned. He continued, "We know very little about Xylor other than it was one of many territories Kelterland annexed during the war. We come from a land that was annexed also. Ravenshire. I'm sure you've heard of it."

Thadus nodded. "If you come from Ravenshire, then you must be aware that not everyone is happy when their homeland is conquered and a new system is forced in place?"

"You could say that," Zephyr agreed.

Thadus leaned back in his chair. "A few years after Xylor was annexed—Annexed? Let's be honest. It was brutally overthrown. Anyway, shortly after Xylor's fall, Luther Reddland came to power. He governs Xylor for the Kelterlanders. Kelterland is a monarchy, hence the Royal Guard, and they crowned Reddland count of Xylor." Thadus was obviously not a fan of the count.

"I take it he's loved by all," Cad said sarcastically.

"Actually he has a lot of support due to the fact he has been great for the economy. We are now major exporters to Kelterland and its territories. Reddland also resurrected the ancient cult of Tanuba, which gained him support from anyone willing to become a pagan radical. It's amazing how many people were just waiting for an excuse to discard their morality for the promise of wealth, wine, and women. Tanuba legitimizes a lot of sin, and sucks up the unsuspecting. Tanuba endorses the vision of being unencumbered by the heavy burdens of sin and guilt. Supposedly without those limits, the worshipers will to soar to their fullest potential. But what happened here in Xylor, as I'm sure happened where you are from also, is quite the opposite."

Thadus did nothing to conceal his look of disgust. "Is this soaring to our fullest potential? Or is it a descent into the dung pile? Hell has been loosed on the people. Everywhere you look are the victims of rape, murder, theft, drunkenness, and oppression. Orphaned children and inappropriate physical immorality are now the norm rather then the exception. Supporters of the status quo are quick to state that these problems have always been around. But now there is more than ever before. Only a fool would deny that fact. Too many people sat astraddle the fence, remaining lukewarm, afraid to take a stand until it was too late." Thadus thought for a moment. "But there is an underground resistance who would love to turn the region back to God."

Zephyr leaned forward in her chair. "Monsieur, you have just described Ravenshire. Both of our homelands suffered similar fates. And if I am not mistaken, Isaac was part of the resistance movement, was he not?"

"Yes he was," Thadus said sorrowfully. "And as you may have guessed, so am I. If anyone finds that out, I'm as good as dead. You saw Isaac meet the fate of those so exposed."

Zephyr nodded her head in agreement.

"So what do you want with us?" Cad inquired. "What was Isaac warning us about?"

"We had information that someone was going to arrive in Xylor to search for a rare medicine. Isaac was one of our best spies. He must have found out that you, your party, were the ones hired for the job. By the way, is it just the two of you who were sent? I thought there were more."

"That's a long story, mate." Cad grinned thinking of Novak. "But how is that so dangerous we need a warning? There's no point in denying that we are here to find a medicine, but so what?"

"Who is that medicine for?" Thadus asked.

"We do not exactly know." Zephyr shrugged her shoulders. "We do not even know what the medicine will cure, or even if it exists."

"You don't expect me to believe that?" Thadus shot back.

"I do not care what you believe!" Zephyr took offense to the insinuation that she was a liar. "It is the truth. A wealthy man's personal physician hired us to find a rare medicine. We never saw the sick man, just his doctor."

"We have some vague idea of who the medicine might be for. If that information is accurate, you are playing with a deadly snake," Thadus warned.

"You obviously don't want this chap cured," Cad deduced.

"I don't even know if the medicine exists. There is no known recipe. Isaac thought he was getting close to tracking down a recipe, but now that hope is lost. As far as a cure for this man, that is of no importance compared to the value of the medicine." Thadus leaned forward to look at Cad and Zephyr to stress the importance of what he was about to say. "You came for Hyacinth Blue, didn't you?"

"Yes." Cad realized the cat was out of the bag so there would be no point in denying it.

"Then let's make a deal. We'll help you acquire Hyacinth Blue any way we can. You share the recipe with us if you find it."

"Look, we don't want to get involved in your bloody political problems. We're here for a job and nothing more. If you want a copy of the recipe, I could care less as long as we finish the job we're hired to do." Cad was adamant. "And thanks for the offer to help, but we work better alone. There is something you can do for us, however. We'll leave you a copy of the recipe in exchange for a hideout. If you are willing,"

"For now that will work; I hope we grow to trust each other, but we are strangers whose paths have crossed involuntarily; maybe in time." Thadus said and saw that his guests nodded in agreement. "I can show you a place you can work out of—"

There was a loud knock at the stable doors. "Open up! Royal Guard! We need to talk to the owner of the stables. Is anyone here?"

A look of panic came over Cad, Thadus, and Zephyr's faces.

"Quick! Follow me!" Thadus instructed.

The three sprang up in such a flurry that an inkbottle spilled over Thadus's desk and Cad's chair fell over. Cad drew his sword as he left the cramped office.

"You two hide. I'll try to get rid of the guards," Thadus whispered.

Zephyr shimmied up a post to the loft and dove over a stack of hay, hitting the floor with a thud. Cad crawled under a tarp that covered sacks of feed. He pulled it up over his head leaving a small crack to see out of.

Thump! Thump! Thump! The Royal Guards knocked on the stable door again.

"I'm coming!" Thadus yelled before opening the doors. "I was feeding the horses. Can't a guy have a little peace?"

Three guards stood at the door. The sergeant did all of the talking. "Sorry to disturb you, but we won't be long. Is Larek here?"

"No, he is not, and he rarely is. Is there anything I can help you with? I manage the stables for him." Thadus noticed the three rugged guards looked tired.

"Perhaps you can. We're looking for a woman to question about a murder she may have witnessed. She also stole a horse. We thought she might have come here. We're searching all the villages around Xylor." The sergeant looked around the interior of the stables. "I just thought she might need another horse since we recovered the stolen one."

"Well, I have four horses rented out right now, one is to a woman. What does this woman look like?"

"Oh, reddish hair, smaller, wearing buckskin and a short cape, a brown cap," The guard described Zephyr.

"No, I haven't seen anyone matching that description," Thadus lied. "The lady who rented the horse was older, in a fancy dress, wealthy; you know, the high-society type. She said she was out to see the sights."

"When was she here?"

"First thing this morning. She came in with her husband around an hour ago."

"Did anyone come in last night?"

"No, we're closed at night."

"Does anyone else work here besides you?"

"Yeah, I hire a couple of kids to come in each afternoon to clean stalls, brush down the horses, do a few odds and ends."

"Any chance they may have seen anything?"

"I'll ask them when they come in, but I'm here with them the whole time. I should have seen whatever they've seen."

"Whose horses are those tied out front?"

"They're mine. Some customers recently returned them. I haven't had the chance to put them up yet.

"Well, okay. Sorry to bother you. Let us know if you see anything."

Thadus closed the stable doors again after the Royal Guard left. He waited until the soldiers rode off. "You two can come out now."

Cad sheathed his sword after coming out from under the tarp. "Thanks a lot, mate. We owe you one."

Zephyr straightened her cap and came to the edge of the loft. She had hay stuck in her hair and clothes.

"It looks like you're popular. You have the Royal Guard looking for you. Then again, stealing a horse usually has that result." Thadus started climbing the ladder to the loft.

"Yeah, Zephyr," Cad teased. "Bringing the local guard into our affairs is Novak's job. Don't you know that?"

"Of course I do, but *I* do not get caught," Zephyr said with a wry smile.

Thadus motioned Cad up into the loft. Zephyr and Cad followed Thadus to the other side of the loft where hay was stacked to the ceiling.

"Follow me," Thadus said and walked behind the stack to a small pathway where one could walk along the rear wall of the loft while being concealed by the hay. No one in the stables looking into the loft would be able to see behind the hay. Walking to the end of the pathway, Thadus came to a dead end.

"You can use this room as your base of operations," Thadus informed them.

"What room?" Cad looked puzzled.

Thadus opened a hidden trap door on the floor. Unless you looked closely, you couldn't even tell it was there. A ladder led down into the dark.

Cad and Zephyr were more than a little surprised, and skeptical of the situation.

"You have a secret room in the stables?" Cad was overtly suspicious.

"Perhaps you didn't believe me when I said I am part of an underground resistance?" Thadus asked. "I assure you this room is safe, and few know of it. It is actually the basement. A false wall conceals this narrow corridor down. This ladder goes to a room under the stables. Follow me."

Thadus lit a lantern hanging on the wall in the secret corridor and then led the way down to a small room with a dirt floor. The room with cedar-plank walls had sparse furnishings. A small table and two wooden chairs stood in one corner. Blank paper, a pen and quill, and a candleholder sat on the table. A pillow on a neatly folded blanket rested on each of the five small beds with straw mattresses in the room. Each bed had two wooden pegs in the wall at its head to hang equipment. Against one wall was a small crate with a wooden barrel on top. A ladle hung from the lip of the barrel. Above the barrel were four small shelves with food items.

"The stables are right above us. You might hear the horses stomping around a bit at night." Thadus proceeded with his orientation. "It's always pitch black down here. There are extra candles in the table drawer. You will have to remain fairly quiet. You will hear when someone is in the stables, and they might be able to hear you. It's muffled voices at best unless you place your ear to the ceiling. Come and go as you wish, but if you make ten to twelve trips in and out in a day, someone might get suspicious. I recommend that you leave once, come back once a day, unless it's an emergency of course. There's food on the shelves and water in the barrel. You might want to keep it stocked from here on out. I can't always make sure that gets done. Other than that, good luck finding Hyacinth Blue; the fate of many lives rests upon your success. I hope that eventually we can come to an understanding of sorts."

"An understanding about what, monsieur?" Zephyr inquired.

"An understanding about the total ramifications of your mission on all of us. And please, call me Thadus," Thadus offered, hope in his voice.

Zephyr didn't quite know what to make of Thadus's remark. "Maybe we will come to trust each other enough to talk about it?"

"For the good of us all, I hope so." Thadus excused himself and started ascending the ladder. "Let me know if you need anything," he called back.

"There is one more thing you can do," Cad asked hesitantly.

"What's that?" Thadus paused on the ladder.

"We are expecting our mates shortly. I have every confidence they will be able to find us. Would you bring them down when they get here?"

"I'll be glad to bring your friends down when they show up."

"Thank you."

Thadus left and closed the trap door.

"Now what?" Zephyr asked

"Now we wait for Scorpyus and Novak. They should be here soon. They've had all blooming night to escape the ship and make it back." A sarcastic grin spread over Cad's face. "I mean, how hard could it have been?"

"Without me there? I can only imagine the difficulty and hardship suffered in the absence of my well-honed escape skills," Zephyr said, then laughed as she plopped down for a quick cat nap.

"I'll go get the gear from the horses. Especially since professional escape artists such as you need their beauty rest. I know how cranky you get when you're tired."

The pillow missed Cad's head as he climbed the ladder.

It had been a long and hypothermic night for Scorpyus, Novak, and Bartus. After escaping the search party and the ravenous dogs, the trio rode the river current to its exit at the port of Xylor. It was a welcome surprise to find the river ending at Xylor. They spent the last few hours thawing out by a campfire while seagulls studied the three curiously.

Now that they were out of danger, at least for the moment, Scorpyus and Novak parted ways with Bartus. Bartus shook their hands, thanking them over and over for saving his life, for helping him when most people would have abandoned such a liability.

Scorpyus and Novak headed for town after leaving the remainder of their food with Bartus. Bartus took shelter under the pier, his home for the last few years. Bartus would need several days to recuperate from the ordeal.

"Let's stop by the stables and get our gear, then go to the inn. I'd like to change out of what's left of Lieutenant Tiberious's uniform and back into my own clothes." Scorpyus inspected the tattered uniform.

"I can't wait to get my armor and two-handed sword back. I feel naked without them," Novak complained, his rumbling voice sounding tired.

"I better not be seen with this. It's too easily recognizable as belonging to the Royal Guard." Scorpyus removed the ornate sword and scabbard and threw it into a ditch along the road. "At least I have this longbow until we get to our gear."

Novak pointed to the bloody stain on Scorpyus's white shirt. "And you have that. It stands out, but there's not much you can do about it."

Scorpyus tucked the shirt in to hide the bloodstain as much as possible.

They walked through the streets of Xylor. As they got near the Shorebird Inn they saw scores of Royal Guards in a flurry of activity.

"Something's wrong," Novak whispered. "Do you think Cad and Zephyr ran into trouble?"

Scorpyus nodded. "It could be. This job is turning into a nightmare. We seem to have stepped into some deep horse manure."

Novak and Scorpyus ducked into an alley.

"Well we can't take any chances and go to the inn and find out. Let's make our way to the livery stables and get our horses instead." Scorpyus led the way and Novak covered their rear. They moved in unison, systematically making their way across town, keeping a low profile.

A short time later they were at the stables. It looked deserted. Scorpyus cased the place, listening for noises and looking for any indication that this was some sort of trap. Novak looked out for approaching danger. When they were satisfied that it was safe, they slipped into the building. The stables were empty except for a few horses.

"Hey, Novak, look at this." Scorpyus pointed to a bloodstain near a stall. "It looks like something happened here."

Novak inspected the stain. "Someone cleaned most of it up. By the way, did you notice the east wall?"

Novak nodded toward the four slash marks that Cad had put on the wall. They were fresh, and contained no residue of blood in the grooves indicating they were not inflicted during combat. Besides that, it was one of many forms of communication the Clandestine Knights had developed through years of experience. Novak knew if the east wall was marked it meant that Cad and Zephyr had left heading east. And four slash marks meant they went to a location that had four letters in its name. And they had to go in a hurry since they didn't have time to leave a more detailed message.

"Yeah, I saw that. What's east of here? Do you still have your map, the one we used earlier?" Scorpyus looked through the stables. "It looks like we're on foot. Our horses are gone."

"I still have the map, but it's wet." Novak pulled a scroll of paper from his boot and gently unfolded it. It was a crude depiction of Xylor. "There are several villages east of here: Kelp, Sage, Dogwood. Sage and Kelp are the only ones with four letters in their names. Sage is also the closest. All are straight out the main road, until the trails branch. Granite and Seacliff are northeast, Moss Gulch, and Whalecove are southeast…and you're right, this map only shows one river on it."

Scorpyus looked at the map. "Sage seems to be the most logical choice. If not, Kelp is the only other option, and it's farther away. We can head that way unless you have a better idea?"

Novak shook his head and refolded the map.

———◆———

Scorpyus and Novak walked east on the dusty road from Xylor to Sage enjoying the peaceful morning. Merchants with small carts of produce and wares passed them headed for the open market in Xylor.

"It looks like these small villages feed Xylor, judging from the number of carts headed that way," Novak observed while sidestepping a pothole.

"I heard a man talking about Xylor being a major exporter to the kingdom of Kelterland. It's a fertile island with a perfect climate. But best of all, it's thinly populated; except for the port of Xylor itself, of course." Scorpyus thought that the island was a good place to go on a job. The climate and scenery were a lot like Ravenshire.

"I knew you were going to say that." Novak knew Scorpyus well enough to know of his dislike of crowds. Scorpyus was accustomed to solitude and preferred smaller groups. But if the need arose, he could smooth talk his way out of a jam and work a crowd better than most. Novak, on the other hand, tended to be quiet and more reserved no matter what the situation. He let his huge size speak for him. Novak was indifferent to crowds, solitude, rain or shine, fast or slow. Nothing seemed to bother him. If anything did irk him, he seldom complained.

Though his family originated in Barovia, Novak grew up in Ravenshire. Novak met Scorpyus when they were in their teens.

A few months after Novak met Scorpyus, he met Cad, whose family hailed from The Dales, now also occupied by the Kelterlanders. In contrast to his friends, Cad was from a prominent family. He also had completed three years of formal education, a rarity in Ravenshire.

Zephyr joined the group shortly after Cad. Her father had come to Ravenshire from Montroix when she was three years old. He ran a horse ranch in southwest Ravenshire. Ravenshire was the hub of trade for the whole territory. It was a melting pot for people from all the surrounding areas. All trade passed through Ravenshire. That fact made it a prized possession of Kelterland who guarded their conquest with a vengeance.

All four considered themselves citizens of Ravenshire and were proud of the fact. Together Cad, Novak, Scorpyus, and Zephyr founded the Clandestine Knights.

As a child, Novak Reinhardt worked with his father, a blacksmith. It was a job he labored at since he was old enough to pick up a hammer. Years of beating metal into new shapes and wrestling horses to shoe them built the boy into a mountain of muscle. The youngest of five children, and the only boy, Novak was expected to help support the family. His childhood also contributed to his quiet nature. He often joked about "living with four jabbering women," and how he "could never get a word in edgewise."

The war brought tragedy to Novak's family as well. His father was part of the Ravenshire Knights and fought valiantly in the war. Cad and Zephyr's fathers belonged to the same group. Scorpyus's father figure, his grandmother's only son, had also been a member. All four of those men were killed in the battle of Saltwater Hill. The battle was so named because those who saw the result couldn't help but weep. The enemy succeeded in ambushing the knights. When the battle was over, corpses were drawn and quartered and hung from trees on a small hill as a final slap at the dignity of Ravenshire. The nearby ground turned to red mud with the blood from the slain knights. Novak had the misfortune of discovering the carnage. He had been a messenger for the army and sent to deliver a message to the knights. Novak was twelve at the time and had to bear the tragic news to not only the rest of the army, but to his mother as well.

Shortly thereafter he was captured while delivering a message. The enemy tortured Novak for eight days to get information out of him. Novak said nothing. Frustrated with the boy, the Kelterland soldiers beat Novak with staves and threw him into a burial pit, thinking they had killed him; but they underestimated the boy's endurance. Though he was badly injured and had a broken leg, Novak escaped during the night, crawling to safety. Had the enemy soldiers not waited for incoming corpses to fill the pit, Novak may have been buried alive.

Worst of all was the rumor that soon spread through Ravenshire. A traitor was said to have betrayed the knights, to have set them up for an ambush. What exactly happened that day was never discovered. Only speculation and rumor filled the void. Without the knights, the remaining army stood little chance. The morale of the region was crushed. Ravenshire fell to Kelterland shortly after that.

Novak dreamed of someday finding out if, and who, might have betrayed his father and the other knights. The uncertainty gnawed at him.

"Take your own advice, Novak; it does little good thinking about it." Scorpyus could tell where Novak drifted off to. It was the only time Novak showed fear in his eyes. Scorpyus knew their childhood changed the course of their lives forever. Novak, like the others, refused to let their shattered childhood turn them into vengeful men bent on hate. Novak also decided to follow God rather then take the path that led to destruction, and helped formed the Clandestine Knights to carry on that decision. The Clandestine Knights would rather be outcasts of society than partake in the world's rebellion.

"Ya, maybe," Novak was solemn. "But if we forget, we lose what drives us to be rid of these jackals."

Scorpyus nodded. "Well, we're in Sage now. Let's find Zephyr and Cad."

The streets of Sage were alive with activity. People milled about, and street side vendors hustled their wares. Scorpyus and Novak caught a few curious glances as they walked about town. A well-dressed, prim and proper lady crossed the street towards them. She gasped at the sight of Scorpyus's bloodstained shirt.

"Not to worry, madam, just cut myself shaving," Scorpyus jested as Novak masked a laugh with a cough. For a moment the lady nodded understanding, but it was soon followed by a look of nervous wonder at the bizarre statement. She watched them walk on. The woman clasped her well-dressed husband's arm and picked up her pace.

"Wait!" Novak tapped Scorpyus on the shoulder and motioned with a nod of the head. "Aren't those our horses over there?"

Scorpyus looked to Larek's stables and saw four horses out front. "They sure are. Cad and Zephyr can't be far away."

They looked over the stables and surrounding businesses as they crossed the street. They stopped at the open stable doors.

"Anyone here? Are you open?" Scorpyus knocked on the doorpost.

Thadus came out of his office to greet the customers. "Yes, how can I help you two today?"

"You wouldn't happen to know where the people are who own those horses out front? We're supposed to meet them." Scorpyus noticed that the two boys cleaning stalls stopped to eavesdrop on the conversation.

Thadus called out to the stable boys. "Fellows, I need you to do me a favor. Take the mare in the end stall to get re-shoed at the blacksmiths."

After the boys left with the mare, Thadus closed the stable doors. Scorpyus and Novak triangulated on Thadus in preparation for a double-flank attack as a precaution. Thadus seemed oblivious to this strategic move.

"Yes, I know where the people who own those horses are. We've been expecting you."

"You have, huh?" Novak was relieved to realize Thadus was definitely not much of a fighter. Any fighter that posed a serious threat would have understood the folly of allowing himself to be triangulated on and would have attempted to counter the move.

"Follow me. I'll take you to them." Thadus climbed into the loft and walked behind the pile of hay.

Scorpyus cocked an eyebrow in wonder. "They're in the loft?"

Thadus led them to a trap door. "They are waiting for you in my hidden room."

"After you," Scorpyus said and motioned for Thadus to descend first. Novak covered the rear, staying in the loft. He watched Scorpyus climb down.

"Novak, it is clear. Come on down," Zephyr shouted up.

Novak joined his friends and shut the trap door behind him.

"It took you long enough to get here," Cad chided.

"We ran into a few difficulties." Novak plopped down on a bunk. "This one must be mine since my gear's on it."

"Why did we check out of the inn?" Scorpyus wondered as he removed his bloodstained shirt, revealing a muscled, lean physique. There was a bandage on his right side. On his cot lay a burlap sack containing his belongings. Scorpyus donned a black cotton shirt, followed by a burgundy leather tunic with black trim. A burgundy tabard followed that.

"Ahh, it feels good to be back in my own clothes."

Zephyr filled the group in on the events of the prior night.

Novak watched Thadus who seemed to be taking it all in as he stood in a corner. "Should we be talking in front of him?"

Zephyr stopped relaying her story. "Je regrette Novak, I understand the concern. But Thadus is part of a local underground. Believe it or not they already know why we are in

Xylor. He knows if he turns us in, his underground movement would be exposed shortly thereafter."

"True," Thadus agreed, "but let's hope your organization and mine can build a working relationship based more on trust than on fear of exposing each other to the authorities."

"So what's the catch?" Scorpyus asked after changing into his own black pants. He pulled on his boots.

Thadus explained again how he would help the party by providing a lair in exchange for some medicine.

"I can't believe the medicine is that important? What's your real gain in helping us?" Novak interrupted.

"I've wondered that myself," Cad confessed. The four waited for an answer.

Scorpyus stared at Thadus, looking into his eyes and reading his mannerisms. Scorpyus was convinced that Thadus was keeping a secret.

"There's more to this than you all know," Thadus said, making sure he had their full attention before he continued. "Luther Reddland came to this island from total obscurity, coming to power without the aid of any Xylorians. Sure, he brought a few people with him, but he was unknown. Then, wham! All of a sudden he was in power. Shortly after the war was over he was appointed count of Xylor by the King of Kelterland. You four are all from Ravenshire, aren't you?"

Thadus paused as his four guests nodded in agreement. "Reddland appeared here shortly after Kelterland claimed your kingdom as the spoils of war. Somehow he had made friends among the upper echelons of the Kelterlanders, powerful enough friends that they would appoint him count of Xylor. He had no such friends here. Have no doubt about it. Luther is a self-made man, and he likes to worship his creator."

The four laughed aloud at Thadus's witticism.

"This Tanuba worship is nothing more then a tool he uses to control the masses who are drunk with thoughts of riches and the very relaxed morals of Tanuba doctrine. It's a cult that has sucked up far too many of this island's inhabitants." Thadus went on to explain a little history of Xylor.

The four learned that Luther Reddland, count of Xylor, had been ruling the island for ten years. A few violently opposed his bid for power and warned others of trusting the charismatic stranger. Luther's opposition soon diminished. His opponents were soon silenced, fleeing Xylor or dying in mysterious accidents.

Despite his being appointed count of Xylor by Kelterland after the war, Luther had to assert his power violently. Thousands died in the struggle. He had since maintained power in the same manner. He has only a few trusted advisors to help him run Xylor, and he keeps those advisors in the lap of luxury. Luther took good care of the Royal Guard, keeping them well paid and fed to assure their loyalty. As a result he set up a government with a strong support base. As long as the tax money and trade goods keep flowing to Kelterland, they let Luther run the island as he pleases. He bought the loyalty of those with power and influence. Those who were not for sale were kept in check with fear of having one of those unfortunate accidents. Luther also gained control of a considerable number of subjects through the cult of Tanuba worshipers. The cult endorsed most vices the people wanted to pursue, so it went over well with those who have itchy ears and want religious justification for their actions. And besides, those who opposed the cult were branded as infidels and ostracized.

Few challenged his authority since he gained power over the island. The occasional outbreak or small revolt was soon crushed. Any challenge to Reddland's authority was difficult since he had many influential and loyal supporters. The common people of Xylor were divided in their loyalties to their leader. About half remained steadfastly loyal to Luther or Tanuba, and the rest hated him with a passion. There was not much middle ground. Those who hated Luther dared not admit it. All people agreed on one thing: Luther Reddland was a man to be feared. Despite this fear, an underground movement worked to rid Xylor of Reddland.

People feared Luther because he ruled with an erratic and inconsistent iron fist. Most citizens could relate stories of public executions, mysterious disappearances, even the arrest of whole families. More than one family had been burned out of their homes. The one thing you could count on was that any "crime" would be punished swiftly and ruthlessly. Few were pardoned. Luther had no apparent system for deciding who he would send to the mainland for trial, who he would pardon, or who he would kill. It all hinged on his pleasure for the day. The only consistencies were that the laws rarely changed. Luther wanted the people to be able to have clear-cut laws so there is no question of his expectations.

Rumors of the underground movement surfaced and Luther concentrated a large portion of his resources rooting out this latest insurgence. Anyone even remotely suspected of being involved in the rebellion was put to death. Because of this, tensions had been high and the environment for covert maneuvers risky at best.

Thadus's audience listened, captivated throughout his account of Xylor's history.

"So you see; this can be a hazardous place to make waves," Thadus finished and waited for his words to be digested. His guests pondered his monologue thoroughly before commenting.

"The count sounds like a bloody tyrant. Most of the new rulers since the war are," Cad said matter-of-factly. "We saw the same thing in Ravenshire. Either a tyrant or a puppet for a tyrant assumes power."

Novak agreed. "It's a sad story, but what does that have to do with us? Like we said, we don't want to get in the middle of a political struggle. We're just here to get some medicine and then leave."

"You really don't know, do you?" Thadus now believed his guests really didn't know whom the medicine was for. "Let me tell you, then. You *are* in the middle of a political struggle. I have reliable information that the Hyacinth Blue you seek is for Luther Reddland. *He* is the wealthy man who sent someone to hire you."

A heavy silence enveloped the room. Thadus watched his revelation hit his audience.

"Let's assume you're right," Scorpyus said at last. "If Hyacinth Blue is for Luther Reddland, why did he hire us to find it? Why not just send the Royal Guard out to get the stuff?"

"Perhaps I can explain. Hyacinth Blue is a medicine that, according to legend, will cure a slew of degenerative diseases; diseases that slowly cripple their victims, eventually killing them. There are a few unfortunate plagues that fit this description. Let me ask you this, if Reddland sent out the Royal Guard to find the medicine, then the Royal Guard, and soon all of Xylor, would know he had a terminal illness. With information like that made public, it would only be a matter of time before a coup would surface."

"What have we gotten ourselves into this time?" Zephyr shook her head in disbelief.

"So you want the bloke dead. You don't want us to find the medicine." Cad thrust a finger at Thadus.

"You are wrong. If the count dies, we have no guarantee that whoever takes over after him will be any better," Thadus explained. "We want you to find the medicine. Having possession of Hyacinth Blue would be a priceless bargaining chip for reform. He who holds the medicine holds considerable power. Luther should want it badly enough to bargain with us. If we get the medicine, we will wield influence for reform. I hope it actually exists. I've never seen it, nor know anyone who has. Isaac said he was getting close to locating a recipe."

"So our choice is to help you or help the count," Novak pointed out. "He's paying us five thousand shillings to get it. Are you making us an offer?"

"No, no, I guess not. The resistance doesn't have that kind of wealth. You four seem like good people. I was hoping to appeal to that, but how can I compete with five thousand shillings. I won't stop you from giving him the Hyacinth Blue, but I do wish you would reconsider. At least let us have some if you indeed find it. It may be useful in the future." Thadus looked sullenly to the floor.

"Maybe the medicine is not actually for him? Maybe there is another who has the disease, and he is the one who actually hired us?" Zephyr was ever the optimist.

"I wish you were right, but I'm afraid that's impossible. We confirmed our intelligence a week ago. At first I didn't want to tell you, but now you know." Thadus was visibly saddened. "In a way it's justice. Xylor was living large. It's been a generation or two since we had a famine or epidemic sweep the island. There are only a few alive who remember hard times. We are so comfortable that we forget about God. Full of pride in ourselves! Witchcraft and the immoral cult practices of Tanuba worship are more interesting. As that cult grows, morals decline and crime increases. I believe God is trying to get our attention."

Thadus was resigned to failure once again. "I just thought that perhaps this was the break the resistance was looking for. If Isaac contacted you he must have felt the same way. His wisdom and insight was usually correct."

"Maybe God *is* trying to get your attention. The story of Xylor is the story of Ravenshire. It's been happening since the beginning of time, and I'm sure it will continue long after we're gone." Scorpyus said and took a chair at the table.

"I can sympathize. Someday Ravenshire will be freed from its dictator. Our fathers died trying to stop that, and we are committed to finishing the fight." Novak pounded his fist on the table.

"Still, this is your fight." Cad added. "We'll have to think about it mate. Whether we help you or finish our job, we still have to find the blooming Hyacinth Blue. Maybe by the time we do, we'll have figured out our next step."

"That's all I can ask. If you'll excuse me, I'll leave you alone." Thadus cordially shook hands with his guests then climbed the ladder and left the room.

Zephyr walked over to the others. "What are we going to do? We cannot help Reddland, no? We would not want someone helping the Prince of Ravenshire?"

"I don't know. I see Thadus's point, but let's find the medicine first and then decide. I mean, it might not even exist." Scorpyus voiced his opinion.

"I agree. What do we have so far?" Cad inquired of Zephyr.

Zephyr read the note aloud. "A legend runs deep in the forest of Xylor....But few will there be who master their fears....The mountains and thicket hold perils and danger, concealing the treasure of sapphire tears." The note also says to meet someone at the Hyssop Creek Oratory at vespers, dusk. And that the codeword for the meeting is Orion. Last, it says Thadus in Sage. Isaac's last words were: Beatus Esse Dominus Deus In Aeternum."

"What does that mean?" Novak inquired.

Zephyr shrugged her shoulders. "Je ne sais pas, maybe we will find out at the oratory."

"Let's hope so." Scorpyus didn't recognize the language.

"Alright mates, here's the plan. Novak and Zephyr, you two keep the meeting at the oratory. Find out what that's about but be careful; it could be a bloody trap. Maybe it will shed more light on things. Scorpyus and I will try to find out more—anything— about Hyacinth Blue. Maybe an apothecary or alchemist shop will have a blooming clue as to where to begin. We'll meet back here tonight." Cad said, then lay back on his cot and stretched.

"Sounds good," Novak agreed and flopped down on his cot and crawled under the blanket. "That gives us time for a nap. I could use it. Scorpyus kept me up all night."

"You mean some dogs did," Scorpyus pulled his boots off, and lowered himself onto his cot, careful not to lie on his sore right side. "By the way, Novak is afraid of puppy dogs."

"Ha!" Novak exclaimed. "They don't make a dog big enough to scare me!"

Zephyr blew out the candle. "What about a mastiff?"

"Mastiff, wolfhound, bring them on! They'd stand as much of a chance as a cat!"

Zephyr feigned shock. "You would not hurt a poor little kitty cat, would you?"

"Hurt it? There's no pain for a cat in death." Novak started laughing, and somewhere in the dark Zephyr's pillow glanced off his head. Zephyr liked to throw things when she feigned anger. Novak laughed harder.

"Don't be mad at Novak. He's helping cats," Scorpyus added.

"How is that?" Zephyr couldn't wait to hear this one.

"Well, Novak figures it's so hard for cats to live outdoors, you know, especially since they all have croup," Scorpyus said with absolute seriousness.

"They do not!" Zephyr insisted.

Novak came to his own defense. "If they don't, then what's with all that huffing and hissing and coughing?"

"You two!"

"That's the price you pay for being the only cat lover among us," Cad explained to Zephyr. "Now let's get some shut eye."

"I like cats." Scorpyus confessed. "But only in stew!"

Roars of laughter echoed in the underground room. Zephyr shook her head.

V

---◆◆◆---

NOVAK CINCHED HIS horse's saddle a little tighter in preparation for his ride back to Xylor. Zephyr waited patiently astride her horse, stroking its mane. She watched Novak secure his saddlebags and give his mount a walk-around inspection. Satisfied, he swung into the saddle with surprising agility for a man of his size, especially in light of the fact that he now carried fifty pounds of weapons and armor. Novak felt more at ease with his trusty two-handed sword. He complemented it with a cuirass, greaves, wrist shields, and a buckler. He was imposing enough without armor; now he was almost scary. He put on his bronze helmet and then signaled Zephyr he was ready. They had an appointment at the Hyssop Creek Oratory. Since they had plenty of time, they headed out at a slow trot.

"Do you have any idea what this meeting is about? Did Isaac give you any clue before he died?" Novak asked again, his cloak fluttering in the breeze.

"No, you know as much about this as I do. Thadus said he knew of no planned meeting at the oratory, but he did say if Isaac said to meet there, then it was good information. I felt that Isaac was going to meet someone at the oratory himself. He wanted me to keep the meeting only because he knew it was the end of his life." Zephyr held the reins loosely in her hand.

"Do you wonder why Thadus isn't keeping this meeting? If he's so sure about Isaac, he should go. I'm suspicious." Novak continued to ponder the bizarreness of the situation, "Even if there is a contact from the underground at the oratory, Reddland's men could have found out and set up an ambush. After all, they caught Isaac, didn't they?"

Zephyr couldn't argue with that. A trap was indeed a possibility. "Oui, you are right. But if there is information to be gained out of this, I want to know it. I am glad Thadus did not insist on going. That way we find out first."

"And that is exactly why I agreed to this. Besides, Thadus couldn't handle the situation if there was trouble." Though Thadus was broad and rugged, he didn't impress Novak as much of a fighter.

Novak and Zephyr made their way through town to the oratory, following the verbal directions Thadus had given them before leaving Sage. His directions allowed them to remain on the outskirts of the city. The oratory was down a cobblestone road and sat atop a small rise on the north side of Xylor. Grass and weeds grew up in the cracks between the cobblestones, and they were slick with moss. The moist damp climate of Xylor was conducive to the growth of moss, and vegetation flourished. Moss-covered buildings, green trees, and flourishing grasses gave Xylor a fertile look.

"It does not look like this road gets much use anymore," Zephyr noticed the unkempt road. "But of course it is against the law to have services here since the count mandated Tanuba worship."

"Ya, you could get arrested for insulting the mother of all fish." Novak smiled broadly. He had no patience for the Tanuba worshipers, especially since the incident at the town square.

They rode up to the oratory and came to an eight-foot high stone wall with an iron-reinforced wooden gate. The wall encompassed the oratory grounds and looked to be quite sturdy, almost fortress-like. The walls had parapets along the inside where men could walk, and there were slits in the outer wall for archers at set intervals. The gate was rusted, and half was torn from its hinges, lying across the cobblestone road. The thick wood-beamed gate that still stood had black charring on its outer surface.

Novak and Zephyr slowly walked their horses through the gate onto the oratory grounds in the dusk. The oratory itself was a large stone building three stories high and looked more like a cathedral in size. Affixed to the top of its two large steeples was a cross. The black slate roof was steep, but a railed walkway led around its border—an ideal place for an observer to watch the grounds. Most of the building's windows were broken out, and ivy was starting to creep over the walls. Leaves from nearby trees lay on the roof, along with patches of moss. Expensive quarried stones were used to build the structure, and three large pillars introduced the entryway. Two thick oak doors with brass hardware marked the entrance at the top of a flight of ten stairs. The building showed years of neglect. The grounds were a jungle of weeds and unpruned trees. Hedges grew wildly around the many walkways. Two other structures stood on the grounds. One looked as if it may have been the stables, the other possibly a tool shed. A once elegant fountain stood in the veranda before the stone-banistered oratory steps. It too sported a growth of moss and was partially filled with stagnant water. Dead insects floated in it. In the center of the fountain rose an impressive stone statue of a woman holding a cistern in her arms. She was tipping the cistern as if to pour its contents into the pool below. From the look of it, pigeons had been roosting on her. Novak and Zephyr dismounted near the oratory steps at a weathered hitching post.

"This was a beautiful place at one time. It is a shame that it is now in this state." Zephyr could see the inherent beauty of the oratory and picture it in its former splendor.

"Ya it was. And from the looks of it, a battle took place here." Novak pointed out the chips in the stone building, and a few scattered arrows on the grounds. One arrow was still lodged in the entryway doorpost. "Strange no one picked up the arrows."

The hitching post collapsed when Novak tried to tie his horse to it. He didn't bother to try another post, letting his horse's reins hang free.

They walked the ten steps to two large wooden doors. Tarnished brass knockers were affixed to each door. Zephyr ran her fingers along the doorjambs while Novak stood watch.

Novak read the sign above the doors: Hyssop Creek Oratory—All are welcome—*For whosoever calls upon the name of the Lord shall be saved—*.

Zephyr stood up after completing an inspection of the threshold.

"Well, did you find anything?"

"Yes, a simple tripwire; it probably runs inside to some bells or an alarm of sorts. Just step over it as we go in."

The door was unlocked, and Novak slowly pushed it open with one hand. He and Zephyr stood out of the doorway or fatal funnel, as they liked to call it. He shoved it all the way open.

"That is odd?" Zephyr whispered.

"Ya, I know? A place this run down and the door doesn't squeak? Someone's been oiling the hinges."

Novak peeked inside. Past the empty foyer he saw rows and rows of pews. Most were damaged, some were reduced to splinters, and a few were missing. Novak drew his sword.

"Go left after a three count."

As Novak entered he slashed from left to right, brought his sword back up to the ready, and then hopped to the right. If there had been an archer waiting for his entrance, an arrow should have struck the wall where he had been standing. Zephyr shot in to the left of the foyer. All seemed to be clear so she closed the door behind them. Cobwebs hung from the ceiling and dust lay everywhere. Footprints were all over the dusty floors. At least a few people had been in and out of the place. An interesting fact since the oratory was off-limits.

Novak and Zephyr walked through the pews after leaving the foyer. The ceiling of the auditorium was over forty feet high. Four steps led up to an altar. Nothing was left on the altar except an overturned table and a few broken chairs. Looking back toward the entry they could see a second-floor balcony. An ornate rail ran the length of the balcony, and miscellaneous furniture, all dust coated, was stored up there. A staircase along the east wall rose up into darkness.

"It looks like the place is deserted," Zephyr whispered.

The once-white walls now had a brownish hue. A large cross graced the wall at the front of the auditorium. Evenly spaced sconces stretched along the walls for light, but none contained torches. The fading daylight filled the place through the many windows. Past rains had leaked through the broken panes, giving the place a musty smell. Old clothing and a broom were strewn on the floor.

Zephyr noticed a paper on the first pew. It was not covered with dust like everything else. She picked it up and read.

"Pssst, Novak, come here."

Novak walked over. "What? What did you find?"

"A note; all it says is 'What's the codeword.'"

They both pulled their swords, eyes darting around the room searching for danger. Satisfied that no immediate danger presented itself, Novak shouted the codeword. "Orion!" His deep voiced shout resonated in the auditorium. He and Zephyr braced for some response.

A door slowly opened at the side of the oratory, and a man in a hooded tunic stepped into view from an adjoining room.

"Who are you? What happened to Isaac?" He asked apprehensively.

"Je regrette but Isaac died. Reddland's men killed him. He sent us in his place." Zephyr responded flatly. If this was an ambush something more should be happening, she thought.

The news floored the man. He stumbled back. Trying to find a seat on a pew, he missed and landed on the floor. They heard stifled sobs coming from under his hood.

This Isaac was well liked, Novak thought as he watched the man weep uncontrollably. He wept for five or six minutes before speaking. Novak and Zephyr waited patiently for him to regain his composure.

Finally he said, "I'm sorry. If you'll excuse me, it's just that Isaac and I were close. Even though I have expected this day to come eventually, it is still quite a shock. I've known Isaac all of my life, and we've been serving together for the past ten years." The man was deeply anguished.

"He's been an underground spy for ten years?" Novak was impressed. "At his age, in this area, that's amazing."

The man was surprised to hear that Novak knew Isaac was a spy. "Yes. His job was a hazardous one. He always gave everything to his work and never swerved from duty." The man replied as he removed his hood and wiped away tears. He was about fifty years old, plump, with short, thinning brown hair graying at the temples. His full beard was gray.

"If you don't mind my asking, why did Isaac remain in harm's way for that long?" Novak asked. "He must have been seventy years old, according to Zephyr. If you were worried about his safety, why didn't you reassign him someplace safer? I'd be ashamed letting a seventy-year-old operate as a spy if I was available." Novak didn't tolerate even the appearance of cowardice. All the young men in the underground should be embarrassed as far as he was concerned.

"Isaac had no choice but to remain underground. When the count took power, a death warrant was put out on his head. He assumed a false identity, and that spared his life this long. We all knew he would be killed if he were ever discovered, spying or not. He was a dead man either way. Isaac himself insisted that if he had to remain underground, he might as well be of service to the cause. He wouldn't have it any other way." The man rubbed his red eyes.

"You are trusting us with a lot of personal information, monsieur. You do not have to talk about it if you do not want to," Zephyr said, hoping the man would not want to involve her and Novak any further.

"Isaac was a good judge of people. God was with him. If he sent you, that's good enough for me."

Novak rubbed his temple slowly. What was he getting into? Thadus's resistance movement must have poor communication. After all, this man hadn't even known Isaac was dead. Novak hoped that the people weren't totally incompetent. Hopefully the resistance was competent enough to keep this meeting a secret.

"So, monsieur, what is the message?" Zephyr was resigned to the fact of further involvement.

"My message is useless. It appears I'm a day late in delivering it." The man broke down again.

Novak didn't want to watch a grown man cry all day. "Um, excuse me, sir, you seem to be taking this hard, and for that I'm sorry. I hate to say it, but we have to go soon." Novak was as polite as possible. ·

"I'm sorry. I haven't introduced myself. My name is Isaac. Isaac Abrams." He shook hands with Novak and Zephyr. "I know you have better things to do than to watch me lose my composure, but my message is worthless."

"Your name is Isaac also?" Zephyr looked at Novak with a hint of disbelief.

"Yes it is. I'm Isaac Abrams, Jr. The old man you met was my father."

"Oh, monsieur, Je regrette. I am so, so sorry. We will not be bothering you anymore." Zephyr felt terrible. What a way to hear of a loved one's death.

"That's alright. Really, I'll be fine." Isaac said. "I just wish I could have been a day earlier. It's my fault my father is dead."

"Now hold on," Novak said. "It's not your fault. Reddland's men killed him. You weren't in the area. There's nothing you could have done."

"I wish you were right." Isaac lamented. "But you see; my message was for my father to go into hiding. I found out his true identity had been recently discovered. Count Reddland's men were in the process of hunting him down to kill him." Isaac shook his head, bereaved with self-blame.

"Your father sent me here just before he was killed," Zephyr said.

"Are you sure that a squad of men was after him?" Novak was curious.

Isaac nodded his head with numbness. "I sent a message for father to meet me here. Well, I guess it's the message he gave you. He had no way of knowing why I sent for him, only that it must have been important. The guards must have been hot on his trail when he found you." Isaac paused while Zephyr confirmed this. "Even knowing he was near the end, his final act was an attempt to further our cause." Tears welled up in Isaac's eyes.

"So that's why you were going to have your father go into hiding?" The story seemed plausible to Novak. After all someone did indeed kill Isaac's father.

"Yes, I called him here to tell him that we had word that his identity was discovered, and that there was an assassination plot against him. I didn't know they were that close. I thought he had more time." Isaac buried his face in his hands.

Isaac pulled out a cloth and blew his nose. "I'm sorry. I'm sorry I can't be of any help."

"I have one question, Isaac…" Novak interrupted.

"Please, please, call me Abrams. Everyone calls me Abrams so I don't get confused with my father."

"OK, Abrams…" Novak conceded. "My question is: What's with the poem about sapphire tears and legends in the forest? What does it mean?"

"What poem?" Abrams gave a quizzical look.

Zephyr showed him the note and he studied it intently.

"I don't know? It's my father's handwriting, but I've never seen it before. He must have written it on my note at some point after he received it. Maybe it has something to do with Hyacinth Blue, although I don't know what?" Abrams spoke so freely it lent a good deal of credibility to his honesty.

"Why do you say that, monsieur?" Zephyr wondered, a bit shocked to hear Isaac refer to the object of her quest. It seemed that every move the Clandestine Knights made was somehow intertwined with this island.

"My father's last assignment was to find that legendary medicine. His last report was that he had located a recipe for Hyacinth Blue. He didn't live to tell us of its location. I don't see how this poem relates to any location. For all we know the recipe may not even work as a medicine. We did have a lot of hope pinned to it, though."

"I don't see how the poem relates to Hyacinth Blue either, but it could be some sort of a clue. Otherwise, it makes no sense." Novak thought aloud for a moment. "Well, maybe we'll figure it out later. I hope you understand, but we must go now." Novak motioned towards the door.

"By all means, carry on." Abrams shook their hands in parting. "Oh, and by the way, God bless you both for helping us out. It's not easy to find someone willing to take a stand for what is right; especially when their help involves substantial risk with little gain. I don't know how much longer we are going to be able to continue the fight."

Novak turned and started to deny any commitment to Abrams' cause, but Abrams continued.

"The Lord has given you both special talents. Nothing in life is coincidence. Your lives have been a preparation for a time like this. He has seen fit to arrange a crossing of paths at this critical moment in Xylorian history. The fate of Xylor is now at the proverbial 'Y' in the road. Which path we embark upon depends solely on all of our actions in the days to come."

Whether Novak wanted to admit it or not, his mission and that of Abrams seemed to be irrevocably intertwined. Novak and the others had stumbled into a revolution.

They left the oratory the way they came in.

Novak and Zephyr's horses grazed peacefully in the tall grass, waiting for their return. "We've stumbled over a pile of trouble," Novak observed as he and Zephyr walked their horses toward Sage. "I don't like the way things are going. I'm starting to wonder if we'll see Ravenshire again."

Zephyr wondered the same thing. All the talk about God and destiny was starting to overwhelm her. She was a believer, but the thought that she and her friends could be used to make a difference in Xylor was scary. Looking down, she noticed an engraved brass plate on the oratory fountain as she rode past.

"Hey wait, Novak, look. There is an inscription."

Novak watched Zephyr dismount and rub some of the moss off of the brass plate. "What's it say?"

Novak saw the look of surprise spring up on Zephyr's face. "What is it, Zephyr?"

She moved out of the way so Novak could read the inscription for himself.

Novak turned red with rage when he read the plaque: Dedicated to Isaac Abrams, Sr.—Pastor, Hyssop Creek Oratory. The past came flooding back to Novak. What happened to Xylor was very similar to what happened in Ravenshire. It was apparent Isaac's death warrant was issued to make room for the new regime, as was the case with Novak's uncle. His uncle denounced the influx of pagan rituals being imposed on Ravenshire. The cult that came to prominence in his hometown had a snake deity, and practiced baby sacrifices. Novak lost a niece to the sadistic cult, and his sister was killed trying to prevent it. Xylor was in the same boat. Reddland shut down the oratory because it was a threat to his plans. As a leader of the people who were against the imposition of Tanuba worship, Isaac had been marked for death. Novak had seen his friends, his neighbors, and his own family including his father, suffer the same fate. There had to be a connection between Ravenshire and Xylor. He wanted to know what it was.

Zephyr could tell this discovery struck a raw nerve with Novak. She knew better than to try to calm him down at times like this. Novak's normally calm nature was punctuated by bursts of anger.

"How widespread is this?" Novak raged. "Are these people everywhere? They slit my baby niece open and burned her as a sacrifice in a demonic ritual! My oldest sister died trying to stop them! For eight days I had to take their abuse! For eight days they tortured me and then left me for dead, beaten and bloody! I lay in a pile of dead bodies until nightfall when I could escape, my friend thrown on top of me. His blood was dripping on my face, his intestines in my lap!" Novak was reliving the ordeal.

Zephyr had never heard Novak talk about his war experience before. She was shocked to learn of his torture.

Novak raged on. "They burned down the church when it was full of people. They mutilated our fathers and hung them from trees! I'm the one that found them! I had to tell my mom and sisters about it all. And now I find out that the same thing has happened in Xylor! And this Reddland is responsible for it. We never knew who the traitor was who betrayed the knights in Ravenshire. But we know Reddland is responsible for the killing here in Xylor. Maybe Abrams is right. Maybe we are here for a reason." Novak was about to explode.

"Now look, Novak, do not go doing anything you will regret later…"

"Zephyr, I know what I'm doing!"

Zephyr grabbed the reins of Novak's horse. "No! You only think you do. Taking on the count now is premature." She knew Novak's intentions. Novak didn't get mad often, but when he did he had a one-track mind and it sometimes got him in trouble as it did when he destroyed the statue of Tanuba.

Novak jerked the reins from Zephyr's hands. "You don't understand. Let me be. I'm warning you."

"I cannot let you do this, Novak!"

"Zephyr, you don't understand. Back off!"

Zephyr had had enough. "Do not tell me I do not understand! I do understand! My brother was killed in the church fire! My father died fighting along side your father. I know what it is like! You are a male. Do you know what it was like for us females? Huh? Do you know what it is like to have your virtue forcibly taken over and over by a filthy pig? Do you? I do! I was left battered and bleeding! Do not ever tell me I do not understand! I was there too!" Zephyr was trembling and in tears.

Zephyr was all too familiar with the horrors that war brought to Ravenshire. In some ways women suffered more then men. Zephyr was twelve when Ravenshire fell: An age far too young to be exposed to the abuses inflicted by the hordes of conquering, Godless, savage soldiers. She had been far too young to lose her father.

After her father's death, her big brother took care of her and her little sister while her mother worked as a cook. That was until he was killed during one of the many purges to rid Ravenshire of "problem people." Her brother wasn't a political citizen, or resistance fighter, but that didn't matter to the new government. Random killing worked just as well as the execution of "traitors" in keeping the citizens' spirits broken. Most of the people who were burned alive in the church with Zephyr's brother hadn't done anything. They were just in the wrong place at the wrong time.

Zander was more than a brother; he had been her best friend. Zephyr's father would be gone weeks at a time. Her father raised horses and would deliver them to customers throughout the land. During his absences, Zander would take care of Zephyr and her little sister, Zenith. He taught them to ride horses, how to care for them, and helped with their chores of cleaning the stables. One evening well past midnight, Zander woke Zephyr to show her something in the barn. Zephyr would never forget the night she witnessed her favorite mare give birth. The miracle of life unfolded before her eyes. Zander even let her help tend to the colt. Her brother was her guide through many such wonders.

Zander was six years older than she, and Zephyr admired him. Losing him and her father were terrible blows. At twenty-eight, she had already lived nine years longer than her brother had. Not a day went by that she didn't think of him. She still had her mother and sister, but knowing that one-day she would see her brother again in heaven was what kept her going.

Zephyr Arrisseau had experienced the war like everyone else. No one was going to tell her otherwise.

Novak was taken aback by Zephyr's outburst. Seeing her breakdown took the wind out of his sails. "Zephyr, I didn't realize—I'm sorry."

Zephyr wiped tears from her cheek. "Let us just go. We have work to do."

Two very old people in young bodies rode on quietly through town.

———◆•◆•◆———

Luther Reddland, count of Xylor, lived in an extravagant castle in the center of the city. The large stone structure with its outlying buildings had been the center of Xylorian government for nearly a hundred years. Since Luther's occupation of the premises, a formidable stone wall had been built around the grounds for added security. The sole entrance to the compound was through a large iron portcullis. The gateway was large enough for wagons to pass through, and had twenty-five feet of vertical clearance. A team of four horses and an elaborate system of pulleys raised the portcullis. The stone wall had a lookout tower at each corner. Royal Guards walked the parapets. Archers, infantry, and catapult teams manned the parapets, providing twenty-four-hour security.

At the castle itself, Luther gathered the most skilled and loyal men-at-arms as his personal security force. The Elite Guard could be distinguished from the Royal Guard in several ways. They were more professional, immaculately kept, and wore red surcoats instead of the blue that the Royal Guard wore. To become a member of the Elite Guard, a soldier first had to distinguish himself in the ranks of the Royal Guard. The Elite Guard lived in luxury with the finest that Xylorian wealth could buy. This made them fanatically loyal to Luther, and they had their run of the island. They would fight for Luther to the death. If he were removed from power their luxurious lifestyle would come to an end.

Luther started people in his government at the outskirts. This gave him time to observe and evaluate their loyalty before bringing them to his inner circle. It also gave the men something to aspire to. He had two trusted men to help him oversee the daily operations of government, and both had been promoted from the ranks of the Elite Guard after proving their loyalty in battle. Most of the Royal Guards were anxious to prove themselves in order to obtain a coveted position with the Elite Guard. The competition to move up through the ranks, for promotion to the Elite Guard, or even the possibility of rising to a position in the inner circle, made the men reluctant to fail Luther. They fought hard, and recruits were easily found to replenish the ranks.

Luther's second in command was a hulk of a man named Marcus. He was a classic example of rising through the ranks. He started as a stable boy in the Royal Guard, and now was second in command. His success could be traced to two personality traits that impressed Luther. Marcus displayed unquestioning loyalty and a total lack of conscience; the fact he was reputed to be the strongest man on the island and intelligent were icing on the cake. He was a seasoned veteran and commanded the Elite Guard and Luther's intelligence gathering squad.

Luther sat in his chambers in front of an immaculate desk. The desk was tidy, with everything in its place. He sat stroking his perfectly trimmed beard and watching an attractive young girl clear the dishes from a recent snack. Marcus sat across from him going over an intelligence report.

"Would you like anything else, sire?" The maid inquired.

"No, that will be all. Dinner will be at six in the main meeting room. I have a late night ahead. You're excused."

Luther was a balding man with a horseshoe of salt and pepper hair. He appeared to be very fit for a man of forty-eight. His lean, athletic look, combined with a jagged scar on his left forearm, identified him as a former soldier. However, the staff servants noticed he appeared a little pale and gaunt as of late. The staff assumed it was due to the worry and stress brought about by the recent flurry of activity of the rebels. Luther received word that a squad of Royal guards had been attacked and a shipment of weapons stolen.

There was a loud rap at the door.

"Enter!" Luther commanded and glanced up over his papers.

"Sire, Lexton is here to see you." Montague, the butler, announced. Montague was in his middle fifties and had been a butler since the previous administration. He was one of the few original staff members who survived the transition.

"Send him in at once. I've been expecting him." Luther held up his index finger. "Oh, and one more thing. I don't want any interruptions during this meeting."

Montague nodded and left. Sir Lexton was one of Luther's generals and commander of the Royal Guard. He was a young, muscular, tall, blonde man who looked every bit the soldier. He wore the blue uniform of the Royal Guard, and as usual was immaculately groomed. He set his helmet on a table near the door as he entered the chambers.

"Good evening, Sire." Lexton stood until Luther motioned for him to take a seat.

"What's the report from the field, Lexton?" Luther poured himself a shot of brandy. He offered a shot to Marcus and Lexton, as was his custom. They declined, as was their custom.

"I have some good news and some bad news." There was a hesitation in Lexton's voice.

"Well, let's start with the bad," Luther suggested.

"The two prisoners who were being transported to Kelterland for trial escaped last night. We had dogs on their trail for a while but they escaped anyway. They are still somewhere on the island." Lexton didn't mince words trying to conceal the failure of his men in retaining custody of the prisoners.

"How did they manage that?"

Lexton was relieved to see the news didn't seem to greatly upset Luther. "They had help. Someone abducted Lieutenant Tiberious, disguised himself to resemble him, and aided the prisoners' escape. It was a faux inside job, so to speak."

"None of the crew suspected the lieutenant's impersonator?"

"No, Sire, apparently not; the imposter was very good."

"So it seems."

"Yes, Sire. Not even the crew members familiar with Lieutenant Tiberious caught on."

Luther exaggerated his rage, "Those incompetent idiots! I trust you'll handle this appropriately."

"Yes, Sire; the surviving guards are confined to quarters."

"Good. Two unarmed prisoners and one imposter outwit a squad of Royal guards and a forty-two man ship's crew!" Luther slammed a fist against his desk. "I will not tolerate it!"

"Forgive me for saying so, Sire, but—" Lexton chose his words carefully—"I was against sending squad six on this detail, or any detail of importance for that matter. They are undisciplined, heavy drinkers, and brawlers; clearly the worst squad we have. Squad six is the dumping ground for the dregs of the other squads. Most have been recommended for courts martial at one time or another. Lieutenant Tiberious always protested having to work with them. That is except this time, and now we know why."

"Yes, Lexton, I am well aware of your recommendations regarding squad six. And as usual your judgment is on the mark. How is the lieutenant, anyhow?"

Marcus spoke up. "I'll handle this one, Lex. He's doing fine. As near as we can tell, he swallowed some sort of concoction that put him to sleep. The last thing he remembered before us waking him up was awaking in the night to see someone standing above his bed. We found him still tied up and unconscious in his quarters with his clothing missing."

"You mean some sort of poison?" A hint of worry creased Luther's brow.

"I don't think so. It just put him to sleep."

"Interesting." Luther thought a moment. "I once heard of an incident where this Gypsy alchemist concocted an herbal cocktail that would render a cow unconscious. It was supposed to help with a breech birth. I wonder. No, that was many years ago, and the old woman would be dead by now anyhow. At the time we laughed it off as just another Gypsy folk tale. You can't trust a Gypsy. They're the rats of the human race."

Marcus and Lexton nodded in agreement.

"Well, what's the good news?" Luther asked and leaned back in his chair, clasping his hands on his chest.

"The good news is, we finally rooted out Isaac Abrams. He has been eliminated," Lexton was pleased to announce.

"Outstanding! The only chance the resistance had of success was Isaac somehow rallying the rebels around their god. With Isaac gone, it's the beginning of the end for them." Luther laughed with pleasure. He was clearly relishing this bit of news. "And it's all thanks to you and your intelligence squad, Marcus. Your men have earned their pay this time. I knew promoting you was a wise decision."

Marcus enjoyed the moment of praise.

Luther reached into a desk drawer and retrieved a box of cigars. He handed one each to Marcus and Lexton. "Fantastic work, men. This makes up for the prisoners' escape. After all this time, to be rid of Isaac once and for all—the bulk of the resistance was once members of his church. I do believe I hear their death knell. Just the same, some of them might want revenge. Start a concentrated hunt for any sympathizers, and kill any that you find. Lexton, you are in charge of this assignment. Kill a few random peasants to blanket the people with fear. I want any potential plot crushed before it starts."

"Yes, Sire. Consider it done."

"I'll get you the latest report on possible rebel activity at first light," Marcus informed Lexton. "By the way, Tanuba's Council of Elders are pleased with Isaac's passing also, Sire."

Luther shrugged his shoulders. "Whatever, as long as our directives are carried forth. What's the word on the rebel attack on our supply wagon?" Luther lit his cigar and held out a candleholder to light the others as well.

Marcus took a long drag off his cigar and blew the smoke toward the ceiling. "Nine dead, three wounded. The rebels ambushed them on Granite Bay Trail."

"Did they take the supplies?"

"Yes, about five hundred arrows, a dozen short swords, and ten coils of rope. They left the rest."

"Does this create a weapon shortage for our men?"

"No, it will be of only minor consequence for our men. We are still well supplied. I am concerned about the rebels acquiring that many arrows though, Sire. I recommend we keep extra guards on duty in the compound until this latest incident is over." Marcus was a well-prepared strategist who took few risks.

Lexton interrupted. "I agree, Sire. The rebels might be up to something. Before Isaac died he made contact with a woman. We were unable to question her on the matter."

"Well, why not?" Luther demanded an explanation.

"She eluded my agents in the forest," Marcus reluctantly confessed. "They report that she was a skilled rider and quite competent in evasive tactics."

"Apparently so if she gave your men the slip," Luther did not wait for a reply. "Do we know who this woman is?"

Marcus answered. "My men tracked her to the Shore Bird Inn. It appears she is a stranger in town. She and three men checked into the inn two days ago. The innkeeper said they told him they were here to do a little hunting. Their rooms were reserved under the name of 'Talon.' It took a concentrated effort for my men to track her there."

"Good work. I assume you had someone waiting for her at the inn when she returned?"

"Yes, Sire, we did. I had a couple of informants inside to let us know when she showed up, and Lex sent two squads along also. She came in last night with one of the three men she checked in with. They must have caught on to us before entering their rooms. Regrettably they were able to evade us again."

"How, pray tell, did they do that?" Luther was starting to get irritated with his men's failures.

"They slipped through an adjoining room and wedged the door shut. By the time we broke down the door they slipped out the window and climbed onto the roof of an adjoining building. They must have run from rooftop to rooftop making their way to the stables. We had two guards with their horses, but they were overcome. The two escaped with all four horses." Marcus's disappointment was evident in his face.

"It appears these four strangers are quite formidable. Do we have any reason to believe the rebels have hired their talents?" Luther was clenching his fists, and Marcus could see his jaw tighten.

Lexton interrupted again. "There's more to this story, Sire."

"And what would that be?"

"The man who was arrested yesterday for defacing the statue of Tanuba at the town square—The really large man?"

"The one I sent to Kelterland for trial?"

"Yes, Sire, that's the one. He is one of the four strangers who checked into the Shore Bird Inn. He is a friend of the woman who spoke with Isaac before he died. It is my belief the person who abducted Lieutenant Tiberious and helped the prisoners escape is none other than the fourth member of that entourage of strangers."

Marcus looked nervously away.

Luther seemed to calm down a bit. "Did we question the other prisoner yet? The tramp who was stealing food?"

"No, Sire; he escaped with the big one." Lexton added.

"What? How could that half-starved derelict escape?"

"The only possible answer is that the other two took him along."

Luther was troubled by this thought. "Well, find him and question him, Lexton. You're dismissed. And see to it the guard is doubled until I direct otherwise"

Lexton stood and started to leave. "One more thing, Sire; I'll let you know if, I mean *when* we apprehend any or all of the four strangers for questioning."

"Very well." Luther waited for Lexton to shut the door behind him. He thought for a good minute analyzing the report thoroughly. "Well, Marcus, how well can we trust these four strangers?"

"I believe them all to be mercenaries from Ravenshire. They shouldn't have any reason to get involved with the rebels. What could possibly persuade them to get involved with a no-win situation like the rebel cause? I think it's a coincidence Isaac came across the woman. As you can tell from the reports, they are very good at what they do. If anyone will be able to obtain Hyacinth Blue it will be them."

"Yes, I suppose you're right. Now you know why I didn't order the big man's death for destroying the statue like the council of elders demanded. And you now know why I chose squad six to take the prisoners to Kelterland." Luther paused while Marcus nodded his understanding. No doubt about it, Luther was a conniving man. "Just in case, I want to know the second there is even a hint one of the four strangers sympathizes with the rebels. I want that medicine but we can't take any chances."

VI

A STRANGE, EERIE glow throbbed in the distance, slowly varying in intensity, its reddish light in sharp contrast to the dim twilight. It held the attention of two curious travelers on the road to Xylor.

"What is that?" Cad shifted in his saddle.

Scorpyus looked at the pulsing glow as he blew warm air into his hands. Besides making the reddish light more visible, the setting of the sun quickly gave way to the brisk nights of the island. "I don't know. It looks like fire, except it doesn't flicker like a flame would."

"Yeah, it just sort of flares up and down, ever so slightly like its breathing." Cad took a moment to contemplate what he was seeing. "You know mate, it reminds me of the embers of a camp fire. The only thing is; that's too bloody big to be a campfire."

Scorpyus agreed. While the glow in the distance had him curious as well, he was more preoccupied with his and Cad's mission. He and Cad had the task of finding Hyacinth Blue. It was worse than finding a needle in a haystack. They were also to try to translate the phrase Isaac spoke shortly before he died. Both missions seemed impossible, but had to be done.

Cad wasn't as worried about the mission. Alchemy was Scorpyus' area of expertise. He could always blame him if they didn't find the medicine. Cad just stared at the strange glow. He didn't have long to wonder about it. The answer to the mystery soon manifested itself.

The pungent smell of smoke filled Cad's nostrils. "I guess it is a fire."

Scorpyus could also smell the smoke and nodded. They continued on toward town in no particular rush, plodding along on their horses. The trail would take them by the apparent fire. Uneasiness slowly built up in Cad and reached its peak when he was close enough to make out the glowing embers of a small farmhouse. Both were on the alert as they neared the burnt-out structure. Parts of the frame were still erect, charred and ashen. The rafter beams, though collapsed, still burned. Smoke wafted from the ashes. A brick fireplace blackened with soot was all that remained. The corpse of a dog lay near the trail that at one time went to the front door.

"I'll check around just in case," Scorpyus said and dismounted on the off chance there were survivors. He cautiously searched the surrounding area.

Cad stayed on his mount and looked over the charred remains of the structure. Reddland burned out another family, probably claiming they were rebels. The scene chilled Cad with a sense of déjà vu. He had already been here. Maybe not in Xylor, but he had been here just the same.

Cad remembered standing atop another hill and looking down into a valley. Near the river was a home engulfed in flame, smoke billowing skyward. The house belonged to friends of his family. There was no movement. He wanted to run down the hill and investigate, find his friend Morton. But he couldn't move. His legs weren't responding. He feared there was more to the ominous scene below.

Nixy was curious also. The family dog was a shepherd mix. He loved these weekly outings with Cad and Morton. Nixy ran ahead ten yards and looked back at Cad. He walked back through the grass then jaunted ahead. Once again, he stopped to look back. He repeated this maneuver as if wondering why his master was no longer playing. Cad just stood there, staring at the structure burning below. Nixy grew impatient and ran toward Cad, then stopped suddenly half way to his master. He caught the scent of something toward the river. With his head above the tall grass and his nose wiggling, Nixy sought out the scent again. All of a sudden he lowered his head and growled.

Cad scanned the horizon in response to Nixy's growling. What did the dog detect? Without warning, Nixy bolted in a dead run. He zigzagged and circled the hilltop hot on the scent. Cad lost sight of the dog when he spotted a group of riders, six men in all, and they were wearing unfamiliar heraldry. One was slumped over close to his horse's neck. They were all leaving Morton's house. Cad couldn't be sure, but it looked like someone was tied up and being led on the last horse.

Panic struck Cad like a fist. Was that Morton? The panic turned to terror when Cad realized the strange group of men was on the trail that went to his house. They were headed toward *his* home! Toward *his mother* and older brother! Toward his baby sister!

"Nixy!" Cad called once and began to run. He ran as fast as his legs would take him. He dropped his gear, a small wooden sword and shield, and the lunch his mother had packed. His mother! It was almost too much for the eleven-year-old to take. He ran faster now. He had to get home before the soldiers reached it.

As Cad ran over the top of the hill, he glanced back toward the soldiers again. They weren't in a hurry, and there were only six. It didn't make any sense. He never saw soldiers this close to the castle before other than the Ravenshire Knights, to which his father belonged. The regular army of Ravenshire was forty miles to the north fighting off an invasion from Kelterland, their eastern neighbor. His father and the other knights stayed back to defend the territory. The castle was only a few miles west of Cad's home. Didn't these soldiers know they were this close to the castle? Cad knew he had to warn his family and get them to the castle. His father helped design and build it. He knew he'd be protected within its walls until his father and the other knights dealt with these raiders.

Cad ran down the hill so fast his legs couldn't keep up with his downhill momentum and he lost his balance and fell. Nixy came from nowhere and ran past him, barking. Cad was tired, breathing heavily, his lungs burning. He quickly scampered to his feet and continued to run. He saw Nixy crest the next hill. That was the last one and then he'd be home. His heart was pounding hard, his pulse throbbing in his neck, and his head hurt. He started to feel dizzy and his vision blurred as he crested the next hill. Finally he got to the top and saw his home. Nixy was coming back for him, but stopped when he saw Cad coming down the trail. Cad felt relieved as he took the final steps to his house. He was breathing hard when he entered.

"We…have to…go!" Cad breathed heavily. His mother could barely make out his words.

"Cadwallader VanKirke! Calm down and relax!" His mother held him still. "Now tell me what has happened." She spoke calmly.

"We have to go to the castle! Soldiers are coming! They're going to burn us out just like they did Morton!"

Thomas, Cad's brother, already had their father's spare weapons out and was holding the sword and shield.

Cad's mother ran to the doorway. Downstream she saw smoke rising into the sky. She quickly turned back.

"Hurry up, let's go!" Cad's mother snatched up three-year-old Megan and started ushering the boys outside.

Thomas led the way with a short sword. He was only sixteen, five years older than Cad, but he knew his responsibilities and was eager to employ his training. Thomas watched downriver.

"They're coming!" Thomas looked hurriedly back at the others.

Cad grabbed his father's battle-axe before bolting through the doorway. The axe was heavy and required both hands to carry. His mother immediately followed him out carrying his little sister. Megan was crying now. She didn't understand what was happening. The family wasted no time in heading for the castle.

"Let's go!" Their mother called. "We have to make it to the thicket. It'll make it real hard for them to follow us on horseback."

The riders crossed the river. When they saw the fleeing family they spurred their mounts to a fast trot. Cad could see a very frightened Morton bound and riding the last horse.

"We're not going to make it," Thomas announced. "I'll try to hold them off."

"No, Thomas! You are to follow us!" His mother called back. Thomas obediently complied.

The strange riders paused at the house, and Cad and his family made it into the thicket. His mother's dress snagged on the brush and she fell sending his little sister tumbling. Megan wailed. Cad set his fathers battle axe on the ground and picked up Megan. As he helped his mother up, Nixy appeared, barking. It looked like his mother sprained her ankle in the fall.

Thomas saw what happened and remained at the edge of the thicket. He knew there was no way his family would make it to the castle unless the soldiers could be slowed down. Thomas was the only one who had a chance of holding the men off long enough for the others to make it to the castle. He decided to stay and fight.

"Come on, Thomas!" His mother cried knowing full well her son was planning to sacrifice himself so his family could escape. Tears streamed down her face as she kept calling for Thomas to join them. She knew it was hopeless, that her son wouldn't come. And if she tried to force him, they would all die. Anguish brewed in the pit of her stomach. Megan continued to cry sensing the gravity of the situation.

Cad was frantic. He didn't know what to do except get his family to the castle. If they could even get close enough for the sentries to see them they would send soldiers out to help. His mother forced herself to walk on. She was heartbroken and weeping bitterly. She knew she probably wouldn't see Thomas again in this world, but she couldn't let all her children die either. It was a mother's nightmare; being forced to choose between the sacrifice of one child or them all. If it weren't for Cad and Megan, she would just as soon die with Thomas. Megan's constant wailing added to the chaos of the situation.

"God be with you, Thomas! I love you!" Cad's mother cried out as she tried to get her family to safety. "My baby, my baby," She gasped, shaking her head among a flood of tears. She stumbled again.

Cad tried to help his mom up. "What do we do now, Mom?"

She saw the tears well up in her youngest son's eyes and forced herself to her feet. For Cad and Megan's sake she would continue on.

Thomas had tears rolling down his cheek as the men entered the thicket. "I love you, Mama!" he yelled as he faced off with one of the soldiers. Trying his hardest to be brave, he prayed his sacrifice would buy his family the needed time to escape.

Cad was choked with emotion as he led his family through the thicket. Branches whipped at him; brush and weeds entangled his feet. Movement was slow and now he had to pull his mother along who was limping badly. Cad took one last look back and saw Nixy with Thomas. The dog growled and barked, prepared to defend her master. Cad also saw two more riders appear.

One of the riders was talking to Thomas. "Laddie, put the sword down before you do something we'll both regret."

Cad heard Morton call out. "Run T-T-T-Thomas!" Morton had a tendency to stutter when he was under heavy stress.

The soldiers cackled hysterically at Morton's speech impediment, "Hey st-st-stupid. Keep your mouth sh-sh-shut."

"Leave him out of this! He's just a kid." Thomas ordered.

"My, aren't we the big man," a soldier mocked. "Who do you think you are? Didn't I hear your mommy crying for you?"

"Ah, look, you're making him cry." Another soldier entertained himself at the lad's expense. One of the men dismounted and circled Thomas preparing to easily crush the boy in combat.

Cad couldn't hear what happened next. Glancing back again, he couldn't see Thomas anymore. He didn't see Nixy either. As he led his family through the thicket he heard Morton scream. Cad started to turn around and go back, but his mother grabbed him.

"It's all in the Lord's hands now." Tears streamed down her face, and she hobbled along on her swollen ankle. Nixy's barking grew fainter and fainter.

Shortly, when they entered a clearing, Cad heard Nixy yelp in pain. The dog yelped repeatedly for the next minute and then stopped.

In no time they were in sight of the castle. It was a few hundred yards across a clearing and up a slight grade.

"There it is! We're almost there." Cad urged his mother on.

Halfway to the castle they saw the gates open and the drawbridge lower across the moat. Soldiers on horseback emerged in formation—the Ravenshire Knights. When he recognized the people making haste toward the castle, Cad's father broke ranks and trotted up to his family.

"What happened, Lara?" he asked.

"Soldiers are burning out homes in the area. Thomas is still back there. You have to go help him."

Cad watched his father trot back to the other knights. In a moment the group of them raced for the thicket.

They waited at the castle for word on Thomas. Later that night they received word that Thomas had been killed, but not before he had taken two of the soldiers. Morton was badly beaten and near death, but survived and was brought back to the castle for recovery. He was the sole survivor of his family. The soldiers killed Nixy also. Later that night Cad snuck out, retrieved his father's battle-axe from where he had dropped it, and has never parted with it since.

Early the next week Ravenshire was stunned with even worse news. A young boy, large for his age, turned up at the castle. He was working as a scout for the army. He had been captured and tortured by the enemy soldiers and left for dead. Miraculously, he lived and made it to the castle with a broken leg to report he had found the remains of the Ravenshire Knights. Cad's father was among those killed. It appeared the knights trailed the remaining soldiers to a verdant valley where they were ambushed and annihilated. By the time a search party made it to where the remains were, there was little left and no way to identify how many had been killed. The people assumed that all were lost, yet stories circulated about possible survivors. Most felt it was wishful thinking since no survivor ever surfaced.

"Well, whoever lived here is gone now. There's no sign of them anywhere. Let's hope they escaped." Scorpyus swung into the saddle.

Cad shook his head. "The dirty vermin—they had to kill the dog."

Scorpyus and Cad left the grizzly scene and headed for Xylor under cover of darkness. Both were quiet and somber along the way. The hill overlooking the city was a great vantage point for observing the citizens as they were winding down from their long and arduous day. The shipyard bustled with activity. The stores were closing for the day, and traffic to the taverns and restaurants started to pick up. Candlelight flickered in a few windows. Xylor seemed to be a town that held many secrets. Maybe Hyacinth Blue was one of them.

The two hitched their horses in front of an inn.

"Smell that roasting meat?" Scorpyus asked as they walked to the inn. It was a welcome scent. They tried to blend in with the population as much as two armed strangers could. Cad knew someone would be looking for them. Perhaps here near the docks among the sailors, longshoremen, and others who continually passed through port they would remain unnoticed. But Cad and Scorpyus did stand out a bit. Most of the citizens wore simple clothes or robes. Few were armed. Fortunately, many armed strangers passed through Xylor on a quest for riches. Many more passed through to peddle their wares, try their schemes, search for fabled treasures, and tell rumors of monsters that were always just over the next hill. The hedonistic spiritual activities of the island lent itself to supernatural tales of all sorts. The cult members of Tanuba imbibed much alcohol and smoked "ceremonial herbs" in their spiritual quests. The most indulgent of the sect, or those the council of elders described as the most devoted, were rewarded with visions of otherworldly things. Many reported seeing shimmering fires, dancing colors, or monstrous beings. All fueled the folklore of the island and enslaved many with fear and superstition. At night, anything could happen.

On an island of considerable oddities, Scorpyus and Cad were just two more adventurers out to seek fame or fortune as far as the average citizen was concerned. No one felt compelled to be overly friendly to people who would be moving on or dead within a few days. Few extended themselves beyond general pleasantries.

"No one seems to be concerned about our presence. That's a good start. Still, we should keep an eye out for the Royal Guard." Scorpyus scanned the plethora of activities and peddlers. "Where do you want to start?"

"Look, the Pelican Inn is serving dinner." Cad drew in another deep breath of the scent of roasting meat. They hadn't eaten since breakfast.

Cad hurried toward the inn leaving Scorpyus in the street. Nothing came between Cad and his meal. Scorpyus followed along.

The Pelican Inn seemed smaller on the inside. The dining area was packed with tables and benches. Patrons sat elbow-to-elbow at most of the tables. The din of utensils and voices filled the air.

"This must be a good place to eat. There are a lot of people here," Cad stated as he grabbed a tray and stood in the serving line. Scorpyus tried to eavesdrop on the conversations around him as he watched the room for anything of interest. Cad's attention was focused on the mashed potatoes, bread, roast, and yams being piled on his plate.

"Don't be stingy with the portions there, mate. I'll pay extra if I have to."

A robust woman wearing a white apron smiled and doubled Cad's portions. She proceeded to serve Scorpyus a regular portion.

Cad paid the woman and the two headed for the nearest table, Cad leading the way. He impatiently began eating as he headed for the nearest seat. He was about to claim his spot when Scorpyus grabbed his arm.

"What?" Cad mumbled through a mouthful of food

"Let's sit over there instead." Scorpyus motioned to where three men dressed in lavish robes were seating themselves. The tallest of the three was adorned with the most jewelry and decorative stitching. Scorpyus thought he heard one of them mention something about a prayer festival and wanted to hear more about it.

Scorpyus picked a seat within earshot of the trio. He sat facing away from them to avoid eye contact during the meal. Cad sat on the bench opposite Scorpyus. If anyone looked it would be blatantly obvious that Cad's only interest lay on the dish before him.

Right away they learned that the men were clerics with the cult of Tanuba. They were on the council of elders, and the taller one in the ornate robe was Drakar, the high priest.

Part way through the meal a weather-beaten dockworker sat next to Cad. Scorpyus glanced at the man. He was burly and sported curly black hair over most of his body. The man looked to be the type who had been around the block a few times. Cad and Scorpyus were uninterested at first. Then the man started to enjoy his food. He ate his food like a dog trying to chew a piece of sticky candy, tongue wagging and lips smacking loudly. Bits of food flew from his mouth. Cad saw a look of repulsion sweep over his friend's face.

Scorpyus deduced that the man's eating 'disorder' was a result of having only a handful of teeth remaining in his mouth. He dropped his fork and pushed his plate forward.

"I'm done," Scorpyus stated, thoroughly disgusted with the display.

Cad glanced at the man then turned so his back would be towards the man. No one, not even some sickening pig, was going to keep him from finishing his meal.

Scorpyus and Cad endured the man another ten minutes. Finally the three clerics rose to leave. Scorpyus focused his eyes on his abandoned plate. The ranking cleric led his party on an exit route that allowed a good look at the two armed strangers.

Cad noticed the high priest staring at him. Cad's look back was equally intense but with one difference. Cad's held a confidence that this cleric and his two lesser sycophants were no threat to his safety no matter how much they gave him the evil eye.

Unwilling to appear weak, the high cleric gave Cad a smug smile and arrogantly looked down his nose, then away. The "little people" of the world shouldn't demand the attention of someone as important as he. Drakar didn't even look at Scorpyus. Gypsies were less than human.

Cad watched the three clerics leave the inn then glanced at the burly man who was still smacking his jowls as he ate. "Let's get out of here."

"Did you hear what they were discussing?" Scorpyus asked when he stepped into the street.

"Yes. There's some sort of festival tomorrow afternoon. It sounds great. Roasted pig, fresh fruits, baked goods…" Cad's eyes widened with excitement as he continued. "Pies…."

"You just ate!" Scorpyus exclaimed.

Cad ignored the comment. "It's too bad we can't bloody well go. I'm not about to kowtow to their mermaid, even for a feast like that."

"Did you hear anything outside of their lunch plans?"

Cad feigned shock. "Of course I did mate. They mentioned some kind of ritual to be celebrated tonight at the temple…the ceremony of the Sea Orchid, I think it was. The Tanuba worshipers are to show their loyalty by partaking in the ceremony where they will drink from the crystal chalice."

Scorpyus was impressed. Maybe Cad wasn't just interested in his food after all. "They also spoke about a laboratory on the temple grounds where they are going to prepare the concoction for the ceremony. If anyone has clues about Hyacinth Blue, they might. The laboratory of the temple alchemist is a good place to start."

"Do we know where the Tanuba temple is? They could have more than one," Cad reasoned. "And besides, I don't think they're interested in medicines. The concoction those blokes were talking about sounds a lot like rum."

Scorpyus couldn't argue that point. "What else do we have to go on?"

Cad shook his head. "I suppose you're right. I'm not thrilled to be at the temple during this ceremony. They're a bunch of pagans who'll be involved in all sorts of daft abominations. Being around all that would be difficult. They would know we weren't one of them. We couldn't fake participation no matter what the reason."

"You're absolutely right," Scorpyus continued. "I don't plan on going there during the ceremony. I was suggesting we break into the alchemist laboratory. We have five hours before the ceremony starts at midnight."

"All right, we'll start at the lab. I don't have any better ideas." Cad was relieved not to be going to a sideshow ceremony. The thought of breaking into the laboratory was only slightly better, but at least it was Scorpyus's forte. "Where to now?"

"Finding the temple should be easy enough. The alchemist laboratory is near. We'll check out the security, if there is any, and then find a way in." As Scorpyus continued to devise his plan, Cad caught a glimpse of a familiar man loading a cart. It was the same man who had been sipping his ale at the Shorebird Inn the night he and Zephyr were ambushed.

Cad tapped Scorpyus's shoulder. "Remember that suspicious chap I told you about at the inn? The one who was watching me before Zephyr and I went upstairs and narrowly escaped from an ambush?"

"Yeah, why?" Scorpyus took a glance in the direction Cad was looking.

"That's him over there loading a cart with supplies." Cad pointed out a slight fellow with short, curly brown hair. The man had a pasty white face and looked to be around forty years old.

Scorpyus's plan would have to wait. There were more pressing matters at hand. Cad led the way up the street to the stranger. He and Scorpyus scanned the street and shops for the Royal Guard or anyone that looked out of place. The stranger glanced up from his cart at the approaching men. He pretended to fumble with a tie-down rope in order to hold his gaze on the approaching Cad and Scorpyus. Once he realized they noticed him, panic stretched across his face and he back-stepped in fear. Cad and Scorpyus picked up their pace in order to quickly close the distance. Out of options, the man shuffled into the alley.

Cad and Scorpyus continued at a brisk walk until they reached the alley, then the race was on. Cad hadn't run more than a few steps before he realized the alley was a dead end and the stranger wasn't going anywhere. Still, he took pride in catching the man in just a few more strides. With a firm grasp, he shoved the fellow against the nearest wall while Scorpyus closed in from the left flank just in case.

The man, who was shorter even than Zephyr, trembled with fear, and his voice quavered: "You…you don't understand—" The man searched for a way out.

"We don't understand what?" Cad asked tersely. The man couldn't be more than five feet tall and weighed about a hundred pounds. It made Cad feel self-conscious as if he were bullying a kid.

"You don't understand…it's not what you think." The man's voice trembled even more; his pale blue eyes shifted between his interrogators.

"What do we think?" Scorpyus added.

"You think I was waiting for you…which I was…but not how you think. What I mean is; I don't mean you any harm. I'm not with the guys who attacked you. I had no idea they were there." The man frantically looked from Cad to Scorpyus hoping to convince them he meant no harm. He convinced himself his life would soon be over and terror washed away his previously fearful expression.

"Relax. Calm down. We're not going to hurt you. You're no threat to us. We're not murderers." Scorpyus spoke slowly, allowing his words to sink in.

"What's your name?" Cad started with an easy question.

"Goral, Myan Goral."

"What do you do?"

"Delivery. I use my cart to run supplies. Sometimes I go to the docks to bring in the catch of the day. Today I'm delivering goods to the Tanuba temple for their ceremony tonight. I get whatever work I can." Myan seemed to be a little more at ease, but not much. He grinned ingratiatingly at his captors.

Cad leaned in close, still clutching Myan's collar tightly. "What brought you to the inn a few nights ago? I saw you watching me."

Fear shimmered in Myan's eyes. "I was sent to warn you. I'd never been to that inn before. I didn't know what to do. I failed…" His voice trailed off and his eyes shifted to the ground.

"Who sent you there?" Cad eagerly awaited the answer.

"I can't say for sure. Somebody in the underground. Since I make deliveries all over town they sometimes use me as a courier.

That evening I found a note in my cart telling me to rush to the Shorebird Inn and warn you of possible danger. The note described you, but when I saw you at the inn I couldn't be sure. I thought you fit the description, but I was afraid to be wrong. I shouldn't have even been sent. Someone must have thought it was an emergency."

Scorpyus and Cad had no reason to doubt that Myan was telling the truth. Everything he said made sense with what they already knew, and he was obviously much too timid to be a hired assassin.

"Who is the leader of the rebellion—and don't think about lying," Cad ordered.

Myan's eyes grew wide, and he looked about nervously before answering. "Isaac," he whispered.

Cad and Scorpyus were satisfied and they were quickly back to their previous business.

"So you're making a delivery to the temple today?" The gears were turning in Scorpyus's head.

"Yes, I have a big one. They're having an important ceremony. I'm taking a cartful of supplies." Myan didn't know where all this was leading. He straightened out his shirt and wiped the sweat from his face.

"We'll go with you and help deliver your supplies," Cad asserted.

"Do you know which building is the alchemist's laboratory?" Scorpyus got to the point.

Myan was puzzled. "Yes, why?"

"It will be safer for you if you didn't know," Scorpyus cautioned.

"We'll help you finish loading your cart and get your load to the temple. While you unload it, we'll need to leave for a while. Before you go, we'll be back and leave the compound with you." Cad gave the itinerary in such a way that Myan didn't have any choice.

"I guess it's the least I can do for not being able to help you at the inn the other night." The three of them finished loading the cart and tied down the load. Myan left Cad and Scorpyus alone for a moment while he got his horse and hitched it to the cart.

"Do you think we can trust him?"

"We should be able to," Scorpyus said. "At any rate, I doubt he'll turn us in once we're in the temple. Since he's the one who will be getting us inside, he'll be considered our co-conspirator. And in this town, being suspected is the same a being guilty."

The trip to the Tanuba temple was uneventful. Myan, in his burlap-brown shirt and dark pants, led his old nag of a horse by a tether while Cad and Scorpyus walked along beside the worn and rickety cart. Its wheels squeaked, and boards groaned every bump of the way. Cad wondered if the ropes tying down the load did more to keep the cart together than in keeping the goods in place. No one paid the trio much attention.

Eventually they came to an ornately decorated iron gate. Golden-robed sentries greeted Myan as he approached.

"Ah, Myan, there you are. The clerics are starting to worry. They want everything to be ready for tonight. It wouldn't be much of a ceremony without the banquet." The sentry looked over the goods in Myan's cart carefully, reading the labels on the crates.

"We'll dine on sumptuous fair tonight." The sentry was excited to see the exotic fish and fresh fruits that were out of season on Xylor.

Myan responded nervously. "I'm sorry I'm running a bit late. The ship from the far south was delayed getting into port. These summer fruits came a long way. I'm just glad they got here at all."

"You always come through. If you can't get the product, no one can." The sentry patted Myan on the back. He was obviously used to him making deliveries.

Myan noticed the other two sentries curiously eyeing Cad and Scorpyus. "Oh, I've hired them to help me unload my cart. Today I had a particularly big shipment."

The sentry nodded and swung open the large gates. "I'll see you on your way out."

Myan coaxed his nag along, and the cart rumbled down the cobblestone road of the temple grounds. The grounds covered perhaps ten acres. Torches lined the road and walkways, bathing the temple grounds in an amber glow. Opposite the main gate was the temple, a two-story stone structure with several recessed alcoves, each containing marble statues depicting Tanuba in various poses. Gold overlay a lot of the decorative stonework. Silver, brass, and copper overlay the pillars up front. Each pillar was engraved with intricate designs. A variety of jewels encrusted the various carvings of people, places, and animals depicted in scenes carved on the outer walls. The temple was the epitome of extravagance and excess. No wonder they had to keep it well guarded, Scorpyus thought. The place reeked of temptation to thievery.

"Apparently the cult's accumulated a lot of wealth," Cad observed in wide-eyed wonder. He had never seen anything like this.

"And all the while the people starve," Scorpyus noted the irony.

Myan agreed. Even though he had been to the temple many times, he still couldn't help but be awestruck by the riches so brazenly brandished there. "Now you know why they have so many temple guards."

Scorpyus and Cad looked around. The bright goldenrod robes of the temple guards could be seen everywhere. Everything was under their watchful eye. This would prove to be more difficult than Scorpyus had originally thought.

Along the wall on the left side of the temple were two smaller single-story buildings. Myan informed them that one was the cookhouse where they were going, and the other was the alchemist laboratory. Stables stood on the right side of the temple. The rest of the grounds were a series of gardens and hedgerows with trees here and there for contrast. Myan explained that the hedgerows were actually a maze. Inside were various gardens of exotic flowers and ponds. The high cleric enjoyed the finer things in life and had imported a wide variety of flora that most people in Xylor had never seen. Coming to see the gardens is what initially attracted a lot of people to the cult. It was a favorite spot for couples, especially in the evening due to its romantic feel.

"Inside the maze, it's very beautiful. There are even a few fountains, one resembling a waterfall. But it's easy to get lost. It took me three hours to find my way out the first time I went through it," Myan explained.

Cad and Scorpyus looked at each other knowingly. If anything went wrong, the hedgerows would be a back up plan.

The kitchen was expecting Myan. A cook directed him around to a back entrance to unload his goods. Scorpyus and Cad followed him to the back, where the cook gave instructions as to where the cargo should be stacked.

"Just put it against the wall. We'll come and get it as we need it. I'm sure it'll all be gone by the morning." Busy, the cook scurried back to the kitchen.

Myan untied his load of goods. "It'll take an hour to unload this. I won't be able to stall much longer than that."

"Fair enough. We can't ask you to risk anymore than you already have. If we're not back in an hour, leave without us," Cad replied. He wasn't sure he wanted Myan around if things got sticky anyway.

Cad and Scorpyus walked the short distance to the alchemist's laboratory. There were no signs of anyone inside the lab. Without a word they set about their tasks.

Cad crouched on the ground, removed a boot, and started to adjust his sock as if he had a burr irritating his foot. Scorpyus was the patient friend.

"How long between circuits?" Cad spoke of the temple guard pacing the wall nearest the laboratory. The golden-clad guard walked back and forth, disappearing around the corner for a length of time before reappearing on his next circuit. The two studied this routine while Myan was talking to the cook.

"Seventy-three seconds."

"Can you get us into the lab in less than a minute?"

"Scorpyus looked at Cad with a hint of scorn on his face. "What do you mean *can* I get us in within a minute? Just leave the door to me."

Cad laughed and slipped his boot back on. They waited until the guard disappeared around the corner again, and then went to the rear door of the laboratory. Scorpyus pulled two metal objects from his boot and started to work on the keyhole. In twenty seconds he had the door open and the two were inside.

Cad quietly closed the door behind them. "That was fast. If I didn't know you I'd say you were a seasoned thief."

"Thanks. I did fall in with the wrong crowd momentarily, but then my grandma caught me and put a quick stop to it. Anyway, the lock was old and of poor quality. That made it easy. I don't think they worry much about people breaking into the lab. There's probably not much here except herbs and things."

"I'm still amazed." Cad reiterated as he lit a candle.

Scorpyus was right. There wasn't much to the lab. The temple clearly spent their wealth on the rest of the property. Aside from two large wooden tables, and a counter full of jars, vials, and small boxes, there wasn't a lot to look at. The counter was strewn haphazardly with containers of various sizes. Two brass candleholders with long white candles stood in the center of one table next to an assortment of jars and boxes. The other table was empty save a few papers. A small fire pit was off against a wall, probably used to cook up concoctions.

Scorpyus started nosing around. "Well, one thing I can say is, even though this place is unorganized and messy; they seem to have everything one would ever need." The scent of the various, portioned ingredients blended into a strange acrid smell.

Cad looked at the assortment of jars. They were of all sorts of shapes and sizes, some glass, some metal, and some even made of wood. Many were left open. Others were coated with dust. A few didn't even have labels on them. Stains spotted the table and nearby floor. When something was spilled it obviously wasn't cleaned up. A few of the spills had partially eaten into the wood table.

Scorpyus started from one end of the counter and worked toward the other. He inspected each jar, opening them, looking inside, and occasionally sniffing one. Many jars had labels tied to them with string. A lot of the vials and small boxes were unlabeled. Scorpyus spent more time on these trying to identify the ingredients.

Cad watched Scorpyus quickly go from jar to jar, pausing to pinch the contents of one wooden box between his thumb and forefinger. Scorpyus worked the yellowish substance between his fingers.

"What did you find?" Cad asked.

Scorpyus shrugged his shoulders. "I have no idea what this is. And to tell you the truth, I don't even know what we're looking for."

"Oh." Cad was disappointed. "I thought you'd found something. We're running out of time so you better hurry."

Scorpyus went through every container on the counter. He inspected each ingredient as fast as he could. He even read the scattered papers that were lying around. Finally, with a look of disgust, he finished.

Scorpyus threw up his hands in dismay. "I don't know. Nothing looks to be unusual. Hyacinth Blue could be made from any of these things. We'll never know without the recipe. Maybe this isn't even the right temple."

"Or else whatever we're looking for is in one of the other buildings." Cad leaned against a table and crossed his arms. The hilt of his sword knocked over a candle sending it crashing into a silver box. He and Scorpyus froze and waited to see if anyone heard the noise. It wasn't that loud but it was better to be safe. They listened at the door. No one appeared to be in the area.

"Be careful, Cad." Scorpyus went to the table and righted the candle, placing it back inside its holder. He picked up the silver box. It was coated with dust. "Nothing looks broken."

Cad apologized. It was very unlike him to make such a blunder; even a minor one like knocking over a candle. "I could have sworn the blooming candle wasn't anywhere near the edge of the table."

Scorpyus ignored Cad. His interest was now intently focused on the silver box. He blew a layer of dust off the lid. The box was ornately engraved with the image of a unicorn and looked to be of some value. Scorpyus tried to open the lid, but it was locked. A key was nowhere to be found. Scorpyus studied the engraving, brushing dust off of it with his fingers. Slowly, as he brushed away the dirt, words began to appear.

"Cad! Look at this!" Scorpyus whispered excitedly. He pointed out an inscription.

Cad read it out loud. "Beatus Esse Dominus Deus In Aternum. It's Isaac's dying words to Zephyr."

Scorpyus hurriedly worked the lock with one of his picks and opened it in no time.

Euphoria quickly turned to disappointment when Scorpyus lifted the lid and found the box empty. "I thought we had found something."

Cad shook his head. "I guess that's it. I bloody well doubt we'll find anything else to fit the clue so perfectly. This box had to be what Isaac was talking about. What are the odds of us finding that inscription someplace else? It was a miracle we found it here. The recipe must have been lost years ago. Isaac would have had no way of knowing."

Isaac unknowingly gave his life in vain. The trail he had been following to the box must have been years old. Someone else must have got to it first. Even the alchemist for the Tanuba temple placed little value in the box as evidenced by the dust and tarnish. The box had no doubt been empty for some time, and had been left forgotten on some table. Without the recipe, it was worthless to them.

"Isaac gave everything in order to get a recipe. I can't believe the bloody box is empty," Cad mused.

Scorpyus just stared into the empty box. He had been so close. The red velvet lining of the box was dusty and worn. The box was clearly old, but well constructed. Scorpyus felt around the lining to see if anything was under it. There wasn't. He turned the box over and studied it from all angles hoping to find some secret compartment but again turned up nothing. Cad admired his tenacity.

"Should we smash it apart?" Cad offered a suggestion on how to find a hidden compartment.

Scorpyus shook his head. "No, I should be able to find it if one exists. I'm going to need some more light though."

Cad grabbed another candle from its brass holder and went to the fireplace. He lit the wick in the still-glowing embers. The two knelt behind the table where Cad tried to shield as much light as possible from the rest of the room.

The light illuminated some details previously undetected, the most noticeable being the color discrepancies between the velvet lining of the box and the velvet lining of the lid. The lid had a slightly redder lining, and looked to be newer.

"Someone replaced the lid's lining at one time. I wonder why that was." Scorpyus removed his dagger and cut a slit in the lid's lining along the edge by the hinge. He slid a finger underneath and gently pulled the lining from the lid, exposing a tiny hole on the lid.

"I think we have something," Scorpyus said and removed a pin-like object from his leather pouch of tools and pressed it into the small hole. Immediately a tiny door sprang open revealing a small scroll. Scorpyus unrolled it.

"It's definitely a recipe!"

Cad slapped Scorpyus on the back. "We've done it, Scorp. Now let's get out of this bloody place before someone finds us."

Scorpyus replaced the lining and put the box back together the way he had found it. He relocked the box with his picks and placed it back on the table.

"What are you doing in my lab?" A gravelly voice asked from the doorway.

Cad and Scorpyus shot around startled and found a rotund man in an ornate cloak standing in the open doorway.

"We seem to have taken the wrong door. Can you be a good chap and direct us to the kitchen?" Cad offered an explanation.

The man was probably in his fifties, but looked much older. He was bald with long stringy white hair on the sides of his head. He had a burn scar on the left side of his face around his eye. His left eye was glazed white, probably a result of the same incident that had caused the scarring.

"The door was locked," the man growled, revealing a mouthful of jagged teeth. Before he could say anymore, Cad and Scorpyus rushed him and forced him to the ground. Cad held a firm hand over the jagged-toothed mouth while Scorpyus bound the corpulent alchemist. After cutting a square of cloth from the alchemist's robe, he stuffed it into his mouth, gagging him. They dragged the rotund man farther from the door. The alchemist was purple with rage, his eyes bulged, and he mumbled profanities through his gag.

Scorpyus poked his head out from the laboratory door. "There are three temple guards walking this way."

"Let's leave like we belong here and see how far we get," Cad offered the only available solution.

The two left and closed the door behind them. They nonchalantly walked back towards Myan as if they were in no hurry. They didn't make it far.

"Hey, you there!" One of the guards pointed at Cad and Scorpyus. "What were you doing in the laboratory?"

Cad and Scorpyus ignored the temple guard and gave each other a knowing glance. Like jackrabbits they bolted for the hedgerows, momentarily surprising the guards. Glancing back just before they entered the maze they could see two guards in pursuit. The other must have gone for help.

"This way!" Cad directed for no particular reason. They took a series of turns, finally finding themselves at a dead end. They paused to catch their breaths.

"Which way is the main gate?" Cad asked unconcerned about being lost on the maze. The guards ran by on the other side of the hedgerow.

"Boost me up." Scorpyus climbed onto Cad's shoulders so he could see over the top of the hedges. "It's that way." Scorpyus pointed to the right.

Before Cad could let his friend down, the two guards appeared at the end of the corridor of bushes. Scorpyus climbed onto the top of the hedge, and then pulled Cad up just as a sword slashed into the thicket where he once stood. They landed hard on the ground on the other side. The hedges behind them rustled furiously as the guards started to climb over also. Cad thrust his sword through the hedge where it was shaking, and a temple guard screamed in agony.

"That will slow them for a while." Cad didn't loiter. He and Scorpyus were off and running again, passing a few citizens who were admiring the gardens. One sat cross-legged near a flower bed chanting.

"Pardon us," Scorpyus said as he and Cad tramped through the flower bed rather than use the trail. They assumed they were in the center of the labyrinth. Myan said there were gardens throughout the hedgerows, but this was incredible. The place was immense.

On the other side of the flower bed lay a sizeable pond fed by a small waterfall that fell from a rocky outcropping. Hedgerows towered on both sides of the outcropping. It was amazing. As a builder, Cad knew the aqueduct system needed to build an artificial waterfall was complex. He never imagined anything like it in his life.

They slogged across the pond towards the outcropping. It was a little over knee deep. Colorful fish swam in the pond, darting away from the intruders as they splashed through. Scorpyus climbed the rocky ledge next to the waterfall. It rose about ten feet above the adjoining hedges. It would make a good vantage point.

"Where to now?" Cad asked.

Scorpyus took a good look around. The entire temple grounds were in view. Guards swarmed everywhere. Two carried a wounded guard on a stretcher towards the temple. Another detachment entered the far side of the gardens by the meditating woman. A look of relief swept across Scorpyus's face. It looked like Myan would help them.

"What is it?" Cad was getting impatient.

"The guards are everywhere. Our best bet is to descend the other side of this outcropping. Myan is waiting by the south entrance with his cart. I think he'll help us," Scorpyus told Cad.

Cad quickly scaled the rocky crevices to the top of the waterfall, his greaves clanging against the stone surface. At the top he was overcome with even more admiration of the architecture. A giant aqueduct fed a large pool at the top of the rocky outcropping. The water ran over the top of the rocks to create the waterfall. The amazing thing was that on the other side of the outcropping were another waterfall and another pond. Each side was a mirror image of the other with hedgerows separating them.

The two waded across the chest-deep pool and descended the other side to the mirror pond. This one had water lilies and leaves on most of its surface obscuring the bottom. Bullfrogs croaked their songs and hopped out of the intruders' way. Cad quickly brushed off the frog that landed on his arm.

Scorpyus stepped from the water and pointed toward a break in the hedges. "I think if we re-enter the maze over there we will eventually find our way out."

The two cut through a stunning floral assortment planted in neat and tidy rows. A young couple stared aghast at the two miscreants who trampled the temple flowers. At the young woman's coaxing, the young man decided he would scold Cad and Scorpyus for their carelessness in not using the trail. He started walking toward them, but stopped when they glared at him.

"It was probably just an accident," he explained to the young woman. She looked at him with embarrassed contempt.

Cad and Scorpyus took a series of turns that seemed to take them nowhere but back and forth across the ten-acre maze. They seemed to be getting no place quickly.

"We have to be close, don't you think?" Scorpyus thought out loud.

"I have no idea, but you better hurry; I hear someone coming from where we were." Cad indicated with his thumb down the hedgerow.

They sprinted down the aisle then turned along a different path in an attempt to leave the maze. This time they seemed to circle back and eventually pass the place they started. At least the temple guard couldn't predict their path. There was no discernible logic in the winding and backtracking route. Soon they came to another dead end.

"This is getting ridiculous. Boost me up again so I can see where we are."

Cad cupped his hands to help Scorpyus climb up onto his shoulders and look over the hedge. Scorpyus wasn't up there long when he heard a shout behind him from somewhere deeper in the maze.

"There they are! One is looking above the hedgerow!" A guard shouted to his cohorts. One temple guard reached in his quiver for an arrow.

Scorpyus jumped to the floor as an arrow shot by his head. "Quick, this is the outer wall. If we get through it, we're free of this maze."

Both drew their swords and hacked a huge gash through the otherwise pristine hedgerow.

Myan was standing next to his wagon when a flurry of swords tore through the hedge. Cad and Scorpyus lunged out, both soggy from the chest down, with bits of green leaves in their hair and clothes. A sizable twig stuck out of the open visor of Cad's helmet.

"Quick, get in the wagon and under the tarp," Myan shouted.

"Thanks," Cad said as he scurried into the cart and got under the tarp with Scorpyus.

"Don't mention it," Myan's voice quivered. "Besides, I didn't have much choice. If they catch you they will have caught me. I don't think the guard at the gate will forget that you two came in here with me."

Myan was near the main gate when temple guards started coming from the gaping gash in the hedgerow. They quickly fanned out on a search of the area.

"Do you think anyone saw us?" Cad whispered. Scorpyus shrugged his shoulders. Myan's rickety cart came to a rumbling halt.

"Myan, I see you're done already. I can't wait to eat some of the scrumptious fare you delivered today." The gate guard opened the gate with his mind on the evening's feast.

"There are some fine foods in today's shipment, that's for sure." Myan's voice quivered nervously. Once the gate was opened he led his horse out of the temple grounds.

"See you tomorrow," The guard said and smiled as he watched Myan go. Suddenly a thought donned on him. "Hey, where are the two men you brought in to help you?"

Myan coaxed his horse along as fast as it would go. "They were lazy so I fired them. I thought they came out already."

The guard looked perplexed. "No, they haven't left yet. They're still here? Wait…you fired them? Where did they go? Are they?…" The guard looked back and forth from the temple grounds to Myan. A slow dawning came over the guard.

Another temple guard ran over to the gate guard telling him to thoroughly search all outgoing parties for two intruders. He described Cad and Scorpyus as being the culprits.

The gate guard looked back to Myan who now had his horse at a quick trot and was well down the road. "Myan! Wait a second. I need to talk to you for a second."

Myan ignored the guard and continued on. He looked back to see a contingent of temple guards running his way. "What do I do now? They're sending men after us."

"Turn down the next alley." Cad ordered while peeking from beneath the tarp.

As soon as Myan rounded the corner, Cad and Scorpyus hopped out of the cart and fled. They sprinted to the next block and mingled into the populace. Myan walked back onto the main street.

"What's wrong?" He asked the rapidly approaching temple guard.

"We need to search your cart. Why didn't you stop sooner?" An angry guard grabbed Myan while others ducked into the alley to search his cart.

"Unhand me, I'm not a criminal!" Myan ordered.

"It's all clear. His cart is empty," a young temple guard reported.

The other guard released Myan. "You're free to go. Sorry for the inconvenience."

The temple guards left as rapidly as the came. They had to find the intruders or face the wrath of their superiors. Myan caught his breath and continued down the alley. The close call scared the color from his face. He couldn't stop trembling as he led his horse on.

VII

THE DISTINCTIVE CLANK of armor echoed through the pre-dawn fog as Sir Lexton led a squad of soldiers down the main street of Xylor. They moved swiftly and with purpose. The crisp air had a bite to it this morning, freezing the morning dew into a thin layer of ice. The ice shimmered in the sunlight that was just breaking over the horizon. The soldiers plodded ahead like horses, their breath coming in visible white snorts. They were well disciplined and professional. There was little talking among the ranks. A few sets of eyes peered out from behind curtains, curious about the troop movement. Some citizens who were out paused to watch the soldiers pass. An uneasy, nervousness, mixed with a dash of fear started to envelop the onlookers. Was this an extra patrol? Was there trouble? This looked to be more than a routine patrol. The soldiers were hurried, quieter than usual. No one dared inquire as to the squad's purpose. The eyes disappeared behind the curtains, and the people on the street pretended they were invisible. Even a stray dog near an alley kept clear of Lexton's men.

The squad paid little attention to the onlookers and made its way to a cottage south of town. Lexton scanned the small fenced-in yard noticing nothing unusual. Smoke gently wafted from the cottage chimney and no light came from the windows. The cottage was either deserted or the residents still asleep. Lexton signaled for his men to fan out and position themselves. They did this with nary a sound. Checking his papers, he verified the address as the same one Marcus had given him. Once confirmation was made, Lexton and three men went to the door. A loud crash shattered the early morning quiet and Lexton and his men barged through the splintered door. Soldiers outside covered the windows in case anyone tried to escape. Inside, the soldiers cleared the empty kitchen then invaded the two bedrooms. Lexton waited in the entryway. A woman's scream was followed by the sounds of a scuffle.

"Just these two kids in this room, sir," a soldier said as he came out of the left bedroom with two young boys in tow. He forced them onto a bench by the window.

The commotion in the other bedroom became louder, and a man in a nightshirt flew through the doorway. He tumbled across the kitchen floor, knocking over a chair. A woman in a nightgown followed him.

"They are the only two in this room, sir," a soldier reported with a scowl. "And the woman bit me."

Lexton looked at the two adults. The man, about thirty-five years old, held his ribs tenderly, trying to catch his breath. The woman, in tears, was attractive for a peasant. She wiped blood from her nose with her sleeve. By now the whole neighborhood was awake. People cracked open their shutters, straining to see what the fuss was all about.

"You are under arrest for treason," Lexton informed the man. "You have been identified as a member of the rebel movement. The penalty for treason is death, and you will be taken in."

"No! No!" The woman shrieked and stood up in defense of her husband. She was met with a fist to the midsection that sent her back to the floor.

"You leave her alone! It's me you want!" The man shouted and turned to face the soldier who struck his wife. A backhand sent him crashing into the table.

"So you acknowledge your association with the rebels?" Lexton glared at the man.

"I…I don't know what you're talking about. What rebels?" Two soldiers jerked the man up from the floor and slammed him into a chair.

"You just said to leave your wife alone because it was you we wanted. Why would you say that? Unless, of course, you were engaged in activity that would make you wanted?"

The man stammered out a response. "No, I didn't mean that…I was…I mean I was upset…my wife was hurt…I didn't mean anything…I…you twisted my words. I'm not a rebel."

Lexton clearly wasn't buying the explanation. "Don't insult my intelligence with an obvious lie. You knew we were here for you. You said it yourself. In my book you gave us a confession." Lexton turned to his men. "Bind him for transport."

"No, wait, I can explain." The soldiers shackled the man's ankles and wrists and pulled him to his feet.

"Take him outside," Lexton ordered.

The two young boys started crying for their father. The woman ran to Lexton, sobbing and pleading for the release of her husband. Lexton ignored her and started to leave. She clung to his arm and pleaded all the more loudly.

"Keep your hands off me!" Lexton ripped his arm from her grasp.

"No, please, have mercy on us. Let my husband stay." The woman was desperate. She held onto Lexton's surcoat.

Lexton pried her hands off and shoved her to the remaining soldier. "Bind her. She's going in too."

"Yes, sir." The soldier shackled the sobbing woman who continued to beg for her family. "What about the kids, sir?"

"Send in two more men. As orphans, the two boys will now be working for the royal government as stable boys."

The woman started to scream at Lexton in an incoherent panic. Suddenly the full realization of what was happening became clear. She now fully comprehended the fate that awaited her and her husband.

"No! No! No! God, no-o-o-o-o!" The woman wailed a cry that sounded like a cross between a howling wolf and an injured cat. The wail unsettled Lexton.

"Get her out of my sight. In fact, take half the squad and get the prisoners back to the compound while I finish up here."

Lexton waited for them to leave, and then lingered in the cottage a moment. The woman's tormented scream still echoed in his ears. It was the cry of an anguished soul, of a woman who feared for her children's future. For a split second Lexton felt remorse for the family. Believing remorse to be a dangerous sign of weakness, he quickly got back to the task at hand. Lexton could remember a time when he felt differently, but that was long ago. His new philosophy was attack first before the other man attacks you. And if the other man wasn't going to attack, oh well, you still win. He didn't care to sort out the difference. That required a blend of patience and compassion; two more weaknesses, to Lexton's way of thinking.

When Lexton left the cottage, a large crowd of morbidly curious onlookers gathered to see what was happening. Lexton seized the opportunity to set an example for the people.

"Everyone, listen up, and listen good." He paused to make sure he had the crowd's attention. He looked each person directly in the eye. Whenever he caught someone's gaze, they invariably broke eye contact and looked away. One robust man kept eye contact, giving Lexton a look of contempt. They locked eyes in a silent dual. Lexton would not tolerate this act of defiance, and motioned to a soldier named Malvagio. The man broke his gaze with Lexton after a gloved fist pummeled his solar plexus. A boot hammered his side after he collapsed to the floor.

"Mind your manners," Malvagio said for the crowd's sake as well as the robust man. His gap-toothed grin was worn in an arrogant manner.

Lexton continued. "Do I have your attention now? Good. These people have been arrested for treason. They have jeopardized our lives by compromising our security. They have plotted against the government. They have rejected Tanuba. Their fate now lies in the hands of the count. Learn from their folly. Do not make the same mistakes. You all enjoy a life of prosperity and protection from harm. We live in a golden era of Xylorian history. Why would anyone want to jeopardize that? Why would anyone raise his hand against the very government that has ushered in this abundant prosperity? Why would anyone forsake Tanuba? But most of all, why would anyone throw away their lives and property? Do any of you have aspirations of rebellion? Does anyone here feel the need to make a name for himself?" Lexton grabbed a torch from one of his men and walked to the now vacant cottage.

"This is what happens to rebels!" Lexton set the cottage on fire. The wooden cottage had a straw roof, and the fire spread rapidly. The flames greedily engulfed the structure, crackling and popping as it advanced. When the flames were shooting high in the air he signaled for his men to form up.

"Are there any other rebels who wish to come forward now? Turn yourself in and you will escape with your life. If you wait until we find you, it will mean death. There is a five hundred shilling reward for turning in a rebel. And to all you loyal citizens, I apologize for this episode."

The citizens stood frozen, afraid to move, much less speak. They just stared at the burning cottage numbly and waited for the soldiers to go.

Lexton set out for the compound with the rest of his men. As they walked Lexton turned to Malvagio and asked, "Something on your mind?" The soldier had been unusually quiet and started to say something twice already, only to stop abruptly.

"Yes, sir, I've been thinking. How did Marcus know these people were with the rebels? Pardon me for saying, but this guy doesn't fit the part."

"A rebel could look like anyone; big strong men, a frail old man, even a child. Don't get fooled by appearances. Underestimating an opponent is the leading cause of death in the Royal Guard. You have to know your enemy well enough to determine the size of a force needed to win." A slight smirk curled the corner of Lexton's mouth. "And besides, does it really matter? Civil obedience can take many forms."

"Yes, sir." Malvagio sported a broad grin. "The cost of being a rebel has certainly gone up."

"That's one way to look at it. I prefer to think the value of good citizenship is what has increased."

Lexton was entering the gates of Reddland's compound when he heard the clacking of horseshoes on cobblestone. He looked up to see a soldier rein in his sweaty horse and dismount.

"You men go on ahead. Tell the count our assignment is completed, and that it went smoother than anticipated." The men left to carry out their order as Lexton removed his gauntlets. He turned to meet his subordinate.

"Sir Lexton, I report on the search for Bartus." The young squad leader removed his helm and wiped the sweat from his face. He had ridden hard across town.

"I take it Marcus was right again? Bartus was found living under the docks as stated in his report?"

"Yes sir, we found his make-shift camp under pier three."

"Outstanding. Bring him in for interrogation as soon as possible. He may have critical information that could help us identify potential rebels." Lexton noticed the squad leader seemed a bit uneasy and was fidgeting with his gloves. "You did catch him, didn't you?"

"Uh, well, sir, he managed to escape."

Lexton flushed with anger. "You have to be kidding! How does a half-starved vagabond escape a squad of highly trained soldiers? Did he learn to fly?"

"I'm sorry, sir. With a few more men I'm sure we can—"

"You don't need more men," Lexton cut him off. "One squad is more than enough to bring in an armed fugitive. It is overkill for an unarmed citizen."

"I'm sorry sir. We'll have him by nightfall."

Lexton interrupted, "Malvagio! Front and center!"

Malvagio came running at once. "Yes, sir. You called."

"You're the new squad leader for squad three. Go to the docks and meet with the rest of the squad. They are on a manhunt for the sly and amazing escape artist Bartus, danger to all!" Lexton reeked of sarcasm. "The count wants him interrogated by nightfall. Find this desperado and bring him here. The men will fill you in on the rest."

"Yes, sir!" Malvagio was thrilled by his promotion. He ran off toward the stables anxious to prove himself.

Lexton turned to his old squad leader. "If you make one mistake, it happens to all of us. Two mistakes, well, maybe it's a bad bit of luck. But this is your third time in as many months. That's unacceptable. Failure is a danger to our organization. The count won't tolerate it, and I can't tolerate it. The rebels might be up to something. It is critical that we discover their plans and put an end to them."

The old squad leader was visibly disappointed but offered no excuses.

"You are now assigned to squad four as Malvagio's replacement. You're dismissed. Go find your squad." Lexton knew full well the importance of the next few days and was feeling the strain. If the rebels were indeed planning an attack, he had to find out where and when. Any significant defeat of the Royal Guard would only encourage other dissatisfied citizens to join the rebel cause. Then the problem would grow even further. If the loss were severe enough, Kelterland would send troops to restore order. A reorganization of the Xylorian government would be sure to follow. It was an unsavory prospect for Lexton. It would be an unsavory prospect with an uncertain future for any surviving Royal Guardsmen. Certainly the rebels knew that even if they staged a successful coup here on Xylor, they had no chance to fend off the swift reprisal from Kelterland. They were crazy if they thought Kelterland would give away the island territory. On the other hand, a crushing defeat for the rebels would end the rebellion once and for all. Then again, maybe the rebels were up to nothing more than stockpiling supplies for some future use. Either way, Lexton was determined to find out.

———— •◆• ————

Bartus narrowly escaped the Royal Guard and was hiding at the docks in a crate of garlic. With any luck the overwhelming scent of garlic would disguise his whereabouts if dogs were brought into the search. He hoped the guards would give up the search before his crate was loaded onto a ship. Bartus couldn't imagine why the soldiers would spend so much time or energy looking for him. After all, he only stole a few loaves of bread? A horrifying thought crossed Bartus's mind. What if they thought he killed one of the sentries on the ship? Impossible. Certainly they would know it had to be Novak or Scorpyus. No one would think Bartus could defeat a trained soldier in battle. He had nothing to worry about. Bartus prayed for the safety of Scorpyus and Novak. They would certainly be dealt with severely if they were captured.

Well, I guess I'll just wait it out. Bartus thought. They shouldn't be much longer. He could hear the soldiers.

Malvagio was directing the search. "You men did good setting up the perimeter around this dock. As long as you know for sure you lost him around here, and no one has caught him trying to break through the perimeter yet, we should find him."

"There's no way he left this dock on foot. We know he ran here, and we searched both ships already. The only thing left is the stack of cargo over there." A soldier brought Malvagio up to speed on the situation.

"Good. He's got to be around here somewhere. He should still be close by unless he jumped in the water; in which case he should be within the wharf area. From what I hear, I doubt he has the endurance to swim very far in this cold water."

Bartus could hear the soldiers opening up crates and barrels and started to tremble. *I'm not going to make it if they search every crate.* He thought about wriggling his way down, burying himself under the cloves of garlic, but decided it would make too much noise.

The lid of Bartus's crate flew off with a clatter. Malvagio and three soldiers looked down on him.

"Well, it appears you're not the sharpest sword in the armory. You didn't think we would notice the lid of this crate was the only one not nailed down? You'll have to learn to hide better than that." Malvagio laughed, clearly amused by his own wit. "Shackle the bum, boys."

Bartus offered no resistance. A deep sense of dread squeezed his chest making it hard to breathe.

The soldiers pulled him out of the crate of garlic as if he were nothing more then a rag doll. They shackled him then proceeded to beat him for good measure. The soldiers cackled joyously as they pummeled their captive. Bartus prayed fervently until he blacked out. A sailor looked on in disgust from the deck of the nearest ship. The count was at it again, he thought.

———•◦•———

"Did he say anything?" Luther followed Lexton down the hall to where Bartus was being held. Marcus followed close behind. A sentry in the Elite Guard unlocked a large iron door, letting the trio into a windowless holding cell. Bartus sat in a large wooden chair, his arms and legs held in place with thick leather straps. He had a bruised cheekbone and dried blood on his nose. Malvagio sat against the wall.

Luther looked to Malvagio. "I hear you're the one who found him. Keep up the good work and you'll go places. I believe in rewarding results, as do my senior officers."

Malvagio's already inflated ego swelled even more.

"Well, Bartus, things may have been better for you had you gone to trial for stealing." Luther pulled up a chair opposite Bartus. "As it is now, you're an escapee, suspected of murdering two sentries, and worst of all, suspected of being sympathetic to the rebellion. Any of these charges in and of itself warrants death."

Bartus's eyes widened in horror. Once someone was linked to the rebellion, whether they were really a rebel or not, their days were numbered.

Luther continued. "Of course if you cooperated with us, maybe I could recommend leniency—at least spare your life."

"Cooperate with you how?" Bartus didn't understand how he could be of any help to Luther.

"Just answer some questions. Tell us what we want to know and I'll spare your life. Refuse, and you'll die—but not before you talk. Rest assured, you will answer our questions. I prefer we avoid all the unpleasantries."

Bartus nodded. His throat felt thick as if he swallowed a cotton ball. Beads of sweat trickled from his brow even though the darkened cell was cold and damp. Torchlight cast an eerie glow on his interrogators making them appear as evil as they really were.

"Could I have some water, please?" Bartus felt parched.

"Certainly, I'm not an unmerciful man." Luther motioned to Malvagio, who brought a ladle of water to Bartus and held it for him to drink.

"Thanks." Bartus downed the ladle thinking it could be his last one. The water was cool and refreshing.

Luther continued, confident that Bartus understood him completely. "Let's start with how you and the other prisoners escaped?"

"Lieutenant Tiberious let us go. He opened the cell doors."

"And he had an escape planned already?"

"Yeah."

"We are aware that an imposter posing as the lieutenant released you. What can you tell us about that imposter?"

"I don't know? What do you want to know?" Bartus was petrified so he planned on talking. He didn't want to be forced.

"What did he look like?"

"He looked like the lieutenant?"

A slight irritation could be heard in Luther's voice. "I know he looked like the lieutenant on the ship. I'm talking about later, when he took off his disguise."

"He never took off his disguise," Bartus lied.

Luther motioned to Marcus. Marcus stepped forward and Bartus head whipped to the left from the force of a massive backhand. Bartus slowly raised his wobbly head, his lip bleeding.

"Is it worth your life to protect these rebels? The lieutenant was seen without his beard as he was climbing a bluff at the beach, where he then proceeded to shoot arrows at my men! Once again, what did he look like?"

Bartus thought a moment. "Uh, a young man, younger than the lieutenant, black hair, not a bad looking fellow, with a dark complexion, about six feet tall, in good shape. The man could run, that's for sure."

"Does he have a name?"

In the chaos Bartus hadn't realized Scorpyus had been seen at the beach, but he was sure Luther had no way of knowing his name. "The big man called him Simon."

"By 'big man' you mean Novak; the other prisoner?" Luther glanced at the arrest report to be sure he had the name right.

"Yeah, Novak."

Luther scratched a few notes on the report. "So they knew each other. Novak recognized the lieutenant to be in reality this Simon?"

"Yes I believe so."

"Did they ever mention any local citizens by name, or speak of their plans?"

"No, they never said anything along those lines. I don't think they trusted me."

"Did they say or do anything suspicious, anything that made you think they were here to contact or help the rebels?"

"No, never." Luther had to know Scorpyus and Novak were new to town. Bartus wondered why Luther suspected them of being here to help with the rebellion. Most people felt the rebellion was about as much of a myth as a unicorn, didn't they? A thing often talked about but never seen.

A flash of light shot through Bartus's eyes; once again his head snapped to the side. This time he remained dizzy after he raised his head. Bartus could feel his right eye swell shut.

Luther was angry. "Do not lie to me! I know they have had contact with at least one known rebel. You were with these two men for some time. They must have said something to you. Wait, wait, wait just a minute. Why would two fit, young, obviously trained fighting men waste their time and risk their lives even further, just to save a weak, untrained bag of bones like you? Certainly they knew you would only hurt their chances of escape, that you were dead weight and would slow them down considerably. That is, unless you were important to them."

A look of revelation lit Luther's eyes, "A rebel with some valuable knowledge, or secret?"

"I...I...know nothing. They didn't...I'm not..." Bartus stammered. His worst fears were becoming reality. Bartus had no knowledge that important, and no prior knowledge about Scorpyus and Novak. He was a man who lived under the docks, always kept to himself, and nothing more. It defied all of Bartus's logic. How could anyone think he was a rebel, much less an important player in some plot? Tears welled up in his eyes. *Oh Lord, please help me.* He prayed.

Luther looked to Lexton. "What time was Novak arrested?"

"Around dusk."

"And what time was Bartus arrested?"

"Um, midday."

Luther snapped his fingers. "Ah, ha! It's starting to make sense. Bartus, who's a man with some valuable knowledge, gets arrested. He probably saw something he shouldn't have down at the docks and now wants to report it. But as fate would have it he gets arrested for stealing bread; he's got to eat. The rebel leaders think Bartus must have some important information, important enough to send a team to rescue him. Novak gets himself arrested by violating a law in the town square, a place where everyone will see him, thus guaranteeing an arrest. This Simon abducts Lieutenant Tiberious so he can pose as him and plans the jailbreak. Novak protects Bartus from possible guard brutality; they have to have him alive to tell his story. And he aids Simon with the escape. Two men would be needed anyway to drag Bartus through the forest. All the while this woman and another man take care of things here on the island; they plan a safe hideaway possibly? And Bartus makes it back alive to tell his valuable secret! Why didn't we see this before?"

Marcus and Lexton nodded in agreement with this new possibility. Malvagio was downright impressed with all he was hearing.

Bartus broke down in tears. "No! No! It's not true! They just felt sorry for me. I know I'm pathetic! Everything was taken from me and my family killed! You know that, Luther. I'm just a broken-down man. I've been nothing since my Lydia passed on. She was all I had left. I'm lost without her. I didn't tell them anything. I know nothing to tell. They just had pity on a broken-down nobody. That's all it was." Bartus quietly sobbed.

Luther took offense at Bartus's denial. "You expect me to believe someone would help you escape if there was nothing in it for them? Just because they took mercy on you? And what about Novak? I suppose he decided to take a stand for his god? That he really feels that strongly about Tanuba being a false idol? That he even cares one way or the other? No, too many things just don't make sense."

It would never occur to Luther, Bartus thought, that someone might show another mercy unless there was something to be gained by it. His mind was not capable of that kind of thought. He couldn't conceive of someone *following* God, much less taking a stand at great risk to his or her life for Him. Helping someone out with no thought for the favor being returned? How ludicrous. In Luther's world you didn't love your neighbor unless he could do something for you. And if he got in your way, you killed him. Power and wealth were Luther's gods. Luther liked his men as long as they did their job. His men liked him as long as they got paid. The more Luther paid, the more loyal his men were. If one died, he bought another. And Luther always had people ready to join him.

Bartus realized his words were futile. He hung his head and sobbed uncontrollably. His fate lay in the hands of God now. He had been so demoralized he almost wanted it to end now. "I swear I don't know anything."

"Lexton, have Bartus here questioned more thoroughly. Make him tell us everything. Its imperative we find out what he knows. The rebels must be crushed once and for all."

Lexton and Malvagio led Bartus from the room kicking and screaming. Malvagio cackled with delight, relishing the thought of putting the screws to Bartus.

"No! Oh God, please no! No! Don't! How can you do this to me? Doesn't it mean anything—" Bartus wasn't allowed to finish, and knew a painful ordeal loomed on the horizon. He began to pray fervently for a quick death.

Lexton was unemotional. He saw Malvagio was definitely the bloodthirsty sort. He would keep that in mind in case he needed any dirty work done. Lexton pondered the uses of his newest squad leader. Malvagio was different from most of the other soldiers. They did their duty because it was their job, and they were paid well. Malvagio seemed to enjoy his assignments thoroughly, especially in gruesome situations like this.

Marcus waited until he was alone with Luther. "Well, I guess this is another possibility. It certainly makes sense. Since these strangers have been in town, things have been happening. The rebels appear to have markedly picked up their activity. But I think it's all a coincidence, that Bartus is just a vagabond. What use could he be to the rebels? Isaac ran across that woman by blind luck. He was about to be captured, and he knew a stranger would be his best bet for help. The woman probably thought Isaac was nothing more then a crazy old man. He only had a few brief seconds to talk to her. That's my opinion, Sire."

"I think you're right, Marcus, but there is something in the air. We must run each theory to its conclusion. We can't take any chances. We have no indication our strangers have abandoned their quest for Hyacinth Blue. There is no logical reason, financial or otherwise, for them to get involved with the rebels. But we have to be absolutely sure. And Bartus is nothing more than a bum; you're right about that."

"Could this Novak really be so loyal to his god? Loyal enough to risk five thousand shillings? That's more money then he sees all year."

"People have been fanatical about lesser things," Marcus observed. "At one time Christians allowed themselves to be boiled alive, impaled on stakes, and set on fire, even crucified rather then renounce their Jesus. It used to be more common. I know it may be hard to believe, but it's true. Novak seems unbelievable because to find someone with that kind of faith anymore is rare. Especially here in Xylor."

"Yes, Marcus, that's true, you have a point. Anyhow, we'll know for sure if we have anything to worry about or not when Lexton gets through with Bartus. A man in his condition should soon be begging to tell us what he knows. He won't last long under interrogation." Luther stood up, and put away his papers. "Let's go get some lunch, I'm starved."

VIII

NOVAK'S BRAWNY ARM brought the meat cleaver down with a thud, cleanly severing the leg. "Thanks for leaving me the drumstick." He slapped it on a wooden plate then tore off a chunk of bread. He generously salted his food.

The group was enjoying a much-welcome meal in the secret room beneath the stables. It was time to relax after the night's adventures.

"This pheasant is delicious." Zephyr sat on her cot taking dainty nibbles from her plate. "Who cooked it?"

"My daughter Emerald is a tremendous cook," Thadus answered and beamed with pride. "Don't be bashful. Be sure to eat all you want. Scorpyus, did you get enough? Do you want seconds?"

As usual, Scorpyus was the first one finished. He had wolfed down his food and now sat sipping some hot tea. The tea was also furnished courtesy of Thadus's daughter. "No, no thanks. My compliments to the chef. You never told us you had a daughter."

"The subject never came up."

"Scorpyus, you are done already? Did you ever consider chewing your food?" Zephyr got a laugh with her wisecrack.

"What? And risk wearing out my teeth prematurely? I may eat fast, but at least I don't nibble on my food as if I only had two teeth in my mouth, one on top and one on the bottom." A piece of bread hit Scorpyus on the head. This made the group laugh even harder.

Cad stood up. "Hey, both of you should be thankful you're not Novak. When he eats it reminds me of a daft dog trying to eat sticky caramel."

The group roared with laughter.

"Don't drag me into this. I could get mad, and then I might break something...like a leg or collar bone," Novak shot back. "By the way, whose turn is it to wipe Cad's drool?"

"If the offer still stands, I'll take seconds," Cad said after he caught his breath. He could always eat seconds and could even out-eat Novak. And what made this feat all the more remarkable was the fact Cad seldom had anything to drink during the meal to wash the food down. Only after he finished eating did he consume liquids.

"Yes, please do." Thadus motioned for Cad to help himself to the food. He could tell the quartet were good friends by the way they joked with each other. He waited until they finished eating before bringing out a bilberry pie. Thadus was pleased to see the quartet's faces light up. Dessert was a rare luxury for them.

"Wow, it has been at least a month since we had dessert monsieur." Zephyr eagerly cut into the pie and served it up. Even Thadus had a piece.

"You're going to have to introduce me to your daughter," Novak told him as he ate greedily. "A woman who can cook this good is worth her weight in gold!"

Thadus was glad to see his guests enjoy themselves. They had done so much to help him already; it was the least he could do. "Well, now that you mention it, you should meet Emerald shortly. I've asked her to join us for our meeting. She'll be the one briefing us on the latest developments concerning the soldiers' activities."

"Your daughter is going to brief us? Is she in the rebellion also?" Novak seemed surprised Thadus would allow his daughter to engage in rebel activity. "Don't you think it's dangerous?"

Zephyr didn't give Thadus a chance to answer. "So what are you saying, Novak? A woman cannot handle the risk?"

"Ahh…They could keep their wits under stress…if they don't get emotional. But what if there's trouble, a fight with a massive guard?"

A wry smile came over Zephyr's face, and she crossed her arms. "Oh, I see. A woman is not strong enough to do the job?"

"Well, ya, fighting takes strength and power."

"I am a woman. I handle myself in dangerous assignments, with you none-the-less."

"But that's different, Zephyr."

"How so?" Zephyr tapped her foot on the floor waiting for a reply.

Novak looked to Cad and Scorpyus who quickly looked away stifling their grins. "Are you going to let me flounder here?" Novak thought quickly. "You're different, Zephyr, because you have speed. And you're so tiny, making it hard to hit you. So there are rare exceptions. But when it comes to a fight, when things get dangerous, a woman could always run like a jackrabbit. That is if she didn't pass out first."

Once again the room echoed with laughter.

Zephyr feigned shock, mouth agape. She knew she was a rare exception. Few women were afforded the opportunity to learn to use a sword. Fewer still had Zephyr's gift of speed and agility. She had great hand-eye coordination. Zephyr had to learn to use a sword for survival in her war-torn homeland. But she knew it was her God-given abilities that allowed her to be successful at what she did. She just wanted to push Novak in front of Thadus. It kept him on his toes. "That was not very nice. At least I do not get myself arrested!"

Cad and Scorpyus enjoyed the exchange, but made sure they stayed way out of it.

Thadus was clearly amused by the conversation. "I know what you're saying, Novak. Exposing Emerald to the cause was a decision I didn't take lightly. But I would rather see her take a stand against all the wickedness then compromise her morals like so many others did. To be a 'good citizen' of this society requires a total betrayal of God. The day Luther's administration forbade the worship of God in favor of the Tanuba cult was the day we were no longer obligated to the government. So when compared to the alternative, assisting the rebellion is really the only option available…unless one is content with turning an apathetic eye toward all that is happening. And I didn't raise Emerald to be apathetic. She is like all of us; interested in restoring her homeland and ending all the suffering. Xylor used to be an ideal, peaceful place and can be again. Besides we need all the help we can get. Will I allow her to engage a soldier in a sword fight? I hope that day never comes, but I do allow her to engage in information gathering, and she has become quite good at it."

All four nodded in understanding.

"How many rebels are there, anyhow?" Cad asked bluntly and took a seat at the table. The candle on the table flickered with the motion.

Thadus let out a heavy sigh. "Not enough. I'm ashamed to admit it, but there are known Christians in Xylor who refuse to participate. Others can be counted on only for their silence or maybe a hot meal for a weary rebel now and again. When it comes to actual participating members, we don't have as many as we should, all things considered. The sad thing is, while some people remain silent, we even have two members who are non-believers, who have no vested interest in restoring the old ways, doing more to help than others who should be helping."

Scorpyus abruptly looked up from his tea. "What? There are non-believing rebels? You don't find that highly irregular?"

Thadus looked puzzled and pulled up a chair with the others. "No, should I?"

"Scorpyus is suspicious of everyone," Zephyr said almost apologetically.

"Wait, just wait a blooming minute." Cad waived a finger in the air. "Scorpyus has a point. To be a rebel means to risk death if discovered. In order to succeed in the current Xylorian society, in order to obtain status, one has to be a worshiper of Tanuba. Unless a chap can gain the count's favor by some other means like being a valiant soldier. To rise in this society means to turn from the old ways and to embrace the new. It is the count's way or the roadway. The more you assimilate the better your chances, and the more wealth you will have the potential to gain. On the other hand, being a rebel requires an uncompromising moral integrity, a code of honor as it were. It means no matter how much wealth or status the new system could offer you, as a believer you would pass on it since it means turning your back on God. Once God was outlawed, a believer would have no choice but to drop out of society and be forced underground. Now, a believer not actively participating in the rebel cause is understandable. Fear for one's life, a lack of faith, maybe illness can explain that. But if you were for Tanuba, or the count, why on earth would you jeopardize everything to help the rebels—unless you were a bloody spy?"

Thadus defended his people. "No one is being paid to spy on us. Maybe they just don't like the killing the count is doing. That could encourage some to aid the opposition. Did you consider that? I don't know. All I can say is they are good people."

"Does one of these non-believers happen to be an open Tanuba worshiper?" Scorpyus leaned forward on his cot with great interest.

"Yes, I believe one is," Thadus replied while crossing his hairy arms.

"Don't trust him!" Scorpyus was adamant. "Take my advice, don't trust him. I wouldn't."

Thadus was getting angry. "You don't even know this person's name, and you've judged him a traitor! How arrogant can you be? Are you saying only a Christian can have a code of honor? Or be the only ones who can get tired of the killing?" He jabbed a finger into Scorpyus's chest.

Scorpyus raised an eyebrow at this aggressive display. The others knew Thadus was crossing the line, and had just been sized up for combat. Cad, Novak, and Zephyr didn't know where Scorpyus was going with this but they prepared to back him anyhow.

"I'm not saying a non-believer; someone who is lost, can't live by a moral code. And sad to say there are believers whose deeds are less then honorable. But a Tanuba worshiper…aiding the fight against the establishment…never trust him."

"I'll have you know this person is one of our best spies," Thadus shot back.

Scorpyus took a deep breath. "Let me ask you a hypothetical question. If one of the Royal soldiers came to you and wanted to join the rebellion, would you trust him?"

"No, of course not."

"What if he came to you and offered information about the Royal Guards activities?"

"I still wouldn't trust him. I'd listen to the information, but I wouldn't trust him."

"And why not?"

"I'll tell you why, Scorpyus, because if he was willing to be a traitor to the Royal Guard by working against them, how do I know that at some point in the future he wouldn't betray *me?*" Thadus realized what Scorpyus had been trying to say, and turned pale at the thought of the possibility. It was a once-a-traitor always-a-traitor theory.

Cad spoke what everyone was thinking. "I'm all for giving someone a chance to forget the past and start life anew. But a chap who has a position on *both* sides of the conflict is only in it for himself. The bloke's motives are certainly suspect. This open Tanuba worshiper who is providing information to the rebellion is being a traitor to his cause. It is impossible to help us without hurting them, and vice versa. The only unanswered questioned is, is this person a double agent? Is information flowing both ways, and does Luther get inside intelligence about rebel activities? You can't play both sides, mate."

Thadus was taken aback. What could he say? He was so focused on the fact this person was assisting the rebel cause, that it hadn't occurred to him the same person could also be a double agent. It made sense. If someone was proving themselves a traitor to their own people, what's to keep them loyal to anyone; especially to a group as different as day and night from the Tanuba worshipers?

"I don't know what to say? I have to admit your theory makes sense. What do we do now? Break contact?"

"No, monsieur, do not break contact. If you do they will suspect something. You have to keep them working so they remain oblivious to the fact they are now suspected of foul play. That will give us time to investigate their activities." The others nodded their agreement with Zephyr.

"What are their names?" Cad got to the point.

"Iris and Wallace," Thadus felt uneasy and disturbed by this possibility. "My God, what if they've been informing Reddland about rebel activities?"

"That's a distinct possibility mate." Cad continued. "That could explain the failure of any rebel mission in the past. It might even explain how Isaac was discovered. The count's men were on his trail somehow. Either way those two chaps have to be taken out of the circle of information. Assign them to finding out about troop movements. That should keep them busy, and unsuspecting of anything being wrong. Whatever you do, don't bloody well tell them anything about rebel plans or activities anymore. Don't answer any questions of theirs…truthfully anyway. Say nothing about locations of equipment, hideouts, and names of other rebels…or anything of importance. The less they suspect, the easier it will be to follow them. In the meantime, Scorpyus has an assignment."

Scorpyus was excited about the task. He enjoyed the patient study of a subject, watching their every move and analyzing their behavior until he found out what their agenda was. "I've got a few disguises in mind that should let me obtain a vantage point into the workings of Xylorian government. I should discover what their intentions are and a few other things while I'm at it. I just have one question: which one is the Tanuba worshiper?"

"Iris is the self-avowed Tanuba worshiper. She makes no attempt to hide that fact. Wallace on the other hand appears to hold no loyalties. He left the cult three or four years ago, and hasn't looked back. They both have provided reliable information about Reddland on several occasions." Thadus was sullen thinking about the whole possibility. He hoped Scorpyus would turn up nothing that would incriminate them, but deep down felt it was a long shot. "By the way, what if you don't find out anything? Or what if you get discovered?"

Novak laughed. "If you saw Scorpyus disguised you wouldn't even worry about it."

"If I dig deep enough, something will turn up." Scorpyus assured Thadus. "Be it good or bad, the truth of this matter will seep to the surface."

In a flash Cad, Zephyr, Novak, and Scorpyus were on their feet and in defensive positions in response to the opening of the trapdoor on the ceiling. Thadus remained seated. Two delicate shoes and the hem of a blue cotton dress appeared on the top rung of the ladder that descended into the secret chamber. Carefully taking each step, a young, beautiful, blonde woman, about twenty-five years old joined the meeting.

"This is my daughter, Emerald." Thadus introduced her to his guests one by one going around the room.

Emerald met Cad first. He seemed courteous, respectful, and well educated; a strapping man with an air of self-confidence about him, and he had a way of making others believe it. Emerald felt it was a trait that would be quite beneficial in a leadership situation.

Next she met Zephyr, and a slight tension developed from the introduction. Zephyr and Emerald sized each other up, engaging in a quick compare and contrast. It was the hidden ritual played out by women everywhere. Zephyr and Emerald engaged in their inner competition all the while speaking so nicely and sweetly to each other. Before the introduction was over, they each made a quick summation of the other's strengths and weaknesses.

Next Emerald met Scorpyus. For some reason she felt a little afraid of him despite his graceful charm. He had such a penetrating stare it made her uneasy. And he seemed a little strange. His dark eyes enhanced his mournful countenance, which clashed with his humorous conversational style. Emerald pictured Scorpyus as the type of person who would always have something to say, no matter the topic.

Then Emerald met Novak. Oh my! Emerald clearly liked what she saw. She couldn't help but notice his bicep flex when he shook her hand. And that boyish smirk, with those deep blue eyes…Emerald was all aflutter. He was so big, strong, and muscular she found it hard to keep her mind on the small talk. Emerald spent a lot more time talking to Novak then she did with the others. They watched her with Novak. She looked so petite standing next to him. Then again, most people did.

Scorpyus walked over to Cad and Zephyr, and put his hands on their shoulders. He pulled them in closer to him and whispered. "I do believe this is an enchanted moment."

Cad and Zephyr grinned as they watched their friend get showered with attention from the vivacious blonde.

Emerald was clearly enamored with Novak. Everyone waited as she made small talk about the weather, or history, anything that came to mind. Novak was aware of the flirtatious undertones of the situation, and was flattered. But he didn't let the attention sink in. Flattery is like perfume; a sweet scent to enjoy while it is around, but if you swallow it, it will surely go to your head and kill you. With Novak's incredibly muscular physique, and rugged good looks, women often entertained him in this manner, sometimes with ulterior motives. Novak knew better than to let it swell his ego. He could remember many times when it had been Cad or Scorpyus in his position. He figured he was due for a turn. Emerald was very attractive, though. The fact that she was also a solid believer put her far ahead of the competition. Novak was content to keep things professional, and too much of a gentleman to press any advantages he may have. Thadus was seemingly supportive of the way the two conversed, each remaining polite and proper. The Clandestine Knights held chivalry, honor, and character above all else, and tried hard to live life in accordance. Birthright didn't make one a knight, moral integrity and values did. Anyone could live by the code of the knight if they so chose.

"She's obviously attracted to muscle rather than genius." Cad whispered coyly with a smirk.

Zephyr elbowed Cad. "Humility is not one of your strong suits, no?"

"Despite what everyone thinks, I'm not perfect." Cad pretended to be apologetic.

Scorpyus feigned sorrow. "At least you didn't scare the fair damsel like I did." Scorpyus growled and made a ridiculous contortion with his face, trying to act frightful. He knew people were often uncomfortable around Gypsies. Anyone with black hair and an olive complexion might be labeled as one. Not that this was the case with Emerald; in fact it was far from it. But most people didn't care for Gypsies, especially in this part of the world. And Scorpyus, not being a typical Gypsy, really didn't even fit in with his own. This was due in part to him being only half Gypsy, but it had more to due with his family not following in the usual superstitious traditions of Gypsy culture. Scorpyus was raised a believer, and this set him apart from the fortune telling mysticism of many of his clansmen. He often mused about how he was meant to be born in another time.

"You did not scare off that seamstress in the Dales," Zephyr offered, knowing full well the seamstress had only been after information.

"The one who wanted to know why we were in town? She was just digging for answers." Scorpyus laughed. "In fact I turned the tables on her and got her to reveal who her superior was."

"Yeah, but the maiden was drunk?" Cad inquired.

"I didn't say she was smart." Scorpyus remembered the scenario with humor.

Zephyr injected her thoughts on the matter. "What gave her away? Was it when she stumbled into the room? Or when she fell off the chair?"

The trio started laughing amongst themselves, amusing each other with observations about human behavior.

"She needed liquor to build up the nerve to approach Scorpyus." Cad stated the obvious.

"Novice," Scorpyus shook his head in disbelief.

Novak spotted his friends giggling in the corner. "Hey, why don't you let us in on the joke?" He interrupted his conversation with Emerald.

"Well, I suppose I should get on with my report anyhow." Emerald turned to Novak. "We'll have to finish our talk another time."

Novak smiled. "That we will."

Thadus took a place at the front of the room next to Emerald. "Please take a seat. I've asked Emerald to bring us up to speed on the activities of the Royal Guard. She is our contact for our agents in the field. They report directly to her. With that said, I will turn the conversation over to Emerald."

Everyone pulled up cots and chairs, gathering around the table. Emerald waited for everyone to get situated and comfortable. Her countenance grew serious as she spoke.

"I'm sorry to say I have no good news to report. Our worst fears are becoming reality and the mood of the city has taken a turn for the worse." Emerald's audience listened with great interest. "Luther's men have been busy. So far the tally is three houses burned, eighteen people captured, including two boys, and six executions."

Novak interrupted. "What? Six executions? What about the trials? They couldn't have taken them to Kelterland so soon, right?" Novak knew from experience that once a prisoner was arrested, they were transported to Kelterland for trial.

Emerald explained. "Yes, Novak, that's true in most circumstances. But in the interest of preserving the status quo, Kelterland lets matters of treason to be dealt with immediately. Their philosophy is that civil unrest interrupts the flow of taxes. All of the arrests included treason in the charges somewhere."

"Will Kelterland allow Reddland to just do what he wants without even checking up on him? They have no interest in what goes on here?" Zephyr was shocked that Kelterland would relinquish that much control.

"Kelterland lets Reddland do whatever he feels it takes to preserve control. It saves them the burden of keeping an armed garrison of their soldiers here. As long as the taxes keep flowing to the king, and civil unrest is kept in check, Reddland has carte blanche to conduct operations as he sees fit." Emerald stated the hard facts of Xylorian policy.

Thadus voiced his concern. "What about the remaining twelve arrestees?"

"The two boys have been put to work in the stables. They should live if they stay out of trouble and do as they're told. The other ten are scheduled for execution after they have been 'questioned.'" Emerald didn't have to explain what the questioning would entail.

"Did we lose any soldiers?" Thadus asked the inevitable.

"Just one; he's being questioned some time today."

Thadus complexion turned ashen. Although he felt bad about the seventeen citizens who were falsely accused of being rebels, he held a special place in his heart for those who were risking their lives to end the terror. Thadus wasn't the highest-ranking member in the rebellion, but he was in the upper echelon. As a result he knew almost all of the rebels personally. "Who do they have?"

Emerald's eyes moistened and she bit her bottom lip to keep it from trembling. Her whispered answer was barely audible. "Uncle Bartus."

The answer set off an emotional charge that shook the room.

"*Impossible!*" Scorpyus and Novak thought simultaneously. "*That frail, timid man was a rebel?*" They both found it hard to picture.

Thadus fell to his knees, burying his face in his hands, and sobbing uncontrollably. This scene was getting played out a little too frequently for Novak's taste. Cad and Zephyr didn't know what to make of the scenario. They never met Bartus.

Scorpyus saw they were puzzled and explained. "He's the man that escaped with Novak and me from the ship."

"You saved my uncle's life. Apparently it was in vain." Emerald directed the conversation to Novak and Scorpyus. "He wanted me to thank you again if I saw you. I know he didn't look like much to most people, but he had lost everything. Two years ago when my cousin—his daughter—died, he collapsed. He lived under the docks a broken man, giving up on the cause. But I tell you this—we knew everything that entered or exited the port of Xylor thanks to him. He may have quit on everything else, but he kept us informed about that. He gave up his position of leadership in the rebellion, but he couldn't walk away completely. You two inspired him. Yesterday he started sounding like his old self again. Seeing the both of you take such a fervent stand for God in these wicked times rekindled his fire. We had hopes he would join us again soon."

The news was shocking. Bartus had once been a leader in the rebellion? Who would have guessed? Circumstances in his life reduced him to such a level that even he didn't consider himself to be a part of the cause anymore. Sure, he still kept in contact with his niece, keeping her informed about the shipping activities of Xylor, but he considered that nothing in light of his former involvement. Bartus considered what he did to be of little worth, and yet he did more than ninety-nine percent of the population who were dissatisfied with the tyranny.

Cad mulled over the possibilities. Maybe Novak and Scorpyus had indeed inspired Bartus to rethink his life. Maybe he was going to increase his efforts and involvement. Strangely enough, more then a few people fancied the belief that Cad and the others were the answer to the rebellion's problems.

As if on cue Thadus spoke, wiping the tears from his eyes with his fingers. "Whether or not my brother survives his current ordeal, I can't say. And if he should pass from us, I know I will surely see him again someday, as I will see Isaac again. In the meantime our work must go on. We can't rest until tyranny is removed from the land. Reddland may think he has already won since he managed to murder Isaac. Isaac not only led our church as pastor, but he led the rebellion too. Reddland underestimates our resiliency; Isaac's son Abrams has already agreed to carry on for his father in both offices."

Judging from the shock on everyone's face, Thadus realized this was news to them. "I have trusted you with everything, and you four now have the knowledge to destroy the rebellion. All cards are on the table, and we stand poised at a crossroads. The next week or two will be either the end of the rebellion, or the end of Reddland's reign of terror. I have consulted with the other ranking officials, and we are all in agreement. We have enough weapons and supplies to stage an attack. Our people have been trained as best we could. I pray their training will be enough. I only hope we are able to make our move before Reddland makes his. What we lack are good, experienced military leaders—leaders who have seen combat, who know how to plan, who have a strategy. Leaders who have experience that can only be gained by having been on the working end of a sword."

Somehow the four knew what was coming next, and the idea was unnerving. Thadus made sure he had their full attention. "We believe it is no coincidence you four should find yourselves in Xylor at this critical time. We believe you have been chosen, by God, to be here now. And based upon this belief, we ask you to lead this rebellion to the conclusion that has been ordained. I can't force you to lead us. The choice is yours. The Lord works in mysterious ways, and I believe He has chosen to debase Reddland by his own hand; for it was Reddland who hired you to come to Xylor. Reddland's evil works have returned to haunt him, and he has become his own undoing!"

The Clandestine Knights were flabbergasted.

Cad shook his head. Thadus was crazy! God chose them to lead a rebellion? Four outcasts from a down-trodden region? Surely it must be that Thadus, Abrams, and the others wanted to believe this so badly that they talked themselves into believing a fantasy? God couldn't use them to liberate his people in Xylor— well, He could but...was all this true? No, it was wishful thinking by desperate people. It had to be. But everything was happening a little too conveniently. Reddland gets an illness requiring a rare medicine, he hires a group of highly skilled adventurers to find it, and they fall into the middle of a civil war. Due to the adventurers past, the people Reddland hired have natural sympathies for the rebellion. Fate has the rebellion befriending the team he hired to find Hyacinth Blue. It was God versus Tanuba, and Reddland unknowingly brings four strong believers with combat experience into the foray. If it wasn't fate, the string of coincidences was amazing.

Zephyr could feel her heart pound. Her sense of compassion led her to lean in favor of helping Thadus, but the prospect turned her stomach in knots.

Novak was numb. He couldn't deny the possibility, but shook the feeling off. He couldn't say if his urge to help was for the rebellion's sake or just because he liked a good fight. Novak thrived on action, and this was a good cause. It also would afford him the opportunity to get to know Emerald a little better.

Scorpyus had a strange gleam in his eye. He always felt he should have been born in another time. Maybe that "time" corresponded to a situation rather then a specific set of years? Maybe for *times* like this where he could do some good, and stop another little boy from having to watch helplessly while his family was victimized.

Cad was excited at the idea of a higher calling for his talents. He knew few people had his engineering and construction skills, and that a victory in Xylor would depend largely on a wide array of aggressively defensive tricks. Still, a part of him wished he had stayed home.

A long, contemplative pause choked all sound from the gathering. One side wondered how to respond, the other side placed all hope on that response. Thadus was nervous. If the four refused to lead the revolt, the rebellion stood little chance. Their answer would likely dictate the future of the rebellion. Odds were against another group of experienced strategists appearing on the scene before Reddland made his move.

"Uh…what you ask…" Cad was speechless. "Give us a moment to talk it over amongst ourselves."

Thadus motioned to Emerald, and they both went to the other side of the room. They gave the four as much privacy as possible. "By all means, feel free to discuss it."

Scorpyus had a few questions for Thadus first. "Before we discuss it, there are a few pieces of information we have to know. How many men does the count have in all his units?"

Thadus pursed his lips. "He has somewhere in the vicinity of twenty-five hundred troops, not including non-combat staff such as maids, stable boys, and the like."

"How many people do you have in the rebellion?"

Thadus let out a deep sigh. There was no point in not letting the four know what would be in store for them. "I guess you have a right to know in light of what I'm asking. We have, not including you four, five hundred and seven people."

The four didn't let the statistics register on their faces. They turned to huddle on the opposite side of the room. They were not only being asked to lead a rebellion, but were being asked to do so while greatly outnumbered.

Zephyr spoke up first. "We would be outnumbered five to one. And out of the five hundred, I would be willing to bet only three hundred or so are prepared for a task such as this."

Cad agreed. "I think it's obvious they would need some training. Either way, with these numbers, an offensive against Reddland's compound would be blooming suicide. The only chance would be to wait for Reddland to go on the offensive. A defensive position requires fewer men, but even then a few tricks would be needed to actually win this war. The count has more than enough troops to lay siege and starve the rebels out."

"I think we're getting ahead of ourselves. What if we're not chosen by God to help them? Maybe we should help Ravenshire first if we help anybody?" Everything was moving too fast for Novak's taste.

"Ravenshire is nowhere near as organized as this place. We don't have an underground rebel movement, just pockets of resistance. There isn't anything we could do to help our own at this time," Scorpyus added.

"You don't think we should do it, Novak?" Cad tried to read his friends views on the matter.

"Hey, I'm ready to fight anytime, anywhere. Maybe this isn't our destiny? Maybe it's wishful thinking. If someone really wants to believe something, they can read into it? Maybe we should try to help our own first?"

Scorpyus answered Novak's concerns. "In a way, these people, as believers, are our own. And in a way, a lot of people in Ravenshire are not. By helping these people we further the cause of the Clandestine Knights, which, if I remember, was to combat the Reddlands of the world. That's why we started? Just like our fathers? Take a stand for what's right?"

Novak mulled it over. He didn't have to have his arm twisted. "You're right. I'm in. A peaceful, serene childhood was ripped from our grasps, and we were handed a nightmare to replace it. Unless someone has the courage to take a stand, the same fate awaits another generation of children, maybe our own."

Zephyr was excited. "Maybe we will really help Ravenshire by helping Xylor. Maybe this is our fate to be here now, and that is the reason we have been led into this mess. It is all a plan to help Ravenshire!"

Cad was puzzled. "What are you talking about Zephyr?"

"Like Scorpyus said, Ravenshire has just pockets of resistance. Thus there is little to be done until that situation changes. On the other hand, Xylor is ready to move ahead—well, actually they are being forced to move ahead; anyway, they are more or less ready to go once they find leaders." Zephyr made sure Cad was following her line of reasoning. "I think God has answered the prayers of His people, both in Ravenshire, and in Xylor. Through circumstance He has brought veteran leaders from Ravenshire together with veteran organizers from Xylor. Together we can win what would have been impossible separated. It is a test of our character. God has arranged an alliance between two sets of his people that will benefit all. But He will help on the condition we help one another…a love thy neighbor test…a 'what you have done for the least of my people, you have done for me' scenario." Zephyr was excited at the possibility. To restore Ravenshire to the way it was, to be rid of the barbarism, and bring back a moral society had been a dream of the Clandestine Knights since their inception. It had been their fathers' dream also.

The others took some time to digest Zephyr's interpretation. People helping people is what true peace is all about. Everyone voluntarily restrained himself or herself so the government didn't have to step in and restrain you. The problem with the current society was nobody wanted to be told what to do. They didn't want to restrain themselves, and they didn't want to answer to anybody. No one was going to hold them accountable, and that's why many rejected God and raised up a false image like Tanuba. Tanuba preached a relaxed moral standard where it was all right to fulfill your lust and greed. Everyone was out for what they could get with little thought for others. People used people, children had no respect for their parents, brother cheated brother, and nothing was sacred. Lies replaced truth in conversation, and people were jaded, lacking natural affection for each other. If someone was being nice, it was because they wanted something.

Amidst the chaos, a man like Luther Reddland rose to power. At first nobody said anything because Reddland told them what they wanted to hear. He legalized a few of the people's favorite vices. He followed that up with the resurrection of Tanuba worship and its inherent tolerance for the people's lustful pursuits, and at the same time outlawed Christianity on the grounds it was "intolerant" of the citizens' desires. Evil was now called good, and good was now called evil. The people believed it because they wanted to in order to live out their every desire. Then Reddland started purging his opposition. A lot of innocent people were killed in the process. People still said nothing. The economy was growing, and besides, if Reddland was judged harshly for his actions, then they themselves might be judged for theirs.

People started tolerating sin, and it soon became acceptable, and then the norm. Citizens who spoke out against it were labeled intolerant radicals. Those who practiced vice didn't want to be told they were in the wrong. People who did not want to be held accountable to God wanted to make up their own moral code. Tanuba offered the solution. Soon the people were held accountable to no one except Reddland. Reddland tolerated the people doing their own thing as long as taxes were paid on time and there was no insurrection. Then he became intolerant. And it grew worse year-by-year until no one dared even speak a harsh word against the establishment. Many lived in fear, and Reddland's hired thugs ran the country.

Zephyr, Cad, Novak, and Scorpyus were fed up. They wanted right to be right and wrong to be wrong. With God everything was clear. He had a standard that, if followed, made life easy. It's when everyone decides for themselves what is moral and immoral that chaos rears its ugly head. There are as many standards as there are people. Soon the chaos builds to the point of destruction. The open tolerance of wickedness leads a society toward decay and makes the times ripe for the Luther Reddlands of the world.

The Clandestine Knights now had a chance to end the chaos, to end the lost wondering of a society looking for stability in all the wrong places, to end the loss of souls to the crafty deception of idolatry. They were presented an opportunity to try to stop Reddland from devouring the people and bring back sanity. A peaceful, consistent, sanity where good was good, evil was evil, and God wasn't a fish.

Cad looked to his comrades and could tell all were in unison. Four people with a mission determined to succeed: they would be up against a larger force, but motivated and optimistic.

Novak raised a slow grin, and held his hand out palm down. "Let's pound them into the dirt!"

Cad placed his hand on the back of Novak's, "To victory!"

Scorpyus added his hand to the stack. "Let the Reddlands of the world suffer the fate they have forced on so many of us."

Zephyr rounded out the stack of hands. "God help us!"

With that the four turned to face Thadus.

"We'll do it." Cad watched Thadus release a huge breath. "But it will take a lot of work. Let's get started on the battle plans. There's no better time than the present."

Thadus was elated. "Thank you, thank you so much. At last, a light at the end of the tunnel, a hope for the future. God willing, Luther's reign of terror will come to an end." A misty-eyed Thadus thanked the four over and over. "I can assure you, you will have the full cooperation of my people. All of our weapons and supplies will be at your disposal."

Emerald was equally delighted. Not only had the four agreed to help, but this also meant she would get an opportunity to get to know Novak a little better, maybe a lot better. "Yes, how can we possibly thank you enough? May God bless you for what you are about to do. Is there anything we can do to repay you?"

"I'm glad you asked. There just might very well be something you can do." Cad directed his statement to Thadus. "If we succeed here—and that's a long blooming way off—we could use your help to organize the resistance in Ravenshire. There are several small groups like us who are good at the military side of things, but to have the whole territory organized to work as one cohesive unit is another story. We have a lot of factions that can't or won't work together. Many more are too afraid to get involved while the resistance is small and disorganized. You may have a lack of military leadership, but you've been able to maintain an elaborate system of supply acquisition and storage, organize a wide-spread system of intelligence gathering and processing, not to mention maintain hideaways and safe houses. All this you've done for ten years through incredible odds without fail. We could use that knowledge in Ravenshire."

Thadus was genuinely embarrassed by the compliment given him. He never thought of it like that before, but Cad was right. Thadus had been so busy noticing the rebellions lack of military prowess and suppressed initiative that he overlooked what he did have. Respected combat leaders who could inspire troops to perform to their fullest capabilities were only half the picture. Behind every squad in the field there had to be someone to supply food, weapons, and intelligence. The Clandestine Knights did it all in their small group, but widespread organization and cooperation was needed to change a whole region. Thadus smiled and held out his hand. "Absolutely. How could I say no?"

Cad shook Thadus's hand. "Great. Now let's get started."

All were content in the new partnership that had been forged in the secret room. It was a partnership that would either change the course of history for Xylor, or become a footnote in a book somewhere.

Scorpyus and Zephyr cleared off the table, and retrieved a quill, ink, and paper. Novak pulled over a bunk to be used as a bench, while Emerald lit a few more candles so there would be plenty of light. The group crowded around Cad who designated himself as scribe.

Scorpyus spoke. "Alright, first of all we need a place to set up a strong defense, one we can defend against large numbers of opponents. We're outnumbered five to one, so an attack on Reddland's compound is out of the question." Scorpyus paused while the others voiced their agreement. "I think we all knew that. The defense has to be more than *just* defense. If all we do is hole up somewhere, Reddland could wait and starve us out. We need a defense with a few offensive capabilities. We have to win by brains, not superior numbers."

Thadus was surprised. "I must be missing something. You came up with a choice for defense rather quickly, it almost sounds too easy."

"Ya, it's as easy as picking specks of dirt out of pepper." Novak jested with a hint of sarcasm.

"The defensive position will be the easy part, mate. It's the offensive ideas that will be tricky. But first we need a base to work from. Then if our attacks don't work, we'll have a place to fall back to; we will also need a plan that will allow us to break out of a siege." Cad explained the matter more thoroughly.

"What kind of attack could five hundred people mount on twenty-five hundred?" Emerald was deeply concerned.

Thadus stroked his beard in concentration. "I see what you mean. So what do we do?"

"First we need a place to stage our defensive lines. Any suggestions?" Scorpyus asked no one in particular.

"Yeah, I have one." Novak tapped Zephyr on the arm. "Remember the oratory? It had an outer wall good for cover, and we could pull back to the main building if we were overrun. It's big, it's made of stone, and it's sort of like a little castle."

"Oui, but it would take some preparation. Fix the gate, reinforce the doors…it would be perfect. It is a sturdy structure, the next best thing to a castle we will find around here." Zephyr agreed.

Thadus evaluated the suggestion thoughtfully. "I think the oratory would hold up well against an attack. In fact it's been the central point of a great battle once before. God willing, any further battle there won't turn out as tragically as the last. The overthrow of the oratory was a massacre from which we have never fully recovered."

"I think it's a marvelous idea," Emerald chimed in. "It's a solid building with two steeples. There is even a walkway along the apex of the roof, ideal for lookouts or archers. The only problem is, since the count has been in power, it's against the law to be on the premises."

"Now you tell us." Zephyr recalled that she and Novak had already been to the oratory. "But that does explain why it looked so dilapidated and dusty. Still, it would have been nice to know we could have been arrested for going there. We could have prepared a little. Instead we just rode up to the place as if we belonged there."

"I didn't think it was terribly important. The Royal Guard rarely sends patrols by. In fact it's practically avoided, probably due to a sense of guilt. But there is a big difference between a meeting of three people, and a contingent fortifying and stocking it with supplies. If it starts looking like its being lived in, or there is abnormal activity in the area, then we're in trouble." Thadus cautioned.

"Do the work at night. Start in the oratory out of sight, and then go to the courtyard and outer wall. Start with quiet work like cleaning. The oratory is far enough from town that noise shouldn't be a problem. It's still a good idea to post lookouts." Novak was right. The oratory was three-quarters of a mile from the outskirts of town. Because of the certain arrest and punishment of those caught in the area; people avoided it like the plague.

"It sounds good to me." Scorpyus agreed with the plan. "Since it looks like I'm going to be going in disguise to see what I can dig up on this Iris and Wallace, I guess Cad will have to be the one to get the oratory ready."

"Oui, plan some surprise tactics just like you did at the Gyptus Marsh incident." Zephyr admired Cad's earlier work. "We are going to need it even more this time."

Cad rolled his eyes and put on an exaggerated air of pompousness. "Yes, I do believe a genius such as I shall be able to come up with something to assist us in our moment of dire need."

A thespian he wasn't, but Cad was an engineer, one of the few in Ravenshire. Cad, like his father and grandfather before him, was part of a long line of builders. They specialized in elegant buildings.

"I'll assist you, Cad, and organize the labor and the delivery of supplies," Thadus offered.

"Sounds good," Cad accepted the help. "Then Novak will prepare the troops for battle."

Novak responded, "I'll organize the troops into squads, delegate responsibilities, and assign them to specialty units. After a few training exercises to see what they can do, I will decide on a ranking structure. I'll need a secluded place to equip the men and conduct the training."

"Yes, of course." Thadus was pleased to see everyone jump right in to get the job done. "The men have been training at Scarborough Field up till now. I think it will prove to be more than adequate. The men have been hiding their weapons in caverns in the area. It's secluded and difficult to find."

Novak was relieved to hear the rebel soldiers had at least some training. It would make his job a little easier. "Good. How do I get there?"

Emerald interrupted. "I'll take Novak there, Father. I mean, I know how to get there, and besides he could use help getting things ready for the troops. And I am a good cook. The troops will need to eat." Emerald blushed slightly at the coy grin on Zephyr's face.

"I see no problem with that if it's alright with Novak. It will be better, safer anyway, to be out of town when the oratory is being refurbished, just in case. And besides, you do know all of the troops and could introduce Novak to everyone." Thadus looked to Novak to see if he was willing to have the company. Thadus wasn't going to force the issue.

"Fine. Can you ride a horse?" Novak could use the help, and he would be a stranger to the others. If he were going to prepare the troops there would have to be mutual trust among all parties. Emerald would be a valuable asset in building some trust.

Thadus smiled. "Good. I'll get word to the men and have them meet you at Scarborough Field. When do you want them there?"

"How far is this place?" Novak inquired.

"About ten miles, north of Granite at the base of the mountains. The place sees few visitors."

"Emerald and I will leave at first light. Give us a few hours to get ready. How about noon tomorrow?"

"It sounds fine. I'll get word to the men." Thadus looked to Zephyr and realized she had been left out, with no task assigned. "Oh, what did you want to be doing during all of this?"

Zephyr already decided what she would be doing. "I get to track down Hyacinth Blue."

"Don't worry, Zephyr; at least you will have the recipe. It's more than Cad..." Scorpyus was cut short by Thadus.

"Did you find the recipe?" Thadus was visibly excited.

"Oh yeah, we forgot to mention it. Scorpyus and I managed to find the blooming recipe." Cad pulled a small slip of paper from a leather pouch and handed it to Thadus. "Isaac was right. He found the recipe and didn't have time to retrieve it. We searched that laboratory from one end to the other and turned up nothing. In fact, we were about to give up when all of a sudden, there it was right before our eyes in this little silver box with a foreign inscription. Once we remembered they were Isaac's dying words, it all made sense. We have the recipe. We just don't understand part of it. And we still don't have a translation for those words."

Thadus read out loud:

> Mix: ¼ cup dried burdock root
> ¼ cup dried lemon balm leaves
> ½ teaspoon mistletoe resin
> 1 cup myrrh oil
> 7 sapphire tears

Boil ingredients in two gallons of water for one hour, or until water is boiled off leaving a blue syrupy liquid. Let cool overnight; makes 8 doses of Hyacinth Blue.

After briefly contemplating the ingredients, Thadus read and reread the recipe. He looked up with a furrowed brow. "This doesn't make any sense? Mistletoe, if I'm not mistaken, is highly poisonous. It'll kill you. And what are sapphire tears? Maybe this is a poison rather than a medicine?" For Thadus the long-awaited mystery was a bit of a let down.

"We don't know what the sapphire tears are either mate. We were hoping you would." Cad was disappointed. "As for the other ingredients, perhaps Scorpyus can explain."

Scorpyus affirmed what Thadus previously stated. "It's true. Mistletoe is highly poisonous. But in very small doses, resin from mistletoe leaves has been known to stimulate your heart, brain, and other organs. Great care is needed in the preparation of the resin. It must be processed properly, and never, never use the berries. They will definitely kill you."

Thadus was impressed with Scorpyus's knowledge on the subject. "I had no idea. How do you know so much about mistletoe?"

"My grandmother worked with herbs. She knew plants and remedies better then most apothecaries. I learned a lot from her. She was a wise woman." Scorpyus words grew quieter and trailed off.

"Do you know what the rest of the ingredients are for?" Emerald was excited to learn more about this legendary medicine.

"Yeah, sure I do. The dried burdock root, or Gypsy's rhubarb as my grandmother used to call it, acts as a blood purifier. We used it a lot for spider and snakebites, or in poisoning cases. It didn't always work, though." Scorpyus reviewed the recipe. "Let's see, dried leaves from lemon balm, that's a mild pain killer. My grandma put it in tea for sore throats. And as for myrrh oil, I'm sure most of you have heard of myrrh before…."

"It's one of the things the wise men brought Jesus as a gift," Novak clarified.

"Right; most of the time it's used as incense. It also makes a very good mosquito repellant. However, if you soak bandages in myrrh oil and place them on a wound, it will help them heal better. You can drink it but it doesn't taste all that good by itself. There are rumors of it curing ailments of all types. Unfortunately it only grows in desert areas, so I doubt there'll be any in Xylor. I did bring some and even used it on my wound." Scorpyus pointed to his side. "And as for sapphire tears…I've never heard of them before."

"Wow, I'm impressed. You learn something new everyday." Thadus had to re-evaluate his impression of Scorpyus. His guests were a perfect team. Each complemented the other and was knowledgeable in their respective areas. Together they made a very formidable force.

Emerald was equally impressed. "You sound like a doctor!"

"It sounds like this medicine is for a nasty disease; that much is sure, no?" Zephyr pieced it all together. "But a disease that affects your organs, blood, and causes pain: that sounds like the symptoms for a lot of diseases. The medicine sounds like it will work on everything."

"Aside from the sapphire tears, will we be able to find the stuff in Xylor?" Novak, knowing the medicine was far from a sure thing, wasn't as excited as the others.

"Mistletoe grows all over the place. It's a parasite on other trees, particularly oaks. As for the other stuff, maybe Thadus can answer that?" Scorpyus turned the discussion over to his host.

"I'm sure the lemon balm and burdock are grown locally. We provide a lot of the agriculture products for Kelterland, especially in the realms of herbs and spices. If we have myrrh it would have to be imported. I can't say for certain if it could be found." Thadus stroked his beard deep in thought. "You know, there was this old hermit woman who lived in the woods in a ramshackle cabin, rarely made it to town, but when she did she always stopped by the alchemist's shop. She had a reputation as a specialist in ancient remedies, much like Scorpyus's grandmother. People dismissed her as an old loon, full of old wives' tales. She was even accused of being a witch once, though I know she wasn't. The accusation filled the old woman with indignation. She has to be around eighty by now. I wonder…if anyone knows what sapphire tears are…I know it's a long shot that she's even still alive." Thadus sketched out a rough map. "She lives in the vicinity where the north trail ends. It's a rarely used trail since the woods are thick and the northern bluffs are rocky and inaccessible by boat, an ideal spot for a hermit."

Zephyr studied the map. "Oui, I will go by the alchemist first and see if they have the other ingredients. I suppose it will not hurt to ask this old woman about the sapphire tears since we have no other clues. How far is it to her place, and is she friendly?"

"It's about eight miles from where the north trail branches off the road to Xylor. And she's as friendly as a quiet, soft-spoken old hermit can be. Friendly when spoken to but a little withdrawn. I never really talked to her much so I can't say for sure." Thadus knew little about her, and what he did know was from brief observations. I realize it's a stab in the dark."

"It sounds like we have a full day planned for us all tomorrow. Good luck to everyone, and remember to bloody well be careful." Cad held up his cup. "Here's to success!"

Everyone joined Cad in a toast. Thadus led the group in a moving prayer for success and safety of all concerned, asking God to bless the people, the mission, and guide the tasks at hand. All gathered knew in all likelihood a battle was soon to take place. Both sides would suffer loss of life. A solemn mood fell over the room as the reality of war seeped into everyone's mind. It was a reality all too familiar, and it caused a feeling you couldn't get used to. The need to be alone for a while surfaced on all faces. With that, Thadus and Emerald excused themselves with plans to meet back in the stables at dawn. Novak saw the guests out.

Scorpyus waited till his host had been gone for a few minutes then addressed his comrades. "No matter what happens to one or more of us, the others have to carry on the good fight. Somebody has to say enough is enough and blaze the path back to God."

"Clandestine Knights forever!" Novak pounded a fist down on the table.

IX

IRIS WAS STARTLED by a noisy splash in the horse trough as she came out of the spare room she rented from the local cobbler. She turned to see a haggard man throwing water on his face. It had become a common sight for her, and she tried to ignore it.

Iris had been staying in this storage-area-turned-bedroom for only a few months, ever since the cobbler needed a little extra money to pay back a gambling debt. She still wasn't used to living in town and preferred someplace quieter.

Iris was a blue-eyed brunette with an abrasive personality and frequent scowl that detracted from her simple beauty. If she was ever happy, no one would ever have known it. In her rust-colored riding clothes and velveteen cloak, she was impeccably dressed despite her lack of funds.

Iris heard a gurgling sound and turned to see the man draped over the trough, his head under the water, vainly trying to regain some semblance of consciousness. He stank so heavily of rum Iris wondered if he bathed in the stuff. Having a drunk camped outside her door was the price Iris paid for having a room facing the main street near all the taverns, but rent was cheap. She eyed the man carefully as she locked her door. It was dawn, and this was an all-too-familiar morning greeting. Up and down the streets of Xylor the nightlife had recently wound down, littering the troughs, alleys, and docks with its aftermath.

Iris wondered what anyone saw in the rotgut served locally. And here was a man who couldn't be more than thirty, yet he looked terribly aged with his greasy hair, scraggly beard, and ratty clothes. At the rate he was going he'd never see forty. Maybe in different circumstances this man's life would have turned out different. But here he was, one bad decision and several bottles later, drinking a horse's backwash, seasick on dry land. Iris watched him as he lifted his teetering head and held it moaning, no doubt begging for the world to stop spinning. He looked up and tried to focus on the shadowy figure before him.

The drunk was about to speak, when Iris disappeared down the street. She didn't wait around to see if he was going to ask for a handout. Besides, she had a very busy day ahead of her.

Once Iris was out of sight, Scorpyus pulled himself up from the horse trough and wiped his mouth with the back of a grimy sleeve.

"The things I have to do," Scorpyus muttered and shook his head. He brushed his hair off his forehead and took a quick look around. The streets were practically deserted so he studied the lock on the door to Iris's room and selected a pick from the pouch he kept in his boot. Scorpyus took another quick look around just to be sure no one was coming before setting to work on the door. Before he could bend down to the lock, two people on horseback rounded a corner and were headed his way. He decided to wait until they were past. It looked like a couple on their way to have a quiet picnic.

As the couple rode by Scorpyus, the man did a double take. Novak recognized the haggard man to be his friend. Scorpyus was equally surprised to see Novak, but neither one made any overt gestures that would betray their missions. A slight smirk slid across Novak's face, and Scorpyus raised an eyebrow in response.

"Disgusting," Emerald said, repulsed. "That's the third one we've seen and we're not even out of town yet."

Novak couldn't help but laugh. "Well that last guy wasn't a drunk, but I know what you mean."

"What do you mean he wasn't a drunk? You could smell him a mile away!"

Novak laughed harder. "Don't tell me you didn't recognize Scorpyus?"

"That was Scorpyus!"

Emerald jerked around in the saddle and look back at him. He gave her a small wave.

Emerald was impressed. "I would have never guessed. How could you tell?"

"It's all in the eyes. Scorpyus has that dark-eyed stare, and they're a little too clear to be a drunk's. Besides, he's used that disguise before." Novak stretched his back shifting his position on the hard saddle.

Scorpyus easily manipulated the lock to Iris's door and gained an unnoticed entry. Scorpyus fully expected to find something that would betray Iris's facade as a loyal rebel. How could a blatantly open Tanuba worshiper feel compassion for the rebel cause?

Emerald sat amazed as her horse plodded along. She tried to picture Scorpyus inside the haggard man she saw, but couldn't. She was equally amazed to find he had disappeared when she turned around again. "Where'd he go?"

"My guess is to try to find out information that will be beneficial to us." Novak stated matter-of-factly.

"Find out information where?" Emerald saw plenty of mystique and excitement in the events. Until now she had been a contact for a few field agents and reported their information to her father. Now things were really getting exciting.

Novak was puzzled by Emerald's question. "Uh, he probably went in one of those doors back there...don't you think?"

"You mean break in! What if someone saw him?" Emerald's eyes grew wide.

Novak looked around quickly to see if anyone was near. "Shhh, keep it down."

"He really broke into somebody's house?" Emerald asked in a stage whisper, clearly flabbergasted.

"Probably." Novak could see Emerald was having a problem with this. "Don't worry. He's there for information only. I can assure you Scorpyus won't take so much as a moldy crust of bread. He'll leave everything as he found it and take nothing. It's for the good of the cause. Sometimes you have to bend the rules when lives are at stake."

Emerald's countenance softened a little. "I agree—but to break in…if the Royal guard saw him.…"

"I understand. Not everyone can condone it. But what if he found information that Reddland's men discovered your father's involvement in the rebellion? That information could save his life. We're battling an evil that goes deeper than we both can possibly fathom. We all have important jobs, Scorpyus included. He *must* find out. If there are spies working to sabotage the rebellion, we *have* to know. Who knows, maybe if Scorpyus had been on the job Isaac would be alive today." Novak put it bluntly, immediately regretting the comment about Isaac. Lord knows the rebellion did all they could to save his life, but this was life-and-death also. Iris and Wallace's motives had to be known. And Novak didn't relish the thought of leading the rebels into an ambush.

Emerald grew quiet. How could she argue? Her mother, Isaac, and now possibly even her Uncle Bartus, had met their ends at the hands of Reddland's men. Her father often said peace was elusive, sometimes only to be found hidden beyond war. And this was a war: not only a war against life and property, but also a war for souls. Luther Reddland, despite his quest for power and riches, was nothing more then a pawn in an evil scheme that stretched back to the beginning of time. Reddland thought he was helping himself to hearty portions of the world, when in reality, unbeknownst to him, he served another master. Emerald had a master as well; one who existed back before the beginning of time, the Eternal Master. And one thing Emerald did know was that if Reddland's regime, with its Tanuba worship, was overthrown, souls would be saved. Sure Reddland had a following, as did the rebellion. But a lot of people followed Reddland out of fear. There was a lost multitude of people who trembled in their tiny homes, meandering, searching for deliverance from their sorrows, not knowing where to look. If Scorpyus could risk his life to help end this dark episode in Xylorian history, she could support it.

"Yes, you're right. It's just shocking at first. Maybe Issac *would* be alive if our agents were more aggressive in their pursuit of information."

Novak was relieved that his point was received, albeit reluctantly. "I'm sure they are aggressive to the best of their abilities. After all, spies will be spies. By the way, I apologize if that remark about Isaac was…"

"Oh, no, it's all right." A demure look came to Emerald's eyes and she turned away shyly. "Let's change the subject. Um, tell me a little about yourself."

Novak shot her a glance. Emerald was not only a beautiful, enthusiastic, and kindhearted woman, she was bold. "What's to tell?"

"Well, what's your homeland like?

"I live by a serene, clear, cobalt blue lake, nestled in the woods in the heart of Ravenshire. Many beachfront villages circle the lake. The lake has two small islands, and we live on one. Politically, it's a lot like Xylor, except about five times worse. Kelterland wasn't as nice to us when they took over. We gave them a lot of resistance. It cost them in blood to take Ravenshire, and it costs them plenty to hold it."

"I'm sorry to hear that. You always think the grass is greener someplace else. It's sad to realize the whole region has suffered so much." Emerald gave Novak a wistful look. "What about your family? Are they still—" Emerald was so afraid she hit on a bad subject she cut herself off mid-sentence.

Novak could see Emerald had a genuine interest, and was flattered. She was much like Zephyr but without the edge of a fighter. Where Zephyr was wise to the world, Emerald still had a naïveté about her. That held some attraction for Novak, but he felt Emerald's infatuation would wane once the harsh realities of his life in the Clandestine Knights became apparent. Novak was away from home as much as he was there. And he never knew which mission would be his last. It was a recipe for life few women would find appealing in the long run, though many found glamorous for a fleeting moment or two. "I have four older sisters, three still living, and a mother who loves to cook. My father was a Ravenshire knight. He was killed in an ambush a long time ago."

Emerald nodded respectfully. "You and your three friends seem very close."

Novak nodded. "Ya, they're like brothers and sister to me. In fact, we're closer than family as only people who have faced death together can be."

A beaming smile set Emerald's face aglow. Novak described Zephyr as a sister! Emerald was relieved to hear that; so much so a small chuckle erupted from her lips."

"What? What's so funny?" Novak grinned inquisitively not knowing if he missed something.

"Oh nothing; someday, maybe I'll tell you. A lady is allowed a few secrets, right." Emerald's joyous mood radiated; she smiled broadly as she gently bounced in the saddle.

Novak and Emerald rode on, pausing several times to admire the lush beauty of the isle. The two were so engrossed in pleasant conversation that for a brief few hours they were able to forget the upcoming battle, the war and the death and destruction that had been so much a part of their lives. It was a needed break, one that had been a rarity as of late.

Novak wondered: could this be the start of something more. Time would tell. In the meantime he enjoyed the awakening of a glimmer of promise, a reason for the day. The unknown may have stretched out ahead, but right now it didn't matter.

The ride to Scarborough Field took the pair through a rich and fertile valley and offered a panoramic view of Xylor's mountain range. Novak learned of Xylor's many crops, and of its small sheep and cattle industry. The road cut through the middle of it all. The trail wove up and into the mountains. After a short climb, Emerald directed Novak off the trail. Towering pines laced the steep horizon as their horses plodded up the grade. They crested a ridge, and after a steep descent they suddenly came to a clearing.

"Well here we are!" Emerald brushed the pine needles from her hooded burgundy cloak. The cloak complemented the burgundy waistcoat she wore over a tan cotton dress.

Novak removed his helmet and wiped the sweat from his forehead with his sleeve. A cool breeze wafted through his hair. Before him in the meadow was a camp of several hundred people. They seemed to be enjoying a leisurely morning. Many huddled around campfires drinking from steaming cups.

"We may as well get started with the introductions. By the way, I wanted you to know I enjoyed the ride...being with you. We ought to do it again sometime."

A huge smile lighted Emerald's face. Novak didn't wait for a reply and spurred his horse on. Emerald followed his lead, and they rode into the camp. Novak was relieved to see the gathered men were at least aware of his presence. He didn't know what he would have done had he caught them off guard. At least their sentries were alert.

A handful of men gathered around to greet Novak and Emerald. They were armed with a wide variety of weapons and armor. This ragtag group didn't have the uniformed look of a professional military unit, but all were ready and eager.

Emerald introduced Novak to a tall man in his early forties. His hair, graying at the temples, gave him a distinguished look.

"Novak, this is Cyrus. He's leader of the troops. He was in the Royal Guard at one time.

Cyrus saw the troubled look on Novak's face. "Don't worry. I assure you those days are long behind me. Let's say I saw the error of my ways."

"Pleased to meet you," Novak dismounted and held a hand out to Cyrus. Cyrus readily obliged with a handshake. "So you have combat experience; good, we need it." Novak thought the man seemed genuine, but would remain apprehensive until Cyrus proved himself.

Cyrus smiled. "Indeed I do. And I hear you and your friends are seasoned soldiers as well. I look forward to working with you."

"Thank you. Shall we start?" Novak replied.

Cyrus told the people to gather around.

Novak waited until everyone was in place and then got down to business. "It's not often I see this many people assembled to take a stand for what they believe. I'll be straightforward with you; this is not going to be an easy task. Odds are we will see fighting, heavy fighting. We will face a well-trained force that will have us outnumbered. If the situation comes to war, we will assuredly take casualties. If you don't feel up to the task, or have reservations about risking your life for this cause, then now's the time to leave. Not everyone can handle it. There is no shame in leaving; in fact it is safer for all concerned if soldiers who can't or won't fight don't get in the way of those who will. Now is the time for the faint of heart to excuse themselves."

Novak waited a while and surveyed the crowd to see if anyone would leave. When no one did he continued. "Good! It's good to see all of you in this together. I know most of you have been waiting a long time for this opportunity. The wait is over. I would like to say one thing. The fact we will be outnumbered is irrelevant. The battle is in God's hands, not Reddland's or ours. I plan on being victorious. And in my opinion, this is as good a time as any to overthrow this pagan system of chaos that's sucking the life out of you people.

Emerald was excited and beamed with pride. She was proud of her friend's willingness to take a stand for what was right, and proud of Novak for his willingness to help a people who were strangers. Emerald realized her four new friends were truly a rare breed. When extraordinary people like that come along, the average person can't help but be inspired. Why Novak and his friends were good leaders had less to do with their leadership ability than it did with their fearlessness in the face of danger. It inspired people to take a stand. They led by example and their standards were high. If they, being strangers to Xylor, could have enough compassion to help the suffering masses, how could any local who claimed to be a good person turn their back?

Novak knew the people were anxious. "Let me explain what I'm going to do, with the aid of Cyrus of course. Today you'll go through some training exercises to see what your strengths and weaknesses are. This will help determine which of four categories each of you will be placed in. Some of you will be placed in squads of archers. A few will go into a cavalry unit. Most will be placed in infantry squads. Those I feel uncomfortable about placing in combat will be used as messengers or other support functions. If you are placed in a supporting function, don't get discouraged. These positions are vital and someone would have to do it even if all of you were seasoned warriors. We need runners to carry messages, some to deliver supplies, others to evacuate wounded, and so on. These people will all perform countless necessary functions. In addition, if we're lucky, I think we might be able to muster up two or three artillery teams to operate catapults."

Novak noticed a group of two dozen women in the assembly. "And, ladies, you're all welcome to try out for a position alongside the men. We need all the help we can get. But I must warn you, positions are given out on merit only. I'm not going to let you, or anyone for that matter, be in the infantry if they have no chance of survival. However, it can be done. I have a friend who can hold her own with a sword. And lastly after I've had a chance to watch you for a while, I'll organize everyone into a ranking structure from squad commander on down. This will be based on demonstrated leadership ability. Starting tomorrow you'll train in your respective units. Any questions?"

No one had any questions although the task seemed enormous, but all were ready to start. Novak seemed to know what he was talking about, and besides if Thadus and Abrams endorsed this move, it was fine with them. The rebel leadership had never led them astray thus far.

Cyrus added a few words. "You heard Novak. We only have a week or so before we report for duty at the oratory, so let's stay motivated. This was Isaac's dream. He died for his dream. We're not going to let him down! Let's work with Novak and his friends and win this battle once and for all!"

The people let out a cheer; they rushed Novak, shook his hand, and slapped him on the back. Some even hugged him. Others had tears in their eyes. Novak was taken aback by the amount of trust they were placing on him and the other knights. The burden of that knowledge was tremendous. The people would follow Thadus and Abrams to the end, and for whatever reason, Thadus and Abrams agreed to place all hope with the Clandestine Knights. Novak prayed these people weren't making a mistake. *Lord, please don't let us lead these people to their death. Please give us a victory. And give us wisdom to accomplish the seemingly impossible,* he said to himself.

Novak was shaken up by all this, but did his best to not let it show. "And, uh, one more thing, does anyone have a medical background? We will need a doctor and a few assistants to tend to the wounded."

A bald man in his sixties pushed his way forward through the crowd. "I'm a veterinarian. I know my experience lies with the treatment of animals, but I can clean and stitch wounds in humans."

No one else came forward. "Welcome aboard, Doc. The job is yours!" Novak got a laugh from the crowd. "Instead of training with the others, I'd like you to gather whatever supplies you think you'll need to make a hospital."

Someone brought a horse forward so Doc could get started on his assigned task. Novak watched the aging veterinarian take to the saddle with a grunt. In his white shirt with ruffled collar and cuffs, and black overcoat, he looked the part.

"Set up a hospital at the oratory. Talk to a man named Cad. He'll set you up in a room somewhere."

The people cleared a path so Doc could ride his horse out of the camp. After he left, all attention was back on Novak.

Cyrus turned to Novak. "Well, where do we start?"

Novak thought a moment then released a heavy sigh. "You take half, and I'll take half. Let's find out who can hit a target with an arrow. Then we can spar against them to see who has some fighting ability. The main thing will be to teach them how to fight as a team." Novak looked the troops over. "How do they stand with their training right now?"

Cyrus furrowed his brow. "Some are good. Some are not. I've only been able to train them in groups of three or four at best. They've never been trained to fight as part of an army. At least I can say they all have been exposed to one-on-one sparring. My main problem has been with their morale. Every time someone was killed in one of Reddland's sweeps, or the rebellion suffered a setback, morale fell. On the bright side, this is the highest their morale has been since I can remember. The troops have been looking forward to this day. I think they're relieved to be getting this over with one way or the other. They can't wait to reclaim their lives." Cyrus looked proudly on the troops. "They're good people. They will do what is asked of them. All I ask is that you and your friends do the best you can. Don't let my people die in vain. If you don't think we stand a chance—" he left it hanging.

Novak was solemn. "We'll do what we can. I don't want to lead anyone to his or her death. Battles are fought and won with a winning spirit as much as they are with skill. If we can shake the Royal Guard's confidence early, that will do a lot to boost ours. It will give us the edge we need. I know we'll be outnumbered, but we'll be holding a defensive position. That will level the playing field a bit. As you are well aware, for every man defending, three are needed to mount a successful attack in most situations. Since Reddland has the numbers, we will need to have a few offensive tricks to shake the Royal Guard. If I know my friend Cad, we will have the needed ploys to rattle the Guard's confidence. They are expecting us to be easily defeated. If we hit them good a few times, it'll give us an advantage." Novak patted Cyrus on the back. "If I didn't think we had a chance I would have told Thadus so. Either way, I think your leaders weren't going to take no for an answer. All I can say is; have faith. And let's get to work."

Cyrus smiled and started separating the troops into two groups. Emerald placed a hand on Novak's forearm as he walked away. "I'm going to prepare some food. The people have brought plenty of supplies, but I could use a little help."

Novak's eyes flashed with an idea. "That sounds good, Emerald. Um…I would appreciate it if you persuaded those three elderly women to assist you." Novak pointed to three women in their mid-sixties who looked a bit out of place holding swords. "It would save me the trouble of…"

Emerald knew where Novak was going so she broke in: "Okay, but you owe me one."

"Whatever you say Emerald. If you need anything else, just let me know." Novak watched her go to the camp, and then started the process of training.

Novak gathered the troops he was to start training around in a semi-circle. "I notice that a few of you men wear your hair long." Novak was not one to mince words. "For you ladies, pull your hair back into a pony tail and find a hat to wear. And for you men, the first lesson we have today will answer the question of why I recommend you get a haircut. You are all soldiers now, not schoolboys, and I want you to look the part."

Novak noticed one of the longhaired troops smirk. Novak singled him out. "You, step forward."

Novak and the longhaired man assumed sparring positions. Novak told him, "Come at me with all you've got."

The man swung at Novak with a series of skilled blows; Novak deflected each to the side. The longhaired man regrouped and lunged again. In a single motion, Novak knocked the man's sword to the side, reached out, and grabbed a handful of hair. He pulled the man off balance and around. Before he knew what to do, Novak had his throat exposed and his blade against his neck. The longhaired man could only grimace as Novak pulled hard on his hair in order to keep his neck exposed. Novak released him with a push and addressed the troops. "Need I say more about haircuts? Don't give the enemy any unnecessary advantage."

The mood of the troops turned serious. The longhaired man clearly received the message and nodded his submission to Novak's directive. Most of the troops already knew that being soldiers was a serious business and came prepared. A few came with other ideas. Novak realized his job for the most part would be to deal with the few who were not prepared for a little discipline. He had to turn this group of individuals into a disciplined team. All their lives depended on it.

<hr />

"How can that be?" Luther Reddland heaved his helmet across the room in a fit of rage. It crashed into a vase on a nearby table and sent shards of ceramic pottery everywhere. Marcus and Lexton gave each other tense looks, each bewildered by Luther's reaction. Luther never lost his temper like this to the point of throwing objects. Being the bearers of bad news had its drawbacks.

"I want results!" Luther paced nervously, wringing his hands. The veins throbbed in his temple. Marcus wondered if Luther's disease was starting to affect his demeanor.

"The rebels are up to something, unless one of you can explain why yet another supply wagon was attacked last night, and why two hundred to four hundred people seem to have disappeared. A lot of people failed to show up for their jobs this morning!"

Luther stopped pacing and faced his commanding officers. "The rebels are obviously planning an attack, or some offensive. And they must realize we would notice so many people suddenly missing and would subsequently search for them. This leads me to believe they are going to make their move soon; sooner than it will take us to track them down. Now, Marcus, I want answers. Where are they? Are they planning the attack for here? Exactly how many of them are there? I want your men on this immediately."

"The rebels must know an attack on our compound would be suicide," Marcus calmly said while trying to read where Luther was going with all this. He knew full well Luther already had an idea as to what was happening. He only asked questions as a means to gain other opinions.

"The rebels should be aware of that. They *should* feel *any* move would be suicide. Because they obviously don't, we have failed in our missions of persuasion." Luther spat his words vehemently. "We can't rule out an attack on the compound. In fact it seems likely. The rebel leaders have rallied their troops around their god. This could very well lead them to believe the task possible. *God* would help them win a victory." Luther's words reeked with sarcasm.

"Sire, do you really believe the rebels could be persuaded to undertake such a colossal military blunder as a direct attack against our compound? They would need seven-to-eight thousand men to stand a chance against our fortifications. Surely some of the rebels must have a little military experience?" Lexton held little respect for the rebels as a fighting force. They were a band of armed peasants as far as he was concerned.

Luther raised his eyebrows and said, "Look how stupid and fanatical the Tanuba worshipers are. Why should the rebels be any different? Their sky god will save them, right? The fools! None of them realize real power comes at the end of a sword. Superior force decides battles."

"Then what are we worried about?" Marcus posed a good question. "I only hope they do attack the compound. Then we can annihilate them once and for all. They won't stand a chance. I for one am sick and tired of dealing with them, and an attack on the compound is the quickest, easiest way to get this over with."

All three paused a moment to ponder Marcus's point. Each man felt confident that the rebels would not stand a chance in any circumstances, but each also felt an uneasiness somewhere deep within his soul.

"You may be right, Marcus. What are we worried about? No matter where this battle takes place, we are going to be victorious. Our men are a well-trained fighting force, and we outnumber the enemy." Luther started to relax a little.

Marcus agreed whole-heartedly. "And besides, they have no trained leaders capable of staging an organized offensive."

Luther thought long and hard about that last remark, going over every possibility in his mind. Stroking his beard he said, "Lexton, I want you to immediately mobilize all the troops as if we are going to war. Cancel all time off until further notice."

"Yes, Sire." Lexton excused himself from the discussion. He was eager to see some action and test his men, showing Xylor what they were capable of.

Luther waited until Lexton was well on his way, and then turned to Marcus. "What's the latest on our four friends? Have they found the medicine?"

"No, Sire, not yet. The female was seen at the alchemists this morning where she bought several medicinal items. The other three have not been seen since yesterday." Marcus filled Luther in on the latest.

"Do we have any reason to believe they are aiding the rebellion?"

"No, Sire; in fact after this morning when the female bought medicinal items, I think quite the opposite. They seem to be working on the medicine. They have not been seen with any of the suspected rebels we've had under surveillance. I still feel the meeting with Isaac was nothing but coincidence."

"Did you question the female?"

Marcus hesitated a moment. "Uh, no, Sire. It looked like she was on the job so I didn't think it was necessary."

Once again Luther was lost deep in thought. After a long silence he spoke, "No matter what, I must cover all angles. Get word to the men that the next time one of our four friends is seen, or if they report in with the medicine—" Luther paused and gave Marcus a flat emotionless stare—"I want them killed on the spot."

"But what about the medicine?"

"I can always hire someone else to get it after the rebellion subsides. In the meantime, as we've seen, those four have too much talent to risk being kept alive. We can't take the chance that their skills might end up being used against us. We know their capabilities. Kill them before they become a problem." Luther was blunt.

Marcus tried his best to hide his shock. "What about your illness? It could take months to find another team to find the medicine."

Luther nodded knowingly. "Marcus, we haven't maintained this reign in Xylor by leaving loose ends, actual, probable, or otherwise. The medicine will not do me any good if we don't crush the rebellion. It won't do any of us any good if we don't end the rebellion once and for all. We've worked together a long time. Our past success is a result of our past thoroughness. Because it is a remote possibility the four might somehow be recruited to help our enemies, we have to eliminate them. Never take a risk when it can be eliminated."

Marcus nodded his compliance. "As you wish, Sire. I'll brief the troops."

Marcus excused himself and set about his full agenda. He felt thankful to be on the same side as such a cold and ruthless man.

X

OVERHEAD A CHOPPY sea of clouds burned red as the embers of a fire, an endless series of crests and troughs making up a fiery ocean in the sky. The waves of clouds cast a canopy that stretched to the mountaintops in the distance. Chipmunks chittered about the early morning trail, and darted out of the way of Zephyr's horse. Their heads jerked as they kept a curious eye on this rare visitor to their part of the woods.

Spring brought forth wild flowers in a wide array of colors. A hawk circled overhead searching for a careless field mouse. Spring, in Xylor, was a haven of beauty. Zephyr, mesmerized, almost forgot where she was. How wonderful that here amidst the killing, amidst Reddland's grinding mill of tyranny and wickedness that had become Xylor, that God would proclaim His presence with a sunrise! Spring shouted a testimony to God for all who cared to listen. Zephyr loved nature, and nature's author graced her with a special treat this daybreak.

Late the evening before, Zephyr obtained the last of the necessary ingredients for Hyacinth Blue, except the sapphire tears. She paid dearly for the myrrh oil, but at least the alchemist had it in supply. All that remained was the elusive sapphire tears, whatever they were. Maybe this hermit woman would know. If she were as old as Thadus thought, she would be a storehouse of knowledge. She should have a strong recollection of the time before Reddland's reign and more than likely the reign previous to that.

Zephyr entered the woods on a seldom-used trail. Tall evergreens flanked her, casting a cool darkness. Evergreen needles blanketed the forest floor, keeping the ground moist and damp. Small trees sprouted up everywhere as if determined to make the forest thicker. Zephyr carefully wove her horse down the trail, on the alert for anything unusual. Certainly she had received the best assignment. Where was Cad? Choking down dust and cobwebs and being saddled with the responsibility of making a defendable castle out of a church. And Scorpyus was disguised as who-knew-what, and no doubt under the stress of remaining undiscovered. Novak was at Scarborough Field preparing the troops. It sounded like a tremendous amount of work. But Zephyr was here in God's country where she belonged. Zephyr navigated the trail with ease. It left her feeling she was born to ride!

The farther Zephyr rode down the trail, the thicker the forest became. Brush overgrew the trail until it finally disappeared. She continued in the northerly direction the trail had been going. After traveling about a mile from where the trail ended, she came upon a clearing. She saw a small shack up ahead. Smoke wisped its way up from a stone chimney. A small garden flourished beside the cabin.

Zephyr dismounted, tethered her horse, and continued on foot. Stealthily she made her way to the edge of the clearing and peered out from behind a huge spruce. She heard nothing and saw nothing through the open door of the cabin. The faint smell of cooked cherries tickled her nose. Immediately her stomach growled its protest of missing breakfast.

The cabin, made from rough-hewn logs, was built against the side of the mountain, utilizing a rocky outcropping as one of the walls. Smaller logs covered with pine branches formed the roof, and on the west wall was a stone-and-mortar fireplace. The cabin blended very well into its surroundings. Shuttered squares cut into the walls served as windows. The door was made from the lids of two packing crates, but looked to be quite sturdy. All manner of vegetables grew in the sizeable garden. Chopped wood was stacked on the small porch next to the door. A small wooden box, probably used as a stepladder, sat next to a lone cherry tree. Judging from the looks of things, someone had been harvesting the very ripe cherries.

Zephyr held her sword to keep it from bouncing against her leg as she snuck her way to an open window. Still there was no sound from the interior. She craned her neck around to peer inside, careful not to move too fast—maybe it was deserted? She moved her head just enough to let her right eye peek through the window opening. No one was there. Shelves were carved into the stone wall of the cabin. Inside was a small straw mattress atop a rickety cot. In the corner of the one-room cabin stood a table with a very fresh and delicious looking cherry pie on it. A few worn wooden chairs were pushed in place at the table. The shelves had all kinds of jars, gadgets, and personal items on them. Hanging over a glowing fire was a small black cauldron. Zephyr's nose told her rabbit stew was cooking. There was no sign of the hermit woman. Zephyr looked again. No, there definitely were no other doors in the cabin. Maybe there was a trapdoor in the floor leading to a cellar? But no, the cabin floor was made of dirt.

"Can I help you, lassie?" An old raspy voice behind Zephyr took her by surprise.

Zephyr turned cautiously around, embarrassed to be caught looking into the window. Standing five feet behind her was an old woman. Thadus was right; she had to be in her eighties. She clasped a walking staff in one hand and a basket of fresh-picked blackberries in the other. The old woman had on a well-worn brown dress and a white apron. Over her shoulder was a rabbit pelt shawl. A tattered velvet hat covered her long, braided gray hair. Looking down, Zephyr noticed the old woman wore a pair of rabbit skin shoes. Apparently the woman was fond of rabbit.

Zephyr replied sheepishly. "Madam…uh…I am looking for—well, I guess you?"

"Looking for me? What on earth for, deary?"

"Someone I know thinks you can help me answer a few questions. He says you have been around Xylor a long time and know a lot about its legends and folklore?" Zephyr estimated the old woman to be a shade over five feet tall.

"Heh, heh, heh, is that so? Well if being around a long time means I know a lot, then I've got to be the smartest person in Xylor!" The old woman cackled. "Oh, where's me manners? I don't often get visitors. Come on in, I've just made some stew. It should be ready by now. A skinny thing like yourself looks to be needing a good home-cooked meal anyhow."

Zephyr followed the old woman into the cabin. She certainly was hospitable.

"Have a seat at the table there and I'll bring you a bowl of stew." The old woman ladled out two large bowls of rabbit stew and placed them on the table as Zephyr took a seat. She tore off two chunks of bread from a fresh loaf and took a seat across from Zephyr. She handed Zephyr one of the pieces of bread.

"Don't be bashful, deary, eat up!" The old woman dug in heartily. "That's enough for you isn't it?"

Zephyr usually ate portions half the size of the one she received. "Oh, yes, madam! This is plenty. I think this generous portion may be more then I can eat."

"Nonsense, deary! A tiny thing like you needs to put some meat on your bones, especially if you have hopes of ever finding a husband. Men shy away from the ones that are too thin in case they're too sickly for childbirth."

"How do you know I am not married?" Zephyr asked between bites. She was famished and this was one of the best rabbit stews she ever tasted.

The old woman let out a laugh. "Now, if you were married would your husband let you come traipsing way out here in the woods all alone? I know you'd pick a better man than that, deary. There's wild cats a-prowl in these parts, not to mention the threat of thieving highwaymen."

The old lady had a valid point. Under normal circumstances these woods on the north of Xylor would be dangerous for anyone alone. But Zephyr could take care of herself. The old lady did make sense though. She wondered if the others worried about her any more than usual because she was a woman. If they did, they didn't let on. She would make it a point of asking sometime.

Zephyr was hungrier than she thought. She finished all of the food given her, which was a sizeable portion, and even had room for a large piece of cherry pie. This made two desserts in as many days. Zephyr felt spoiled. "You are a good cook, madam, that is for sure. Uh…" Zephyr suddenly realized she didn't even know the old lady's name. "By the way my name is Zephyr. Here I am eating your food and have not introduced myself."

"Your name is Zephyr? That's a mighty lovely name for a lass pretty as yourself. It seems I've forgot me manners also. Its not often I get visitors. In fact it's been three years." The woman counted on her fingers as she thought back to her last visitor. "Yes indeed, three years this month in fact. Oh, and you can call me Maggie."

"Your name is Maggie then?" Zephyr replied.

"Well, no, but I've always liked that name. It sounds a darn sight better then Hester. I don't know what me mum was thinking." Hester chuckled and offered Zephyr another piece of pie.

Zephyr laughed and declined the second helping. "It has been three years since you had company? That is a long time to go without visitors! If you do not mind my asking, why do you live way out here by yourself? You seem like someone who would readily make friends."

Hester smiled at the compliment, and rocked gently in her rocking chair. "Oh no, deary, I couldn't live in Xylor or one of the villages any more. Things have changed so much since I was your age, all of them for the worse I'm afraid. I mean, can you picture an old lady like me fitting in with all the worldly wickedness that has come to Xylor? I'm afraid I just wasn't made for these times. Why, when I was a young lady you could feel safe walking the street. You didn't have to worry about the count then either. He's a murdering man, he is! And he has caused many to fall into all sorts of evil." Hester was visibly saddened as she spoke. "No, me mum and dad didn't raise me to partake in those matters, God rest their souls. I had to come out here. It broke my heart to see my homeland's downfall."

Zephyr thought about what had happened to her own Ravenshire, and her heart went out to the old woman. "Oui, but do you not ever get lonely? There are still good people left in Xylor."

"Oh I know there are still a few upright people, but I do better out here in God's country. Besides that, I always had my tabby for company, until last month. She just disappeared. She may have been killed by some wild critter, I suppose. She was eighteen so she led a full life anyhow."

"Oh, madam, I am so sorry to hear that."

"Oh, I'll be alright." Hester liked Zephyr. She was a polite and thoughtful young woman who seemed sincere and caring. "Now I know you didn't come all the way out here just to ask me how I've been doing. What's on your mind, Miss Zephyr?"

"Where do I begin? So much has happened in such a short time...."

Hester waited patiently for Zephyr to collect her thoughts.

"Let me see...my friends and I were hired to come here and find a medicine. After a lot of hunting we came across an actual recipe for it. We know what all of the ingredients are but one. And I was hoping you would know what exactly that one ingredient was. The medicine is from a forgotten era, and I was told you would possibly have knowledge of it?"

"What's the name of the medicine?" Hester was listening intently.

Zephyr took a deep breath. "A lot of people think the medicine is nothing more then a myth, but it is called Hyacinth Blue." Zephyr braced for Hester's reaction.

Hester's eyes grew wide with excitement. "You found a recipe for Hyacinth Blue? My stars it's been ages since me ears heard that name. Oh my, this is exciting. So many people have been looking for that medicine in years past and not found it that it has been relegated to legend."

"What do you say about the medicine? Is it real or legend?"

Hester smiled knowingly. "People believe what they want to believe. How strong is your faith, deary?"

Zephyr hesitated a moment. "If you are talking about faith in God, well then I have faith. But if you are suggesting a belief in this mythical medicine, I do not know. I mean, if the medicine did exist, would not more people have heard of it? I just do not know."

Hester stopped rocking and leaned forward. "What would you say, Miss Zephyr, if I told you I saw it cure a dying eight-year-old girl once?" Hester sported a wide grin.

Zephyr's interest was piqued. "What are you saying, madam? It cured her just like that? Like magic?" Zephyr was apprehensive about anything magical. "If you are suggesting it is a magical potion I do not want anything to do with it. Magic, sorcery, and the like are abominations."

"On no, deary, I would never condone sorcery either. This is a real medicine with real ingredients. I saw me grandma use it to save the life of a little girl. Don't get me wrong, the medicine will work only if the Lord's willing, as it did in the case of this little girl." Hester started rocking again. "I can assure you the medicine is like any other, except it is shrouded in years of mystery." Hester watched her guest ponder the idea.

Zephyr was relieved and relaxed a little. "If Hyacinth Blue worked, why did it vanish?"

Hester searched her memories. "Well, deary, the medicine disappeared during the war, not this last one that placed the count in power, but the one before that, around fifty years ago. Unlike this last war, we were victorious and managed to fight back the invaders. You're too young to remember. It happened before you were born." Hester laughed.

"Well, any way, the war lasted two or three years, and the few who knew how to make the medicine were killed. I supposed all records of how to make it were lost in the chaos. I remember people sifting through the aftermath trying to find it without luck. Me grandma had watched a batch being made, but couldn't remember the exact ingredients. She had me help her try to make several batches, but none of them turned out. After a few years we lost hope. Since so few people had the opportunity to see the medicine work, many began to doubt its existence. It wasn't long before it was considered a myth." Hester scratched her head.

"I do seem to remember me grandma saying something about old Samuel hiding a recipe before he died. He's the one who made it for me grandma. He was a local craftsman who made the most beautiful jewelry boxes. He liked to dabble in herbal medicine as a hobby. Unfortunately his shop was looted and burned during the war."

"Really? That is an amazing story. I had never heard of Hyacinth Blue before. And you say it worked? You saw a little girl get cured with it! I will bet you have seen some incredible things in your life."

Hester laughed. "Yes, that's what getting old will do for you, give you stories to tell some youngster about the way things were."

Zephyr chuckled and nodded her head in agreement. "I suppose you are right. Do you know if the little girl made a full recovery?"

"You can say that lassie. I've lived 74 years since then. Is that considered a full recovery?" Hester reeled joyously with laughter.

"Madam, it was you! It is all starting to make sense. You said Samuel was a craftsman? We found the recipe in an old jewelry box. Or I should say we had some help. Isaac picked up the trail somehow. We just finished what he started."

"Yes, deary, it's amazing how things work out for the best. And Isaac is a good man too. You are lucky to have met him."

Zephyr remembered the events surrounding Isaac's death somberly. She decided not to relive that event by telling Hester how Isaac died right before her eyes.

"If you have taken the medicine, then you might know what sapphire tears are?"

"Yes, but that, deary, brings us to another legend." Hester gave Zephyr a wink.

"What do you mean?"

"Sapphire tears are where Hyacinth Blue gets the 'blue' part of its name. Sapphires are blue, so sapphire tears are nothing more then an eloquent way to say 'blue tears.'"

"So the secret ingredient is actual tears? Blue tears? From a human?" Zephyr was excited and fascinated at the same time.

"Not quite, deary, it's not that easy. Human tears are clear. The tears needed for the medicine are blue. Like all tears they are salty. But these saltwater tears are special. It's their unique medicinal quality that makes them blue."

Zephyr was ready to burst with anticipation. "If they are not human tears, what are they from?"

"That, Miss Zephyr, is the other legend." Hester paused, leaned in close to Zephyr and stated in a voice just above a whisper, "Sapphire tears are the tears of a unicorn."

Zephyr was speechless. Was Hester serious? She did say unicorn, right? Was this the fantasy of an eccentric old woman? Unicorns weren't real. They were the stuff of legends. And now the medicine's success hinged not only on finding a unicorn, but collecting its tears! Hester had to be wrong about sapphire tears, or Hyacinth Blue really was nothing but legend.

"Are you sure sapphire tears come from a unicorn, madam?" Zephyr's disappointment showed in her face.

"Don't look so sad, deary. I assure you it's true." Hester had a warm smile for Zephyr. "I can see the doubt in your face. Such a pretty, young lass to be burdened with heavy thoughts. Maybe I can put your mind to rest a bit? Let me tell you something, believer to believer. Isaac said even the Bible mentioned unicorns?"

"Oui I had heard that, but…" Zephyr couldn't deny that. "I always thought it meant…I do not know…not literal unicorns." Zephyr was looking at the floor. "Have you ever seen a unicorn? Has anybody? If they existed, would not someone have seen one by now?"

"Now, lassie, I think unicorns would avoid human contact and remain in only the most secluded areas. And besides that, there probably are not many in existence, making them very rare. So I wouldn't expect them to be seen except by a precious few."

Zephyr couldn't have foreseen what Hester was about to say next.

"But to answer your question, deary, yes. I saw a unicorn once, a long time ago deep in the forest near here. Granted there be few who will master their fears, and brave the danger and perils in the mountains; and thus few will find the treasure of sapphire tears." Hester responded with a knowing wink as one who had seen and believed. She spoke without a hint of doubt in her voice.

Zephyr was so shocked to hear Hester recite verbatim the poem Isaac gave her she nearly jumped out of her seat. Could it be Hester really had seen a unicorn? Maybe there was something to all of this. Zephyr realized there was some sort of a connection, a common theme as it were, in the events before her. The possibility was exciting but then again, Hester could have heard that poem anywhere. She was certainly old enough to have heard a lot of things in her lifetime. Wasn't that the reason Thadus recommended Hester as a possible source of information about Hyacinth Blue in the first place? Zephyr was intrigued and slightly skeptical. "Are you saying there are unicorns here in Xylor? And you have seen one?"

Hester gave Zephyr a huge smile revealing a few gaps where teeth once were. "Oh, yes, deary. There is a rare few deep in the woods north of here. Through the thickest part of the forest runs a meadow. In that meadow, many, many years ago, I saw the most beautiful unicorn! What a sight it was! Only heaven itself could surpass it in beauty. As far as I know, I'm the only one who has been there in years. Most people avoid that area because they believe it to be haunted." Hester let out a chuckle. "Silly superstitions, anyhow; that's what paganism will do for you. Of course it works out well for the unicorns not having people trouping through their home."

Zephyr was at a wondrous loss of words, her head awhirl somewhere between the surreal and the insane. Zephyr decided to set aside reason and follow the inner child who still wanted to believe in unicorns. "How would you ever collect its tears for the medicine?"

Hester smiled, slowly rose from her chair and went to a shelf. She retrieved a small dust covered book and handed it to Zephyr. The book was well worn and aged. "That was me great-great grandma's. Written in her own hand, on the inside cover, is an inscription. I don't know where she heard about that inscription, or why it's there, or even if she wrote it herself or copied it from someplace. All I know is that's how me grandma was able to obtain the medicine for me. It will also explain why very few people will ever be able to obtain Hyacinth Blue."

Zephyr looked down at the thin little book, its leather cover so worn the title was no longer visible. The bindings were so worn the pages were loose. Zephyr turned to the inside cover, careful not to damage the yellowed pages. The inscription was still readable and written in a flourishing penmanship.

> Be there a young maiden of carnelian locks
> Who for truth has taken a stand,
> Who's borne injustice and grievous deeds
> And not walked in the ways of the land,
> Who is a kind soul, pure of heart
> Washed clean by the Blood of the Lamb,
> The unicorn shall, assuaged and appeased,
> Accept the touch of her hand

Zephyr looked up pale and sweaty as if she had seen a ghost.

Hester spoke and brought Zephyr back from her dizzying thoughts. "I must confess, deary, when I first saw you outside looking into me cabin, it was like watching destiny unfold. Here I am in the middle of nowhere, and out of nowhere comes the maiden of me great-great grandma's inscription. I don't know how many times I've read those words, but when I saw you I thought

Could it be? Now after talking to you, deary, I know this is one of those rare instances where legend and real life come together."

Zephyr had just heard the same speech from Thadus who felt the Clandestine Knights were the long-awaited answer for Xylor's rebellion. One fact stood out; the impossible series of coincidental events clearly showed God's sovereign reign over the affairs of men. Resigned to the fact there must be some purpose for her and her friends to be in Xylor, Zephyr was awestruck. She was deeply moved to near tears with the realization that God indeed had a plan for her life; that he could use someone like her for His purpose, someone the world placed little value in. When Zephyr thought about it, she had no explanation for her surprise. She knew full well God often used the downtrodden and outcast. Those who were discarded or spurned could at anytime turn to God and find open arms. It was God's way to love the unlovable, accept the rejected, take in the orphaned, and forgive those who asked. A lump of clay could be made into something beautiful by the Master's hands.

Zephyr had no idea what the future held. She had no idea about the existence of unicorns or their tears. She could not say if the inscription in Hester's book had anything to do with her. And if the Clandestine Knights were the answer to Xylor's problems, she couldn't see exactly how. All she knew was she was going to do her best to do the right thing, hoping it would please God. Even though she may not fully understand where all of this was heading, wherever He led, she would go.

Zephyr decided to give it a shot. "Well, I do not know what to say. I guess I will go to the meadow to look for the unicorn. The inscription does not really say how to collect the tears though, does it?"

Hester clasped her hands for joy. "Oh, I knew you would, deary! I wouldn't worry about how to gather the tears. It is believed unicorns are very empathic creatures. Somehow everything has a way of working out. If it's meant to be…" Hester started gathering a few food items for Zephyr to take with her.

Zephyr was concerned for Hester. "If the Royal Guard finds out you helped me, your life could be in danger. I want you to go to the oratory. It will be safer there. My friends are there. Tell them I sent you and they will protect you. At any rate, things are sure to get rough in the weeks to come." Zephyr decided she could trust Hester based upon their conversation. "I may as well tell you since the news has probably spread across Xylor by now anyway. A battle is brewing between the rebels and Reddland's men. Who knows what could happen?"

"Don't worry about me, deary. You just go find that unicorn. If there's a war coming, having some Hyacinth Blue around may not be a bad idea. I'll be praying for you and the others. This moment was bound to come sooner or later. I hope this will be the start of getting things back on track." Hester gave Zephyr a hug as she left, and watched her disappear into the woods to get her horse.

Zephyr followed Hester's directions to the meadow. It was hard to find. More than once she had to dismount and lead her horse on foot because of the thick undergrowth. There was no trail and she had to snake her way between the trees. Zephyr estimated the meadow to be about five miles from Hester's cabin, and it was all uphill. At the crest of the mountain was a small grassy meadow in a slight valley. Waist high grass; perfect for grazing, covered the meadow floor.

Zephyr crisscrossed the one hundred acres a couple of times hoping to cross the unicorn's trail. She assumed unicorn tracks would resemble horse's tracks. Aside from some bear tracks, and a single panther print, there wasn't much to see. A small herd of deer had grazed on the meadow. Judging from the moisture in their manure, they were there earlier that morning.

The day wore on and she turned up nothing. There was no trace of anything remotely resembling horse tracks. She really thought there would be some sign; hoof prints at least. Hester did say sightings were rare, though, that she had only seen a unicorn once herself. Zephyr grew discouraged and was ready to call it a day. Maybe there was a wild horse living in the area and Hester mistook it for a unicorn. How good could Hester's eyesight be at her age anyway? Serious doubts crossed Zephyr's mind. She didn't know what to believe and was too tired to think about it.

Daylight was fading so Zephyr made camp. She wasn't about to try to negotiate the woods in the dark. The mountain was much too steep for that. After the sun went down the meadow grew chilly fast. Zephyr built a campfire and sat on her bedroll in front of it. The warmth felt good as she cooked some beans on the fire. She thought on the week's events. Who would have guessed she would be out in the middle of nowhere looking for a unicorn? Zephyr didn't know why she hoped to find the unicorn so badly. Maybe she just wanted to believe she could be the young maiden in the inscription. Everyone wanted to feel needed. And to be a special maiden sounded even better. Maybe she just wanted to believe Hester couldn't be wrong. She didn't want to believe the old woman was a little crazy.

As Zephyr pondered these thoughts, somewhere out in the blackness, a wolf howled his sullen song. She felt that somehow the wolf knew a human was looking for a unicorn. Instead of its ode to the moon, Zephyr decided the wolf was howling with laughter.

———•◦•———

Drex couldn't believe it. Here he was, an experienced soldier with the Royal Guard for the better part of the last six years, taken captive. Drex mulled it over, feeling like a fool. How could he have fallen for such a ruse? Especially one he had seen used once before, by the Royal Guard at that. It was the old, "get the cat to chase the mouse right into a trap" routine.

Earlier that day while on patrol, Drex caught a man breaking into an alley door, rather noisily now that he remembered it. The man appeared startled upon being discovered and ran around to the back of the building with Drex in pursuit. The last thing Drex remembered was rounding the corner. Drex bemoaned his predicament. *How could I have been so stupid?* What would the others say when they found out?

None of that mattered now. Drex regained consciousness in a dark and musty warehouse somewhere near the docks, judging from the smell of rotting fish. He had been stripped of his uniform and now wore only a tattered cloak.

Drex strained at the ropes that bound him to a wooden support beam. It was no use. The ropes were too tight, and even if he could break the wooden beam it would only bring the roof down on him. His wrists and ankles throbbed from his bonds, and other ropes that tied him in place restricted his breathing. A scarf effectively gagged him. It was tied around his head, in his mouth, and forced his tongue to the rear of his palate. He could utter nothing more than a stifled mumble. Aside from a case of cottonmouth and a pounding headache, he was unharmed. Things could have been worse.

Drex heard a door open and close behind him. Footsteps pattered around, followed by the sound of someone opening a crate. Shortly, a chiseled man with black hair and a moustache appeared carrying a pack in one hand and a large clay jar in the other. A tall thin reed protruded from the jar. Drex was infuriated to see the man wearing his uniform. He could say nothing, but he hoped his contempt showed in his eyes.

"I thought you might be thirsty." Scorpyus said and dropped the pack. He set the clay jar next to Drex and adjusted the reed so it would be within reach of Drex's mouth. "It's hollow so you can get some water up through it. It won't be easy to drink with a gag on, but I assure you it can be done."

Drex gave Scorpyus a scornful look and turned his head away from the makeshift straw.

"Suit yourself. If you get thirsty you know where it's at."

Scorpyus rummaged through his pack and retrieved several items. He arranged them all in front of him, each one having its place. "This is going to be a stretch, but you were the best I could find at such short notice. I guess you'll have to do."

Drex watched with growing interest that blossomed into amazement as Scorpyus started the process of his transformation. Drex was close to the same height as Scorpyus, and he also had black hair and olive skin. But that's where the similarities stopped. Scorpyus was a fit, lean man in excellent shape that employed proper hygiene. Drex had an ale belly that hung over and obscured his belt. He had rather bland features and rarely had time to waste on keeping clean. Even though as a soldier Drex lived an active life that provided plenty of exercise, his overindulgence in tobacco products left him winded during even slightly strenuous activity.

Scorpyus set about his task. Drex watched as Scorpyus smeared lard into his hair to give it a greasy sheen. He then took a dry leaf and some hay, and crushed them up between his hands. He put the tiny bits of leaf and hay into his hair to complete the unwashed look he was after. Using his fingers he worked his hair into the same general position that Drex wore his. Scorpyus was careful not to use a comb. Soon he had duplicated Drex's hairstyle.

Scorpyus looked from Drex to a mirror and back again continually. Next he mixed ashes with a touch of water and smeared the paste under his eyes to give them a dark, sunken look. After that he rubbed onion powder in his eyes to make them bloodshot. Drex watched him put a red dye on his nose to mimic the look of a heavy drinker. Scorpyus also pressed small, thin metal rings into his nostrils to make his nose flair into a more bulbous snout.

Scorpyus shaved the small patch of whiskers from under his bottom lip and adjusted the shape of his moustache with scissors. He used berry dyes on his cheeks for a gaunt and sunken appearance and on his eyelids so he would look like he had been up for three days. He also added blotchy marks to his skin as best he could to mimic those on Drex's face. Scorpyus clawed at the dirt floor to get plenty of dirt under his fingernails, and applied some to his face. Scorpyus's transformation, though not perfect, was quite remarkable.

Scorpyus knew he probably wouldn't fool Drex's close friends for long, but he needed to get into Reddland's compound somehow. He also knew a Royal Guardsman in Reddland's personal area of the compound was unusual, but felt he had no choice. Knowing Reddland was more familiar with the Elite Guard since they served him as personal security on a daily basis, he couldn't take the chance of disguising himself as one of them. He counted on the fact there were so many Royal Guardsmen going in and out of the compound that it would be difficult to remember them all.

Drex was already angry at being taken captive, but watching Scorpyus disguise himself sent him over the edge. Drex hatred his captor. He strained at his bonds until he turned red and his wrists were rubbed raw. Scorpyus had unknowingly insulted Drex's pride. It was one thing to watch Scorpyus mimic his look, but to watch him take step after step to make himself uglier was a slap in the face. Scorpyus was unaware; insulting Drex never crossed his mind. He had more important things to worry about. But the steps Scorpyus took to disguise himself all detracted from his appearance, making him ugly. This fact was not lost on Drex who had always fancied himself a lady's man. It was a fantasy he entertained despite the fact he paid for his companionship.

Scorpyus looked up to see that Drex was very upset, his tobacco stained teeth gritting down on his gag.

"Oh, that reminds me." Scorpyus poured a syrupy butternut colored liquid into a cup and took a drink, swishing it around in his mouth. He spit on the ground then inspected his teeth in the mirror. They were now a dull brown like a cigar leaf. He then stuffed cloth under his shirt to give the illusion of a bulging belly. Satisfied with his work, Scorpyus got ready to leave and packed up his bag of tricks.

Drex was apoplectic at this final insult and grunted and strained at his ropes. His face glowed red with rage and his pulse throbbed in the veins on his temples. He wanted Scorpyus with a vengeance.

"You may as well relax. I can assure you those ropes won't break. Save your energy. Don't let your ugly temper get the best of you, or else before long you'll make your wrists bleed." Scorpyus offered his advice and departed for his mission. Drex mumbled unintelligible curses at Scorpyus as he was left to writhe in solitude. So even his temper was ugly now!

⸺ ◦•◦ ⸺

First light crept over the mountains and stirred Zephyr awake from a sound sleep. "No, not time to get up yet," she yawned and stretched in her bedroll. Squinting, she saw a faint blue over the horizon confirming the sun's report. Zephyr stayed in her warm bedroll awhile longer and pulled the blankets up tighter around her neck. There was no rush to get up. She felt the chilly salt air on her face, and heard the rustle of the tall grass. Birds were already up feasting on a cornucopia of insects. Spring's tranquility hovered above the foggy meadow. Zephyr took this all in for a solid ten minutes, drifting in and out of sleep a few times in the process. Finally she sat up rubbing her eyes. Another yawn escaped her as she pulled her hair back and donned her cap. She retrieved nuts, berries, and some bread from her saddlebags, her usual breakfast. More than once the others ribbed her for eating her "bird feed," but she didn't care. Even though she packed the dried fish and meats the others carried, she always paused to gather edible "goodies" from the indigenous plants in her surroundings.

Zephyr was thoroughly enjoying her meal when she froze mid-munch with a slight gasp. Her eyes grew wide. There, about one hundred yards away was the most dazzling white horse, its head down as it browsed in the ground-level fog.

Beautiful. Zephyr watched the animal as she resumed chewing slowly. It almost seemed to radiate light as it grazed in the meadow, its tail twitching lazily. Zephyr knew horses, but had never seen one like this. This one looked perfect and flawless from this distance, and it was so very white. Zephyr couldn't take her eyes off of it.

Could this be the unicorn? Did not unicorns have wings? This horse had none.

Mesmerized, motionless, not wanting to scare it off, Zephyr waited patiently for a better look. So far it had not lifted its head from the fog.

Finally Zephyr's patience was rewarded when the horse suddenly lifted its head and looked away from Zephyr's location. Zephyr's mouth dropped and she felt clammy. Her stomach fluttered.

Is this real! Zephyr grinned, barely containing her excitement. There stood a horn on its head. Unicorns did exist!

Zephyr's pulse pounded. Hester wasn't crazy after all. Or maybe she was and now Zephyr was crazy too. Whatever, she felt a wondrous joy. Just in case, she pinched herself. No, she was awake. The others would never believe this. This isn't even a story you could tell your grandkids and be taken seriously. Was it?

Without warning the horse walked off into the fog, its head bobbing to no particular rhythm. *No! Do not go away!* Zephyr screamed in her mind. She had seen the place where imagination meets the world. A week ago unicorns were legend, were the hopeful wishes the fantasies of young girls were made of. Today they were as real as a horse or dog. For a fleeting moment she had witnessed the impossible, a fantasy come alive. It was a lot to take in all at once.

The problem was it disappeared as quickly as it appeared. And what were the odds of seeing it again? And if she did see it again, how would she ever gather its tears? Assuming the best case scenario—that she was able to somehow capture the unicorn— what would she do? Put pepper in its eyes? Tell it a sad story and make it cry? Yeah, right. But according to legend, unicorn tears were real and somehow collectable. Hester's grandma had managed to pull off the improbable.

The more she thought about it, the less likely the whole thing seemed. Could the unicorn have detected her presence? It did disappear in quite a hurry. Maybe it got scared away. But it didn't look like it was frightened off; it had casually trotted away. Zephyr licked her finger and held it up. The unicorn couldn't have smelled her as she was downwind from the animal. And she was pretty sure it hadn't seen her either. How could it have with only the top of her head sticking out above the tall grass? Besides, Zephyr had been careful to stay motionless.

What if something else spooked the unicorn?

Zephyr slowly stood up to get a better view. She scanned the meadow for anything unusual, any irregularities in the grass. There was nothing and yet the hair stood up on the back of her neck.

Relax, Zephyr told herself. *I am starting to spook myself now.* Maybe the unicorn caught the scent of something upwind?

Zephyr's horse neighed and snorted, shifting its hooves on the ground. It started to rear a little and pull at its reins which were tied to a stake in the ground.

Zephyr stroked the side of her horse's neck. "Shh, what is it, boy? Easy now." She scanned the meadow again, and again there was nothing to—

What was that! She stared intently at the spot where she saw a ripple in the grass. There it was again! But this time closer. Zephyr's horse reared up again, trying to pull free. Clearly spooked, it nervously stomped its hooves.

"Easy, boy! Easy!" Zephyr tried to control her horse as it started to buck and stomp. She knew there would be no way to saddle her horse or retrieve her gear as long as it was frightened like this. The horse grew more and more terror stricken by the second and a lesser handler would have lost control of the animal.

Glancing back, Zephyr saw the grass rustle again. Her eyes were wide with alarm. Whatever it was, it had closed a lot of distance in a short time. It was much too fast to be human. Zephyr knew that could only mean one thing. She was being stalked by a predator, a stealthy and quick one at that.

Zephyr frantically tried to mount her horse bareback as it reared up on its hind legs. Her gear and saddle were no longer important. She fought the horse, trying to mount it as it reared. With one hand firmly gripping the harness at the side of the horse's head, and the other clutching its mane, Zephyr repeatedly tried to swing a leg over the frenzied steed. Eyes rolling wildly, the horse bucked and spun, thwarting all attempts to mount it. Time was running out, and Zephyr knew she had to act fast. Even though she was getting lifted off the ground and thrown against the horse with each buck, she refused to yield her grip on the harness and mane.

This cannot be happening! Fear crept into Zephyr's heart. It was the type of fear she knew all too well from her childhood. It was the fear of helplessness. Valiantly she struggled to control the horse and swing a leg over its back. The steed was beyond control. It wanted only to be rid of Zephyr so it could flee.

With each buck, Zephyr could feel a jolt in her shoulder socket as if her arm might be ripped off. She felt a sharp pain on her right forearm just as the horse let out a blood-curdling whinny. Zephyr looked to see a crimson stain spreading from slash marks on her forearm.

To Zephyr's horror, there next to her arm on the horse's neck was a brown claw. The claw dug deep into her horse's flesh where blood flowed freely.

Zephyr was horrified. A panther had claws dug into each side of her horse's neck for support, and its jaws were clamped tight on its throat. In agony, the horse spun and reared, attempting to free itself. Both Zephyr and the cat held firm as the horse bucked, tossing them around as if they were rag dolls. The cat was determined, drawn and gaunt, badly in need of this meal. It flailed its back claws, slashing at the horse, trying to bring it down. The horse was crazed with fear, spinning in a wild frenzy, trampling Zephyr's gear in the process.

She had to act. She dropped to the ground, landing on her back; her cap fell over her eyes. Zephyr flung her cap aside in time to see hooves coming down on her. Without a moment's hesitation she rolled to the side but felt a violent jolt to her left hip anyway.

Oh my God, I have been stomped! Zephyr knew that being stomped by a horse was often a mortal injury. She also knew her extreme fear would mask the pain long enough to do something.

She scampered to her feet. If I can stand it probably did not break my leg, she thought.

She saw her horse starting to succumb to the panther's attack. It wasn't rearing as high, and blood flowed from several slash marks on its chest. There was no time to lose if the horse was to live. Zephyr grabbed the hilt of her sword and pulled, but nothing happened. She couldn't remove her sword from the scabbard.

Zephyr saw that her scabbard was bent, effectively lodging her sword inside. Her horse must have landed on it rather then her leg.

Zephyr drew her dagger and waited for an opportunity; the horse wasn't rearing up, she lunged at the cat and stabbed it in its left shoulder. Surprised by the attack, the panther dropped to the ground and let out a raspy snarl. Jerking its head to face Zephyr, the cat paused for a second, as if startled to find another creature beside the horse in the vicinity. It crouched low on the defensive against its new attacker. It was wounded but not out of the battle. Zephyr stepped back as the panther crept toward at her. It growled, teeth exposed, its yellow eyes fixed on its new meal. Zephyr's horse took full advantage of the momentary confusion and trotted off across the meadow, leaving Zephyr to fend for herself.

The wounded and angry panther circled Zephyr, not about to be cheated out of a meal.

The cat sprang. It slammed into her, knocking her back as it dug claws into her shoulder. Zephyr thrust her dagger deep into its chest with everything she had left. They both fell to the ground, the cat on top of her; a flash of white shot through Zephyr's eyes as she struck her head on a rock. Her vision faded to black.

Her forearm no longer hurt; neither did her head or shoulder. She could feel her pulse in her temples as she drifted deeper and deeper into another realm. A tear trickled from her closed eyes.

Zephyr remembered she was being attacked by a panther and struggled to get up but couldn't move. Besides, it was so peaceful here. Zephyr saw herself lazily drifting down a slow-moving river, her raft gently bobbing in the water. She lay on her back watching clouds shift shape as they trekked across the sky, just like she had done so many times as a child. This was so very peaceful and quiet; Zephyr couldn't help but smile. Her right hand hung over the edge of the raft, fingers trailing through the water. The river puzzled Zephyr. It wasn't how she remembered it. The river back home had always been cool and refreshing. Now the river felt warm and sticky.

Scenes from her life replayed themselves slowly. There was her childhood house! The ranch looked just as she remembered it. And there were her father and her brother Zander! She hadn't seen them in so long. They were talking by the woodpile and had no idea she was hiding behind it. Zephyr strained to eavesdrop on the conversation. Her dad and Zander talked about her upcoming birthday! Zander had made a little bow and arrow set for a gift. Her father thought it would be a great gift, but said that since Zephyr was only nine she would only be able to use it with supervision.

Nine years old? Why did her father say that? Zephyr knew there was something she was supposed to be doing, but couldn't bring it to mind no matter how hard she tried. It was on the tip of her tongue. Before she could recall it, a barking dog distracted her. Zephyr looked to see her dog Jasper running towards her on the trail. Jasper jumped and leaped down the trail trying to catch birds. The birds were much too fast, but the dog was unwavering in his determination. That black dog loved to chase birds. He was a natural hunter, a real bird dog. Zephyr remembered old Jasper to be a frolicking and fun-loving dog right up until the end. He was a scamp until that day in his twelfth year when he suddenly took ill—and died? No, Jasper was alive. Zephyr could see him as plain as day, could feel his breath on her face as he sniffed her where she lay. Jaspers breath tickled her ear.

"Cut it out Jasper, stop it!" Zephyr laughed and moved her face away from the playful dog. A sharp pain shot through her neck and her head throbbed with a pounding headache.

What happened? My head is killing me. Zephyr strained to open her eyes, squinting to focus. The white blur above her slowly resolved into a dazzling white horse. The horse was curious, sniffing at Zephyr, investigating the scene.

What is that? Zephyr focused on a single horn protruding from the horse's forehead.

Zephyr cascaded back to reality in a wave of vertigo that left her dizzy.

The Panther! Zephyr snapped upright, and looked around. Her forearm was stiff and bloody, and it hurt to move so fast. She moved fast anyway, frantically searching for the cat. She didn't have to look long. There, to her left, a dead panther sprawled on the ground, a dagger deep in its chest. Relieved she let out a sigh. Looking back, she saw that the unicorn had retreated a few steps at her sudden movement.

The unicorn! Zephyr was in a state of euphoric shock. There before her eyes, up close and very personal, was a live unicorn. Zephyr was thrilled to see it again, and grateful to be alive. She moved slowly so she wouldn't scare it away any further.

The unicorn cautiously evaluated Zephyr, looking her over carefully from a distance. Zephyr froze and just stared at it. She could hardly believe her eyes. The unicorn scraped a hoof on the ground and stared back.

The unicorn had a sorrowful look in its eyes. It didn't flick its tail, and its head hung down. It was almost as if the unicorn were sad or mournful. The unicorn's big brown eyes even appeared misty.

Zephyr had seen the same look before with dogs. She wasn't sure if she had seen it with a horse, but she didn't think so. Dogs knew when their masters were sad or sick, and seemed to sympathize. Zephyr's own dog, Jasper, had been quite good at it. Whenever she was sick, Jasper moped around the foot of her bed until she was well enough to play again. And when she was happy, Jasper was right there, tail wagging, ready to go out and frolic. After Zephyr's father was killed, Jasper took it as hard as she did.

During the long months of mourning that ensued, the dog would wake each morning at the foot of the bed, and go to Zephyr's pillow placing his paws next to her, checking on her. If Zephyr were still sad, Jasper would lay his head on his paws and look at her with the saddest eyes. Sometimes Zephyr would manage a small grin. If she smiled, the dog's ears would perk up, and his tail would start to wag. Jasper wasn't happy unless Zephyr was happy and he always knew the difference

Many times after her father's death, Zephyr cried herself to sleep. And many times Jasper would let out a soft whimper in sympathy. The two played together, slept in the same room, and mourned the loss of family members together. Zephyr could even remember a story of a dog that slept on his master's grave after the man died. The dog slept there for the rest of its life.

And now this unicorn had that same look that Jasper had. Boy did it ever remind her of beloved Jasper. Zephyr decided to take a chance and move. Slowly she reached into a leather pouch and pulled out a carrot. The unicorn's nose twitched.

"Come on," Zephyr whispered and waved the carrot back and forth.

The unicorn cautiously approached. It sniffed the carrot, and then started to eat it. While it ate, Zephyr stroked the side of its face.

"Well hi there. My, are we pretty." Zephyr talked to the animal as if she were talking to an infant. The unicorn seemed to like her, and even to enjoy being stroked. But the unicorn's eyes, they were so sad. In fact, the more contact Zephyr had with the unicorn, the more sorrowful it became.

A chill went down Zephyr's spine when she noticed a blue tear form at the corner of the unicorn's eye and she felt a mixture of awe and fear. What was happening here? Despite Zephyr's amazement, she had the presence of mind to remember her mission; she quickly retrieved a vial from her pouch and collected the tears as they trickled from the unicorn's eye. Why, she wondered, was it shedding tears? Hester said unicorns were rumored to be empathic creatures, but Zephyr felt more amazement and disbelief than sorrow. She didn't feel sad in the least.

Zephyr tried to make sense of it all. Unlike Jasper, who was sympathetic and shared Zephyr's emotions at the time she had them, could this unicorn somehow empathize, or identify with Zephyr's life as a whole? The inscription in Hester's book made a lot more sense if that were the case.

One-by-one the tears welled up in the unicorn's eye. One-by-one they rolled down its cheek into Zephyr's vial. If it were possible to read an animal's mind, she would have known what the tears were for.

Was there a tear for rape? A tear for famine? A tear for a father who never came home? Was there a tear for a child's broken heart, a tear for lost innocence, and a tear for a brother who would never grow old? All in all, Zephyr collected seven sapphire tears.

And then it was over as quickly as it started. The unicorn took one last, long look at Zephyr. She knew her friend would soon leave. After giving her a quick nuzzle with its nose, the unicorn was gone, leaving Zephyr with seven tears and an incredible story to tell. Her eyes misted as the unicorn trotted off across the meadow. Zephyr was living in a moment bigger than herself. She no longer believed in coincidence. Everything happens for a reason. God has a plan for everyone's life. Until this day, she hadn't totally realized it. She would never have doubts again.

XI

A BEAD OF SWEAT trickled down Scorpyus's temple and his neck was starting to cramp. Luther Reddland had returned to his room unexpectedly, forcing Scorpyus, who was disguised as a Royal soldier, to take cover under the bed. He had managed to only briefly survey the room before hearing a key work the lock on the door. Now under the cramped confines of the bed, Scorpyus stifled a sneeze, waiting for Reddland to leave. And what a wait it had been. For the last half-hour Scorpyus had been watching the count's feet pace about through the gap where the comforter nearly touched the wooden floor. Apparently Reddland had gone out on a patrol with the Royal Guard and now wanted to freshen up a bit for a late lunch. He clanked his armor in the corner, and then spent considerable time deciding what to wear. Reddland's large wardrobe gave him a lot of choices, and he took nearly thirty minutes. Most women could pick an outfit faster.

The count, who was always refined in manner when around others, was quite the opposite when in the privacy of his personal quarters. Scorpyus was privy to the sounds of all manners of grunts, belches, and other bodily functions. Another fact Scorpyus found odd was Reddland's habit of spouting mumbled curses sporadically. It shed doubts as to the condition of his mental state. It was almost as if he were conversing with himself. Perhaps this was the early stage of the disease for which Hyacinth Blue was hoped to cure. Then again maybe Reddland was just an angry, frustrated man. With all of the atrocities he'd committed in his life, it would be no wonder he had a lot of pent up rage. Scorpyus knew people often used rage to express guilt, especially if they refused to acknowledge their sin.

Scorpyus pinched his nostrils to stifle another sneeze. Even a count had an acre of dust under his bed.

Reddland sat down to put his boots on, and the bed sagged, putting pressure on Scorpyus's back. He had scarcely finished the task when there was a sharp rap at the door. Reddland got up and answered the door, and a pair of large feet entered the room. Scorpyus ascertained from the greeting that the feet belonged to Marcus, captain of the Elite Guard. Judging from the enormity of his polished black boots, Marcus had to be the size of Novak. Whoever ended up tangling with Marcus would have his work cut out for him.

Scorpyus strained to keep still and eavesdrop on the conversation. Reddland and Marcus spoke only briefly, but fortunately for the rebels it was about some important issues. Scorpyus learned of the standing order to kill all known or suspected rebels on sight, including Scorpyus and the other three. Reddland felt he could no longer take any chances with "unknown problem potential." Reddland also planned to mass his troops at his compound for the time being, in preparation for an attack. It was a wise decision, and it showed he was taking the rebels as a serious threat. The good news was this meant some time would be afforded to Cad to prepare the oratory. Finally, and most importantly, Reddland didn't know what the rebels were up to yet. He didn't even know where they were. All he did know was that a lot of people suddenly disappeared. Roving patrols were out in search for them. Scorpyus prayed Novak would be ready if Reddland's men found him.

As quickly as Marcus came, he and Reddland departed, locking the door behind them. Scorpyus slowly crawled out from under the bed and tried to massage some feeling back into his neck. His right arm tingled as it woke up from its momentary restriction of circulation. He had just started his reconnaissance of Reddland's compound, and already he had learned a few beneficial tidbits of information.

Once circulation returned to his arm, Scorpyus began to search the room. He was methodical, starting from one side and working to the other. He wanted to be thorough, but he also wanted to be fast. The longer he was in the room meant not only the more he could find, but also the more the likelihood he would be found.

Scorpyus looked around the lavishly decorated room, deciding where to start. The wardrobe held little of interest and stood primarily as a testament to Reddland's expensive taste in clothing. A trunk at the foot of the immense bed yielded only a slew of pricey items such as a jewel-encrusted dagger and golden trinkets that neither shed light on current events nor furthered Scorpyus's mission. Scorpyus surmised from the objects Reddland collected that he was a vain man who reserved only the best for himself. Everything found in the trunk was expensive, flashy, and even gaudy. Perhaps the most intriguing items found in the trunk were the silk-padded iron shackles. The shackles provided a rare glimpse into the mind that ruled Xylor, a glimpse Scorpyus would much rather have not taken, but such was the nature of his work.

Moving to the desk, Scorpyus found the usual: ink, quill pens, rolls of parchment, Reddland's official seal and wax, and candlestick holders. The lack of official documents led Scorpyus to believe Reddland must have an office elsewhere. Still, there were a few interesting pieces of information. Reddland had composed a list of supplies needed for the compound. The list mentioned no weapons, but a tremendous amount of foodstuffs had been ordered for delivery to the compound.

There was enough food ordered to feed an army. Why was Reddland gathering food now? He should have had a supply on hand. Had another supply wagon been ambushed?

Reddland wasn't taking any chances. It was Reddland's way of looking at situations from all angles that kept him in power this long.

Scorpyus mulled it over. The count was gathering his forces at the compound before making his move. That meant he was in no hurry. The lack of weaponry on the list indicated the Royal Guard was *already* well armed for battle. Reddland was biding his time and was not about to panic and make a brash move. Eventually he would track down the rebels and attack. Once Reddland realized the oratory was again being occupied and had been fortified, he would act. More than likely he would lay siege. Reddland had the patience for it. An all out attack wasn't out of the question. Whatever he did, he would be a formidable foe. Luckily Cad was making preparations for both scenarios.

Moving to one of the drawers, Scorpyus found a stash of love letters. They were written by a slew of women, and some still held the scent of sweet perfume. Scorpyus was amazed that any woman would want to be with a man as evil as the count. But here was written proof that there was a sizable cadre of females vying for his attention. There were no signs Reddland returned their affections among his possessions.

There were several books on military tactics. But for the most part, Reddland's reading interests seemed to revolve around the occult; especially the subject of necromancy. There were also a few books on astrology. A newer book about herbal remedies was there also. Scorpyus opened to where Reddland had a bookmark. It looked like he had been reading about elixirs to help stave off sleeplessness.

Scorpyus opened a polished wooden box that sat atop the desk. Inside were a dozen or so cigars. Assuming they were expensive, Scorpyus was surprised by how much they stank. He thought a man of Reddland's means should be able to afford cigars that smelled better. Shrugging his shoulders, he moved on.

There was a partially-written letter in the top desk drawer. Scorpyus helped himself to its contents:

Phineas,

> *Well old friend, it is with great reluctance that I am writing you today. I regret to inform you that the rebel uprising here in Xylor has not yet been dispatched. In fact, recent events have the rebels taking a bold step toward an attempted coup de grace. This will lead to the exposure of the identities of the rebels once and for all. Now that they've made this bold move, they will no longer be able to remain anonymously underground. I offer my sincerest apologies for not handling this matter in a more expeditious manner. However, I can assure you that the situation will be resolved shortly. Once we defeat the rebels, all survivors will be put to death.*
>
> *By the way, Phinehas, considering our former 'line of work' I discovered an interesting bit of information relating back to those forgone years. History has a strange way of repeating itself. Remember those mercenaries I hired? Would you believe that I know...*

The letter suddenly ended with a small blotch of ink. While Reddland's intentions for the rebels were clear, Scorpyus could only wonder about the mercenaries. The paragraph bothered him. He suspected that Novak, Cad, Zephyr, and himself were the mercenaries in question, but didn't see how it would relate to history repeating itself for Reddland. The Clandestine Knights would have been small children in Reddland's "foregone years." Could Reddland have hired another group of mercenaries?

Scorpyus searched the rest of the desk to no avail. No secret compartments or false-bottomed drawers could be found. A systematic search of the bed and nightstand was fruitless as well. There were no big clues, no revealing answers, and not even a hint to shed light on the partially-written letter. The ruling regent in Ravenshire was Prince Phinehas, and Scorpyus wondered if he could be the recipient of Reddland's letter. For Reddland to be addressing Prince Phinehas as casually as the letter indicated, they would have to be close friends. Seeing as how Reddland had not been to Ravenshire at any time in Scorpyus's memory, that seemed improbable. And certainly Reddland had hired countless mercenaries to do his bidding. Besides, Scorpyus had been hired to find a medicine, hardly to work of a mercenary.

Scorpyus gave the room one last look over, and then headed for the door. On his way out, a small dark spot on the frame of a painting hanging by the door caught his eye. Scorpyus reached over and grabbed the portrait. The dark spot on the lower right corner of the frame lined right up with his thumb. A grin crossed his face.

What have we here? The picture swung out on hinges to the left revealing nothing but more bare brick wall. Scorpyus felt around on the wall until he found a loose brick. Using his dagger he pried it out until he could get a grip on it with his fingertips. Scorpyus found a small hollowed out cavity containing a black velvet bag behind the brick. Scorpyus removed the bag then slid the brick partially back into place. He loosed the drawstrings and emptied the pouch into his hand. Dozens of large uncut gemstones poured into the palm of his hand. It was more money then he had ever seen in his entire life. Temptation was pounding on Scorpyus's door. Reddland couldn't possibly miss a few of these little beauties. Scorpyus quickly put the idea out of his head. Many times he, as well as the others, found themselves in positions like this, and each had successfully kept focused on the mission regardless of the temptations. Scorpyus's grandmother always preached against stealing, even if it was from someone like Reddland.

Scorpyus sifted through the gems and retrieved a signet ring with a large gold band. Turning it over, he noticed it sported a black gemstone. The gemstone had an elaborately engraved "RK" on it.

Scorpyus's eyes widened in shocked disbelief and a wave of nausea swept over him. His mouth flooded with saliva and he knew he was on the dangerous verge of throwing up. He had to suppress a few coughing wretches. After all these years to finally have an answer to the question that had been eating away at him since he was a boy made him feel sick. Quickly he fumbled the gemstones back into the bag and drew its strings tight. He shoved the bag back into the wall and replaced the brick as he found it. He had to tell the others fast. This couldn't wait. This changed everything.

The more Scorpyus thought about the ring, the more his shock turned to rage. The missing piece of the puzzle in the lives of the Clandestine Knights had been found. How would Zephyr react? The news would devastate her. And Cad, what would he say? Scorpyus shuddered to think how Novak would take it.

Rage surged through Scorpyus. He tightened his jaws. Scorpyus half expected to wake up and find this had all been a nightmare. But he didn't wake up. He was stuck with this reality and would be forced to deal with it. Vaguely-remembered rumors from the past bubbled to the surface of his memory. If there was any doubt as to what actions he and the others should take, this would put it to rest. For now, the most important and only mission Scorpyus had was to tell the others.

No sooner had Scorpyus finished putting the brick back into place than footsteps echoed in the corridor. They stopped in front of the door. Scorpyus instinctively froze and cocked an ear toward the sounds. He heard a jangling of keys. In a controlled flurry, Scorpyus put the painting back in place over the secret compartment and rolled a blank piece of parchment from the desk into a scroll. He turned just in time to meet Montague as he entered Reddland's chambers.

Montague was astonished. "What are you doing here?"

"I suppose I shall ask you the same." Scorpyus had no idea who he was talking to, and was merely trying to buy some time while he formulated a plan.

Montague shot Scorpyus a look of conceit. "I'll have you know that daily I tidy up Sire's personal chambers. He has trusted me alone to this task, and in fact I am the only person besides the count himself who has a key." Montague was cocky and confident because of his relationship with Reddland. "And you haven't answered my question; what are you doing here?"

Scorpyus was unimpressed. "Well then, since you work so closely with the count, I'm sure you are aware of the current state of affairs with regards to the rebellion?" Scorpyus waited for Montague to respond with a nod.

"Good. The count has sent me to retrieve a document he needs to further our plans." Scorpyus held up the blank parchment.

"What document? Let me see that." Montague was highly suspicious.

"I'm afraid I can't do that. This is sensitive material. Even I haven't read it." Scorpyus was pressing his bluff hard.

Montague relaxed a bit with that explanation, but still seemed suspicious. "Why would the count send you and not Lexton or Marcus? Or even one of the Elite Guards since they are more familiar with the compound." Montague saw that Scorpyus was wearing the blue uniform of a Royal Guard regular and not the red of the Elite Guard. "It's not often we see one of you, especially in the personal wing of the compound."

"I don't know what to tell you. Maybe they were busy. You'll have to ask the count when you see him. And if you haven't noticed, there are a lot more of us around since the recent turn of events with the rebellion."

Scorpyus had enough talk and seized on the momentary lull in the conversation. "Now if you'll excuse me, I have work to do." He stepped around Montague and headed down the hall, scroll in hand. Montague pondered the encounter as he slowly started dusting Reddland's shelves.

Scorpyus knew it was only a matter of time now before his cover was blown. It was time to abort the mission. He had decided to do that anyway when he found out Reddland's dirty secret. That news couldn't wait. The others had to know.

Scorpyus made his way down the hall and was briskly crossing the grand ballroom when someone called out to him.

"Drex! Hey, Drex! Wait up!" A Royal Guardsman ran up to Scorpyus. Scorpyus turned to meet the soldier.

"Hey, Drex, I've been looking all over for you for nearly four hours now. Where have you been?" The young soldier was exasperated.

"I've been around here the whole time. What did you need?" Scorpyus imitated Drex's gravely voice as best he could and acted surprised he was hard to find.

The soldier bought it. "I just wanted to find out if you wanted me to have the squad set up the catapult or just stand by?"

"No, go ahead and set it up by the back wall." Scorpyus figured he may as well keep one squad busy with the catapult. It would be one less squad to discover his identity.

Back in Reddland's chambers, Montague made a startling discovery. He hadn't been dusting long when a sparkle on the floor caught his eye. He brought the lamp from the night table to get a closer look. On all fours, after a brief search, Montague found a large uncut diamond. He knew Reddland would not have been so careless to leave it out. And no one other than Reddland and he knew of the gemstone's existence. Suddenly his nagging suspicions gained relevancy.

Montague knew he should have stuck by his first instincts. Never, in the last ten years that he had known Reddland, had anyone other than the count been alone in this bedroom except Montague; and that was only to clean. Montague ran to the door and stuck his head into the corridor. Scorpyus was nowhere to be seen.

"Guards! Guards!" Montague was too timid to actually go after the intruder himself.

The Royal Guardsman speaking to Scorpyus spun around. "Montague's in trouble! Let's go!"

"You go on ahead. I'll get more men." Scorpyus tried to bow out gracefully but the guard was persistent.

"GUARDS! We have an intruder!" Montague bellowed in the background.

"What? Montague sounds like he's in trouble, Sarge. Don't you think we should get there?"

"I don't know, just go on. That's an order!" The conversation was taking more time than Scorpyus had patience for. Soon guards would arrive, and Montague's continuous calling in the background was unnerving.

The Royal Guardsman had a look of contempt on his face. "You don't know or you don't care?"

"Pick one!" Scorpyus glared at the soldier with a look that induced fear in those who received it. What Novak could do with his physical size, Scorpyus did with "that look." Knowing time had run out, Scorpyus was done talking.

The guardsman was taken aback by his sergeant's uncharacteristic frankness. He remembered the incident with Lieutenant Tiberious when an imposter posed as him. He also thought he heard Drex roll an "R" once or twice. He never noticed an accent before. "I've never known you, Drex, to hesitate when it came to a fight. In fact, that's what has kept you a sergeant instead of moving up through the ranks faster. Now you're acting a little cowardly, not wanting to help Montague. Normally you're the first one to go." The guardsman drew his sword and grabbed Scorpyus's arm simultaneously.

"Who are you anyway?" He held the sword to Scorpyus' neck.

There would be no way to avoid a fight now. Scorpyus knew the soldier must still have a trace of doubt in his mind or else he would have attacked immediately. But who could blame him? No one wanted to kill their friend accidentally, and Scorpyus' disguise was convincing enough to cause hesitation. Unfortunately that hesitation would cost the Royal guard his life. He was so intent on trying to see through Scorpyus' disguise, trying to see behind the mask, that he didn't notice Scorpyus slip his dagger from his sheath. Often a disguise proved to be a psychological advantage for Scorpyus. For many, seeing is believing, and people refuse to accept what they can't see, even if deep down they know the truth in their heart. A lot of people use that excuse to justify a rejection of God. The guardsman was no exception. He *knew* he was confronting an imposter, but could only *see* his sergeant. His friend was acting so uncharacteristic as to be suspicious, yet he looked like Drex.

Scorpyus stepped into the guard and drove his dagger home. He twisted the guard's sword arm back away from his throat, and then forced the guard's arm into a hammerlock. For a brief moment the two stood face to face in an awkward embrace. The guard tried to pull away from the dagger, or release tension on his arm that was twisted up to his shoulder blade. But Scorpyus held him close until the end. Slowly the guard collapsed against Scorpyus, a victim of hesitation. Scorpyus lowered him to the floor just as three more guards ran into the room.

"Quick! They've killed him! They ran out the west door!" Scorpyus shouted, thinking fast, sending the three guards on a wild goose chase. All the while Montague could be heard in the background sounding the alarm. Royal soldiers were scurrying in the corridors.

The situation deteriorated rapidly leaving little time to think up a plan. Scorpyus was forced to make it up as he went. For the first time in his experience as a covert operative, he felt a sense of dread. He wondered if after all these years he was finally in over his head.

Scorpyus would have to make his escape with Royal guards swarming all over the compound. He had to get word to the others about his discovery.

Scorpyus fled the grand ballroom and found himself in a long hallway. Stealthily he snaked his way down the hall, pausing to check a few doors. They were all locked. He paused where another hallway intersected the one he was on. It branched off to the right.

Voices came from down the corridor, so Scorpyus took the hall to the right. By now the whole world had to be looking for him. Scorpyus sprinted down the hall holding his sword to keep it from clanging against his leg. He had discarded the cumbersome shield and helm used by the Royal Guard.

At the end of the hall was another locked door. As Scorpyus was about to pick the lock, he heard keys rattle in the keyhole on the other side. He quickly turned aside and bolted for another door and entered the first one he came to. This door was unlocked and the room unoccupied.

Scorpyus found himself in another bedroom. Judging from the floral décor and the shear volume of perfume bottles on the vanity, the room belonged to a woman. Wasting no time, he emptied a pitcher of water into a washbasin. Knowing the guards would be looking for Drex, Scorpyus set to scrubbing all the makeup from his face and teeth. The soap left an awful taste in his mouth, and the scrubbing reddened his olive complexion. He splashed water over his head and forced an ivory handled brush through his hair, slicking it back. After Scorpyus left the dresser a mess with water everywhere, he opened one of the dresser drawers. Pulling out a skirt, he dried his hands and face then tossed it aside. Quickly he pulled the padding from his artificial "belly" and tossed it aside.

"You two search all the rooms in this hallway. The rest of you come with me." A gravely voice in the hallway gave orders.

Scorpyus headed for the window and threw open the shutters. In a flash he was over the sill and landed in the courtyard. His heart pounded as he made his way across the compound grounds. For now no one noticed him. Soldiers were scampering everywhere. A squad was posted at the main gate, and both side gates were closed and heavily guarded. Archers readied themselves along the parapets.

A lieutenant readying his men on the guard tower saw Scorpyus walking by. "Hey soldier, come here. We could use a hand up here."

Scorpyus looked to the parapet. "Yes, sir, I'll be right there. I just have to get something real quick." Scorpyus ducked into the nearest door. He didn't give the lieutenant a chance to reply.

A captain walked over to the lieutenant. "Who was that?"

"I don't know?"

"Have you seen him before? I don't recognize him."

"He might be a new recruit? We are always in the process of enlisting new men." The lieutenant shrugged his shoulders.

The captain thought a moment. "Let's get a half dozen men and check this out just to be safe."

Unknowingly, Scorpyus walked right smack dab into the jail. At a desk were two young guards reclining with their feet propped up. Behind them were four small cells with thick wooden doors. Each door had a tiny barred window. Reddland didn't keep prisoners alive long enough to need more then four cells. The guards were startled when Scorpyus burst in.

"Um, uh, hi…what do you need?" One guard nervously stuttered his words, embarrassed to be caught in such a leisurely state.

"The captain wants to see you both right now. He sent me to relieve you." Scorpyus was surprised to find himself in the jail of all places. He blurted the first thing that came to mind.

"Are you sure? We just came on duty." The other guard was worried he was in trouble for something.

"Yes I'm sure. And if I were you I wouldn't keep him waiting. He's not in the best mood right now." Scorpyus opened the door for them.

The two guards were still in their teens. Both complied and left looking rather scared. "I hope we're not in trouble." One expressed as they left.

Scorpyus closed the door behind them and watched them through the small window.

A moan escaped from one of the cells. Scorpyus went to take a quick peek. He looked through the small metal grate that served as a window. What he saw inside made him sick. Hanging limply from his wrist shackles on the opposite wall was a scrawny gaunt man, nude and bloody. His nose was swollen and grotesquely twisted to the side. He had black raccoon eyes, and dried blood was all over his mouth and down his chest. The old man had been brutally beaten.

"Bartus? Is that you?" Scorpyus was horrified. He could barely recognize Bartus anymore.

Bartus slowly raised his head and looked out the slits of his swollen eyes. His voice cracked and was barely audible.

"Kill…me." Tears streamed down Bartus's face as he pled with Scorpyus. Clearly he was in unbearable pain.

Scorpyus's eyes misted over. "My God, what have they done to you?"

Scorpyus glanced all around the room frantically. On a wooden peg on the wall by the desk was a set of keys. He tried them all on Bartus's cell door until he found the one that unlocked it.

Scorpyus entered the cell and tried the keys on Bartus's wrist shackles.

Bartus groaned an incoherent response. Scorpyus freed his wrists then gently lowered him to the floor. Bartus, slick with blood, was hard to keep a grip on. His back looked like raw meat. Slash marks from the whip crisscrossed his back, some curling around the sides. Each one oozed blood.

Scorpyus retrieved a water skin from atop the guard's desk, and cut the upholstery from the chairs. He rinsed the blood from Bartus's back and fastened some makeshift bandages.

"Arghh!" Bartus cried out in agony.

"Here, take this." Scorpyus forced open Bartus's mouth and emptied a ceramic vile containing a red powder into it. The powder quickly dissolved on Bartus tongue.

"It'll help with the pain." Before Scorpyus finished with the bandaging, Bartus was in a drunk-like stupor feeling little pain.

"This stuff works well." Bartus slurred his gratitude.

Scorpyus removed the Royal Guard surcoat he wore and dressed Bartus in it using a piece of rope for a belt. He wasn't going to let Bartus lose any more dignity.

To compensate for the added weight of packing Bartus, Scorpyus relieved himself of the Royal guard's heavy chain mail armor, keeping only the sword. This left him wearing royal blue pants, black boots, and Drex's stained white linen shirt, much less cumbersome attire when carrying the wounded.

Scorpyus slung Bartus over his shoulder and peered out the jail door. The courtyard was a bustle of activity. Soldiers were filing in the main gate where officers gave them instructions as to where to post themselves. Reddland, Marcus, Lexton, and a small entourage had gathered, no doubt making plans for a speedy capture. Scorpyus oriented himself with regard to the stables.

At least it's a straight shot there. Not that I have much choice.
Scorpyus walked along the south wall at a brisk pace, Bartus
flopping limply over his shoulder. It was a cool afternoon and yet
Scorpyus was sweating profusely; the only indication of stress he
displayed. He knew there would be little chance of making the one
hundred-yard trek undetected. It was no shock when he was finally
spotted.

"There he is!" A sentry on the parapet sounded the alarm.

Scorpyus ran the last twenty yards amid a barrage of arrows,
one striking the stable door near his head. Before a second volley
could be launched, he was inside and the door was barred.

Scorpyus retrieved his horse. Someone had unsaddled it. This
was all he needed. Why don't people leave other peoples things
alone? He wasted no time in draping Bartus over his horse's back
and retrieved a length of rope from a peg on the wall to secure
Bartus. Scorpyus made sure Bartus was firmly in place.

The Royal soldiers had to be closing in on the stables.
Scorpyus had been so intent on escaping and securing Bartus to his
horse that he suddenly realized he had gotten tunnel vision. By the
time Scorpyus realized there was someone behind him it was too
late. A scythe caught him on the right thigh.

Scorpyus bellowed in pain as he spun to face his attacker,
drawing his sword in the same motion. A burning pain throbbed
through his thigh, and blood soaked his pant leg.

Much to Scorpyus's surprise, his attacker was not a soldier, but
a stable hand armed with only a scythe and wearing no armor, a
stocky man apparently meaning business. At around forty, he had
to be the oldest stable hand in Royal service. It was a job usually
reserved for young boys.

"Are you sure you want to do this?" Scorpyus squared off with
his attacker.

The stable hand answered by swinging his scythe wildly at
Scorpyus. Scorpyus easily deflected the blows with his sword and felt
that once the stable hand realized he was taking on an experienced
fighter, he would conclude he was in over his head and flee. It was

not to be. After blocking a few more wild swings with the scythe, Scorpyus gave his attacker a kick in the chest. It sent the stable hand sprawling against the wall, knocking picks, rakes, shovels, and other tools from their place and clattering to the ground.

The stable hand quickly sprang to his feet, this time with an iron poker in hand. He exuded a hatred for Scorpyus that went beyond reason.

Did I offend this guy somehow? Scorpyus couldn't understand why the man insisted on fighting. Surely he knew he was a novice and didn't stand a chance.

Bartus, who was tied in place across the horse, was powerless to help. All he could do was watch as the horse stepped away from the fracas.

The stable hand frantically swung the poker time and again at Scorpyus, sometimes striking the walls or stall doors. The fight hadn't even lasted forty seconds before the stable hand was exhausted. Scorpyus had enough. Seeing his opportunity he swung with all his might. His sword crashed against the stable hand's iron poker with such force it caused a shower of sparks and knocked the stable hand to the floor. The poker flew against the ceiling before bouncing to a stop across the stable floor. Scorpyus leveled his sword and slowly advanced on his now unarmed and exhausted attacker.

In a panic, the stable hand scampered to his feet and stepped frantically backwards in a retreat from Scorpyus's impending attack. In his haste, the stable hand tripped on the scattered farm tools, landing on his back with a thud. He didn't get back up.

Scorpyus cautiously approached the fallen man expecting a ruse. As he neared, he noticed the ashen face of the stable hand. Scorpyus heard the man taking short rapid breaths, as red foamy sputum formed at the corners of his mouth. When the stable hand fell he impaled himself on a rake.

Scorpyus knelt down beside his wounded attacker. The prongs of the rake punctured the stable hand in several places between the shoulder blades. The wound was mortal, and the man was fading fast. Bartus looked on from the horse, helpless to the situation.

"You've impaled yourself on a rake. Even though you have been mortally wounded, there is still hope for you as long as you have a breath of life in your lungs. Don't die without knowing…" the stable hand cut off Scorpyus.

"Leave me…alone…you…filthy…Gypsy!" The stable hand spat curses between gasps of air, clearly uninterested in what Scorpyus had to say. His words revealed his true interest in the fight. "It's your kind…that always…stealing and…cheating…like you did…my father…so don't you…go telling me…" The rest of the stable hand's message was lost in a bubbling cough.

Scorpyus was undaunted by the racial undercurrents in the hand's voice. He knew the dying man had only moments left on earth, and was going to try to help him despite his requests for Scorpyus to leave him alone. Scorpyus bent down and whispered in the stable hand's ear.

Unbeknownst to Scorpyus, Marcus watched the whole scenario unfold. Marcus had only popped into the stables to retrieve a horse, where by pure coincidence he stumbled across Scorpyus. Confident that Scorpyus would by no means escape, Marcus decided to take the opportunity to study the enemy. Out of morbid curiosity, he watched the stable hand attack. From his vantage point peering through the partially open back door to the stables, Marcus could see it all. He shook his head in disgust when the stable hand fumbled the surprise attack. Marcus watched transfixed, as Scorpyus fought the stable hand while holding back his full potential. The stable hand could have been killed at any moment, but Scorpyus seemed reluctant to kill an untrained man. Marcus believed he had discovered a weakness in the enemy's defenses. And now when Scorpyus had the perfect opportunity to finish off the mortally wounded stable hand, he chose instead to waste time talking to the dying man about his religion. Didn't Scorpyus know time was of the essence? Marcus had always felt religion was nothing more than a crutch for the simple minded. Now he felt it was also a weakness to be exploited. Apparently, these rebels had a hard time killing, especially killing untrained citizens who were no match for their skills. They preferred to only kill in self-defense, or in defense of another, and then only as a last resort. It was preposterous! Marcus had always found killing easy. Especially average citizens; they offered little resistance.

Marcus recalled that the survivors from the ambush of the supply wagon told a similar story. In that case the rebels only fought until they overcame the resistance. Then they chose to spare the wounded. The rebels had even talked with the wounded about their God also. It was totally mystifying to Marcus. The Royal Guard always killed the wounded and survivors. Even those taken prisoner were executed within a short time after interrogation was completed. Why let the enemy live to fight another day? The actions of Scorpyus defied the good sound logic of warfare, and yet he seemed to be successful.

Marcus was puzzled because he also felt a twinge of respect for the code of honor displayed by this man. He didn't understand it, but it stirred something down deep, a feeling he hadn't felt since he was in his teens.

Marcus looked on in bewilderment as Scorpyus whispered to the dying stable hand in what seemed to be genuine concern. What was with these people? They were somehow different. They had a certain confidence, a fearlessness that Marcus admired. It was almost as if death was no threat to them. Nothing could have prepared Marcus for what he saw next.

The stable hand remained uninterested in what Scorpyus had to say. He didn't want to be confronted with this new possibility no matter how true it rang. Instead the stable hand swelled with pride for Tanuba, and started chanting a Tanubian curse at Scorpyus. Tanuba worship had always fit in with the stable hand's way of life, especially the ceremony of the temple prostitute. No Gypsy was going to come along and tell him he was wrong. Some other person had tried to sell him the same bill of goods years earlier. As far as the stable hand was concerned, Christianity was old fashioned and outdated. It was nothing more than a list of rules that filled the stable hand with resentment. That was the appeal of Tanuba; you could do what you felt was right and decide your own morals. He was more comfortable forming a god to his own standards than conforming himself to a god's standards. The stable hand was going to answer to nobody. Sure he had heard all the spiel a few times, but who were these people to impose their way on him? And now to be harassed, by a gypsy nonetheless, was too much. He gathered up what little strength he had left to spit in Scorpyus's face.

Scorpyus wiped the spit from his forehead and continued without missing a beat. "Listen. Deep down you know I'm making sense. I can see that you are wondering if I might be right. Don't…" Scorpyus watched as the stable hand slipped away. Marcus looked on from the doorway intensely curious, and mesmerized by the scenario.

A look of abject horror slowly drifted over the stable hand's face, like a cloud slowly passing before the sun. His eyes grew ever wider as his body stiffened up. The dying man dug his fingers into the sod floor, gritting his teeth, trying desperately to claw onto something, anything that would stop what was happening. His skin grew pale and clammy, as he tried to recoil from the ghastly images only he could see. If it were possible to have sunk into or beneath the sod floor he would have done so. Now there was no escape.

"Arghh, my feet are on fire!" The stable hand's scream went from a low guttural growl to a crescendo of wails, his teeth gnashing his bloody tongue.

"No!" Scorpyus beat his fist against the ground in dismay. Never in his life did he witness anything like this and now he wished he never had. His stomach was in a knot to the point of cramping. He shook his head in anguish, fully realizing what transpired, and feeling worthless for not being able to help. He had witnessed the death of others in the same fate as the stable hand, but none had been so chillingly graphic. Now emotionally drained, Scorpyus felt numb. He couldn't even feel anger about the lies and deception that claimed another soul.

"You did all you could. It's not your fault." Bartus's slurred words couldn't even comfort him.

Scorpyus made no reply, and started to finish preparing the horses for escape. Nothing in the world seemed to matter anymore.

"You can't blame yourself. It was his choice. Pride comes before the fall." Bartus was worried about Scorpyus. He was grateful he hadn't seen the stable hand's demise. Hearing it was bad enough.

After arriving and stumbling across the stable hand engaging the intruder in combat, Marcus had been observing the melee for intelligence-gathering purposes, after which he intended to finish off the intruder. But Marcus didn't attack Scorpyus, he couldn't. He was frozen with shock, mouth agape. He wanted to say something, but what? And for the first time in as long as he could remember, he felt genuine fear, a fear of the unknown. The contorted face of the dying stable hand was burned into his mind. Marcus could see the man's gnashing teeth every time he blinked, his scream echoed down the corridor of his mind.

Marcus felt a stirring queasiness deep within his being, the same feeling he had when around Malvagio, especially when he was "interrogating" Bartus. There was no explanation for the feeling. Marcus didn't even know what it was. It was like a sense of dread, but somehow not entirely a bad feeling. It made no sense. For some reason the feeling was occurring with more frequency as of late.

Marcus tried to move, but halfheartedly. He didn't try to stop Scorpyus from slipping out on horseback with Bartus. He knew the others would take care of them. There was no escape anyway. All Marcus could think about was what had happened to the stable hand, some unspeakable horror. And somehow the intruder knew it would happen and tried to stop it.

It took Marcus a few minutes to regain his composure. He felt like his mind had been sifted like flour. By that time Scorpyus was long gone. Confused, Marcus didn't know if he were going crazy, or if he was already there. He had seen scores of men die, but none like this. He had no idea what happened to the stable hand. He didn't know much about what the intruder was trying to tell the dying man. He didn't even know if he would live to see tomorrow.

All he knew was he did not want whatever happened to the stable hand to happen to him.

Scorpyus rode low and barebacked leading the horse with Bartus draped across it like a saddle blanket. The sentries discovered the escape almost immediately as the two left the stables. Scorpyus quickly got his bearings, then dug his heels into the horse's side, making a mad dash for the main gate. Arrows darted all around, far missing their mark as the lookout blasted the alarm on his horn. Not expecting such a brazen move by the intruder, the surprised archers fumbled their first volley. Other sentries scrambled to lower the portcullis.

Hooves pounded the pavement spurred on by Scorpyus who clung to the side of his horse to avoid the archers. A band of soldiers was forming up to his left.

Scorpyus flinched when an arrow shot by inches from his face and struck his horse in the head. With only forty yards to go, the horse collapsed in a heap and sent Scorpyus flying over its head and tumbling across the courtyard. Bartus's horse kept going, bouncing and jostling the injured man every step of the way.

Scorpyus bounded to his feet and sprinted for the main gate, a squad of soldiers in pursuit. He dug his heels in, pumped his arms, and gave it all he had in an attempt to beat the portcullis. Right now the pain in his right thigh was the least of his worries.

Bartus cleared the compound just as the portcullis started to come down. The agile Scorpyus was outrunning the soldiers, but he didn't beat the portcullis. It slammed down when he was yards from the gate, and he crashed into the grate. Trapped! Panting, he saw Bartus fade into the distance down the road.

Scorpyus looked back at the guards approaching full force; he veered south along the compound wall and entered the first door he came to.

Two surprised guards turned toward him.

He was in some sort of receiving room or foyer. *Well, God, I think I need a miracle,* Scorpyus prayed and swallowed hard as he drew his sword and met a barrage of blows. Scorpyus blocked blow after blow. Seeing an opportunity, he went on the offensive and drove one of the soldiers back until he tripped over a chair. Before he could move in for the kill, the other soldier was on him hard. Scorpyus deflected a series of blows from the soldier's sword into the surrounding furniture.

Scorpyus kept one step ahead of the soldiers until he had another opening. He locked swords with one man, and the other charged him from the rear. Seeing the maneuver out of the corner of his eye, Scorpyus waited until the man was about to thrust with his sword, then suddenly dropped to the floor. The charging soldier plunged his sword into his friend's chest instead of Scorpyus as planned. The soldier hesitated in shock and Scorpyus moved in. One thrust to the solar plexus and it was over as quickly as it started.

There was a ruckus at the foyer door followed by the pounding of a battering ram. Soldiers wanted in and now. Scorpyus noticed he was dripping a trail of blood from his thigh, a trail that would be easily followed. He hurriedly wrapped his thigh in part of a dead soldier's surcoat and ran from the foyer; taking the stairs four at a time, he ran the four flights to the top where he came to a long hall. He charged into the first room he came to, a bedroom.

He went to the fireplace and looked up the chimney. It was small but it would have to do. He shimmied up the chimney and peered out the top. The courtyard was a hive of activity. He saw a small window thirty feet away along the crest of the roof. It was caked with dirt and hadn't been cleaned in a long time. It had to be the attic. Sweat combined with soot to make Scorpyus look like he had been splashed with black ink.

Scorpyus waited until it was clear then slithered out of the chimney and crawled the few feet to the window along the crest of the roof. Four stories up, he had a good view of the compound. The window was easy to force open, and Scorpyus was in within seconds.

The attic was filled with old furniture, trunks of clothing, broken household items, tapestries, and other detritus. The thick layer of dust and rat droppings confirmed the room rarely had visitors. In the corner was a large trunk. Scorpyus emptied the mildewed clothes out of it into a battered dresser. It would be an adequate hiding place until he could make his escape. He placed the trunk near the window just in case he was discovered in the attic and needed to leave fast. The soldiers were sure to search up there eventually.

He needed to formulate some sort of a plan. Circumstances had played against him, but he was still in the fight.

He hoped Bartus made it to safety. Scorpyus wasn't going to hold his breath, but if the others found Bartus first, maybe they could help bail him out of this situation.

———◦•◦•◦———

"What do you mean he disappeared? He was right there!" Reddland roared and furiously stabbed his finger at the doorway Scorpyus had gone through.

"He barred the door, Sire. By the time we broke it down, he was gone and two soldiers were dead. We're searching the compound right now." The sergeant hated reporting bad news.

Reddland shook his head in disgust. "I want him found. This is embarrassing. How will it look if the citizens find out a single man eluded hundreds of Royal soldiers within their own fortress?" Reddland didn't wait for an answer. "Lexton, where's Marcus? Why doesn't he have the men posted yet?"

Lexton managed to stay out of this so far. That came to an end. "I don't know, Sire."

"Well it appears no one knows what's going on." Reddland reeked of sarcasm. "Sergeant, I want every room searched thoroughly. And keep a squad on horseback in case the intruder is spotted outside the compound. He'd better not make it that far. Do whatever it takes to get this imposter."

"Yes, sir." The sergeant promptly left to carry out his orders.

"Sire, the Royal Guard should be ready by morning for full mobilization, and prepared for battle. Archers, infantry, and cavalry are all ready to go. The catapult batteries are all that's left." Lexton felt now was the time for a little good news.

"Good! At least something is going as planned. We're ready for an attack here, or so I thought until recently. At any rate, as soon as we find the rebels we'll cut them to pieces. I want no survivors. Make sure the men understand that." Reddland scanned the courtyard. "Ah, here's Marcus now."

Marcus rode up and lifted the visor of his helmet. He still looked a little pale. "Sire, I heard the intruder eluded us somewhere within the compound. Is there any change in orders for my men?"

"No, post them as planned." Reddland noticed Marcus was acting a little different than usual. "Is something wrong, Marcus? You look like you've just seen a ghost."

Marcus took a deep breath. "No, I'm fine. I just found one of the stable hands dead. He was impaled with a rake."

"What? How barbaric! Impaled with a rake? I want this vicious animal exterminated. Be sure word of this gets out to the citizenry. It will show them how no one is safe from the rebel menace, not even unarmed men."

The irony of Reddland's words was not lost on Marcus or Lexton.

Reddland looked inquisitively at Marcus. Clearly his friend was troubled. "It's not like you to be so upset by the death of a soldier, much less by the death of a servant."

"I'm fine, Sire," Marcus said. "I can assure you, we will have this uprising under control and behind us soon. The men are anxious for action." Marcus was a professional soldier. What he had seen bothered him and he couldn't wash the scene from his memory, nevertheless, he had a job to do and he would do it. Years of being a soldier would carry him through this episode.

"Very well." Reddland surveyed the compound. "But first, let's settle the task before us. Find this snake!"

Marcus snapped the visor of his helmet down and was off.

Novak rose before dawn, prepared for another day of training the rebel troops. The first day had gone smoothly, with all the men being assigned to squads. He had been relieved to see Cyrus had brought most of the troops up to an adequate level of proficiency over the past several years; the major task left was to turn the individuals into an organized team. Without an unwavering willingness to follow orders, the rebels would stand little chance against the trained and organized Royal Guard. Novak started the task of getting the troops to react to his orders and the orders of the appointed officers without hesitation, no matter how strange those orders seemed. If Novak knew Cad, there would be some unconventional methods employed during the campaign. Unconventional methods were a must if the rebels were to stand against the superior numbers of the Royal Guard.

Novak walked over to where Emerald was cooking breakfast. "Good morning. What's in the pot?"

"How does venison stew sound?" Emerald helped Novak to a bowl and a large slice of fresh bread.

"Umm, very tasty. A good cook is a priceless commodity in my way of thinking," Novak smiled, and then eagerly ate his stew. The smell of cooking venison began waking up the others who started to make their way to Emerald's makeshift kitchen area one-by-one.

"So, Emerald, is there anything you can't do?" Novak asked as he sipped on some hot tea and grabbed a seat on a barrel. "You can cook, ride, sew, and you even put a few stitches in that soldier who cut his arm sparring yesterday. You seem to be a woman of many talents."

"Why, thank you for noticing, Novak." Emerald was pleased to be making a positive impression. She watched Novak sip at his hot brew. He didn't really like tea, but he never complained and drank what was available. "Am I the type of girl a gentleman would want to take to meet his family?"

Novak choked on his tea. He rapped on his chest as he coughed. "Remind me to…*cough*…add surprising…*cough*…to your list of attributes."

Emerald laughed joyously at Novak's reaction.

"What's so funny?" a hungry soldier asked as he wandered over for some food.

"Emerald thinks I look funny." Novak said with a deadpan expression.

"Well, I have eyes!" Emerald hit Novak lightly on the arm.

"She said my eyes bulge like a bull frog's."

"They just made me think of the story of the princess and the frog, that's all," said Emerald.

Novak was having fun with this, a girl who could tease as well as he could.

The soldier laughed at the exchange. Emerald served him up some stew.

"I think I walked in at the wrong time." The soldier grinned sheepishly.

Emerald retrieved a kettle from the fire. "Do you want some?…" Emerald was cut off.

"Novak! Novak!

Novak looked up from his last sip of tea. A sentry led a horse with a man draped over the saddle toward him. "What is it? What happened?" Novak rushed to meet the sentry.

"This horse trotted up the trail to our perimeter carrying this man who appears to be badly beaten," the sentry reported. "He's wearing the surcoat of a Royal Guardsman and nothing else."

Novak recognized Scorpyus's horse. The frail man was definitely someone else. "Here, help me get him down."

Novak and the sentry untied the man and lowered him gently to the ground.

"Go have Emerald bring some water and fresh bandages. I'll remove these old ones." Novak watched the sentry hurry off.

The wounded Bartus was weak from hanging over the horse all night. He had a pounding headache and strained to open his swollen eyes. "You have to help Scorpyus."

Novak did a double take. "Bartus? What happened? Who did this to you? I didn't even recognize you."

"Reddland's men tortured me for information about the rebels, but I didn't say anything. Somehow, Scorpyus appeared on the scene and freed me, saved my life, but he didn't make it out of the compound with me. He was trapped after his horse went down. You have to help him." Bartus gave Novak a brief rundown of what transpired.

Emerald hurried over with water and bandages. "Uncle Bartus! What happened?" Emerald froze and stared in horror at the pulverized flesh on her uncle's back.

Novak stood and placed his hands on Emerald's shoulders. "Listen, I have to go. Reddland has Scorpyus trapped. I'm going to get Cad and Zephyr, and then we're getting Scorpyus out of Reddland's compound. I'll meet you at the oratory. Have Cyrus carry on as planned. I'll be back as soon as this is taken care of."

Novak strapped on his sword and retrieved his buckler and helmet. He paused to turn to Emerald. "Take care until I get back." Novak left in a rush to help his friend. A sentry had his horse ready.

"Novak," Emerald called and waited for him to turn. "Be careful yourself. Come back." Emerald couldn't bring herself to say more. She knew the extreme danger Novak would be in going to Reddland's compound.

Novak looked into Emerald's worried eyes. She was going through a lot with the rebels about to fight a war and her uncle beaten to a pulp. And now he was riding into the heart of the enemy stronghold to help Scorpyus.

Emerald walked up to Novak. Her eyes welled with tears and her bottom lip quivered. Novak felt terrible that Emerald was going to worry about him on top of everything else she had to deal with.

"Hey, don't worry; I'll be back before you know it." Novak managed a half smile. Oh how he so desperately wanted to give

Emerald a comforting hug but couldn't. This was the reason why he had always been so wary of these types of situations.

Emerald bravely bit her lip and stayed strong.

"I'll be back. You can't get rid of me this easy." Novak gave Emerald a nod then swung onto his waiting horse. He had a lot on his mind when he left the camp. He gave Emerald one last look then spurred his horse on down the trail as fast as it would go. Emerald watched him disappear into the forest.

"It looks like you'll be the first customer in our new hospital." Cad informed Zephyr of her dubious honor. "It's too bad your horse didn't make it. But the important thing is you did."

Zephyr grimaced as Doc sewed up the slash on her forearm. She had traveled most of the night to reach the oratory after surviving the attack of the panther. Her horse brought her most of the way, but after a valiant struggle it succumbed to its wounds short of their destination. Zephyr walked the last mile on foot. She relayed her amazing story to Cad piecemeal, pausing every time Doc pushed his fishhook shaped needle through her flesh.

Cad shook his head in amazement. The story, coming from almost anyone else, would have been dismissed as lunacy; not that he didn't believe someone could survive an attack from a panther; it was the unicorn part that was hard to swallow. But if Zephyr said she saw one, then Cad believed she thought she did. The vial of blue fluid lent some credence to the tale while at the same time adding an air of mystery.

"That's a blooming incredible story, Zephyr. I don't know what to say. I wish I could have seen it too. And the inscription in Hester's book, what do you say to something like that?" Cad threw his hands up in resignation.

"As amazing as the story sounds, the panther was real." Doc paused from his work and told Zephyr and Cad. "And I can tell you you're very lucky your arm isn't worse. Your wound is just down to the muscle. You're lucky the cat was after your horse and not you, or you would have more than superficial slashes."

"Oui. I think the cat caught my forearm accidentally on its way to my horse's neck. I do not think it saw me until later."

"You very well got lucky. Someone is watching out for you." Cad added.

"I noticed you did not comment on the unicorn, Doc." Zephyr said.

The doctor thought a moment. "Well, you don't have a fever so I assume you're not delusional. I've been around long enough now to have heard of many strange occurrences. And the legend of the unicorn has been around for years. Others have seen it also. You never know. Anything is possible, with the grace of our Lord."

She decided to change the subject. "Any word from Scorpyus or Novak?"

"Nothing from Novak; he's still at Scarborough Field. He sent Doc our way to start setting up a hospital. Scorpyus checked in yesterday with a report on Iris. And as you can see I've made a lot of progress around here. In fact we're ahead of schedule. I have a talented group of blokes to work with." Cad briefed Zephyr.

"What did Scorpyus say about Iris?" Zephyr inquired. Doc paused from bandaging Zephyr's arm to hear the report.

"Well, he found no evidence of Iris betraying the rebellion. From what Scorpyus could find out by watching her and going through some of her personal papers, it appears that revenge is her motivation. She is angry at being passed over for appointment to a priestess position in the Tanuba temple. She is getting back at the ruling clerics by helping the rebellion. Either way, we're not going to let her in on our plans. We can't be too careful," Cad replied.

"That sounds like a good idea. Let her seek us out after the battle starts if she truly wants to oppose her own." Zephyr agreed with Cad's decision to keep Iris in the dark.

"Exactly. And now Scorpyus is at Reddland's compound to dig up what he can." Cad watched Doc finish bandaging Zephyr's arm.

"I do not know how Scorpyus can stand the stress of all that subterfuge. I know he is good at it but, it seems kind of crazy to want to do it, no?" Zephyr wondered out loud what made a person become a spy.

"A lot of blokes think the same about all of us. Why do we do what we do? Surely there are easier and safer ways to earn a living?" Cad asked.

"I guess you are right." Zephyr stretched her arm to test Doc's handiwork.

"It's not crazy to use your talents to right some of the wrongs in the world. It's honorable. Look at Xylor. Not even five hundred of us are willing to lend a hand with this upcoming confrontation, and yet I know there are thousands who would like to see true peace and freedom come to the island. Take pride in yourselves, especially your friend. It is always the few doing the work that benefits the many," Doc remarked sagely while cleaning up his supplies.

The door to the hospital suddenly swung open with such force that it slammed into the wall. The raid-like entrance startled Cad, Zephyr and Doc. Novak and Thadus strode in with great urgency.

"What's wrong?" Cad could tell by the expression on Novak's face there was an emergency.

"Saddle up. Scorpyus is in trouble." Novak dripped sweat from riding hard all the way to town.

Zephyr hopped off the examination table, alarm on her face. "What happened?"

"Bartus rode into camp at daybreak, badly beaten and tied across Scorpyus's horse. Things went bad for Scorpyus at Reddland's compound. He found and managed to free Bartus, but the archers shot his horse out from under him when the two were making their escape. Bartus made it out, but Scorpyus was trapped in the compound with the Royal Guard swarming everywhere. He's still there as far as I know." Novak recounted the highlights of the story as fast as he could.

"Let's get going." Cad grabbed his gear. "Do we know his status?"

"No. Let's hope he was able to hide, but the compound is so heavily guarded he'll need help in order to escape, if we're not too late." Novak expressed everyone's worst fears.

"Fresh horses are waiting. I had the men get some ready when Novak showed up," Thadus informed the group as they headed for the door.

Zephyr's face creased with worry. "I am sure he found a place to hide," She said, trying to convince herself more than inform the others.

"Do you want to take any other men with you?" Thadus inquired.

"No, we'll handle it. We work better as a small team. Besides, you have to take over here just in case." Cad wasn't too reassuring.

The group ran across the oratory grounds. They swung into the saddles and headed for Reddland's compound. Though they didn't have a plan yet, they all knew they had to get there, evaluate the situation, and get Scorpyus out any way they could.

"Stay focused, Novak." Cad could see Novak was tense, was starting to contemplate the possibilities, possibilities that could cause a flash of rage in his friend.

"Oh, I'm focused all right, right on the first fool that tries to stop us from getting Scorpyus out of there. By the way, Bartus said Scorpyus found some information about our fathers," Novak announced.

Cad and Zephyr looked at each other. "Did Bartus say what?" Zephyr asked, her imagination running wild. So much had happened on this trip that it left her head spinning.

"No; we'll have to get to Scorpyus to find out," Novak replied.

The three rode, each praying for another miracle in a string of miracles, each torn between their confidence in Scorpyus's abilities and their fears of the harsh realities of the Royal Guards' sheer numbers. The next hour would be pivotal in their lives. They prayed to God it wasn't too late.

They reached Reddland's compound. Keeping out of range of the archers, they circled the perimeter. The compound jumped with activity, and the parapets crawled with guards. Sentries saw the riders in the distance. They were too far away to be readily identified, but just the same they were being watched as a precaution.

"Let's not make any sudden moves. Just act like we belong here and are in no hurry. We're just a few chaps passing by." Cad spoke softly while surreptitiously scanning the parapets. A commotion caught his eye.

"There he is!" Cad was careful not to point.

"This is lucky. At least we do not have to find him, and he is still alive." Zephyr watched Scorpyus run north along the parapet of the west wall, forty feet above the ground. He wore part of a Royal Guard uniform, but there was no mistaking their friend. "He is limping," she added. Four armed Elite Guards were in pursuit with swords drawn. Scorpyus had a good lead on his pursuers but it was vanishing quickly.

"We've got to help him somehow." Novak carefully evaluated their options. There weren't many to choose from. "Let's go. If we can get a rope up to him, he can get off the wall. It's the only thing we can do with all the gates locked down. Scorpyus will be down the rope before they can get the gates open and the men out to face us." Novak pulled a rope from his saddlebag.

"Sounds good; if we can get ahead of him we can have the rope in place by the time he needs it," Cad added. "Scorpyus has no choice but to turn and run east along the north wall. Let's get the bloody rope in place in the middle of the north wall somewhere."

Zephyr nodded approval. "Let's hurry, though. It looks like he is almost ready to turn onto the north wall now."

They spurred their horses to a full run. There was no time to waste. The Elite Guardsmen had closed the gap and were now only seventy-five feet behind Scorpyus. They managed to cut the gap in half in the last ten to fifteen seconds. All attention was on Scorpyus. So much so that Cad and the other's movements went unnoticed.

Scorpyus rounded the corner where the west and north walls met. He gave a quick glance back at his attackers as he took the corner. Six more soldiers were now on the parapet, running to join their comrades. Scorpyus climbed up from the parapet to the outer edge of the north wall, and pulled his sword. That's when he saw his friends on horseback and he quickly formulated a plan. It was a gamble, but the odds looked better now. His friends would provide a distraction that would help him to make his escape. And it was just in time. He was near exhaustion from playing this cat-and-mouse game with the Royal guard.

"What's he doing?" Cad wondered. "Is he going to take a stand against the soldiers there?"

"If Scorpyus did it, he must have a reason. He would not climb up off the parapet unless he had to." Zephyr was worried. The move made little sense to her.

Novak was equally dumbfounded by the move. "I don't know. Let's keep going. Maybe a soldier is coming up through a trapdoor or something."

They whipped their horses on; frantic, knowing something was happening on that wall. Not knowing what filled them with anxiety.

"Oh my God! Scorpyus fell off the wall!" Zephyr's voice broke with emotion.

"What!" Cad yelled. "How?"

Scorpyus was no longer on the wall. Zephyr was right. A sense of dread swept them. The wall was forty feet high! Would a fall from that height be survivable?

"Come on! Faster!" Novak yelled through gritted teeth as he spurred his horse on.

The three rounded the corner only to find a peasant's rickety hay wagon moving along the north wall. Scorpyus was not in sight. They slowed their horses to a walk.

They found him. He lay twisted on the ground, his face covered in blood; his arms sprawled out, his sword just out of reach. Blood oozed slowly from a wound on his thigh, and there was blood in his ears, nostrils, and mouth.

Novak dismounted and felt for a pulse. He turned to look at the others with a grim look on his face and shook his head.

"No, no, this can not be happening! He is only twenty-seven" Zephyr dismounted and ran to Scorpyus, tears rolling down her cheeks. She reached a trembling hand to touch his head. His hair was wet and sticky. She jerked back her hand as if a snake had bitten her and sobbed, staring at her bloody fingers. "No, God, no! No, no, this did not happen!" Zephyr looked for an escape that wasn't to be found. Scorpyus Verazzno was gone.

Cad's throat tightened as he choked back emotion. He clenched his teeth and rubbed his mouth as though trying to massage feeling back into his lips. He didn't want to lose control at this time as the nightmare unfolded.

Guards arrived on the wall above where the three stood near their fallen comrade. They shouted that they had "gotten him," and someone gave the order to "get the other three."

The trio had been discovered and there would be no time to grieve. One of the guards looked down on the tragedy from the wall and cackled happily finding humor in the death of the intruder. He shouted taunts at the trio about how they were next. Little did they know but Drex especially enjoyed taunting the trio after the humiliation he suffered after being captured by Scorpyus. He had been discovered and freed in the middle of the night, and laughed joyously at seeing Scorpyus pay for what he did.

Novak erupted. "Reddland! Do you here me? You're going to die, do you hear!" Drex stopped laughing as a bolt of fear shot through his body.

Cad knew he would have to be the one to keep it together. Novak was in a rage, and Zephyr was too emotional. It was only a matter of time before the soldiers arrived. "We have to bloody well get going. Soldiers are on their way, a lot of them I'm sure."

"They have a fight coming and I intend to give them one." Novak drew his sword and waited.

"Novak, we have to get moving! They outnumber us heavily!" Cad grabbed Novak's arm.

"They're going to pay first!" Novak roared and jerked free of Cad.

"I'm not going to let you do this!"

"I said I'm staying!"

"Are you daft? Committing suicide won't bring Scorpyus back! They outnumber us a hundred to one, more actually." Guards streamed from the east gate and one was prepared to rappel down the wall. It was Drex.

Novak turned from Cad and eyed the soldier coming down the wall.

Cad grabbed Novak. "Listen! Do you want to honor Scorpyus? Then live to fight another day; a day when we can win." Cad started forcing Novak to his horse. "Don't be a fool! Look to the east. They'll be here soon!"

Novak saw them coming and didn't care. And he wasn't about to be forced to his horse like he was a child. Not even by Cad. Cad twisted Novak's arm forcing him to his horse, but Novak broke free.

"I said no!" Novak dealt a blow to Cad's chin knocking him to the ground.

"Novak, you're being a fool!" Cad turned to Zephyr who still knelt by Scorpyus's corpse and said, "Get on your horse, we have to go."

"Ok, but we cannot just leave Scorpyus here like this. Help me put him on a horse." Zephyr grabbed Scorpyus by the wrist and started dragging his body to his horse. His arm was cold, limp, and lifeless, his olive complexion now ashen.

"There's no time!" Cad grabbed Zephyr by the shoulders and shook her, forcing her to let go of Scorpyus. "Look, Zephyr, time is running out. There are forty to fifty men coming right now." Cad pointed to the soldiers who were on the way. Whoever carried Scorpyus's body would never escape. It would be too much weight for one horse, a horse that would need to be able to run long and hard.

When Zephyr saw the soldiers she came to her senses and mounted her horse. She was still crying. "I cannot believe we are not even going to be able to bury him."

The thought of leaving Scorpyus hurt Cad too, but he knew his friend was in a better place. His corpse was now an empty shell. Staying longer would only sacrifice three more lives.

Novak was already battling the guard who had rappelled down the wall. Driven by anguish, Novak brought his sword down again and again on the soldier with everything he had. All Drex could do was cower against the wall and hide behind his full shield. Cad had never seen Novak wield his sword with that much force before. Novak had snapped.

"I'll smash through your shield if I have to!" Novak roared and pummeled the cowering Drex.

Novak paused, dripping with sweat. Drex could no longer hold up his shield, his arm broken and twisted from the last blow, still entangled with the distorted metal that was once a shield. Drex trembled with fear, holding his twisted left arm.

Before Novak dealt the final blow, Cad rode up and handed Novak the reigns to his horse. "It's now or never. You have about five seconds left."

Novak glanced to the approaching soldiers then let out a powerful yell. "Ahhhhh!" He swung his sword with one last ferocious blow. Drex's head toppled to the ground.

In a flash he mounted his horse and the trio was off with the Royal Guards close enough to almost strike Novak with a sword.

"Follow me to the forest. We'll try to lose them there," Cad instructed the others and they all turned their horses for the woods.

Cad questioned Zephyr. "Can you lead us through the forest?"

Zephyr wiped away some tears and nodded. She was the fastest of them all at navigating the woods. The others could do it if they had to but not as fast as Zephyr. Right now they needed every advantage they could get.

"Oui," Zephyr sniffed. She moved to the lead and the others moved in behind, single file. Cad made sure he was bringing up the rear. They entered the woods at a full gallop, with the Royal soldiers close behind.

XII

EMERALD PACED NERVOUSLY in the oratory's main auditorium. Novak and his friends had been gone now for quite some time, nearly six hours. Soon it would be dark. She feared the worst. Rescuing Scorpyus would be difficult at best. At worst, she didn't even want to think about it. All around her rebel soldiers bustled with activity, and yet nothing could distract her from her morose mood.

Shortly after Novak left with Cad and Zephyr, rebel troops began to arrive from Scarborough Field. Cyrus ensured the movement of troops was a slow trickle so as not to arouse suspicion. The first waves brought much-needed supplies. Each man carried his own weapons as well as additional arrows and food. Thadus and Abrams directed the distribution of supplies. The kitchen was being organized for the preparation of an evening meal. The logistics of feeding five-hundred-plus people was formidable. A dozen or so women, wives or sisters of some of the rebel soldiers, came from town to assist. Abrams was thrilled to see more people come forward to take a stand and help with the rebellion. Now was not the time to be a fence sitter.

Emerald watched the latest arrivals as they went to work barricading the shutters, preparing the oratory in case the rebels were pushed back from the courtyard walls. Doc reported he had a functional hospital in an upstairs conference room. Everything seemed to be going smoothly so far, but that was of little consolation to Emerald.

"They should be here soon." Thadus knew his daughter was worried and gave her a consoling hug.

"I hope so. I pray this whole thing will be over soon." Emerald rested her head on her father's shoulder. "It's been so long since we've had peace in Xylor; I can hardly remember a time without strife."

Thadus nodded, stroking his daughter's golden locks. "It's been ten long years. You were just fifteen when the war started. I don't blame you for wanting to start having a normal life. We all do."

Emerald smiled. "Wouldn't that be wonderful? I feel like I've missed so much because of the war and Reddland's terror. Oh how I would like to settle into a normal life, one without all the fear, death, and uncertainty."

Thadus wished for the same thing, but often wondered if it would ever really be possible. He knew that even if the rebels succeeded in overthrowing Reddland, there was bound to be repercussions from Kelterland, that the battle could in fact go on for years, and that a lasting, solid peace would come if only the whole land could be reclaimed and rid of Kelterland's influence also.

"Would you, by any chance, fancy this Novak as playing a part in that?"

Emerald's eyes widened with surprise and her head jerked up to look at her father. He placed his hands on her shoulders. "Am I that transparent, Father?"

Thadus laughed and nodded his head several times. "It's pretty obvious you're smitten with the man, dear."

Emerald's cheeks flushed, "Have I been so obvious that Novak knows?"

"I would say yes, unless he's a fool."

Now Emerald was beet red. "Oh, my! How do…what do…do you think I've scared him off?"

Thadus smiled reassuringly. "Oh no, dear, the feeling looks to be mutual." Thadus watched his daughter radiate joyously at that proclamation.

"Do you really think so, Father? I think about him all the time, ever since we first met at Larek's stables. I'm not saying this is…well you know…but I haven't felt like this for a long time. It's just that it would be nice to let things progress, and that's why I'm so worried; if something happened to him before we had a chance to…before I found out…" Emerald was rambling excitedly.

"Calm down, dear," Thadus chuckled. Where did the time go? It seemed only yesterday Emerald was a little girl.

Emerald laughed at the realization. "You're right. I guess I'm going on a bit. Well, now that I've said that, what do you think?"

Thadus answered after a long thoughtful pause. "First, let me say I think Novak is a man of integrity, of character, and a man who is willing to fight for what is right. Most importantly he is a loyal follower of God. But he is a Clandestine Knight. While what he does is very honorable, and Lord knows we need more people like him, his career is hard on a family. Being a soldier's wife is not an easy task for those who undertake it."

Emerald was reflective. She had thought about that already. "I know, father. I just pray I'll have the time to find out for sure, and pray to have the wisdom to know if it's the right thing."

"Well, if it's meant to be, everything will work out," Thadus reassured his daughter. "Let's take things one day at a time."

Emerald gave her father a hug.

Scarcely had Emerald the time to enjoy the moment before a soldier burst through the door and ran to her father.

"Riders approach! It looks like the newcomers." The soldier breathed heavily.

Thadus ran from the oratory with Emerald on his heels. The main gates were opening to let in three galloping riders. Although it was almost dark, Thadus could make out Cad, Novak, and Zephyr as they entered the grounds.

The three rode to the large stone steps of the oratory and dismounted. Novak's horse hadn't even come to a complete stop when he dismounted and started taking steps two at a time. Thadus and Emerald waited at the top of the stairs. Novak bounded up with Cad close behind. Zephyr lingered and brought up the rear hoping no one would notice her, the tears in her eyes. Thadus motioned for a nearby soldier to tend to the horses.

A curious soldier went up to Novak as he hit the top of the stairs. "What happened?"

"Not right now." Novak scowled.

The soldier was persistent and stepped into Novak's path. "No, seriously, how'd it go? Is your friend alright?"

The muscles in Novak's jaw tightened. Without breaking his stride, Novak placed his hand on the soldier's chest and shoved hard. The soldier lurched backward and fell, landing on his hind side with a thud. "I said, not right now!"

Much to Emerald's anguish, Novak continued past her without a word or even a look. He disappeared into the oratory. Emerald started to run after him but was stopped by Thadus's grasp on her arm. Emerald turned to face her father, her eyes welling with tears

"Give him some time alone, honey," Thadus advised.

The soldier Novak shoved was fired with rage. He sprang to his feet and started after him. Before he could get far a hand grabbed his shoulder. The soldier spun around in anger.

Cad gave the soldier a look of warning. "Take my advice, mate, and let it go. He's not himself right now, and it's not worth risking your life." Cad was firm in his tone. The soldier hesitated a moment, and then acceded to Cad's suggestion.

Zephyr entered the door unnoticed.

Cad was left alone to explain to Thadus and the others what happened. He didn't feel like staying around either, but someone had to hold it all together. And once again the task fell to him. He didn't know where to begin. He had to think fast.

He asked, "Who did Novak pick to be officer in charge of sentries and support?"

Cyrus stepped forward. "I guess that would be me. My name's Cyrus."

"Cyrus, glad to meet you, I'm Cad." Cad shook hands. "You need to finish placing the sentries and find positions for the catapults. Then have the cavalry gather by the stables, the infantry by the greenhouse, and the archers inside the main auditorium. I'm sorry, I'm not more organized right now but some unexpected things have come up. I'd appreciate it if you could help us with those things. Tell the troops either I or Novak or Zephyr will be by to brief them as soon as possible." Cad wasted no time in getting things moving.

"Consider it done." Cyrus turned to the soldiers who had gathered in front of the steps. "You men, come with me."

Cad watched Cyrus and the troops hurry off to carry out his orders. It was reassuring to see that Novak picked a disciplined professional to help lead the troops. At least there was some good news.

"Is there anything you need me to do?" Thadus had been waiting patiently.

Cad removed his helmet and wiped his brow. His hair was dripping wet. "No, not right now. I'll get with you and Abrams later, hopefully with Novak and Zephyr. We'll go over battle plans. Right now I've got a few things that need to be done, a few surprises for Reddland's troops."

"Do what you have to. Emerald and I will check on Bartus and help Doc with the hospital. If you need us, that's where we'll be." Thadus asked the inevitable: "The rescue failed, I assume?"

Cad shook his head and rubbed his temple. "Yes. We would have been here sooner, but it took us four hours to lose the Royal Guard in the woods. Scorpyus is dead, in case you couldn't figure it out…and, well…." Cad's voice trailed off at the end of his report. He saw tears gleam in Emerald's eyes. "Now would be a good time for prayer. That's what we're going to need the most of," he added

Thadus nodded in agreement.

A memory flashed through Cad's mind—he saw a drop of blood on the rickety cart near where Scorpyus lay dead. How odd. Why would he remember something like that out of the blue? Before he could dwell on it further a soldier walked up wanting instructions. For now Cad would have to do the work of all the Clandestine Knights.

—•◦•—

Novak sullenly plodded his way to the perimeter wall through a light rain. It was a dark night, overcast, with no moon. It looked like the clouds were trying to decide whether they should rain or drift away in the slight breeze. At any rate it would rinse some of the dust off Novak's armor.

Elijah, sentry on the parapet, was cold. At seventy-three he was the oldest member of the rebel forces. His thin, frail frame rattled in the night chill, and this drizzle wasn't going to help. He bundled up against the night, pulling his tattered cloak around tight, but his old circulation wasn't what it once was. He squinted into the darkness trying desperately to see like a twenty-five-year-old again. A short sword looked out of place hanging awkwardly from his bony hip. Cyrus had placed him in the least likely point of attack.

Novak was walking along the parapet when he noticed Elijah. Here was an old man doing his part while people half his age were sitting it out. It goes to show that character doesn't wither with age, if anything it matures, ripens. And it does no good to be young and able-bodied if you don't have the fortitude to go with it. It was a sad testimony for those who were young and wanted the end of Reddland's reign of terror, but were hiding under tables somewhere instead of standing up like men.

Novak could tell the sentry needed a break.

"Hey, how are you doing?" Novak startled the man.

"Oh, as well as can be expected, all things considered." The sentry smiled and massaged his knuckles.

"Why don't you go rest a while? Get something hot to drink and thaw out by the fire. I'll take your post for an hour or so." The night air felt good to Novak. He felt bad for the sentry. If the man was feeling chilly already, what would the poor fellow do in the early morning hours when it was really cold?

The sentry wiped rain from his face. "Are you sure?"

"Ya, go ahead. And besides, I kind of want to be alone for a while anyway." Novak motioned for the man to go on.

"Yes, sir. I'll be back in an hour." The sentry smiled broadly revealing worn and crooked teeth. He didn't wait around for Novak to change his mind.

"Don't hurry. Hey, and one more thing," Novak waited for the man to turn around. "Have Thadus get you a blanket or cloak or something before you come back out. Tell him I said so." Novak nodded for the sentry to carry on.

"Thank you again." The aged sentry headed for rest, both grateful for the break and impressed that one of the commanding officers would undertake guard duty in place of one of his men.

Heavyhearted, Novak stared out over the parapet wall. The random patter of rain hitting his helmet, the ground, wall, and vegetation added a certain spookiness to the air. The night was otherwise quiet. Novak scanned the vast darkness in search of evidence of an enemy attack. Each drop of rain hitting a leaf out in the blackness had the potential of being an enemy probe.

As Novak stood watch his mind raced. The shock of Scorpyus's death was starting to set in, and he could barely face it. He knew the others were going through the same thing. The reality of it all seeped in slowly; Novak would never see his friend again. Images of his father's corpse hanging from a tree and Scorpyus's pale and lifeless body intertwined.

Novak covered his eyes and shook his head. He stifled a sob and looked around quickly. Thank God nobody was anywhere near. He sat on an empty crate and peered into the night. The crate was just tall enough so he could rest his chin on his hands and still see out over the parapet wall. After one more look around he felt confident enough to release his emotions undetected. The light rain would provide a measure of disguise.

Tears cascaded down Novak's face and mixed with the streaking raindrops. A wave of sorrow escaped Novak as his chest heaved repeatedly, straining the leather straps of his cuirass. He was careful not to make a sound.

Novak thought of the first time he met Scorpyus when they were both teens. Novak had been walking by a butcher shop and noticed a commotion. Two grizzled men, both portly and stout, were arguing with Scorpyus. At the time Scorpyus was gaunt from lack of food. The war caused shortages and he hadn't been eating regularly. Few people had. The two portly men were rare exceptions.

"You said you would give me a ham if I cleaned out your pig sties. That was our deal; my choice of ham for a full day's work. I did my part and now I want my ham," the young Scorpyus demanded.

The portly men laughed so hard their bellies jiggled. "I know what I said, you ignorant half-breed, but the deal's off!" One of the men bellowed.

"Not after I already did the work, it's not!" Scorpyus started for the hams to take one, but one of the men pushed him back away from the open smokehouse door.

"You better hightail it out of here before we give you a good beating." One man waved a fist at the scrawny kid. His bad breath stung Scorpyus's nose.

"Yeah, what's the matter? You thieving Gypsies don't like being taken at your own game?" The other man chimed in.

"I'm not leaving without a ham," Scorpyus stated bluntly.

One of the men jabbed a finger into the boy's chest. "Unless you think you can whip us, those hams are staying in the smokehouse." The two portly men were very brave as they faced the thin, teenaged Scorpyus.

Scorpyus didn't even flinch. "I've been shoveling manure all day. I guess shoveling two more big fat piles won't hurt me."

It took a while for the portly men to process the insult. Then their faces turned a salmon color. Neither of them noticed Novak eavesdropping throughout the whole exchange.

"Why you little…" Scorpyus ducked and dodged a barrage of blows with the swiftness of a jackrabbit. One of the men slammed his fist into the smokehouse when a punch aimed at the youth missed. Angry that Scorpyus sidestepped his punch, the man cursed again and held his hand in agony.

In a flash Scorpyus was in and out of the smokehouse and running down the road with a sizeable ham. Both men lumbered along after him. Like a gazelle, Scorpyus went up and over the corral fence. He paused when he saw Novak. At fifteen, Novak was already six feet tall and a shade under two hundred pounds. Scorpyus squared off not knowing if Novak was friend or foe.

"I saw everything. I'm with you." Novak joined in the fracas. Even back then he was always ready for a fight, especially if it was for an underdog. Scorpyus smiled and nodded.

The two fat men squeezed between the corral fence rails in the time it took for the two youths to decide if they were friends. Scorpyus turned to face the first man. He dodged blow after blow, letting his overweight adversary tire himself out. The man was slow and threw roundhouses, which made the task rather easy.

Novak didn't have the speed of Scorpyus, but didn't need it. All he usually had to do was connect with one punch. After taking a blow, which brought a slight trickle of blood from his left cheek, Novak connected. The well-muscled arm that had reshaped its share of metal, reshaped the second man's nose farther to the right.

The second man bellowed in pain as he fell to the ground. Novak waited, ready for him to get back up.

It didn't take long for the first man to grow winded. He was snorting like a racehorse and sucking air heavily into his lungs. Scorpyus continued to dance around the gasping man. The fat man knew he was in trouble. His arms were heavy and hard to raise, and he had to hunch forward in order to breathe. Scorpyus kicked the man's leg out from under him and he crashed to the ground. He lay there panting, saliva foaming at the corners of his mouth.

The second man looked through watery eyes to see the blurry image of his friend sprawled on the dirt. He also saw Novak waiting to knock him down again.

"Get up! Come on, get up!" Novak waived a fist at the second man.

The second man decided he needed help. "Paulo! Paulo!"

Several men with blood-stained white aprons ran from the butcher shop. On the other side of the corral fence they saw one of their friends sprawled on his back and the other seated fondling his bloody nose. A gangly youth and a mountain of muscle stood over them.

"Paulo! They're robbing us!" The second man yelled while cupping his hands to his broken nose.

The men in white aprons raced for the fence. As the first one scaled the top he was met simultaneously with a right hook from Novak and an eighteen-pound ham to the forehead by Scorpyus. The man's head snapped back. He dropped straight down and didn't get up. The rest of the men decided to spread out along the fence and cautiously scale it while yet more men came from the butcher shop wielding cleavers and knives. They had been in the process of butchering swine, but now came to see what all the fuss was about.

Novak had just made short work of another man when he felt a tap on his shoulder. He looked to see Scorpyus with a concerned look on his face.

"Hey, they're surrounding us and they have knives." Scorpyus pointed to the men coming on both flanks. "We have to get out of here. Follow me!"

Scorpyus led Novak down alleys and side streets, across fields and fences, zigzagging their way across town until they lost the pursuing men. They eventually came to the run-down farmhouse in need of paint that Scorpyus called home. A large garden was planted to one side. Most of the fence had been torn down, and a lot of the yard was burned and charred. The place looked like it had been recently vandalized and a large fire started out front. A young, raven-haired girl who was visibly relieved to see Scorpyus came from the house.

Scorpyus introduced Novak to his seventeen-year-old sister, Isabella, a demure and beautiful girl.

"Hey, Izzy, you don't mind if…" Scorpyus paused and turned to Novak. "I just realized I don't even know your name."

"I'm Novak." Novak courteously held out a hand.

Scorpyus shook hands. "I'm Scorpyus, and this is my sister, Isabella."

Scorpyus turned back to his sister. "You don't mind if Novak stays for dinner do you? He helped me out of a situation today." Scorpyus never told Isabella of any danger he faced, or of any even remotely unsettling activity he became involved in. He knew Isabella couldn't take hearing about the risks, not since the death of their grandma. Her worst nightmare was losing Scorpyus, the last of her family.

"Sure, he's welcome to stay for dinner if he doesn't mind eating tomatoes and ham." Isabella went on to apologize for the lack of choice for dinner. She explained that tomatoes were all that was ripe from her garden.

Novak accepted the invitation, and the three talked well into the night. They all had a lot in common. They were surprised to find out their grandma's son and Novak's father served together in the Ravenshire Knights. It became the start of a strong friendship.

Scorpyus's speed and agility went well with Novak's tremendous strength. The two complemented each other quite well and decided to form a team. At the time it was to aid in their mutual survival. By their early twenties, and with the addition of Cad and Zephyr, the team had grown into the Clandestine Knights. Forming a partnership was natural. Both held the same ideals and values.

It had been a long adventure since then, but now it was over. What was Novak going to tell Isabella? Scorpyus's death would devastate her. Now she would be alone.

"How are you doing?" Emerald's question startled Novak. He hadn't heard her walk up to his post. He took a couple of seconds before turning to greet her.

"Hi…uh, how long have you been there?" Novak panicked at the thought of appearing weak before a woman, especially Emerald.

"I just got here. I didn't interrupt anything did I?"

"No, no, have a seat." Novak stood and let her take his seat on the crate. "So what brings you out here in the cold damp night?"

"I just wanted to see how you were doing." Emerald looked shyly away. Novak could scarcely see her face in the depths of her hooded cloak. She also had her hands pulled into her sleeves for warmth. Had she worn a black cloak rather than the turquoise one she had on, she may have passed for the grim reaper.

"Why don't you pull your hood back so I can see who I'm talking to?" Novak maneuvered to try to see under the hood.

Emerald slid the hood back so her face peeked out, but not too far because she didn't want her hair to get wet in the drizzle. "There, is that better?"

Novak nodded. Emerald was a beautiful woman; her soft features a pleasant beacon in an otherwise dreary night.

"So, how are you doing? Is there anything I can do?" Emerald reiterated her question.

Novak sighed deeply. "I'll be fine, all things considered. Since we have a job to do still, I'll have to carry on. Which reminds me, Cad was sort of left holding the bag. How's he doing?"

Emerald shrugged her shoulders. "He's building all kinds of things, getting stuff ready; it all seems to be progressing rapidly."

"That's good. Cad comes up with these new ideas, unconventional ones no one can predict. Reddland is in for a few surprises." Novak paused to reflect. "Too bad Scorp won't be here to see it. Then again, he's probably up there looking down and glad to be missing it all. Who knows, we may all be joining him shortly."

"The two of you must have been quite close."

Novak nodded. "We're all very close, closer than brothers and sister. When you go through a lot with someone you develop a bond. Scorp and I were especially close."

A curious look graced Emerald's countenance and prompted Novak to continue. He smiled coyly. "I'm not saying I'm exactly proud of this, but…ah…on occasion I've gotten into a few sticky situations, like when I was a prisoner on that ship. When the others bailed me out, it was usually Scorpyus who handled the task. Sometimes I wonder if my confidence in the others has kept me from restraining myself once or twice when I know I could have. Anyway, Scorp was good. Don't get me wrong, though, I make no apologies for the last time. I'd take that stand again."

Emerald took it all in. "I know what you mean. Going through ordeals can bring people together. That's how we feel about Isaac."

"And you know when it ends…" Novak stiffened up and swallowed hard, then shook his head in disbelief. "It wasn't even two weeks ago we were all together at my sister Krysta's wedding. What a great time we had. We had to have it secretly since the ceremony is against the law, as is anything to do with God. The temple of Balar, Ravenshire's brand of Tanuba worship, does not authorize it. You have the mermaid, whereas we have a serpent. Be it statues, jewelry, artwork, or pottery, back home snakes are everywhere. Anyway; we had the wedding on our island…"

"You have an island?" Emerald interrupted.

Novak held up a hand. "It's not my island. We live near a town on a mountain lake. In the lake, towards the center, are two small islands; remember, I told you about them earlier. The serpent people believe evil spirits haunt the islands, so they stay away. Fishing boats steer clear of them. So, they became a natural refuge for us. Since we were being forced from our land we needed to find a place to go. The islands were the logical choice. We call the place Ravensclaw. Anyway, we had the ceremony there, right where we live." Novak reminisced. "It was a good time, Scorpyus always the jokester, Cad with his sarcastic remarks, and Zephyr pretending to be shocked by it all, with all of our families present."

Emerald smiled. "It sounds like you had a lot of fun. You can't always be off on one of your adventures I guess."

There was a long pause in the conversation when the two just looked at each other. Emerald broke the silence: "If I remember correctly, the last time we talked you said you had four sisters."

"Ya, the oldest is Krysta. She's the one that just got married. Janek is next; she was murdered five years ago trying to save her child from being sacrificed to the serpent cult. Her widower husband is still with us. Kara is next; she and her husband grow a lot of the food we eat on the island. Ingrid's the next in line; she's the spunky one. Cad's been courting her for the past six months. We'll see where it goes; I've already warned her about the life of a soldier's wife. It's not for all women. And then there's me, the youngest of the Reinhardt clan. All four of us have our families on the island. Our little adventures fund the bulk of the island's expenses." Novak spoke about personal matters more with Emerald than he had with anyone else for a long time. "What about your family?" He decided to ask the questions for a while.

Emerald looked briefly skyward. "It's been me and my dad for as long as I can remember. My mother died giving birth to my sister when I was four. My sister died a few days later. I grew up with my cousins, Uncle Bartus' kids. But now Uncle Bartus is all that's left of his family. My aunt and cousins were all killed by Reddland's men during one of his purges." Emerald looked like she was trying hard to remember something. "I have another uncle somewhere. I don't even know if he's still alive. I never met him. No one talks about him much. He disappeared, ran away when he was sixteen. He's my dad and uncle's oldest brother."

Novak furrowed his brow. "What do you mean he disappeared?"

"He left when he was young. I don't know any more. The subject is almost taboo. He left and became a great warrior of some sort, but he also turned his back on the family. He broke all contact with everyone. I seem to remember someone saying he went down the wrong path, turned bad." Emerald shrugged her shoulders and threw up her hands. "I guess no one's heard from him since. He just rebelled against my grandpa and vanished."

Novak commiserated with Emerald. "Who knows why people do the things they do, why things happen, why some die untimely deaths." Novak stretched. "Scorp always used to say 'It's not our job to question God, only to follow orders.' He was most serious about matters of that sort. Then again, he also said cats and persimmons are proof God had a sense of humor." Novak got a laugh recalling that statement.

"It doesn't sound like he was much of a cat or persimmon lover," Emerald observed.

"No one in their right mind is," Novak said and laughed joyously.

Emerald said seriously, "I like cats."

Novak's eyes grew wide feigning shock. "Here I was thinking you were the perfect woman. But now I find *this* out."

Emerald didn't react the way Novak expected her to. Instead of replying in the same joking manner, she just sat in silence and stared, her face all aglow.

"You've been thinking of me as the perfect woman?"

"I…um…well…ah." Novak felt cornered. What could he say? It was his turn for the unexpected. Rather than continue in the bantering manner, Novak grew serious. "I guess what I mean is, you're a very beautiful woman, with a kind heart, who is taking a stand for what is right when many others fail to act. You also have been able to maintain an innocence and an ability to see the good in people, even amidst all the depravity and turmoil. Any man would be proud to keep company with you."

Emerald's jaw dropped. It was her turn to be speechless.

Novak continued. "And when all this is over, I would be honored if you would allow me to be your escort for an evening. Of course, I'll ask your father's permission first." In true chivalrous form, Novak pled his case.

Emerald's eyes welled with tears and she flushed with emotions. "The lady accepts the gracious offer from the handsome Knight. And with that I think I should go before I do something impetuous."

Novak nodded his agreement. "The scandal would sweep the island. And besides, the sentry I relieved should be back soon." Novak held out his hand to help Emerald from the crate.

Her hand seemed so small in his, so soft and delicate.

"Your name suits you well, Emerald, for you are indeed a rare gem in a world of ordinary things."

Emerald blushed more.

Emerald reluctantly removed her hand from Novak's. "I'll be praying for you, and for all of us, and for success in the coming days."

"Thank you. I think we all will be. Lord knows we're going to need it."

———◆———

"All right everyone, listen up and gather around." Thadus assembled together the latest arrivals from Scarborough Field. "Those in front, grab a knee so those in back can see."

Cad and Cyrus made their way across the courtyard to the assembly. Halfway there a soldier walked up to Cad and handed him a paper. After a brief exchange where Cad pointed to several items on the unrolled parchment, the soldier carried on. Cad and Cyrus continued to the assembled rebels. The small talk ceased, and the soldiers quieted on their approach.

"Good evening, men and women," Cad addressed them. "We don't have a lot of time so I'll be brief. First things first. Will those of you who Novak selected to be sentries and support personnel fall out to my right. Cyrus will get you positioned and brief you on your duties, shifts, and all else." Two dozen soldiers gathered to Cad's right.

"I can get the catapult batteries set up like we planned also," Cyrus offered.

Cad stroked his goatee. "Yeah, that sounds good mate. How many did we end up with anyway?"

"Five, the other two couldn't be repaired in time."

"Well, we knew we would have to win by brains more than brawn."

Cyrus nodded. "I'll let you know when I'm done."

Cad waited until Cyrus gathered his men and left, then spoke to the remaining assembly "Now, the next order of business; will those selected to be in the cavalry form up to my right." Ten soldiers gathered in the place ordered.

"OK, you ten meet me at the carriage house. It's the building at the far end of the grounds. Cad motioned to where some horses were tethered. "Some of your friends are already waiting. I'll get there as quickly as I can. In the meantime, make sure all the horses are shod, fed, and ready to go. I'll lead the cavalry when the action starts." As they walked off, Cad couldn't help but think how rag-tag the rebel troops looked. Each wore his own clothes and armor. Cad knew an army in matching uniforms was an impressive sight, and played big in striking some fear in the enemy.

Cad addressed the remaining troops. "Next are the archers. For now, go to the main auditorium until further notice. Many of your friends have already arrived and are waiting. Zephyr will be your commander. She will meet you there."

Cad waved for Thadus to come closer and whispered. "Can you find Zephyr and tell her that her troops are ready and waiting."

"Consider it done." Thadus hurried off, pleased. He had agreed to lead the small squad of messengers and litter bearers.

"The rest of you will be under Novak's command in the infantry. He has spent considerable time with an army and knows what he's doing. He will be joining you later. In the meantime we have a lot of blooming work to do. Reddland's men may discover us at any moment, and we have to be as ready as we possibly can. I prefer to be completely prepared when the enemy arrives. And believe me, it won't be long now. This means we won't be getting a lot of sleep tonight." Cad proceeded to dispatch squads to complete various tasks. He assigned some to repair the wooden doors to the oratory compound. Some he had clear away the weeds from around the building. Others were to secure supplies for the sentries on the perimeter wall.

Cad called a dozen men forward. "Here's what I need you guys to do. Get about thirty to forty water skins and fill them with lamp oil. But first you will have to process the lamp oil. In the carriage house is a device used to make rum. I had Thadus find a still. I'll be there to help you with this, but anyway, once the lamp oil has been processed, once it has been distilled, it becomes more flammable. I know it sounds strange. I can't explain why that happens right now, but trust me; the oil will be more flammable. The oil is not much use in this state except for what we're going to use it for."

The men looked inquisitively at Cad. "Once the water skins are full of the processed lamp oil, I want you to tie them to ropes that stretch across the road to the oratory gates." Cad pointed to the rows of trees that lined the road to the main gates of the perimeter wall. "Tie them up high and close to branches in order to conceal them as best as possible. It shouldn't be too hard since some of the branches from the trees on either side of the road almost touch in the middle."

"Why? How is that going to help us?" One soldier asked.

"I'm glad you asked." Cad smiled. "When those water skins are hit with flaming arrows, it'll rain fire down on whatever is below. It should rattle Reddland's soldiers; maybe take some of the bloody wind out of their sails. It'll give them something to think about."

Cad selected another group of soldiers and gathered them around. "You men have an important job too. You need to get two big cauldrons and set them up on the perimeter wall about a hundred feet on either side of the main gate. Have them filled with the processed lamp oil. Behind the oratory are sections of reeds in varying diameters. Find the biggest one you can and attach a funnel to it. Then take ten-foot sections of reeds, each decreasing in diameter from the first, and fasten them together until you have two hundred-foot pipes. Make sure the reeds start from big at the funnel side, and get smaller gradually to the other side. Put one pipe on the wall at either side of the gate, the funnel side next to the cauldrons. When the time comes, I'll show you how to employ them." Cad went on to assign other squads tasks. Some were as unconventional as the ones just assigned. Soon everyone had an assignment. There was a lot of work to be done and no time to lose.

One of the soldiers grumbled about the workload. "I don't think there is any way we can get all this done in one night. We don't even know if all this will work. And besides, there is just too much to do." Some of the others shook their heads in agreement.

Cad was fired up with anger. He realized he would have to waste time to address the grumblers, and motivate the men. It wasn't unexpected, as there is dissent in every group. "Let me start by saying the last time I checked this wasn't a bloody democracy. I was asked to command the rebellion. Some of you chaps may not like that, and that's fine. What matters is that you follow orders, not question them. If one of you were qualified to lead, I'm sure Thadus and Isaac would have put you in charge long ago. I don't make it a habit to answer when someone questions my orders. But since we are all just getting to know each other I'm going to make an exception."

Cad looked the troops in the eyes. "First up; whatever a person says aloud he will eventually believe. Someone could wake up in the morning, see that it's cloudy, and raining, and decide it's going to be a terrible day. And for that person it will be. Another person could wake up to the same day and think, 'We could sure use the rain,' and have a good day. Whatever your mouth spews forth will dictate your actions. It will also affect everyone else."

Cad looked the grumbler in the eye. "You have decided the task is impossible before even attempting it. You have already chosen to fail. I'm pretty sure you haven't attempted anything like what I've asked you to do before. And no one else here has either for that matter. Yet you have formed an opinion based on no prior experience or information. In doing so you have become a mindless voice heckling from the sidelines about something you have no knowledge of. This can only serve to discourage those who have a can-do attitude, and are ready to accomplish something in this world. We can't have that in an army, especially in the heat of battle."

Cad softened his tone and now spoke towards the entire group. "I assure you all, this can be done. I've seen or heard about all the tasks I've assigned before, and they do work. At any rate, now is the time to think victory and have a positive attitude. Don't defeat yourself with an attitude of hopelessness and failure. And by all means don't inflict gloom and doom on your fellow soldiers. If for some reason you can't keep your blooming mouth in check, I would encourage you to sit this battle out. We all have to watch what we say. Your tongue will run your whole life. That's why we put a bit in a horse's mouth; for where the horse's mouth goes, his whole body will follow."

Cad could tell his message sunk in. The grumbler would not look up and seemed to regret shooting off his mouth. After Cad's monologue, he doubted anyone else would have anything negative to say. All of the troops were basically good people. They wanted what was best for the rebellion. They just weren't used to the discipline of being soldiers. The troops had to maintain an attitude for victory at all times. The pros and cons of logistics and talk of worst-case scenarios had to be left to the commanders. It was the leader's job to think of all the things that could go wrong and correct them. The leaders had to instill a confidence in the troops. They had to appear under control and have solutions. And under no circumstance could the leadership waiver or act defeated in front of the men. If leaders appeared afraid or uncertain, it would bleed down to the troops in the form of chaos. A good commander always knew what to do, even if he really didn't.

As Cad watched the men go about their assignments, he went over the troop totals in his mind: sixty-one archers, twenty-seven cavalry, twenty men on catapults, fifty-four sentries, three-hundred-fifty-two infantry, and the thirty-to-fifty who remained for support and medical aid.

XIII

———◆•◆———

THADUS WALKED BRISKLY towards the oratory, the gravity
of the situation starting to sink in. All around him people were
gathering armaments, clearing weeds, and preparing contraptions
of Cad's design. Torches flickered everywhere in testimony to the
intense work taking place. Catapults had been positioned and
ammunition readied. A squad of soldiers worked on the oratory
roof. Sentries walked the parapets at the outer wall. Thadus's
friends were going to war. Each time he passed someone as he
walked, he couldn't help hope the soldier would be alive in the days
to come. With the loss of Isaac, and now Scorpyus, he knew that
even in victory, there would be sorrow. To those who had to pay for
it, sweet freedom came with a bitter side. Many would shed their
blood so future generations wouldn't have to shed theirs.

At the oratory gate, Abrams was thinking much the same
thing, his bearded face poking out from his hooded cloak. All
around him bustled soldiers who could very well be living their
last week. Some were already coming to him for spiritual guidance.
The fact they stayed to fight spoke highly of their character.
Abrams took time with each one and promised to address the
whole force shortly.

All of the troops were now looking to him for reassurance, and he felt sorely inadequate to fill the shoes of his father. Isaac had been their minister for nearly fifty years. Isaac had seen them through the war and the persecution that followed. Abrams wondered how he could ever live up to that. And yet he was the only logical choice. Abrams had been his father's assistant since he was twenty-two and had seen Isaac handle a variety of situations. He had plenty of on-the-job training. Abrams had been to seminary. Most of the rebel soldiers had no formal education. Those who did had a few years at best. Abrams knew he had to succeed his father. He prayed he wouldn't let his people down.

"Thadus! Thadus!" Abrams ran up the stone oratory steps.

Thadus was just about to enter the oratory doors. He turned to see who was calling him. "Abrams! Thank God you finally made it. I was getting worried."

"I wanted to make sure everyone made it over from Scarborough Field," Abrams explained. "Fill me in on what's been happening here."

Thadus waived for Abrams to follow him. "Come with me. We'll talk along the way. I'm trying to find Zephyr. The archers are waiting for her. She's upset over the loss of Scorpyus."

Abrams lowered his head. "Yes, I've heard about that. It serves as a testimony to the other three. They continue on with us even after the loss of their friend."

"They're good people. They truly live up to all the title 'knight' implies," Thadus added. "The world could use more like them."

"Yes, and as I look around I see the few doing what the many should be doing. I know that for everyone here, three are in hiding some place. It leaves us spread thin. I pray we don't suffer too much loss."

"We knew only those who had helped all along would be here now; and as for losses, they were killing us one by one anyway. The only way to end this is to take a stand."

"You're a good friend, Thadus." Abrams was grateful for the loyal support. "I know you're right. It won't make the loss of life any easier, but you're right."

Thadus said, "I'm curious to see Cad's devices employed. I'm certain Reddland's troops have seen nothing like them."

Abrams shot Thadus an inquisitive look. "Really? That's good, I think."

The two men entered the oratory. "You know," Abrams continued, "I received our latest intelligence report today, and probably the last one until this is over. In the last two days Reddland has killed eighty-four people in his raids. That's more than at any other time in the last ten years. I think he would have continued at that pace as a means of eroding our support with the friendly citizens. It would have meant an end to the rebellion. I don't think I could continue to ask for support under those circumstances."

Upon hearing the number of citizens killed, Thadus shook his head. "Eighty-four people. What else could we do? It seems all things are coming to a head at once. And I don't believe in coincidences."

———— ◆—◆—◆ ————

Zephyr was still numb with grief and sat alone in the storeroom staring blankly at the wall. She heard men in the other room preparing for battle. Everything was going on as if nothing happened. Did anybody care? Few of them even met Scorpyus, or knew that he died to help them, and none would remember him tomorrow. It was a bitter irony that tore at Zephyr's heart. She didn't have to close her eyes to see Scorpyus's pale and lifeless body lying in the street. *We did not even bury him! We just left him in the street.* A solitary tear streamed down her cheek.

The door to the storeroom opened with a creak and startled her from her ruminations. "Ah, there you are." Thadus entered the storeroom. Abrams followed him.

Zephyr wiped her red eyes. "Oh, hi Monsieur. I suppose the archers are waiting for me?"

Abrams removed the hood of his cloak. "They are, but you can still take a few minutes." Both Abrams and Thadus sat on a crate across from Zephyr.

"I tell you this, I do not know what is going to be harder, coming to terms with Scorpyus's death myself, or breaking the news to my little sister." Zephyr paused a moment to think. "Zenith has had a crush on Scorpyus since she was seventeen. He never showed any interest for the longest time, but she never gave up. Out of the blue, about a month ago, I noticed they were talking more, spending more time together. Finally, a couple weeks ago when Novak's sister got married, Scorpyus escorted her to the event. I have never seen Zenith as happy as she was that night. She was so radiant and beautiful in her blue dress."

Zephyr paused to wipe away another tear. "And worst of all, Scorpyus's sister Isabella will be devastated. He was the only family she had left."

"I'm sorry." Abrams searched for the right words. "Scorpyus died to help us regain our freedom and to restore peace to Xylor. For that we will forever be in debt to him, as we are in debt to all four of you. And should we all perish in the days to come; God will remember. He will remember Scorpyus, He will remember you, and He will remember all of us and what we tried to do here for Him. We can't do it without Him. And He knows that we are willing to lay down our lives rather than swerve from the path we know is right."

It was as if Abrams had been reading Zephyr's mind and knew her concern for the memory of Scorpyus. She felt a little embarrassed for thinking no one would appreciate what he had done. After all, she reasoned, preparations *had* to be made. No matter who or how many died, the survivors had to carry on and do whatever it took to ensure success.

"Merci…I thank you, Monsieur. I know in my heart you are right. I also know we never really get used to death." Clearly Abrams had a lot of wisdom packed into his fifty-odd years. "There are two things that are going to get me through this. One is the fact I know where Scorpyus is as we speak. It is the only thing that can give those left behind any semblance of peace. The second is, I am not going to let what he did be in vain. Reddland must be stopped. He will pay."

Abrams was in full agreement. "That's absolutely true; you will see him again. Your faith is strong. Without faith, we all would be lost in more ways than one."

"I suppose I should get my archers ready." Zephyr managed to force a small smile. Thadus and Abrams nodded appreciatively. Zephyr placed her cap squarely on her head and opened the door.

"And, Zephyr," Abrams added. "I know you and your friends are giving us your utmost effort. If I didn't believe that, I wouldn't have trusted the lives of all the troops to your leadership."

Zephyr raised her eyebrows and shook her head. "I know, Monsieur. That is what makes this all the more unnerving. We do not want to cost anyone else his or her life. We will do our best."

Zephyr had sixty-one archers depending on her, and Novak had over three hundred infantry under his command. But for Cad, she now felt the most sympathy. He was in command of the whole operation. A good portion of the battle would sink or swim, depending on his ideas. Sure she and Novak, and even Cyrus, would have a say in the matter. But when all was said and done, the final responsibility fell to Cad. He was the one who came up with the bulk of the plan.

She could at least have the archers ready.

Zephyr found the archers waiting in the main auditorium. All of the pews had been removed and placed upstairs. The archers sat on the floor chatting. Zephyr walked in and greeted them. "Bonjour; for those of you who do not know me, my name is Zephyr. We are going to be the archers for the upcoming battle. My first order is that everyone is to carry a sword. I know we will primarily be using long bows, but in case of an emergency, I want everyone to have a sword handy." She wasted no time in getting down to business.

Zephyr continued. "Everyone should have two quivers of arrows. We are going to need to be mobile enough to move to wherever the attack is coming from, and we won't have a lot of time to resupply. At first we will be at the outer perimeter wall ready to launch volleys at Reddland's troops. No matter how tempting it is, unless it is an extreme emergency, let the sentries handle the defense of the wall itself. All of us need to concentrate on getting arrows down range."

Zephyr could tell the archers already understood their role in the battle. It was pretty much standard tactics. A third of the archers were women. Novak told her the few women who came forward with the desire to be part of the fighting force wanted to be archers when they found out Zephyr would be their commander. Maybe these women, like her, had borne the cruelties of war personally. The savage loss of virtue could easily make one want to lash back, if for no other reason than to spare their daughters the same fate. The thought gave Zephyr a feeling of fellowship with the female archers. They were all younger women. Maybe they were looking to her with the same thoughts?

"We need to place some extra arrows on the perimeter wall, and some on the oratory roof. If the need should arise for us to fall back, we will be positioned on the catwalks on the roof. Let us get our supplies in place now where we think we will need them." Zephyr led her troops in the preparations.

All around the oratory grounds the rebel soldiers set about their work to flickering torch light. Catapult teams gathered ammunition, soldiers set in place the devices Cad had designed, and still others cleared weeds from around the oratory itself. Sentries paced the perimeter wall keeping their vigils. The work continued until midnight when it was finally decided the bulk of the preparations were complete. Further plans were put on hold in favor of letting the troops get some rest before daybreak. Word spread for all the people to gather in the courtyard before turning in so Abrams could address everyone. The sentries remained on watch while all others gathered in front of the oratory's steps. Cad brought the cavalry soldiers, Zephyr the archers, and Novak the infantry. Novak found himself a seat with Emerald on the steps. Cad and Zephyr stood nearby talking to Thadus.

It had stopped sprinkling a few hours earlier, and the clouds began to part. Novak looked up at the recently unveiled stars and half moon.

"That ought to make it harder for them to launch a surprise attack. The added light will make it easier for the sentries to see what's coming."

Emerald gazed up at the night sky. "All that space…it makes you realize how small we must be."

Novak laughed. "It's not often I think of myself as small, but compared to the sky, I guess I am."

"You know what I mean. It's just that the clouds look so vast the way they tower up like huge columns of smoke."

Emerald and Novak enjoyed a moment of beauty, courtesy of the passing clouds.

Cad also noticed the passing of the storm. "It looks like the weather's going to break in our favor."

"Is that all you think about? How the weather will play into our battle?" Zephyr chided.

"Right now, yeah; look around, Zephyr, that *is* why we're here." Cad motioned all around.

Zephyr shook her head. "You men are all the same."

"Why, what were you thinking? 'How beautiful the sky looks?'" Cad teased Zephyr. "You blooming women are all the same."

"Maybe I was! Maybe it is." Zephyr crossed her arms forcefully. "What about you, Thadus? What were you thinking?"

Thadus gestured with a hairy arm to the vicinity where Emerald sat with Novak and smiled. "I was wondering if I might be losing a daughter."

Cad and Zephyr looked to where their friend sat with Thadus's daughter. It certainly looked like the two were getting along well. And judging from the whispering and laughing back and forth, they were having a good time.

Just then Abrams came out of the oratory and walked down the steps to where Cad, Zephyr, and Thadus stood. He looked tired and a bit nervous. Everyone knew he had the tremendous responsibility of carrying on in his father's footsteps. It was a responsibility Abrams did not take lightly and gladly accepted. The people needed him to take over, perhaps now more then ever. What he was about to say was of the utmost importance. And soldiers awaiting battle were at one of the few times in their life when they were most willing to hear what he had to say. Abrams prayed he wouldn't let the troops down. A hush fell over the crowd, and all turned to face the steps from whence they would be addressed.

Cad stepped forward. "Could everybody move in as close as possible? Gather around. Abrams is here to say a few words to all of us tonight."

And with that Cad stepped aside and Abrams stepped forward. A hush drew over the gathering of soldiers. Abrams looked out on the sea of faces flickering in the torchlight.

"Some of you may wonder why we are gathered here, the five hundred or so of us, poised ready to risk life and limb for the cause of truth and justice. Most of us can think of others who are in complete agreement with our reason for being here, and yet they are nowhere to be found in this moment of crisis. These fair-weather members of the faith hide while others do their bidding. And still there are countless others, who for various reasons, not necessarily the same reasons as us, would love to be rid of Reddland and his tyranny. And where are they now? This is nothing new. For it has always been the few doing the work from which the many will benefit. You are all to be commended for your courage, for your faith, and for your willingness to stand against injustice. You are an elite group."

Everyone sat in silence respectfully listening. Abrams continued. "You are among the elite that few men of prominence can boast of being in."

Abrams related a story to illustrate his point. "Back during the war before Kelterland finished conquering the territory, I was on the mainland in seminary school. There were twenty-five men in my class, all of us in our early twenties. We were in our third and final year of seminary, and due to graduate soon. We all thought of ourselves as men of faith, strong faith, as men who had chosen a life of service to God. After all, that is why we were in seminary. We thought of ourselves as elite, that we had been trained, educated, and prepared more than most other people to take a stand for God. We all had big plans of going out to congregations and putting our expertise to work. If our faith was tested, we felt confident we would come through."

Abrams spoke softly. "And the proud shall be humbled." He looked out over the gathering of soldiers with a hint of sadness in his eyes.

"Well, the town soon fell to Kelterland. The new authorities burned down the seminary and murdered the instructors. My classmates and I were thrown into 'reform' prison. After two months of filth, starvation, and beatings, they gathered us back together. We were told that if we renounced our God, and signed papers affirming that decision, we would be set free."

Abrams lowered his head and paused. "Eighteen of my classmates renounced God and signed the papers. They were readily set free. The seven of us who refused to sign were thrown back into prison. Three years later they released the four of us that were still alive, but not before deporting us to the far ends of the world."

Abrams stroked his graying beard. "God is not partial to anyone based on worldly status. He uses those who are willing. The faith of all of us here in Xylor is being tested. It has been tested for over ten years. You gathered before me right now have risen to the occasion. Not only are we willing to risk our lives for the highest of causes, but we are risking our lives so that others can have a better future. You are fighting for those who can't or won't fight for themselves. You are fighting for the children of Xylor who have no future under the current dictator. You are fighting so those who have yet to be born can have a life free of premature death, torture and spiritual depravity. You are willing to risk your lives to usher in a real hope for a future. It is written; 'Greater love hath no man than to lay down his life for his friends.' You are all to be commended for having that kind of integrity, character, and honor. Let us not worry where the others are who should be here beside us. Not many have what it takes to do what you have been called upon to do. And let us not hold any ill will against those who are not here. Let us just put forth our best efforts and show the world what can be done by a few people who have the faith to take a stand."

Abrams continued. "Now I have some good news and some bad news. First the bad news. Some of us will indeed lay down our lives. Some of us here now will not live to see next week. It is even a possibility that *all* of us will perish in the days to come. Scorpyus, Isaac, and eighty-four others in the last two days alone have crossed to the other side. We must be prepared in case we are asked to make that ultimate sacrifice."

Abrams looked back and forth across the crowd. "I encourage you all to give some thought to the afterlife. Let us not be among those who put more thought and preparation into a Saturday picnic than we do into that permanent and eternal trip into the afterlife. And this brings me to the good news. I said earlier 'Greater love hath no man than to lay down his life for his friends.' I'm going to talk to you about a friend who laid down his life for us, and I strongly suggest you listen. Because when you are lying in your own blood mortally wounded on the battlefield, or at some future date on your deathbed, this friend will be all you have. It won't matter how much money you have, how smart you are, how good a life you led, or how well you fought; all that will matter is whether or not you've accepted this friend's sacrifice of his life."

Some of the troops were shifting around uneasily. A few wondered if Abrams was trying to cause a desertion with his talk of death and dying.

Abrams let it all sink in. "Let me tell you about a friend who had a sack put over his head, who was beaten repeatedly about the face by an angry mob, and when the bag was taken off, his hair was matted with blood, his lips split, his eyes swollen shut, his nose flattened—basically he was so disfigured his face was unrecognizable. And yet the mob wasn't finished. They pulled his beard out, and then they took a cat-o'-nine tails and whipped him mercilessly, almost to death. They flogged him until they tore the flesh from his bones. He was scourged so heavily that ribs and internal organs were exposed. They beat him with staves, even rammed needle sharp thorns down into his head. That still wasn't enough. The mob wasn't finished yet. Then they forced him to carry a heavy wooden cross through town to the place of his execution. They scorned, and spat, and mocked him all the way there. He had been so beaten that he fell down several times as he made his way through town. Each time he fell, the mob would whip and beat him to his feet, forcing him on. Finally, even the mob realized he couldn't go on, and they forced a bystander to carry the cross the rest of the way. Eventually they came to a hill on the outskirts of town. There they robbed this friend of his clothes and lay him on the cross. Large iron spikes are hammered through his hands and feet. They lifted up the cross and slipped it into its mount. It landed with a thud. The force causes this friend's shoulders to dislocate. Hour after hour, the mob watched this friend pull himself up with his hands, and push up with his feet in order to gasp a breath. All the while the mob cursed him and laughed at him, enjoying their savage handiwork. Finally he died."

Abrams looked over his audience. They were listening attentively. He wanted to make sure what he was saying was understood. "And why did this friend die? Because of us. Because of each and every one of us. You could even say we were the ones who killed him. If it were not for us, he wouldn't have had to die a bloody death. He did nothing wrong. He died because we have done wrong. Think of it like this: If we only commit one sin a day, in thirty years we would each accumulate ten-thousand sins. Those sins have to be paid for, and ten-thousand is a very conservative estimate. I can guarantee we all sin more than once a day in our thoughts alone. In a perfect justice system all crimes have to be paid for, all ten-thousand."

Abrams held up two fingers. "We all have two choices. We can reject this friend and pay for our sins ourselves. That's not the wise choice. Hell is where people who reject this friend pay for their sins. But there is another way. Here's the good news. This friend will pay for our sins for us. In fact he has already pre-paid them as a free gift. All we have to do is accept that free gift. This friend has shed his blood for us already, because without the shedding of blood there is no remission of sins. Now the choice is up to us. Don't let pride or vanity keep you from accepting what this friend has done for you. Being saved from having to pay for your sins is your choice, and no one can force you. The gift must be accepted voluntarily. All this friend asks is that once we've accepted his offer, we should love God, and love each other."

Abrams paused again. "As you all know by now, this friend I'm talking about is Jesus. He gave his life as a ransom for many. It's pretty hard *not* to love God when you realize what he's done for you. And yet some do. Some men hate God so much and those who represent Him, that they will kill His people as an ultimate expression of rejection. Let us not be so hard of heart. I encourage you now, if you have never done so already, to accept Jesus as your savior. There are some of us here who have but a day or two remaining to decide. Novak, Cad, and some of the others can attest to that. No military action is without its casualties."

Novak, Cad, Zephyr, Cyrus, and Thadus nodded their agreement in unison. A sense of reverence came upon the gathered soldiers. Most were moved by what Abrams said, and a few had tears in their eyes. Abrams knew he struck a chord with the troops, as he had expected. Not because he was a great orator or public speaker, but because men who were soon to be facing death were often the most ready to think on spiritual matters. The most disturbing thing to Abrams was the knowledge that even in their last minutes, some people still reject the message.

Most of the rebel soldiers had long since accepted the Gospel and knew beyond a shadow of a doubt their destiny. That knowledge is what brought Cad, Novak, and Zephyr sane through several tragic events in their lives. Still, a few soldiers came forward, troubled and uneasy. Abrams took them aside and went over everything again with them. He would stay with the troops as long as he was needed, and he was in no rush.

Cad stepped up to address the soldiers. "If you have no questions for Abrams, you are all free to swing by the kitchen and get some grub before turning in for the night. We have a big day ahead of us. I highly recommend taking heed of what Abrams said. If you have any questions don't hesitate to ask. I know most of you chaps have already got it all taken care of and that's why you are here in the first place."

Cad watched the soldiers fall out. There would be a lot of somber reflection that night, and more than a little praying. Cad knew the mission could use it. The fight wasn't going to be easy.

Emerald parted with Novak for the night, and Thadus headed for the chow line. Abrams was still talking to a small group of soldiers.

Novak walked up to Cad and Zephyr. "Abrams did a good job with that message. I guess you don't survive three years in prison if you don't really believe in what you are doing."

"His devotion is obvious," Zephyr agreed.

"Yeah, that's true. Let's go get something to eat. I have a few last minute details to go over with you two," Cad said.

"Should we invite Abrams? We could wait," Zephyr asked.

Novak shook his head. "No, Emerald told me he hasn't eaten for the last two days. She said he's going to fast and pray continually for all of us until this is over. He's intent on doing all he can."

"We can use a chap like that right now." Cad placed a hand each on Novak and Zephyr. "Let's get some grub. We still have a few bugs to work out of the plan. I'd appreciate your input."

—•◆•—

An urgent rapping on the door startled Luther Reddland from a sound sleep.

What is it now? Reddland flung his blankets off in anger and forced himself out of bed. Lantern light flickered in the crack under his bedroom door. Sleepily he groped for his robe draped across the bench at the foot of his bed and walked barefoot to the door.

"Who is it?" Reddland snarled as he drew the sash of his robe tight.

"It's Lexton, Sire," a muffled voice announced.

Reddland opened the door. "What is it that couldn't wait till morning?"

Lexton normally dreaded contact with Reddland when the count was in an agitated state, but not this time. He knew full well his commander would want to hear what he had to report.

"Sire, we have found the rebels." Lexton was smug.

"Outstanding!" Reddland smiled and his mood shifted abruptly for the better. "Come in, Lexton, come in…uh…give me a minute. Have a seat at the table."

Reddland used Lexton's lamp to light a few candles at the table, then went to the other side of his bed and kicked the mattress. "Get up. Something's come up."

A mound moved under the blankets and a bunch of blonde hair with a face poked out the top. "What is it, Luther?" a sleepy feminine voice asked.

"News of the rebels. I'm going to need you to leave now. I have work to do." Reddland pulled the blankets off the woman and grabbed her arm to encourage her to her feet. "Come on, hurry up. I don't have all night."

The blonde woman reluctantly stood and rubbed her eyes. Her eyes focused and she noticed Lexton at the table. "Oh, hi, Lexton," She brazenly replied not even the slightest bit embarrassed to be standing unclothed before one of Reddlands men. She made no attempt to cover up, and Lexton pretended not to notice anything amiss.

Reddland gathered her clothes from the chaise and shoved the bundle into her arms. "Here you go. You can stay in the guest room down the hall if you want." Reddland pushed her towards the door.

"When will I see you again?" The woman asked as she was moved across the threshold.

"I'll contact you soon." He closed the door in the woman's face the turned to Lexton. "Well now we can get down to business. So what do we know?"

Lexton cleared his throat. "Sire, the rebels have been located at Hyssop Creek Oratory. They're roughly three hundred to five hundred strong. Some fortifications have been made; the usual fare: cauldrons of oil on the front wall, a reinforced gate. They've been working into the night so I suspect a lot of their preparations have been hastily made. We have reason to believe all the top instigators are present, including the remaining three mercenaries."

Reddland chortled. "So they're at the old oratory, huh. I should have known. How fitting. We beat them there once before, rather brutally as I recall. If they insist on repeating history then so be it. This time we will finish the job properly. I want all of their relatives, children, friends, and acquaintances put to death. I will not have these fanatics rise up again. Marcus's intelligence squad is to be commended."

Lexton nodded approvingly but was skeptical of being rid of the rebellion forever. He had been around long enough to know that no matter how many purges, battles, and deaths were inflicted on the rebels, a few somehow always managed to survive. But Lexton intended to stay on top. "If we crush them that thoroughly, Sire, I'm sure we won't have to worry about another uprising for twenty years at least."

Reddland wanted more details. "How strong of a fight can they mount? How capable is their leadership? Is there any indication they are preparing an offensive?"

"We don't take them lightly. The three mercenaries have proven to be exceptional as a small squad. I would even say outstanding. Yet it would be difficult at best for them to take a mixed force of rebels and turn them into anything more than an average, mediocre army. But it does look as if they've broken into specialized units."

Reddland was taken aback. He didn't expect the rebels to be sophisticated enough to break into specialized units. "They've actually formed up a cavalry and artillery? How many catapults do they have?"

Lexton continued. "Not many. We don't have any exact numbers. Neither unit can be too big. They only have five hundred men at most. But the fact they did separate into specialized units at all shows they have some knowledge about battlefield tactics, and that they are thinking. With this added information, it would be a mistake on our part to think of them as mere peasants with pitch forks."

Reddland wanted solid proof. "How do you know they have any catapults?"

"We found catapult wheel tracks in the forest."

"And they have horses?"

"There is a fairly strong scent of horse manure coming from the oratory's carriage house."

"Well, aren't they the resourceful types." Reddland tapped his fingers on the table, sifting through this information. "And as far as an offensive?"

Lexton shook his head. "No, I don't think they're planning one. They seem to be digging in; besides, I don't think they're dumb enough to attack us. That would make our job too easy."

The wheels turned in Reddland's head. "We'll assume they are a skilled army and conduct ourselves accordingly. Still, they have only a few hundred men." Reddland retrieved a piece of paper and started writing.

"We'll leave the five-hundred Elite Guard soldiers here to secure the compound. Have them ready to respond just in case we need reinforcements. Mobilize the rest of the forces. I want our complete cavalry, and every catapult team mobilized. We'll hit them with everything we have; there's no sense in holding back now. Have the catapult teams get in place tonight. By dawn I want our forces ready to move against the rebels. We're not going to give them another day to prepare. Rest the men and make sure they are given a hearty meal." Reddland signed and folded the paper and gave it to Lexton. "Here are your orders. We move at dawn."

Lexton took the orders and stood. "It sounds good, Sire. Everything will be ready." The rebels may have obtained a few skilled leaders, but we'll just see how they react in the morning when they discover two-thousand Royal guards ready to rain down death upon them." Reddland escorted Lexton to the door.

"See you in the morning, Lexton. You and Marcus have done good work. I knew I could count on you two."

Lexton smiled and then departed to prepare the Royal Guard. He made his way down the hall with a somber devotion to duty.

Reddland called out to Lexton from the doorway to his room. "And, Lexton, one final thing: make sure the men know they are to take no prisoners."

Lexton disappeared down the hall. Within a few days the rebellion would be over.

XIV

———◆◆◆———

"**H**OW LONG HAVE they been out there?" Cad peered out into darkness. He could clearly hear movement in the grass and the occasional whinny of a horse. There was no doubt about it; Reddland's army was forming up.

"We've been hearing noises for the better part of an hour. It sounds like a lot of them," a sentry reported.

"The sun should be breaking over the horizon anytime. We'll know soon enough exactly what we're up against." Cad could hear an occasional voice and what sounded like a wagon rolling over rough ground. He knew Reddland would be coming with everything he had. Cad would if he were in Reddland's position.

"We came as soon as we heard. What is the situation?" Novak appeared on the parapet next to Cad. Zephyr was right behind him.

Cad pointed out into the night. "They're setting up on this side. They'll be moving toward the gate."

Novak said, "Getting troops through the gate is easier than getting them all up ladders and over the walls. On the other hand, he wouldn't have to smash through anything going over."

"No, I think he'll choose the gate no matter what. Except for a cauldron one hundred feet on either side of the gate, he'll think we don't have any burning oil to rain down on his men. That should convince him he's in the right place." Cad pulled the spyglass from his pouch that Scorpyus had carried.

The black of the night slowly bled away revealing ever so gradually an army outside the oratory walls. It was an impressive sight: two thousand soldiers, all in royal blue surcoats lined up by units. The sheen of their chain mail shone brilliantly in the sunlight.

The rebels could see rank upon rank of infantry with their matching shields. Behind them were the ranks of archers. Several catapults were also in plain view, and somewhere not seen, but sure to exist, lurked the cavalry. The display of the organized and disciplined army was awesome and unnerving.

"Oh my," Zephyr echoed the thoughts of everyone present.

Cad looked through the spyglass. "They brought everybody," he told them.

Several Royal banners flapped in the cool morning breeze. Three horsemen broke rank and rode forward, stopping fifty yards from the main gate. The rider to the right, a hulk of a man comparable to Novak, wore a burgundy surcoat unlike the others. He carried a white flag on a lance. The middle soldier wore a uniform more ornately decorated than one Cad had ever seen. He wore a golden cuirass and sat tall upon a brilliant white horse, also adorned in armor. His flowing purple cloak covered his steed's flanks. A feather-crested helmet rested on his proud head and set him even further apart from his men. No introduction was needed. Everyone within the gates knew this ominous man's identity. Reddland obviously took great satisfaction in his position as count and as commander of such a formidable force.

Thadus's burly frame appeared on the parapet. He looked at the three riders. "What are they doing?"

"They want to talk; probably to offer terms of surrender," Novak joked.

"You think?" Cad asked. "Thadus, let's meet them and find out what they want." Cad turned to Novak and Zephyr, and with a deep sigh said, "Well, this is it."

"Let's go. We owe them for Scorpyus. My men are ready and waiting." Novak began cinching his armor tighter.

Zephyr drew her bow and aimed into the mass of Royal soldiers below them. "My archers are positioned along this wall and are ready also."

Cad and Thadus mounted their horses and waited for the sentries to open the oratory gates. Thadus held up a staff with a square of white cloth tied to the end.

"Close the gates behind us," Cad called back as he rode to meet the Royal contingent, the visor of his helmet raised.

"I guess we get the honor of speaking to his highness."

"Yes, and as always, he's dressed for the occasion," Thadus answered. "The soldier to the right is Marcus. He is head of the Elite Guard and one of Reddland's top men. The other rider is Drakar. He is head cleric in the temple of Tanuba."

"The temple cleric, aye? He wants to make it official," Cad stated whimsically.

Cad eyed the three men carefully as he rode closer. Drakar was an ancient looking man in a beige jewel-encrusted robe; his long, stringy gray hair hung down to his shoulders. A large medallion emblazoned with a mermaid, hung around his wattled neck. In his hand he held a staff with a crystal orb on the end of it. Marcus was expressionless and appeared to be a formidable opponent; his massive muscular form rested heavily in the saddle. He carried himself like a true professional, holding the lance with a white flag. Reddland was the ultimate expression of grandeur he had come to be known by. Cad assumed he had no plans of partaking in the battle himself, which would explain why he dressed so formally. Under his golden cuirass, Reddland wore a purple jerkin with silver trim. He clutched the reins of his mount with golden gauntlets.

Reddland leaned over and whispered to Marcus out of the corner of his mouth, "We'll see if the rebellion is indeed prepared to fight."

From the parapet, Novak and Zephyr kept a close watch on Cad and Thadus as they approached Reddland. At the first sign of a trap, Zephyr and her archers would unleash a volley of arrows. Of course, Reddland's archers were sure to be thinking the same.

Reddland didn't try to conceal a look of disgust as he eyed his buckskin-clad adversary. "Well, well, well, Thadus. I should have known you'd be a party to this rebellion. You never did have an ounce of common sense." Reddland noticed Thadus's white shirt was soiled from his labors, dirty hands protruding from the rolled up sleeves. It was repulsive to Reddland's refined tastes.

"I could say the same about you, Luther." Thadus motioned to Drakar, "I see you brought him along. Is he here for show or have you degenerated to paganism over the last ten years? It's been that long since we last spoke, if I remember correctly."

Reddland nodded. "Your memory is correct. I assure you, however, that I do not follow Tanuba or any figment of someone's imagination. I'll leave that crutch to the simple minded such as yourself."

Thadus shook his head and looked visibly saddened. "I'm sorry to hear that, Luther." Drakar showed no surprise at Reddland's attack on Tanuba.

Reddland glanced to Cad. "So who is this?" Reddland stopped abruptly and his jaw dropped. The color drained from his face and he just sat looking at Cad. There was a long silence. Cad furrowed his brow in bewilderment.

"What? Is there something in my nose?" Cad wiped his nose and mouth and then looking around laughing at his own statement.

Reddland stammered. "No, I, uh, there's nothing, I, uh, you just look like someone I used to know. But that was a long time ago. You would have been just a kid then."

Cad shrugged his shoulders. "We've never met. But you didn't come here to discuss my look-a-like, did you, or to insult Thadus? I suggest we get to the bloody point of this meeting." Reddland said nothing. The color had yet to return to his cheeks.

Cad, emboldened by Reddland's sudden lack of presence, seized upon his momentary hesitation and took the initiative.

"Here are our terms: if you surrender now, and step down from power, not only will you spare the lives of your men, but we will spare your own. We will allow you two days to leave Xylor with the condition you never return."

Reddland's face now flushed red as he rose in his stirrups and gathered his wits about him again; he shook an armored fist at Cad. "How dare you make threats against me! Look around! You are outnumbered five to one. You are faced with certain death! I will make the conditions for *your* surrender." Reddland shook with the force of his words.

Thadus spoke before Cad could respond, trying to avert a premature confrontation. "What are your conditions, Luther?"

Reddland drew a deep breath, and focused his gaze on Thadus. "If you surrender now, I give you my word you all will be given a fair trial in Kelterland. I will send letters recommending leniency for your cooperation."

"What happens if we don't accept these terms?" Thadus asked.

Reddland looked Cad and Thadus directly in the eyes. "If you choose to fight, all of you will die. We will take no prisoners. We will not accept any future surrender. Your only opportunity for surrender is now. Once the battle begins, we will not stop until every last one of you is dead."

Drakar added his own threat in an ancient, raspy voice. "If you don't surrender now, I will place the curse of one thousand plagues upon you and your people. You will die in utter misery."

Cad wasn't fooled by the temptation of a fair trial for surrendering. All of Reddland's actions—the burnouts, the purges—all showed his resolve to exterminate those who were even remotely suspected of being a rebel. There was no reason to believe a man like Reddland would show mercy now. If the rebels surrendered, Cad knew they would be executed before the day's end.

"If you..." Thadus began to respond, but Cad stopped him placing a hand on his shoulder. "I'll handle this mate."

Cad addressed Drakar first. "Listen to me, you daft imbecile. When we win this battle, you and your bloody mermaid goddess, and everything else you stand for, will be the first to go!"

"As for you," Cad turned to Reddland. "When we win, you're going to be dethroned and arrested for the murders of countless innocent civilians. Your reign of terror is over and you will be held accountable for the shedding of innocent blood!"

Reddland smirked. "You have the reckless overconfidence of youth. I assure you, your pathetic little band of pretend soldiers will crumble under the onslaught of my forces. If you had any knowledge at all about military tactics you would realize that. By fighting you are only committing suicide."

"I know what I'm doing." Cad smiled knowingly. "After all, isn't that why you hired my friends and me? Because we were good at what we do?"

Drakar was now the one who had a look of shock on his face.

"Oh, yes, mate. Didn't Reddland tell you? He hired us to find a medicine for him. Don't tell me the 'all knowing' fish goddess didn't tell you?"

"Your ego is clouding your judgment. Your men aren't that good. As I recall, one of your friends is already dead," Reddland said sarcastically. He maintained his composure at the sudden revelation that Cad now knew who hired him.

"Have your laugh now, Reddland. But it may interest you to know we found the Hyacinth Blue," Cad added.

A flash of deep concern spread over Reddland's face. "You're lying!"

Thadus confirmed Cad's claim. "Yes, Luther. They found the long lost recipe. Hyacinth Blue is real. It is not merely a myth. Cad and his friends found all the ingredients and were able to prepare a batch. I didn't believe it either until I saw it."

Reddland absorbed it all in stunned silence While Drakar tried to piece together what he was hearing.

Thadus continued. "Isaac told us all about your plans, Luther. We know you sent someone to hire Cad and his friends. We know you are sick and need the medicine. At first, all we wanted was to find the medicine ourselves, so that we'd have a bargaining chip to use in negotiations with you. But, a miracle happened, Luther. The people you hired turned out to be honorable. When they discovered the extent of your evil, they had second thoughts about helping you. You see, they too have suffered at the hands of evil men and wanted no part of furthering your tyranny in Xylor. Ironically, the people you hired to lengthen your reign of power will now play a major role in ending it. How is that for justice? I always knew your past would return to haunt you. Who would have guessed your demise would be by your own hand?"

Reddland was caught between another bout of rage and having his curiosity about Hyacinth Blue satisfied. He twitched nervously. Had this rag-tag band of rebels actually been successful at finding the mysterious concoction? Or was this just a bluff? With his failing health, could he afford to take the chance? If they did, indeed, have the medicine he so desperately needed, he couldn't let the opportunity slip from his fingers. He could barter, perhaps. Deep inside his ruthless heart, Reddland knew he couldn't have it both ways. The rebellion would not volunteer the medicine for anything short of the surrender of the Royal forces. Reddland could either crush the rebellion or have the Hyacinth Blue.

Or was there another way? Reddland's army could cripple the rebellion and bring them to the brink of total annihilation. Then he would offer to spare the survivors in exchange for the medicine. If they had it, they would certainly give it up to save themselves from a hopeless situation. Reddland decided on this course of action. Why had he been so worried? The odds were the medicine didn't exist anyway. Marcus's men had spent more than a year trying in vain to find it.

While Thadus and Reddland debated the existence of Hyacinth Blue, Cad was busy surveying the enemy lines. The Royal forces had seventeen catapults that Cad could see. He also spotted a battering ram, a huge log suspended by ropes from a wooden framework. The log would be swung on the ropes into the gates.

The top of the framework had a covering to protect the soldiers operating it from objects and burning oil that might fall on them. The battering ram sat on a platform with wheels so it could be rolled right up to the oratory's gates

Looking down the road, Cad could see townspeople fleeing. Citizens with carts loaded with their possessions were headed for the mountains. No one wanted to be around during this time of unrest. If Reddland won, there was no telling how far he'd take his rampage, maybe into the towns again to purge the land of so-called "rebellious sympathizers." If the rebels were victorious, no one knew what kind of changes would take place. It seemed only a handful of citizens would remain to take their chances.

"Well, Thadus, that was clever. For an instant you almost had me believing you obtained the Hyacinth Blue." Reddland signaled Marcus and Drakar to move back to their lines.

Thadus was expressionless. "Believe what you want, Luther."

Marcus and Drakar turned their horses to leave. Reddland reined his own horse in preparation to do the same. "I'll give you one last chance to accept my conditions for surrender."

"Sorry, Luther, that's not possible." Thadus declined.

"Hey, Reddland! I'll give you one last chance to accept our terms for surrender," Cad called out, a smile above his goatee.

Reddland looked at Cad with disgust and shook his head. He held nothing but contempt for his young, blonde adversary. Then he jerked his horse's head around to the left and trotted back to join his ranks and prepare for the next step.

Cad and Thadus started back to the oratory. As the gates opened, a commotion could be heard from Reddland's lines. A woman attempted to ride past the Royal Guard and make a break for the oratory, but was stopped by Reddland's men. One soldier grabbed the reigns of her horse while others pulled her from the saddle.

"Let me go! Let me go!" The woman screamed in vain.

"Who is that?" Cad asked Thadus.

"It's Iris! I think she's trying to join us!"

After a brief scuffle, Reddland's men disarmed the woman and bound her with ropes, striking and kicking her several times in the process. Reddland went over to find out what was happening. Cad could not hear the exchange of words.

Suddenly, Reddland's angry voice could be heard by all near the oratory gates. "You want to join the rebellion? Good! Then you shall be the first to suffer the fate of all those who rebel against my authority. Guards, take her away!" Iris was led away kicking and screaming.

"I guess Iris's conscience finally directed her toward our cause." Thadus was deeply saddened by her fate. "I wish there was something we could do."

Cad motioned for the sentries to close the gate. "Scorpyus was right. Iris's loyalties were not with the rebellion until now, when it was too late. What a shame she hadn't joined us sooner. I wonder why she changed her mind? Wallace never showed up either, did he?"

Thadus shook his head. "And Reddland claims another victim."

Cad tethered his horse then took the ladder to the parapet two steps at a time. He walked to where the others stood and surveyed the Royal army. "Get ready! They should start their attack at any moment."

"Things went that good, huh?" Zephyr cracked and motioned for her archers to prepare to launch a volley at her command. The archers drew arrows from their quivers and notched them on their bowstrings. Poised, they waited for the next command to draw back their bows.

Cad shook his head in disgust. "Reddland never had any intention of calling a truce. I could tell the moment he started talking. 'Surrender and I'll see you get a fair trial,' he said. How absurd. No one would live to get a bloody trial at all. But I think I scared him. He must feel a little threatened because he went pale when we met, like he had seen a ghost. Something unnerved him."

"Maybe it was your breath? No?" Zephyr laughed.

"Well, ghost or no ghost, if he meets up with me I'll give him plenty of reasons to turn pale," Novak said and slapped Cad on the back. "Let's do it. I'll give the infantry the signal to ready themselves. Let me know when you need us."

"Will do; I've got a horse so I can make the rounds faster and guide the battle. I'm going to stay on the wall as long as possible, though." Cad looked Novak in the eye. "And another thing, don't get yourself killed."

"You either." Novak smiled at his friend before he moved down the ladder.

Cad watched Novak descend, and then turned to Zephyr. "Well, Zephyr, here we go again." Cad released a heavy sigh.

"It is the story of our lives." Zephyr added whimsically. "Your breath smells sweet as apples, Cad."

———◆◆◆———

"Shall I give word for Marcus to start the attack?" Lexton asked.

"In a minute." Reddland carefully surveyed the oratory gates and wall. "What do you make of those two cauldrons the rebels have on the wall?"

Lexton was already aware of their existence, but studied them again. "They're thirty yards or so on either side of the gate. I would say the rebels either have confidence their gates will withstand whatever force we use, or they didn't have the time to place more cauldrons. The latter seems the more likely explanation."

"If they only had time to prepare two cauldrons, why not set them at the gate; the most likely place of attack?" Reddland tried to decipher his opponent's intentions.

Lexton thought about it. "And if they placed the cauldrons at the gates, the walls would be lacking. They could feel the walls were the weaker point of their defense."

Reddland nodded his head in agreement. "I can't see any other reason for the move." He analyzed the situation a bit more. "If we attack the gates, it will take the rebels a while to move those cauldrons in place to use them."

"Certainly. We would have plenty of time to move out of the way before they could dump the cauldrons' contents on us."

Reddland smiled broadly. "That's what I wanted to hear. Have Marcus start the attack."

Lexton motioned for his trumpeter to sound the signal for Marcus to proceed. The trumpeter's blast echoed across the oratory grounds, sending shudders down the spines of many of the rebels. In unison, Reddland's infantrymen and archers assumed a defensive position behind their shields. They were not to be used for this first action, so they shielded themselves in case of incoming rebel arrows. The rebel archers were at the ready and the Royal army was prepared. A sense of excitement and thrill swept across the Royal forces; they would soon be in battle, and this was a fight they felt confident they would win.

The grinding sound of wooden wheels on cobblestone soon permeated the morning air. From the parapet, Cad saw about twenty Royal soldiers pushing the battering ram up the tree-lined cobblestone path that led to the oratory gates. A metal roof of interlaced shingles protected the soldiers pushing the battering ram. Two squads of infantrymen followed a short distance behind them. Cad made a mental note to dig up the path directly in front of the gate in the future. He would not make that oversight again.

Tension ran along the parapet like a rabid dog. All the rebels could do was wait. One of the sentries walked up to Cad. "What are we going to do? We're not going to just let them walk right up and smash down our gates are we?"

Cad gave the sentry a look of warning. "No mate, we are not. Just sit tight and watch." Cad motioned for Zephyr to stand ready.

Marcus followed behind the battering ram with the two squads of soldiers. He sat on his horse and surveyed the entire scene. The rebels didn't seem to be concerned so far. No one was attempting to move the cauldrons into place, and there was no activity on the parapet to indicate any type of projectiles or boiling liquid would be cast down on the soldiers with the battering ram. The rebel archers were at the ready, but were making no attempt to stop the battering ram either. Marcus was perplexed. What were the rebels thinking? Weren't they going to take a few shots at the soldiers pushing the battering ram? Were they just going to let the Royal troops waltz right up and batter down their doors? The situation did not sit right with Marcus. He knew the rebels had some sort of plan, but what? Marcus shifted nervously in the saddle and studied the oratory walls, searching for clues. Marcus's every instinct told him something was amiss.

He watched the battering ram move into position. The soldiers immediately grabbed onto metal bars that protruded from the side of the metal-tipped log and started swinging it against the oratory gates. Soon a rhythmic thump shook the gate every ten seconds, but still no response came from the rebels. Marcus was deep in thought when something splattered on his forearm. He looked to see a drop of clear liquid. Was it water? Marcus touched it, rubbed it between his thumb and forefinger, and held it to his nose. It felt oily and smelled like something similar to lamp oil. Marcus wondered how he could get lamp oil on his arm. Looking up, he scanned the tree branches. The sick feeling in his stomach grew worse when he saw dozens of water skins suspended from ropes tied to the trees.

He looked back down in time to see the rebel archers light their arrows aflame. One archer lit his arrow from the comrade on his right and passed the flame to the person on his left. In seconds, all the archers' arrows were lit.

Realizing the imminent danger his men were about to face, Marcus did the only thing he could. "Retreat! Retreat! Pull back!" Marcus's order startled his men as well as Reddland, who was watching from a safe distance.

Zephyr's archers loosed their arrows and sixty streaks of fire shot across the sky. Twenty-seven of them pierced oil-filled skins that erupted in flames and spilled their flaming contents on all below. Fire danced on the roof of the battering ram and ran between the cracks on the roof of interlaced shingles onto the men. Their surcoats suddenly blazed. The soldiers cried out and spun around frantically trying to slap out the flames.

The rebel archers launched a second volley into the frantic Royal troops who fled from beneath their burning shelter. Zephyr took careful aim at a particular soldier who was spinning madly and flailing his arms. He fell face down in the road and lay still. Several others soldiers fell from the volley also. The sound of arrows clanging against armor indicated that others were lucky.

"Retreat! I said retreat!" Marcus rode up to his men. "Lie on the ground and roll! Roll on the ground!" Many soldiers already figured this out and had extinguished their flames.

Lexton watched, as surprised by this unconventional maneuver as everyone else. He immediately ordered the Royal archers into action. He knew Marcus would need covering fire in order to withdraw his troops.

Zephyr heard the trumpeter and saw the Royal archers ready their arrows. "Get down! Archers down!" Cyrus already had his sentries taking cover since they weren't being utilized at this stage of the battle. Cad had the visor down on his helmet and peered out over his shield.

The archer next to Zephyr hesitated not understanding why the order was being given. He was intent on getting another arrow off. He looked from side to side and saw that everyone else was taking cover so decided to do so also. It was too late. Two hundred and fifty arrows flew toward the oratory walls seeking targets. Four of the arrows found the archer next to Zephyr and he fell back, landing across her legs. Other arrows splintered against the stone walls, and some dug deep into the ground after arching over the walls.

On hands and knees on the parapet, Zephyr turned to see the archer bleeding on her boots. He was gasping for air. "Stretcher!" Zephyr called for medical aid and instructed the nearest sentries to lower the archer from the wall. They crawled over and lowered their wounded comrade by his legs to the litter bearers.

Zephyr looked for Cad and saw him motioning for her to keep everyone down. This could only mean the Royal archers were preparing to launch another volley.

"This is why you have to do what I say immediately!" Zephyr yelled at the archers, upset at having lost a man needlessly. Seeing their friend get carried away with four arrows in his body drove the point home.

The two squads of Royal soldiers that had been following the battering ram were in a dead retreat. Marcus ordered the others back in place under the battering ram. The fire blackened the interlaced shingle roof, but failed to ignite the wooden framework. "The battering ram will provide cover for you as you maneuver back to our lines."

The soldiers didn't have to be told twice. Marcus didn't realize the burdensome ram could be pushed that fast. Clearly, the men were spooked by this unconventional tactic. Liquid fire from the sky had that effect.

Zephyr crawled over to Cad. "How did we do?"

"We got eleven by my count." Cad's voice was muffled under his full-face helmet. "But, I definitely think they're spooked. How did they fare?"

Zephyr shook her head. "We lost one."

Cad turned to Zephyr and lifted his visor momentarily. "It's not your fault mate. They didn't have enough time to be drilled as a team. We have to expect these things."

Zephyr shook her head knowingly.

"What was that?" Reddland asked from atop his horse while watching his troops scurry back to their lines like frightened mice.

"I've never seen that before, Sire." Lexton was angered by the fact the rebels were able to outwit his experienced soldiers.

"If they can dispatch eleven of my men while untrained, we should be grateful they aren't more learned in the proper techniques of warfare." Reddland's words bit with sarcasm.

Marcus rode up to Reddland and removed his helmet. His hair was sweaty. "Sorry, Sire. By the time I realized what was…"

Reddland interrupted. "Don't worry Marcus, you recovered quickly; you too, Lexton. You wasted no time calling in the archers. This was all unforeseen."

Lexton appreciated the compliment. Words of encouragement from his superior had been rare as of late. "What now, Sire?"

"Marcus, did you see any more surprises hanging from the trees?" Reddland inquired.

Marcus shook his head. "No. Nothing else, Sire. A few more water skins of oil, but not enough to do that much damage again. But who knows what other tricks they may have."

Lexton ordered one of his men to dispatch the remaining skins from the trees. This would help eliminate the threat of any future liquid firestorms.

"No, Marcus. I think this was the rebels' only moment of glory. Clever little games like this will only delay the inevitable." Reddland had been surprised by this event but seemed relatively unconcerned.

Lexton was in agreement. "I think we should send the battering ram again."

Reddland could see that Marcus was unconvinced. "You disagree, Marcus?"

"Yes, Sire. I fear the rebels may have more surprises, more unconventional tactics we can't plan for." Marcus searched for words carefully. He had been feeling quite strange since witnessing the death of the stable hand back at the compound and didn't quite know if that experience was playing into his current sense of dread.

"I respect your opinion, Marcus. But see for yourself. You have stated there is nothing more in the trees, so the path to the gate must be clear. The rebels have two cauldrons on the wall, and they are far from the gate. Nothing else can be seen. The water skins in the trees would have been spotted had we looked closely. We still wouldn't have known what they were for, but perhaps they would have served as a warning." Reddland continued with confidence. "The rebels have had their moment. Now we are expecting the unexpected. We will try the battering ram again. This time, scan the wall for anything unusual. If you see any ropes or water skins or anything else that looks out of place, pull the men back."

Marcus agreed. "Yes, Sire. But I would like to make one request."

"What request?" Reddland asked.

"That I don't take the two squads of infantry men forward as we usually do. If we start to breech the gate, I'll signal for them to be sent up then. Their only purpose is to maintain a breech until the bulk of the infantry can come through anyway."

Reddland thought this through. "Request granted."

Once again Lexton signaled the trumpeter and the battering ram rolled back toward the oratory gates. Marcus followed behind on horseback.

"Here they come again!" Cad signaled Novak. Cyrus readied his men in case they were needed.

"Zephyr, go back with the archers and have them notch up an arrow, just for looks." Cad's eyes never left the approaching battering ram. Zephyr re-formed the archers along the parapet.

Marcus followed his men from a safe distance. He scanned the walls for anything out of the ordinary. He saw the rebel archers notch their arrows. His men were safe beneath the charred roof of the battering ram. Again, the rebels made none of the usual responses he had seen so many others do in similar situations. And again, Marcus had a bad feeling about the whole thing. The rebels acted as if they were not concerned in the least that they were about to be attacked. They offered no resistance to the positioning of the ram at their gates. They shot no arrows at his men.

A bead of sweat trickled from under Marcus's helmet and down his cheek. Finally, he noticed something peculiar. Two sentries, one directly on each side of the gate, held a torch. It was daylight and they had torches. They didn't wave them or throw them on the men below. They just stood there. Marcus noticed Cad raise his visor.

What Marcus didn't know, couldn't have known, was that by raising his visor, Cad had signaled the sentries by the cauldrons. The sentries were sitting on the parapet out of sight of Reddland's men. On Cad's signal, the sentries loosed the corks that plugged two-inch holes near the bottom of each cauldron. Instantly, Cad's processed oil spilled out and into funnels attached to hundred-foot sections of pipe. Every ten feet the diameter of the pipe decreased. By the time the oil reached the end of the hundred-foot section, it was highly pressurized.

If Marcus had been closer he would have seen two freshly bored holes in the oratory wall just above the gates. He also would have seen small metal grates covering those holes.

In an instant, high-pressured oil sprayed out of the holes onto the battering ram and much of the surrounding area. Before Marcus realized what happened, the two sentries held their torches in front of the oil. The result was explosive, and unlike anything he had ever seen.

Marcus's horse reared up in terror at the flames shooting out of the oratory wall. He felt a blast of heat as he tried to regain control of his spooked mount. Every Royal soldier watching from the distance took a step back in utter shock. For a full thirty seconds the battering ram and the twenty-four men operating it were engulfed in a ball of fire. For a brief moment Marcus believed in fire breathing dragons. Reddland and the entire Royal force stared at the spectacle aghast.

This was the first time Marcus did not know what to do in battle. Black smoke billowed up from the battering ram. Shrieks from the twenty-four soldiers sent chills down the Royal lines. The smell of burning flesh stunned Marcus's nostrils. He knew his men were lost and turned sullenly for the Royal lines riding slowly. At that moment, he didn't care if he took an arrow.

Reddland and Lexton watched fire consume the battering ram and the soldiers beneath it. Reddland filled with rage, a rage brought on by fear. For the first time he felt uncertain. He had suffered losses before to be sure, but none as bizarre as this. Many of his men held strange and strong superstitions, and this certainly played hard on their fears. Reddland was determined to have the victory, determined that those dirty rebels would suffer losses before this day was through.

"Sire! What just happened?" Lexton stared, mouth agape as burning soldiers stumbled from the flames, only to collapse a few yards away. Lexton did not have the same cocky self-assurance he began the battle with.

Marcus rode into the ranks and stopped by Reddland. His face was moist and pale. He stared vacantly ahead and said nothing. There was nothing to say. Everyone had witnessed the flames shoot out of the oratory wall and no one could explain it. Many in the Royal ranks felt it was an omen.

"That does it! These rebels have had their fun. Let's just see how good they are at playing my games! They will regret the day they ever heard the name Luther Reddland. I want them dead. I want their horses dead. I want the whole place destroyed. If they think for one minute that I am impressed with their little fire show, they are kidding themselves. We will show them a display of force that will make them think the entire world has come to its end!" Reddland was purple with rage. He paced his horse back and forth. "Lexton, call in all of my commanders."

Lexton rode off to carry out his orders. His voice could be heard shouting for the unit's captains. Reddland turned to Marcus who continued staring at nothing in particular.

"Marcus, we need a victory." Reddland cooled a little and now spoke in a more normal tone.

Marcus raised his eyebrows and nodded. He still remained silent. He removed his helmet and slicked back his sweaty hair. The breeze felt good on his face.

"And you, Marcus, gather yourself together. You look like a nervous wreck. Act like a leader in the Royal army, not like one of the men. They're going to need us to be strong." Reddland didn't like weakness, especially in his officers. Marcus hadn't been himself recently, and Reddland was becoming annoyed by it.

Marcus's jaw tightened and his countenance grew hard. Thirty-five men under his command had just died in the last half hour while he could do nothing but stand by and watch. Didn't Reddland care about them? They were his men too. Marcus put on a good face, but deep down he had grown weary. And quite frankly, he didn't feel like sending his men into battle if they didn't have a chance. Sword fights made sense. What just happened defied his logic.

Lexton rounded up the unit commanders and brought them to Reddland. Each hoped for orders that didn't involve battering the gate.

Reddland addressed his commanders. "Here is my plan. I want a full barrage from the catapults. Smash those gates to pieces and bring the walls down on all sides. These imbeciles must not be allowed to enjoy another success. Archers, I want a volley of flaming arrows. Spread the shots out and try to catch something on fire." Reddland's tone was dusted with sarcasm. "Then, I want you to fire at will at any available target until I say otherwise. I want the infantry ready to charge through the gate the moment it comes down, and the cavalry will be right behind them in reserve. I want the rebels knocked so hard it throws them from their boots. Does everyone understand their orders?"

Marcus had another idea. "Maybe we should attack another wall in a feigning maneuver to draw some of their men away, and then suddenly attack from the opposite side. I think the situation needs more analysis. We could even attack in shifts through the night, keep the rebels exhausted. I believe we should take the time to formulate more of a long-term strategy. They can't very well leave."

Reddland's impatience was obvious. "No, Marcus. We cannot allow them to gloat over their success. We heavily outnumber them. The rebels will be no match for a full scale onslaught."

The other commanders seemed to agree with Reddland. Logically, Reddland was right. But the rebels were not using logic, and Marcus knew it. If they had, odds were they wouldn't be in this situation in the first place. Marcus was outvoted and would obey his orders. He only hoped the others were right.

"Well, now that we're all in agreement, begin the attack on my signal. Have the archers fire heavily enough so the rebels keep their heads down." Reddland smiled.

"What are they doing now?" Thadus climbed up to the parapet and found Cad. Cad had been watching Reddland through the spyglass.

"It looks like we've managed to rattle their nerves a bit. It is a big advantage for us to be fighting a group of men who are unsure of what to expect. The need to be prepared for the unexpected will distract them from their duties in battle."

"Well, I'm glad you're pleased thus far. Things are going well." Thadus was relieved at the positive report. "But what are we going to be doing next?"

Cad shrugged his shoulders. "As soon as I know what their next move is, I'll know what our next move is. It looks like they're formulating a plan. Reddland called all of the commanding officers together."

"May I?" Thadus pointed to the spyglass. Cad obliged his friend. Thadus scanned the ranks of the Royal soldiers. "This is a powerful spyglass. I can see their faces as plain as I can see yours. I don't believe it! Wallace has joined the Royal Guard!" Thadus gasped.

"You mean the rebel spy Scorpyus was suspicious of?" Cad inquired.

Thadus nodded. "Yes. Scorpyus was right all along" Further discussion on the matter was cut painfully short.

Thunderous cracks from the catapults springing loose echoed from behind the Royal lines. Trumpeters sounded their instructions to Reddland's men. Simultaneously, the Royal archers prepared flaming arrows and the infantry started to move. Reddland sat atop his mount keenly watching the activities. Marcus and Lexton readied their men. Drakar blissfully chanted a curse on the rebels, holding his arms up and muttering gibberish that only the Tanuba clerics understood.

When Cad heard all the Royal catapults release, his heart skipped a beat. "Get down!"

Cad dove, bringing the sentry next to him down also. "Stay down until the barrage stops. They won't charge as long as they're firing the catapults."

Pandemonium broke out on the rebel lines. Boulders rolled through the air, slamming down with ground-shaking ferocity. One boulder struck the wall near the gate knocking a stone from its place. Another boulder crashed violently into the earth, spewing dirt onto Thadus and a stretcher-bearer who hunkered down against the perimeter wall. And another stone tore a branch from one of the few trees on the grounds.

After the first volley, Novak knew the oratory and his men were out of range of the Royal catapults. Only the outer wall and half of the grounds appeared to be reachable. The rebel catapult teams were not as lucky. They were well within the strike zone.

"If our catapults are in range of theirs, then theirs are in range of ours." Novak had a plan. "Infantry men, stay here! I'll be right back." He sprinted across the grounds.

Meanwhile, Cad crawled rapidly toward Zephyr who lay prone along the parapet; his greaves scraping along the stones. "Zephyr, get the archers out of here! I think they're going to hit us with everything they have. Form up somewhere out of range of the catapults and be ready in case they breach our defenses."

Before Zephyr could answer, a jarring impact rattled her bones. Pebbles and sand showered her and Cad as a crack appeared on the wall near their heads. Streaks of fire whizzed overhead.

"Flaming arrows!" Zephyr cried out following the flames with her eyes.

"I think this will bloody well continue until they breach our outer wall. Then they will send in their men. When they do, we are going to need you to get some arrows on them. And you will need to be behind our troops to do that; not on the wall." Cad brushed dust from his face and goatee.

Zephyr concurred and crawled along the parapet giving her archers instructions, pausing at each one to make sure they understood. When she gave the word, they would follow her toward the main building.

Novak reached the first catapult and ordered, "Fire back at them! Aim in the direction their boulders are coming from. Maybe we will get lucky and take out a few of their catapults." He wanted to get some use from the rebel catapults before they were disabled. At the current rate the Royal army was firing, that wouldn't be long.

Novak saw a brief blur and the crewmen he was speaking with disappeared. Then there was a huge crash and the sound of splintering wood. Something hit Novak in the chest and threw him onto his back. After shaking the shock out of his eyes, Novak saw an arrow buried it the ground near his head. The crewman he had just been talking to lay crushed to death in the rubble of the catapult, the man's blood splattered everywhere. Another crewman was also wounded, and still another lay crying out in pain as he held his leg. Novak realized he had been struck in the chest by a piece of wood from the fragmenting catapult, and hit hard enough to put a small dent in his cuirass.

He sprang to his feet and rushed to the downed crewmen: two seemed to be fine, just a little shaken; the other had an arrow in his calf. Two others had been killed. "You two, get him in to see Doc." Novak pointed to the man with an arrow in his leg then ran to the next catapult crew, and gave them instructions. Soon, he had the remaining rebel catapults firing back as fast as the crews could work. Satisfied, Novak returned to his troops.

"Alright, men, prepare to move! We could be needed at any moment." Novak could see Cyrus riding along the three other walls, apparently instructing some of the sentries to move toward the main gate. So far the Royal army was concentrating their efforts on the main gate. It looks like Reddland was going to keep things simple and hit them in the front door.

———◆•◆———

Zephyr had the archers pull back toward the oratory. She was in the last group to leave the front wall. Arrows flew all around as she sprinted for safety. A boulder crashed into the ground thirty feet away and sent her heart racing. An arrow shot by dangerously close to her head. Out of the corner of her eye, Zephyr saw the archer running next to her suddenly lurch forward. The lurch was followed by a ground-pounding thud. She turned to see a headless body run a few more steps before faltering to the ground. Zephyr held back the nausea by swallowing hard. She continued on without breaking stride. Another arrow darted by her a few feet away.

Almost out of the strike zone, Zephyr paused to assist another archer who had been struck with an arrow in her right hip. The archer gritted her teeth in agony. Zephyr helped her to her feet and supported her as she limped to safety. She decided to take the wounded archer to the hospital.

Emerald met them at the oratory doors. "Let me help you with her."

Zephyr gladly accepted Emerald's help. "How's Doc doing so far?" She inquired.

"Right now we are keeping up. How are you doing? It sounds so terrible. Every time a rock hits the wall we can hear it in here." Emerald had bloodstains on her apron and hands, and her blond hair was now up in a bun. Both women helped their wounded companion into the building for treatment.

—•◆•—

Cad ran to the gate. The Royal catapults had perfected their aim and were pounding away at the entrance with regularity. A breech was inevitable.

Before leaving the outer wall to form up the cavalry, Cad flipped his visor down and peeked over the wall, taking one last look at Reddland's position. The Royal troops were kneeling behind their shields. Farther in the distance, out of catapult range, Royal cavalry troops were in formation, no doubt in expectation of a breech at the gate. It did not take long for a Royal archer to find Cad. An arrow slammed into his helmet and ricochet skyward. Cad ducked, albeit too late had he not worn head protection. He leaned over the parapet into the courtyard and called, "Hey, Thadus!" Cad waived his cohort closer.

"What is it?" Thadus had a worried look on his face and a dazed sentry clinging to his shoulder for support.

"The Royal Guard is preparing to send the infantry against us. As soon as the gate is smashed, they will attack. When they attack, they'll also stop lobbing arrows at us to avoid hitting their own men. Once the barrage stops, get all the support personnel out of here to a position behind the archers and near the oratory. The battle will be too intense to try and help the wounded until after we push them back." Cad explained his predictions for the immediate future.

Thadus's expression changed to a look of horror. "What do you mean they're going to smash through the gate?"

Cad held up a gauntleted hand. "I expected them to eventually breech the walls and I fully expect to push them back out again."

Thadus did not look convinced. "Alright, if you say so. I'll move behind the archers when the arrows stop."

"Good. You need to prepare yourself. The fight will be messy." Cad lifted his visor in order to make the conversation he was about to have with Thadus more personal. "It's going to be bloody, and men will be maimed and killed. Some of our men will probably break down. Escort those out with the wounded if you can."

Thadus nodded, wide-eyed and pale at the thought of seeing his worst nightmares come to life.

The relentless barrage continued. Boulder after boulder crashed into the rebel fortifications. With a horrendous crash, another rebel catapult was silenced, debris exploding everywhere. Immediately, litter bearers moved in to help the wounded crew. Cad noticed that Cyrus now had the bulk of his sentries on the front wall. Cyrus saw Cad looking in his direction and raised his thumb up to show all was well. Both knew the true test of rebel courage lay just ahead of them all.

⸺⋯◆⋯⸺

Reddland sat atop his mount, puffed up and proud, watching with satisfaction the gradual deterioration of the rebels fortifying wall. The gate was near collapse, and Marcus and Lexton were ready for an all-out assault. The Royal troops were more confident after witnessing the terrible barrage of arrows and projectiles the rebels were receiving. It was a welcome departure from the fire show they endured earlier.

Reddland was unaffected by the sporadic retaliation from the rebel catapults, even when one of his own catapults and a few archers were struck by lucky shots. When Reddland felt confident, casualties were acceptable. He would not have to wait much longer now. The gate would be breached, the Royal infantry would storm the oratory grounds, and the rebellion would be crushed. The plan was all so simple.

Cad peeked over the wall again. Several hundred Royal soldiers were now formed up, shield to shield with swords drawn, their bright surcoats a blue river. Cad glanced back inside the oratory grounds. Thadus had rounded up his stretcher bearers and a few wounded soldiers. He was ready to lead them to the main building once the barrage stopped. Several sentries fought to keep the gates closed, bracing them with four-by-four beams. Cad climbed down from the parapet and went to the gate. Cyrus barked out instructions to the sentries, preparing them for a breech.

Cad mounted his waiting horse. "I'm going to get the cavalry ready. Stay sharp. It won't be long now." Cyrus reigned his horse in next to Cad and nodded. The breach came sooner then expected.

Suddenly, with a huge explosion, the stone archway above the gate blew apart leaving only a jagged outcropping to mark where it once stood. Debris showered the sentries as they fought to brace up the gate. One sentry had been knocked unconscious by a falling stone.

Cad and Cyrus and their horses recoiled from the blast. The Royal onslaught was imminent. Cad spurred his horse and galloped to where Novak had the infantry formed up into two companies. "Are you ready?"

Novak's cape fluttered in the breeze. "Definitely; I'll attack with one company as they enter the grounds and wait for your signal." Novak could feel his pulse quicken in anticipation of combat, a feeling he thrived on.

"It sounds good. Just fight. Don't worry about watching the Royal soldiers. I'll keep watch over them. When you hear a long blast on the trumpet from behind you, start your maneuver. Do all your men know what to do?" Cad was a stickler for details.

"Ya, they all know what to do."

"Is Zephyr ready with her part?"

Novak nodded. "She's got her archers formed up behind us."

Cad smiled and reached down from his horse. He and Novak clasped forearms. "Stay alive."

"You too," Novak's brow furrowed. "Let's get them for Scorpyus. They have a beating coming the way I see it."

Cad nodded his head approvingly and the two friends parted company. He pitied the first Royal soldier that tangled with Novak. Cad spurred his horse and rode hard to his cavalry troops. "Mount up and grab your lances."

They had fashioned lances out of wooden poles and added sharpened metal tips. They looked more like gigantic spears then lances. Cad had his men line up side-by-side, lances held in tight. The soldier to Cad's right held a trumpet in his free hand, waiting for his orders. All rebel eyes sat fixed on the gate knowing that as soon as it was breached their war machine would be put into action.

———◆———

Abrams stood on a catwalk on the oratory roof. From there he would have a clear view of the entire battlefield. He had been in prayer all morning and now wanted to see those who he would be praying for throughout the upcoming battle. Perhaps he could direct his prayers toward critical incidents as he saw them arise.

Abrams looked upon the rebellion with each person in his place, ready to take on a larger force. Each was ready to make a sacrifice for their fellow citizens who lacked the courage to be here with them; each taking a stand for what was right, each taking a stand for God.

On the other side of the gate Reddland and his men fought for what they could get by way of spoils. They were driven by the promise of wealth, food, and women. They believed what they wanted to believe and heard what they wanted to hear. Most weren't even practicing Tanuba worshippers. They only supported the cult because it endorsed their ways of life. The Royal soldiers stood in sharp contrast to the rebel troops.

It was a strange phenomenon. How does one group come to a knowledge of God, while the other creates a god from their own imagination? If someone was ignorant about God, it was not due to a lack of information. It was because of rejection of it. For various reasons, the Royal soldiers molded a god to fit their beliefs instead of molding their beliefs to fit God's.

Abrams watched boulder after boulder strike the perimeter gate. The sentries scrambled to brace the crumbling wall. Others tried valiantly to douse flaming arrows. However brave the rebel fighters were, the pounding of the Royal catapults was too intense. The inevitable happened. With a resounding crash, a boulder came splintering through the gate, ripping most of it from its hinges. One sentry lay wounded as a result of the hit. All chaos unleashed, shouts erupted from both sides of the wall followed by a series of blasts from a trumpet. With a shout, the Royal soldiers surged forward, swords drawn, toward the breach in the rebel defense. Some of the Royal soldiers carried ladders.

At that instant, Thadus led his group back to the oratory.

Cyrus waved his arms directing his sentries to the parapets where they could defend against the Royal soldiers with the ladders. Abrams saw Novak and half of the infantry thunder towards the gate to meet the attackers. Zephyr had all of her archers notched and drawn, ready to send a volley into the Royal lines as they funneled through the gate. The three remaining rebel catapults were adjusted and aimed in preparation. Cad had the cavalry maintain position. He sat atop his mount and watched the scene unfold.

Abrams expected a lot of things about witnessing a battle. One thing he had not foreseen was the sheer enormity of it. The sound was deafening: metal clanging, men shouting, the wounded screaming, and horses neighing all blended into one large wall of sound. How could anyone hear their orders? The noise grew even louder.

A barrage of arrows mowed down the first of the Royal soldiers to reach the courtyard. A boulder from a well-aimed catapult punched a hole through the next rank. The screams of the wounded Royal troops echoed through the oratory grounds, but the soldiers kept flooding into the courtyard. In an explosive clash of metal, Novak and his infantry slammed into the advancing soldiers like two great rams butting heads.

Abrams stood transfixed, mouth agape, watching the battle unfold. Arrows flew everywhere as the blue surge of the Royal troops continued spilling onto the grounds, mixing with the rebels.

Novak threw himself into the fracas. Soon, he was lost in a sea of swords, shields, and men. All around, he could hear the angry clash of metal against metal. Scowling, with teeth gritted, he swung, chopped and jabbed with his sword. It seemed that two new soldiers replaced each one he killed, and the two he now faced were experienced. While Novak parried with one, the other tried to flank him to the left. Novak blocked the flanking attack with his buckler, then side kicked the soldier in the groin, all the while maintaining a defense against the first soldier. Novak's flanking attacker collapsed for the time being. Novak heard a loud scream to his immediate right. Ignoring the sound, Novak advanced on the remaining attacker. This one swung his flail toward Novak's head. Again, Novak blocked the blow with his buckler. Two of the flail's spiked balls clattered against the shield, the third swung over the top and whipped down into Novak's forearm. Blood ran from the puncture wound halfway between his wrist and elbow. He grabbed the chain of the flail and jerked it to the left ripping the weapon so hard from the soldier's hand that it spun him sideways. Taking a step, he thrust his sword into the soldier's armpit above his cuirass. Another Royal guard came at Novak. Feeling a blow to his left shin, Novak glanced down to see that he was stepping on a soldier's arm. That soldier was swinging his sword at Novak's legs with his free arm. Novak brought his other foot into the soldier's chin with such force that it sent the man's helmet clattering into a tangle of feet. Novak stepped on through his kick and engaged the advancing soldier.

Novak was beating a few dents into the soldier's shield but could not find an opening. After another flurry of blows, he found himself face to face with the man, swords locked, each trying to push the other off balance. Out of the corner of his eye, Novak saw yet another soldier charge him. This one had a pole arm with a long slender spearhead. Without hesitation, Novak reached around and grabbed the surcoat of the soldier he had locked swords with. With a grunt Novak swung him into the path of the charging soldier with the pole arm. Both Royal soldiers' eyes went wide, one because he had been pierced in the back, the other because he had inadvertently done the deed. Novak finished off the other soldier before he had a chance to remove his pole arm from his friend. Novak stepped on somebody else. This time he looked down to see a dead rebel soldier.

Another rebel had been knocked down and was frantically trying to reach his sword. His attacker had his battleaxe raised above his head and was going in for the kill. The Royal soldier brought the axe down full force only to have it blocked at the last second by Novak's sword. The rebel found his own sword and scampered to his feet, grateful for the assistance. The Royal soldier looked to see who had thwarted his kill. It was one of the largest men he had ever seen. Unlike his predecessors, he immediately realized he was in for a whipping and hastily retreated. Novak did not bother to pursue, as there were several other opponents close at hand.

—◦•◦—

Abrams watched the carnage from the roof. He saw the rebels beat back the Royal Guardsmen time and again only to have them replaced by more men charging through the gate. Other soldiers tried to climb over the wall on ladders. At first, the sentries pushed the ladders over and fought the Royal Guard off. Then some Royal soldiers who had entered through the gate went to the ladders leading up to the parapet. Furiously, the sentries defended their wall, but the parapet ladder nearest the gate was soon taken and Royal soldiers started filing up to the parapets. Cyrus saw this and spurred his horse into a gallop. He plowed right into the soldiers waiting their turn to climb to the parapet, sending two of them bouncing along the dirt. Cyrus struck down the Royal Guardsmen on the ladder. Turning, he started viciously defending the parapet's access point. If the Royal soldiers gained control of the parapets they would be able to funnel their troops into the compound faster. The infantry could barely keep up with the current pace of infiltration.

Cyrus single-handedly defended access to the parapet. He shouted orders for the sentries to bring more men from the other walls. He could see his sentries busy with the dozen or so Royal soldiers who had made it to the parapet.

Several other of Reddland's men rushed toward Cyrus and plunged daggers into his horse. They wanted onto the parapet badly. Cyrus swung frantically at them until his wounded horse started rearing up in pain. The horse turned, and Cyrus felt a thunderous blow to the side of his head. The blow knocked his helmet into the fray and he felt warm blood run down his face. His horse staggered and began to collapse. Dazed and light-headed, Cyrus grabbed the top rung of the ladder. Quick-thinking sentries pulled him to the parapet just as his horse collapsed. They leaned a semi-conscious Cyrus against the wall. He sat momentarily dazed. While the commotion swirled all around him, making his head spin even more: one sentry pushed a Royal soldier off the ladder with his spear while another worked to dislodge the ladder from the wall and another joined in and started jabbing his spear at the invaders. The sharpened point kept them at bay while the ladder was briskly pulled onto the parapet. Reddland's men would have to find another route up the wall. The delay in finding one would buy the rebels time.

Cyrus's double vision cleared, and he regained his bearings enough to stand. Blood ran down his cheek. It had been a close call.

The three remaining rebel catapult teams worked feverishly to launch projectiles as fast as they could over the breached gate and into the advancing Royal troops: ropes creaked under the strain of being wound tightly to load the catapult, the crew rolled a boulder into the apparatus, and then a man pulled a lever to send the boulder sailing through the air. The catapult crews repeated this process over and over as fast as they could.

With the gate smashed, the Royal Guard's catapults were now turned against the rebel catapults. They were increasing their accuracy, making adjustments in their aim, slowly finding their mark. It was a slow and brutal duel.

Zephyr positioned her archers near the oratory and instructed them to fire volleys over the rebels toward the gates into the advancing Royal troops. She took the four best marksmen with her to the periphery of the main battle that raged on the grounds. She had an idea she hoped would work.

"Alright, I want each of you to target the soldiers fighting your friends! Take your time to aim. If you miss your target, there is a good chance you will hit your own men! If you are not confident in your ability to hit your target accurately, do not take the shot. There will be dozens of opportunities. Our men need all the help we can give them and you four are the archers with the best chances of being successful under these circumstances. I know this is unconventional, but it will work. The Royal army must concentrate on defending themselves against our infantry. They won't expect us to be shooting at them. One last thing, by all means do not get yourselves drawn into the fight. Stay on the outskirts. If a Royal soldier leaves the battle and advances toward you, retreat. Go to the cavalry or to a group of archers; go anywhere there are greater numbers of our men." Zephyr set her plan into motion and she and the other four archers began circling the battle. It was a good plan. No one expects arrows to be shot into a pitched battle where the odds of hitting one of your own are high. But Zephyr was a gambling woman. She knew she had the marksmanship skills for the task; and she prayed she had chosen wisely the other four archers.

Zephyr stalked the outskirts of the fracas, waiting patiently for an opportunity. The carnage was sickening. Amidst the clash of steel upon steel, she could hear the cries of the wounded. Zephyr had seen her share of the mortally wounded, but no one should ever get used to the carnage of battle or the screams. Zephyr pressed on.

A Royal Guardsman was about to bring his raised battle-axe down on a fallen rebel. Zephyr took aim just above the breastplate and loosed her arrow. A half-second later, the arrow appeared in the guardsman's throat buried up to its fletching.

The Royal soldier's eyes grew wide in shock and he froze, battle-axe still raised. Unable to make a sound, he dropped the axe and slowly sank to his knees, his hands gripping his throat. The rebel soldier scrambled to his feet and gave Zephyr an intense look of gratitude. She nodded her acknowledgement. The rebel was soon engaged in a melee with another opponent.

Cad surveyed the battle with his spyglass. So far, the rebellion was doing better than expected. Cad knew it wouldn't last. Eventually, enough Royal soldiers would struggle through the gate and the rebels would be too heavily outnumbered and too weary to hold their lines. Cad planned to mount his cavalry charge at that precise moment.

Through the spyglass Cad found Novak. Scorpyus had always been impressive to watch in combat with his speed and agility which made his opponents feel like they were fighting a shadow. Novak, on the other hand, was awe inspiring. What he lacked in speed he made up for in raw power. Even if a Royal soldier were to block one of Novak's blows, the force would knock them back two or three steps. Royal Guardsmen had to fight him three-to-one. Still, Novak was clearing a path wherever he went. It reminded Cad of a farmer with a sickle during wheat harvest.

Cad put away the spyglass and looked to his men. "Get ready. It won't be long now." The cavalry readied their lances and waited for the trumpeter to sound the charge.

Abrams watched the three remaining catapult crews valiantly fight a lopsided battle. The Royal Guard had a lot more artillery and the rebel catapults could not hold out much longer. For fear of hitting their own troops, the Royal catapult crews had long since ceased firing on the rebel infantry, and were concentrating on the two remaining rebel catapults. The Royal crews finally perfected their aim. The consequences were disastrous for the rebels.

Two boulders came hurtling over the wall in rapid succession, just as the rebels launched their own toward the other side. One boulder slammed down on a rebel catapult and shattered wood and bodies flew in all directions. The other Royal projectile smashed head on into the rebel projectile. It was a display that could only happen once in a thousand years. The boulders exploded into a shower of fragments.

Cad realized Novak and the infantry were about to be overwhelmed. Enough Royal troops had entered the fight to start giving Novak's infantry trouble maintaining their position. Now was the time. Cad signaled his trumpeter to sound the charge. The horn blasted across the grounds and Cad spurred his horse on. Thirty horses galloped at once into the heat of the battle. Each rider clung tightly to lances braced against their sides. On the field, Novak heard the cavalry sound their charge and gave the order for his men to flank left and right. In unison the infantry's lines parted to the sides, making a hole for the charging cavalry. The Royal troops continued their flow into the grounds.

Spear tipped lances hurtled toward the Royal soldiers, each propelled by fifteen-hundred pounds of equestrian might. Cad pulled his lance in tight to his side. Looking through the slits of his visor, he aimed his lance for a thick group of Royal soldiers. Perhaps his horse would trample those escaping his lance. Novak already orchestrated the rapid parting of the infantry. They were safely to the sides of the charging cavalry. Without missing a beat, the Royal troops pursued Novak's infantry as they made their maneuver, many mistaking it for a retreat. Other Royal soldiers funneled into the perimeter gates. These were the ones Cad targeted.

Cad leaned forward and braced for the impact. His horse let out a nervous whinny as it sensed the collision, but stayed on course. Cad made one last-second adjustment to the aim of his lance, then all of a sudden he jerked back violently in the saddle. The force of the impact nearly tore him from his mount, rattling his bones and blurring his vision for a moment. The resounding crash of the rebel cavalry impaling the Royal infantrymen echoed across the grounds, momentarily drawing the attention of the other combatants. It was a fatal loss of concentration for the soldier fighting Novak.

Shouts and screams now mixed with the whinnying of horses and the clanking of swords. The battle around the gate was in chaos. Cad's arm had been jerked violently to the right. His shoulder felt like it had been dislocated, but he could still move it. He felt other lesser impacts brush against his legs as his horse plowed through the enemy ranks. Cad quickly pulled himself back into a seated position. In his right hand were the splintered remains of his lance. The rest of the shaft impaled two Royal soldiers and wounded a third. The Royal soldiers suffered a serious blow and were in a state of panic. The influx of blue surcoats stalled.

Cad swung the nub of his lance into the chin of a soldier who grabbed his horse's reins, knocking him off his feet. Throwing the shattered stick down, he drew his sword. He yelled orders for the cavalry to continue to push through and out the gate.

Novak had held half of his infantry back from the first attack. Now, that other half was right behind Cad and his cavalry, moving up to help push the Royal soldiers back. Novak and his other men were ready to deal with whomever was left from the cavalry charge. Cad gritted his teeth, determined to push the enemy out.

Cad found himself in a sea of blue surcoats, his mount stepping nervously amid the clamor. He reined around and spurred his horse on, cutting a swath through the Royal army.

Angling to the right, he engaged a hairy soldier who took offense at being nudged by a horse. The melee was short-lived. After Cad successfully blocked two wild swings, his mount reared up and came down on the soldier's foot. With a yell, the man lowered his weapon to push on the horse's neck and shoulder to relieve the pain. Cad took the opportunity and brought his sword down on his opponent's clavicle near the neck. As Cad engaged the next soldier, he felt a massive blow to his back. The jolt shot up his spine, pounded his head, and rattled his teeth. He had never felt such a blow and he thought that maybe a catapult had struck him.

Cad started to turn to see who or what attacked his rear and saw a flash to his left out of the corner of his eye. Reflexes brought up his shield and with a clang something big crashed against it. Cad lurched to the right and was nearly knocked from the saddle. Again, he felt the vibration in his joints. Now Cad was angry. Quickly he reined his horse around and saw a huge man wielding a battle-axe. Marcus had found him.

Cad spurred his horse towards the behemoth soldier, determined to use the horse's weight to his advantage. Cad swung and parried, looking for an opening. Marcus returned the favor. Cad blocked blow after blow with his shield.

The exchange lasted a long time as the two well-trained soldiers fought. Sweat ran into Cad's eyes and the air grew thick in his helmet. The fight dragged on, each soldier battering the other. Finally Cad backed Marcus up against the wall with his horse, effectively pinning his huge adversary. Cad swung his sword repeatedly down on Marcus. Marcus blocked each blow and searched for an escape route.

Cad pushed Marcus even closer to the wall to where there was scarcely room between his mount and the wall. There was no room to swing his sword and he could only stab at Marcus. Cad tried to spur his horse in to crush his opponent while simultaneously trying to impale him.

Letting go of his battle-axe, Marcus braced against the wall and pushed Cad's horse with all of his might. The horse didn't budge. Marcus pummeled Cad's thigh and hip.

The formidable foes locked in close-quarter combat, each almost oblivious to the battle raging on around them. Realizing he was too close to use his sword effectively, Cad brought his hilt down on Marcus's head. Ignoring the pain shooting through his thigh, Cad hammered away at Marcus. He saw dimples appear on Marcus's helmet. Blood blossomed on Marcus's cheek and the bridge of his nose as Cad drove his hilt downward as hard as he could. Marcus regretted his choice of a visorless helmet. Using all of his strength, Cad delivered blow after blow, refusing to let up, all the while driving his horse into his foe. Marcus had been in tight spots before but this one had to end fast. Blood poured from his nostrils.

When Cad brought his hilt down again, Marcus grabbed his wrist and started twisting Cad's arm back. Cad rolled his body forward and strained with all his strength to keep his arm from being rotated. Pain shot through Cad's tendons, and it felt like his shoulder was about to burst. Quickly, he loosed his right foot from the stirrup and brought his knee up hard into Marcus's face. Marcus's jaw slammed shut with a snap, and Cad tore his arm free from his adversary's clasp. A flash of light and a welt above his eyebrow told Marcus that Cad was pummeling him with the hilt of his sword again. Marcus had had enough. Cad was too skilled to allow this to continue.

This guy is bloody incredible, Cad thought, and dealt yet another blow. How much punishment could one man take? For a split second it looked as though the fight was over and Marcus dropped his arms. But then there was the flash of a dagger.

"Arrgh!" Marcus let out a yell as he buried his dagger up to the hilt in the side of Cad's mount. He twisted and pulled up on the blade with enough force to slit open the side of the animal. The horse immediately reared up on its hind legs and let out an agonizing whinny. Cad hit the ground with a thud, his left foot caught in the stirrups. The horse's intestines fell out as it galloped madly away. Marcus was relieved to see his threatening opponent go bouncing across the battlefield.

In its final, frantic gallop, Cad's crazed mount bolted for nowhere in particular, blood spilling from its side. Cad could not free his left foot from the stirrup and was dragged through a tangle of legs and fallen soldiers, plowing a swath with his body through the crowd, occasionally bouncing into the air like a stone skipping across the water. His sleeve caught on a fallen soldier's armor and made his arm whip above his head and dislodge his sword. His mount trotted on, not caring that Cad's arm was caught in a snag. The horse dragged both bodies for several feet until Cad's sleeve tore away and he found himself freed from the snag, but still being carried away from the fight. Cad's mount continued on, but slowed.

—•◆•—

Zephyr had just loosed an arrow, taking down another Royal Guardsman, when she saw a riderless horse running toward her. It didn't look like the animal was going to swerve. The panicked horse dragged something behind it. She had just enough time to scramble a few steps and dive out of the way, her cap falling to the ground.

It was Cad. Zephyr looked back and confirmed her suspicion. He tried to brace himself against the bouncing ride and to dodge obstacles. Any thoughts of investigating further were dashed by a Royal soldier barreling down on her. She quickly switched from longbow to sword.

The Royal soldier swung down on Zephyr with a mace that slammed into the earth where she had been one second earlier. Zephyr could see the vain overconfidence all over his face. She could also see the soldier's love of ale spilling over his belt buckle. He still smelled of ale. He turned rapidly on Zephyr, jiggling as he stepped towards her for another swing. He missed again. This time, Zephyr's sword came down on his helmet. Judging from his one-eyed, squinting grimace, he was nursing a hangover. The glancing blow should not have caused that much pain. The soldier tried a third swing. Zephyr blocked it with her sword and brought her foot hard into his groin. The soldier froze, momentarily paralyzed. A guttural groan escaped his gritted teeth. Zephyr finished him off quickly and retrieved her hat. She sheathed her sword and switched back to her longbow.

—◦•◦—

Cad's wild ride came to an abrupt halt. Battered, but grateful it wasn't worse, Cad pulled his dagger and cut the stirrup from his foot. His horse lay on its side breathing heavily, pink froth foaming from the puncture wound. A three-foot gash was torn into the animal's belly. It had lost a lot of blood and was partially disemboweled

Cad's saddle was twisted to his mount's left side making it easier to cut the leather above the stirrup with his dagger. A stein full of dirt fell from Cad's head when he removed his helmet. Sweat and dirt combined into a muddy paste on his face and his mouth was gritty. He lost his sword somewhere along the way. He retrieved his battle-axe from its ring on the saddle, and with a mighty chop, mercifully ended his mount's suffering.

Cad took his waterskin from the saddlebag. He spat the first mouthful of water out after rinsing some of the dirt from his teeth. After gulping down several mouthfuls of the warm water, Cad poured the rest over his head. He worked his hands through his hair and goatee. The breeze felt good on his moistened skin. Full-face helmets had their drawbacks but Cad knew today why he still preferred them.

Not wasting any time, Cad banged his helmet against a boot, knocking as much dust out of it as he could. Donning it again, he proceeded on foot back into the battle. From what he could tell, half of the cavalry were either wounded or dismounted for other reasons. Novak had set aside very capable men for the cavalry and they had done a good job in stemming the flow of Royal soldiers into the oratory grounds. That maneuver, combined with the sudden influx of the other half of Novak's infantry, had the desired result. The Royal forces were being pushed out of the perimeter walls.

Seeing this gave Cad a surge of energy. Reddland would soon attempt to regroup his men and stop their retreat with a cavalry charge of his own. The Royal troops still in the oratory grounds were fighting their way back to the gate in retreat, realizing their comrades were no longer able to gain access and assist them. The next minutes were pivotal. The rebels had to push the Royals completely back before Reddland could counterattack with his cavalry.

Cad ran back into the battle and started commanding the rebel troops to follow him. "Come on! Charge the gates!" He ran down the line shouting for everyone to charge. The Royal troops within the grounds would have to find a way out or be trapped.

On the other side of the battle, Novak was doing the same.

The combined tactical effort was successful. The Royal troops outside the gates had been momentarily halted by the onslaught of the rebel cavalry and remaining infantry. Marcus and Lexton had also been driven back by the intense battle. This left the Royal troops without leadership.

Sensing the wavering retreat of the Royals, the rebels had a surge of confidence. The ferocity of the rebel attackers increased at the first glimpse of victory. With that surge, the Royal troops still trapped in the oratory grounds grew even more apprehensive. Many panicked and started to flee.

In the absence of Marcus and Lexton, the Royal sergeants tried in vain to get their men to hold the line. If they could just maintain a little longer, their comrades would break back through the gates to their aid. The red-faced sergeants screamed at their troops, trying to stall the retreat but they needed more time. Cad and Novak had other ideas.

"Come on! Let's go!" Novak roared at his men, sword flashing, leading the attack. "They're starting to run!"

This was the time to keep pressure on the Royal troops. Novak only had a small window of opportunity. The Royals had to be driven into a frantic retreat before Reddland could muster his remaining forces and counterattack. Timing was everything.

Novak brought his sword down hard, partially severing the head of one opponent. He immediately advanced, swinging, thrusting, and slashing his way through two more men. Novak's men were with him all the way. Seeing the large man tear a path through the enemy would inspire anyone to fight on. The Royals were starting to turn tail and the scent of victory filled the rebels with an aggressive euphoria that bordered on bloodlust.

Novak was in his element, clearly on the offensive now. Both of his hands were free to wield his two-handed sword with all his might. He punched, slashed, kicked, and cut his way forward foot-by-foot, his square jaw tight with determination. Droplets of blood splattered over his face and cuirass. He was drenched with blood from his forearms to the tip of his sword. Realizing they weren't going to hold the line, the Royal sergeants tried at least to organize the retreat.

But Novak wanted the Royal troops in a chaotic and fright-filled retreat. He started hooting and yelling as he attacked. Soon all the rebels were making euphoric shouts as they drove the Royal troops toward their own lines.

Sparks flew as Novak's sword contacted helmets, shields, armor and other weapons. Sometimes he made contact with rib cages, shoulders, and foreheads. Novak lashed out at everyone around him wearing a Royal blue surcoat. A couple of Royal soldiers found out the hard way that a chain mail sleeve might keep your arm from being severed, but when fighting Novak, it couldn't keep your bones from being broken.

On the other side of the field, Cad rallied the infantrymen around him to launch a brutal attack as well. He led the attack, battle-axe ablaze. After blocking several sword blows with his

shield, Cad brought his axe down on the nearest Royal helmet. On
the back swing he drove the pointed side of the axe through a Royal
chain mail shirt. An enemy soldier dropped his sword and winced
in pain as he grabbed his shoulder. After Cad removed the point of
his battle-axe, the wounded man fled. The other soldier with a dent
in his helmet decided to swing again at Cad, this time at his legs.
Cad tried to jump above the blade, but taking on two opponents
had its disadvantages. Because Cad had his attention split, the Royal
soldier got a couple of seconds jump on him. The blade struck
Cad's greave and sent a throbbing pain along his shinbone. When
Cad came down so did his axe, this time on the soldier's shield. The
two fought, Cad forcing his opponent backward in a slow retreat.

Then Cad dealt three swift blows in rapid succession. The
Royal soldier blocked two with his sword and one with his helmet.
When the soldier tripped and fell over a wounded rebel, Cad went
in for the kill. He finished him off with two more blows of the axe
then advanced on the next opponent.

Zephyr watched the Royal attack slow, stall, and then fizzle
out into a panicked retreat. They were in a full run, jumping over
wounded in a mad dash toward their own lines. Some fought
their way out of the compound. Seeing their comrades fleeing like
jackrabbits caused the Royal soldiers outside the oratory to panic
also. Zephyr ran to her archers and gathered them up, bringing
them towards the main gate. She directed them to fire volleys into
the fleeing Royal troops.

Lexton stood his ground outside the gates barking orders.
He managed to get a few retreating Royal soldiers to form up a
defensive line and offer resistance. But that wouldn't be enough.

Marcus ran back to the cavalry units who had formed up
and were ready to ride. With two-hundred Royal cavalry troops
barreling down on them, the rebels were sure to retreat. Soon
Marcus would have the battle turned back around.

Reddland decided to get involved with his own plan. He had
the Royal archers notched and waiting for orders to fire. Reddland
was only waiting for his retreating men to get out of the field of fire

before giving the order. Volley after volley of arrows would force the rebels to break off their attack and run for cover within the oratory behind the perimeter walls.

"Get ready!" Marcus readied the Royal cavalry for a counterattack to end the mad flight of his infantry.

— ⋯ ◆ ⋯ —

Somewhere outside the gate Novak came across Cad. "What in the world happened to you?" Novak gave Cad the once over and saw he was speckled with blood and dirt. One of his sleeves was torn off and bunched up at the top of his gauntlet. But what stood out the most was a tear in the back plate of Cad's cuirass.

Cad gave Novak a wink. "There's a war going on, mate, in case you hadn't noticed. I could ask the same of you; you're a bloody mess!"

Happy for the brief reunion, Novak grinned and gave a quick lick to his cut lip. "Don't worry. Most of the blood's not mine!"

The two surveyed the scene before them. Marcus rode along the line of the cavalry. As he did, each soldier donned his helmet and lowered his lance. The Royal archers were still at the ready.

"Let's go back into the oratory grounds! They're mounting a cavalry charge!" Cad immediately started shouting orders. Novak raced about and did the same. Together, they halted the advance of any more rebel troops.

Reddland saw this and ordered a volley of arrows.

Novak was waving his men back into the oratory grounds when he felt something bite him on the neck. He flinched and gripped the spot where the pain was. Almost simultaneously an arrow appeared in the back of the man in front of him, driving him to the ground. It was then that Novak realized what was happening. As he ran he grabbed the man with the arrow in his back by a wrist and dragged him as he headed for the gate. "Arrows! Incoming!" Novak shouted a warning.

Zephyr and her archers scrambled up to the parapets and returned fire. Arrows flew everywhere. One buried itself deep in the chest of the sentry next to Zephyr. He staggered back and fell from the parapet.

"Fire as fast as you can!" Zephyr yelled down the line of archers. It was risky keeping her troops exposed to the incoming arrows, but she had to defend the retreating rebels.

Cad entered the main gate and saw sentries waiting to prop the severed gate back into place. Others had hay wagons ready to help form a barricade. Cyrus directed the sentries, coordinating the building of a makeshift barrier across the gate. A sentry with an arrow in his chest fell from the parapet, landing in front of Cad. Cad knew he was dead, but still pulled him out of the way.

<hr />

Marcus was furious. *That idiot,* he thought as he looked at Reddland. Marcus held up a hand halting the cavalry. He wasn't going to order a charge and have his men ride into the path of the Royal archers. It would be bad enough to ride into rebel fire, but at least they had shields to protect them from that. Reddland's premature deployment of the archers blew the chances of Marcus deploying the cavalry and cutting through the rebel lines before they had a chance to get back on the oratory grounds. Marcus was confident two hundred cavalry soldiers would have been more than enough to push the rebels back. Now they would have the task of breaching the gate again. Reddland panicked and underestimated the rebel's ability to push his men back. Marcus wondered if his boss was starting to crack.

<hr />

Cyrus directed the sentries who were pushing a hay wagon into place to help barricade the gate. Others brought timbers and braced them against the door. Soon, the breach was closed, albeit haphazardly.

"Scatter the hay around. Don't leave it stacked on the wagon. We don't need a fire ball burning out the gates permanently." Cad instructed a nearby soldier. As he continued to jam a timber between the gate's crosspiece and the ground, another rebel pounded it firmly in place.

Lexton was irate. Marcus was supposed to bring up the cavalry. Instead, Lexton and his men were abandoned to fend for themselves. He rode up to Marcus and removed his helmet.

"What happened? If we got pushed back you were supposed to bring up the cavalry! Why did you order those archers? If we had attacked, our own archers would have struck us. What is going on here?"

Marcus was equally irritated and his anger showed on his bloodied face. "I'll tell you what happened." He waved off his junior officers, ordering them to regroup the men and take care of the wounded. He and Lexton rode off a few paces for some privacy.

Marcus continued. "I was prepared to set the charge when that…" Marcus paused to regain his composure. "When Reddland ordered the archers to fire. That is why I did not charge. I am not taking my men into the battle when several hundred arrows will be screaming down on their backs!"

Lexton was not appeased of his anger. "Why would he do that? It doesn't make sense. He knows our plans. We went over everything with him. Reddland certainly knows the folly of such a decision." Lexton shook his head in angry amazement. "Were you aware the archers were preparing to attack?"

"Of course I did! I assumed this was merely a precaution against another advance. It is my opinion that Reddland is losing his command presence. He hasn't been himself at all lately. He became frightened. That is the only logical explanation. In not waiting for our counterattack, he has allowed the rebels to secure the gate."

Lexton shook his head in disgust. He too realized Reddland's mental prowess had not been what it used to be of late. "He should have trusted our judgment. I could have had my trumpeter signal the archers. I knew better than he did just how long our men could have lasted. I was in the fight. The rebels pushed us out of the compound, but the cavalry could have regained that ground."

Marcus agreed. "The cavalry could have pushed them back across the island too. Now the point is moot. So far, all the breaks have been for the rebels."

Lexton couldn't argue with that. "The problem is we have been going after these rebels as if they were a typical army. They clearly are not; they are different. We have to convince Reddland to change our tactical approach. Let's spend a little more time in preparation for what we will do next. We must not rush in as we have been doing."

"I agree." Marcus removed a gauntlet, moistened a piece of his surcoat, and dabbed at his bloody brow and nose.

"I mean, these rebels have been incredibly lucky. We could have had them beaten; they just got lucky." Lexton offered further comment.

"Maybe." Marcus gently wiped the dried blood from around his right eye. "Then again, maybe there is something at work here we just aren't aware of."

Lexton furrowed his brow. "What? What are you implying?"

Marcus shrugged his shoulder, offering no answer.

XV

THADUS AND THE stretcher-bearers shuttled the wounded
to the rebels' makeshift hospital. The dead were taken to the
gardener's shed where they would stay until they could be buried
after the battle was over. The walking wounded made their own
way to the hospital, some with the aid of a friend. There they
waited until the more seriously injured were tended to.

The Royal army had fled leaving their wounded and dead
on the battlefield. Cad and Novak allowed an unarmed Royal
contingent to bring a wagon and collect their people.

Cad surveyed the aftermath of the heavy conflict. Dozens of
soldiers were being carried toward the oratory. Cyrus set about
posting his sentries again, as did Zephyr with her archers. Even
though there was a momentary lull in the battle, the rebels weren't
taking any chances.

Doc and his volunteer nurses were swamped at the hospital.
Doc separated patients into three groups as they entered. To the
storeroom were directed the wounded that could get there on
their own; these could wait until the doctor had taken care of
everyone else.

He directed those who had a chance of living if they received immediate attention to a hospital bed. He directed the mortally wounded to the other end of the hospital to a row of cots where they would be given an herbal concoction Scorpyus previously made for the pain. A few lesser-wounded soldiers and the nurses would comfort them while they waited to die. Most of the soldiers directed to the cots already knew they would soon pass on.

Abrams had watched the whole battle from the first attack to the retreat. He numbly stared out over the scurrying rebel troops as they evacuated their fallen comrades, tears streaking his cheeks. "May God have mercy on them all," he murmured to himself. In some ways mankind had made no progress since the Garden of Eden. In fact, maybe they became worse. Abrams knew this battle was necessary. It was either fight or let Reddland eventually hunt you down. The only other path to survival was to abandon God and turn to Tanuba and Reddland.

Abrams still wondered why the bloody carnage seemed to be the only answer. He guessed as long as there were men like Reddland who insisted on totalitarian control and conquest of others, there would always be some who would resist and fight for freedom.

The rest of the rebel soldiers were busy preparing a defense for whatever came next. Reddland seemed to be regrouping his men also. For the moment, Abrams had time for reflection. He felt a profound sorrow for the loss of rebel soldiers, but deep down felt confident in their eternal destination. Believing he would one day see them again offered some solace. Ironically, he also felt a sobering anguish over the lost souls of the Royal dead. The final state for those who rejected God was not good. The thought cut through Abrams and left him wondering if maybe he couldn't have done more to reach them. The phrase "wailing and gnashing of teeth" went around his head, leaving him sick to his stomach. This was now reality for most of the dead Royal soldiers. But what could he have done? All people were free to make their own choice. Not choosing was tantamount to rejection. Coercion was futile. God accepted any that volunteered.

A rebel soldier interrupted his ruminations. "Abrams, the wounded are calling for you."

Abrams was jolted back from his meditative thoughts. He wiped his red eyes and turned around. "Yes, of course. Let's go at once."

He followed the soldier to the hospital. Inside, he lowered the hood to his cloak. In one short minute he had left the quiet of the oratory roof and entered complete pandemonium. Abrams lips slightly quivered through his beard, and tears welled up again. Everywhere he looked wounded soldiers were crying out in pain. The floor was slick with blood. Used bandages and pieces of clothing littered the floor. Two nurses held down a squirming patient as Doc made an incision on his thigh to remove an arrow. The rum given to the wounded soldier did little to quell the agony.

Emerald approached Abrams. "Some of the dying are asking for you. Many don't have much time."

"Show me there at once."

———◆———

Cad, Novak, and Zephyr met on the oratory steps to discuss the battle. From there they could keep watch over and direct the preparations of the soldiers as needed. Cyrus joined them in the discussion.

"Well, how did we fare?" Cyrus asked. By now all the squad leaders had reported in to Cad.

"Let's see. As near as I can tell, we've lost close to one hundred troops dead or severely wounded. I'd say another forty are wounded but will be able to return to duty. You're one of those I see." Cad pointed to the gash above Cyrus's ear. "We have one catapult left, and the cavalry is now non-existent. Twenty-three horses were killed and eighteen men. But the charge was incredibly violent. We drove right into the thick of them. We paid a price to drive the Royal soldiers back. But they suffered far worse."

"How many casualties do you think Reddland took all together so far?" Zephyr inquired.

"I estimate about four hundred or so." Cad removed his helmet and ran his fingers through his sweaty hair. "We won't know for sure; but when they retreated they took a good hit."

Cyrus's face lit up. "Really? That is fantastic! We beat them four to one."

Novak removed his helmet and laid it near his buckler on a nearby bench. "That isn't good enough, Cyrus. If we continue winning at that rate we will still lose. We need five to one to tie; ten to one to have a real victory. Or, we need to somehow convince them to surrender before then." Cad and Zephyr nodded in agreement.

Cyrus thought a minute. "So then, what happens next?"

"Don't get me wrong mate, we won that battle." Cad tried to offer some encouraging words. "We just won't win the war that way, and as for what happens next, I think Reddland will make his next move at dawn. He definitely was not expecting to be forced to retreat by us, and losing four hundred men should send a shock through their command structure. They're not used to losing large numbers of men and haven't suffered defeat since Reddland has been in power. I can't see him making another move without thinking it through very thoroughly. They don't want a repeat of today. There are only a few hours of daylight left, so I think he will wait until morning. But rest assured, whatever they decide to do, it will be better than their last plan. It will require us to be even more alert and flexible than today."

"Are you saying we will need a miracle?" Zephyr responded.

"I don't know about a miracle, but we can't do it alone. We knew that going in. I wouldn't worry. If it is God's will, then we will win. If it's not, nothing we do will circumvent that. Let's just hope God is ready for Reddland to be removed from power. Then this island can return to the way it should be." Cad offered his thoughts on the matter.

"It sounds good. I'm going to get something for this puncture wound on my arm and some food for this pit in my stomach. A gallon of cool water sounds good right now." Novak announced and parted company with the others.

"He seems to be taking this well," Cyrus noted.

Cad smiled. "Novak keeps life simple mate. He has often said, 'What God decides is fine with me.' Novak knows he's been called to be a warrior and he's been tremendously blessed to meet his calling."

Cyrus nodded in agreement and the movement caused his head to throb. "Well, I think I'll be going too. I'm certain I need a few stitches."

"It sure looks like it, mate." Cad looked at the wound and then slapped Cyrus on the shoulder as he walked off. He then turned to Zephyr. "You may as well get something to eat too."

"Definitely. What are you going to do?"

"I'm going to hammer the crease out of my backplate. It's starting to irritate."

Zephyr looked at the deep crease. "Wow, it must have been a powerful blow!"

"It bloody well was! My back hurts when I take a deep breath." Cad and Zephyr walked into the oratory, both looking as tired as they felt hungry.

Reddland summoned Marcus and Lexton to the command tent. When they arrived, both men handed their horses to a waiting stable hand.

"Have them fed and watered," Lexton ordered. Then he and Marcus parted the tent flaps and entered. They both took a seat across from Reddland at a simple wooden table. Reddland excused his servant and waited for him to leave. It was obvious to Marcus and Lexton their boss was enraged.

"What happened out there today? How did this happen? The rebels are supposed to be easier to defeat than this!" Reddland cursed and slammed his fist on the table, knocking his helmet off. He didn't bother to retrieve it.

Neither was too anxious to reply. Marcus, who now sported a bandage above his right eyebrow and two fresh stitches on the bridge of his nose, decided to speak first.

"Well, Sire, to be quite honest, we underestimated them. The men had been conditioned to believe the rebels were poorly trained and without leadership. I believed this to be an error, but we marched right up to their gates anyway. When we began the campaign this morning, we were taken aback by two unconventional tactics involving fire. As you know, many of the troops are ignorantly superstitious. The fire shooting out of the walls spooked some of them into thinking the rebels possessed supernatural powers. With two such conflicting perceptions about the enemy, our men did not know what to believe and became hesitant. When we breached the gate, the rebels met our attack with only half of their strength. They suddenly hit us with the rest of their forces, pushing us back. The men retreated and Lexton and I tried to turn them back. Because of all that happened they were hesitant to do so. And as you are aware, Sire, hesitation on the field of battle is often fatal." Marcus paused a moment, and after taking a deep breath continued on.

"Lexton and I came to the conclusion we would need a cavalry charge to turn the battle around. I have no doubt this tactic would have been successful, as it is doubtful the rebels could stand against a charge of two hundred horses. Before I could deploy our cavalry, our archers opened fire. As you know, Sire, our men cannot advance under fire of our archers, lest they expose themselves to the very arrows that should be helping them."

"Are you suggesting that I am the cause of today's defeat?" Reddland was beet red.

"No, Sire." Lexton blurted out. "We're just saying that had we mounted a cavalry charge and the men not been hesitant and uncertain we could have…" Lexton's defense of Marcus was cut short.

"That's exactly what you're saying, you insolent fool! I had no choice but to order the archers to strike! We were being overrun. You two failed to keep the men under control. They were fleeing like jackrabbits. The rebels would have soon been on us. The archers had to be deployed to save the rest of our men." Reddland cursed in a purple rage, his neck veins bulging. Saliva flew from his mouth as he spoke.

"Now, Sire! They were still one-hundred-fifty yards from our lines; we had ample time to launch a cavalry charge. And had they been foolish enough to attack our lines we could have cut off their retreat back to the oratory and annihilated them. They need the protection of the oratory. They are too few in number to take us on equal footing, and the rebel leaders know that," Lexton replied quite puzzled; surely Reddland knew that? He could understand if Reddland did not want to own up to panicking and making a mistake, but it wasn't such a mistake that the Royal army couldn't recover.

Reddland flew into a greater rage and flung the small wooden table over. He jumped to his feet and screamed at Marcus and Lexton, his mouth inches from their faces. "How dare you question my judgment! I tell you I had no choice! None! They were going to overrun us and I saved the men!"

Marcus and Lexton sat in stunned disbelief. Reddland could not possibly believe that three hundred rebels were going to march out of their protective walls and conquer a two-thousand man army. They were not about to say anything further, though. This was all too surreal for comment.

Reddland paced back and forth for a long minute and then abruptly turned to Marcus and Lexton. "Aha! What is that supposed to mean? Which one of you said that?" Marcus and Lexton had no idea what Reddland was talking about.

"Uh, said what, Sire?" Lexton was getting worried.

Reddland calmed slightly. "Didn't one of you just say in a deep voice *'Luther, this is the last time I'm going to call you.'* I heard it plain as day."

Lexton and Marcus looked at each other in wide-eyed amazement. Now their superior was hearing voices.

Lexton's breathing came in sporadic gasps as if he had jumped into a cold pond. He was downright scared. What was happening? The thought that the Royal government was unraveling made him sick to his stomach.

"We haven't said a thing, Sire." Marcus was sure Reddland was going insane from the pressure. He had seen it before with soldiers in battle, soldiers becoming so unnerved they could no longer function. Marcus feared Reddland was reaching his limits, probably in part due to his illness. At any rate, Marcus was having second thoughts about life anyway; especially since seeing the stable hand die earlier. He wasn't sure he wanted to be a part of this anymore. Being by himself, isolated from all problems like a hermit suddenly sounded like a good idea.

Marcus changed the direction of the discussion. "I've been thinking about the battle, Sire. If it would make any difference, I'd like to tender my resignation. In case today's fiasco was in any way my fault, I would not feel right remaining in command." Not even Lexton could have predicted this from Marcus.

The room grew quiet. The entire meeting dumbfounded Lexton. First Reddland erupted in anger, then he heard a voice, and Marcus resigned. What would happen next?

Marcus's resignation seemed to jolt Reddland back from the edge. He immediately calmed down and lowered his voice to a mellow whisper. "No, Marcus. That won't be necessary. I want you to stay in command. You are a good soldier. We will overcome today's mistakes." Reddland righted the table and picked up his chair. He sat again with his men prepared now for a cordial discussion. He couldn't lose a top officer now. The possibility sobered Reddland dramatically.

"Let us get down to business. We have lost three hundred eighty-four men today, plus twenty-seven others with minor wounds. Are there any suggestions for our next step?" Just like that Reddland was back to business as usual. His mood shift left Marcus all the more uneasy. Lexton breathed a sigh of relief at the newfound normalcy.

Against his better judgment, Marcus withdrew his resignation. Soon the tension bled from the room, and Reddland had a servant bring in something to drink.

The three formulated a new plan well into the night. No longer were the rebels going to be taken lightly. This time Reddland painstakingly went over every detail with his top officers. It was time for the Royal army to get serious. All felt confident of its success; they were now going to take things slower. The idea was to put the battle on the rebel's level and Reddland was not holding anything back. The Royal troops would have a few surprises of their own this time.

"Alright men," Reddland sounded cocky and sure. "Implement our new plan at daybreak. In the meantime, have a squad of men harass the rebels throughout the night. Shoot a few arrows, probe their defenses; at least awaken them during the middle of the night a few times, keep them tired."

Marcus and Lexton departed with their new orders. Both men were relieved to see their superior set aside his tremendous ego and treat the rebels as the threat they had proven to be.

After Reddland dismissed his men he plopped himself down on his cot and pulled off his boots. He was exhausted. He had been having nightmares for the last few nights and was short of sleep. He blamed the nightmares on the rebel insurrection since both started about the same time.

Reddland's dreams were bizarre. In them, he was being pursued by a dark, invisible force. He would run as hard as he could but would hardly be moving. He was alone, and his feet were like lead. He would awaken just as the creature that had been chasing him caught him. It had a beastly growl that rattled his nerves. Not only had the dreams cost Reddland valuable sleep, but now he was hearing voices. Reddland's brow was wet with worry. He lay back on his cot, resting his forearm on his forehead. This was all too much. Although exhausted, he feared falling asleep. It would be another long sleepless night. He had to get this battle behind him before his hauntings worsened. Victory might be the only way to make them stop; victory and Hyacinth Blue.

———————◦•◦•————————

Offshore fog rolled in shortly after the sun sank slowly below the horizon. The rebel troops were set in defensive positions waiting for Reddland's next move. Most would camp at their posts for the night. Cad had the troops break for supper in squads so as not to overload the cooks. A dozen elder women worked the mess line and had prepared a big cauldron of bacon and bean stew. They ladled out a bowl to each soldier as he passed, and gave each a generous cut of bread. Novak shuffled past the food line with a small sack in his hand.

Novak entered the oratory and made his way to the hospital. The cries of the wounded grew louder the closer he got. It reminded him of his days as a messenger for the army of Ravenshire.

The hospital was a place of suffering and death. The smell of blood hung thick in the air. Novak headed for the area where those with minor wounds were being treated. He had to step carefully because the stone floor was slick with blood.

Doc was preparing to amputate the crushed and partially severed leg of one of the catapult crewmen. While two of his friends held him down, Abrams held his white knuckled hand and whispered in his ear. With a purple face and teeth biting into a piece of leather, the wounded man groaned loudly. Saliva foamed at the corners of his mouth and he panted hard like a woman in labor. Abrams stroked the man's head as Doc set to work with a wood saw. Novak doubted the wounded soldier would survive the procedure.

To Novak's left lay a man with a gaping slash across his side just below his cuirass. The ashen man was soaked in blood. As Novak drew closer he realized the man was already dead.

The older women who volunteered to help Doc were given the business of tending to the severely wounded. They had been around during the war ten years earlier and had some experience. The women could do little more than clean the wounds, stop the bleeding, and comfort the men as best they could. Many were mortally wounded and nothing could be done aside from easing their pain. A couple of barrels of strong wine were used to those ends.

"God help them," Novak said, moved by the carnage and suffering he saw. Few things made him feel more useless than the inability to do anything to help. He comforted himself with thoughts of how well things had gone so far for the rebels. Continuing to help the rebellion was something he could do for those who were going to live.

Novak moved on to where the moderately wounded were being treated and poured a basin of water. He removed his wrist plates and set them and the small sack to one side. Grabbing some soap, he washed both arms to above the elbows. The basin water quickly turned light red. He concentrated especially on cleaning the puncture wound on the inside of his forearm. It was an inch deep and was quite sore. The flesh around the hole was red and inflamed. Novak grimaced as he cleaned it.

"What happened to you?" Emerald was horrified when she saw Novak. He had blood splattered on his chest and face.

Novak held a hand up and replied with a grin. "Don't worry. Don't worry, Emerald. Most of the blood is not mine. You should have seen the other guy. I just have this one puncture wound. One of the balls of a flail wrapped itself around my buckler. But thanks for your concern."

A look of relief came over Emerald. "Oh, thank God. You look terrible, like you were hurt bad."

"Not this time. What have you been up to?" Novak dumped the basin and poured another. He grabbed a nearby cloth and dipped the end of it in the water and began to wash his face.

"Doc has me working with the less severely wounded over here, cleaning, bandaging, and sewing up their wounds."

Novak shot Emerald a glance. "You can stitch wounds?"

"I can now. Doc gave me a quick lesson on the first wounded soldier and I have had a lot of practice since then." Emerald watched Novak slick back his hair.

"Ahh, it sure feels good to clean up a little."

Emerald looked at Novak's wound. "Would you like me to throw a stitch in that?"

"No, thank you. I'll let it drain. I'll bandage it up after I put some of this on it." Novak pulled a big jar out of the sack he had brought.

"What is that?"

Novak opened the jar and showed Emerald the green paste inside. "It's some sort of medicine Scorpyus made. It helps the wound to heal faster. If it is applied quickly this stuff will prevent gangrene, usually. It's better than using maggots to eat off the infected flesh like you might otherwise have to do."

"Really? I've never heard of such a thing."

"Not many have. It's a Gypsy remedy. If people would stop hating the Gypsies and trying to kill them, they would see they have a thing or two to offer, "Novak replied while smearing some of the medicine on his wound.

"Do you know what's in it?" Emerald inspected the green pasty substance.

"Not exactly; plants and stuff. Nothing too hard to find. Scorpyus has all kinds of goodies in his sack. Like this stuff; it is a painkiller." Novak took out another jar full of a brown, syrupy liquid. "Use these things on the wounded. It will help them recover. Scorpyus doesn't have anything for the mortally wounded."

"Thank you, I'll use it. By the way, I wonder if Hyacinth Blue would help these men?" Emerald remembered a batch of the medicine had been made.

"Hyacinth Blue is a cure for some sort of disease, I think. I don't see how it would help with combat wounds. It might even kill if used improperly." Novak shrugged his shoulders.

"Yeah, I suppose you're right." Emerald watched Novak bandage his arm. As she spoke several more soldiers walked in. "It looks like I have more patients waiting."

"OK. I need to eat and meet with Cad and Zephyr anyway. You're doing a good job in here." Novak gave Emerald a wink.

Emerald placed her hand on Novak's arm. "Take care of this wound; and I don't want to see you with any more."

Novak smiled and gathered his gear. As he turned to walk away he commented, "I wish we…this was over so we could spend some real time together."

Emerald returned a smile. "Me too," she whispered as a worried tear welled in the corner of her eye. She watched Novak walk out of her hospital and into who-knew-what kind of danger.

Cad, Zephyr and Thadus were sitting on the oratory steps eating their stew when Novak walked up with a bowl in his hand.

"Mind if I join you?" Novak saw Cad was missing a sleeve. "Nice shirt. Were you feeling a little warm?"

Cad smiled. "No, some bloke wanted the shirt off my back but we compromised."

Cad's remark drew a laugh. Thadus shook his head in amusement.

"I'm amazed I can still laugh." Thadus stared on into the distance for a moment. "After seeing some of the wounded…" Thadus's voice trailed off. "So how did we do today?"

"If our forces were of equal size, we would be on the road to victory." Cad replied. "But since they're not, we'll have to go at it another way. We did show our chaps they can win. We also showed Reddland he can lose. In those ways we have done well."

"So now we just wait for Reddland's next move?"

There was sudden shout of activity at the south wall. The sentries scurried about briefly, then all quieted down again.

"What was that all about?" Thadus had been busy with the wounded and unaware of Reddland's mission of harassments.

"Reddland's probing our lines. A squad will sneak up to the wall somewhere and fire off a few arrows and cause a disturbance. It'll break up everyone's sleep; force us to stay alert all night." Novak stated the facts without concern about the commotion at the south wall. Cad didn't even stop eating. Zephyr continued to nibble on a piece of bread. Thadus was surprised at their lack of concern.

Cyrus walked up and sat down with a bowl of stew. Cad noticed the stitches on his head where his hair had been shaved. "It looks like you took quite a hit mate. You have a lot of bruising."

"I'll say. I've never been hit that hard before. It definitely rang my bell and nearly knocked me out. This was with my helmet on." Cyrus was still amazed at the power behind the blow that had so forcefully dazed him.

Cad nodded and said, "I think I ran across the same guy. He hit me hard enough to put a separation in my armor."

Novak didn't seem surprised at either report. "Ya, I've done that a time or two." There was a hint of pride in his comment.

They all finished their food and discussed the events of the day further. They decided everyone would camp with their own squads. Cad placed the surviving cavalry troops into the infantry. With only a few horses, not much else could be done. He would now share command of the infantry with Novak and break them into two squads. Zephyr hit the parapets with her archers. There was nothing to do now but wait for Reddland's next move. A thick anticipation hung in the night air. Sleep would be light tonight.

XVI

———◆•◆•◆———

NOVAK FELT A stabbing pain in his ribs. The rock he had
been laying on finally coaxed him awake. He stretched his
stiff and sore muscles and groaned. He sat up, rubbed his face,
and let out a sigh. It would be light soon. The sky at the horizon
was already turning saffron. Oh how his ribs ached where the
rock had been poking. No matter how well a person thinks he has
cleared the area of rocks, one always seems to find its way back.

Novak pulled his damp blanket off, shook his boots out, and
slipped them on. They were very cold and the leather was hard.
As he fastened his greaves, he noticed the puncture wound on his
arm had seeped fluid through the bandage. It was draining nicely.
He donned the rest of his armor and shoved the blanket into his
pack. Pouring out a handful of cold water from his water skin,
he managed to splash a little of the sleep out of his eyes. Novak
scanned the grounds and saw Cad was already awake and walking
for the main gate.

Novak buckled his two-handed sword in place, slapped on
his helmet, walked over to where one of his men was sleeping, and
nudged him with his boot. "Rise and shine."

The soldier reluctantly forced his eyes open. "Already? Didn't we just go to sleep?"

"It's been five hours," Novak replied. He had been thinking the same a few minutes earlier.

"Get the men up and ready. Make sure they eat. We'll need our strength today. I'm going to the main gate. I'll be back as soon as I find out what will happen next. We should know something soon."

The awakened soldier sat up and acknowledged his orders.

Novak walked briskly to the main gate, stretching and warming his arms and shoulders as he went. Cad was already on the parapet talking with Zephyr.

Zephyr saw Novak appear on the parapet from a nearby ladder. "Hey, sleepy head, it is nice of you to join us."

Novak rubbed his eyes. "Ya, some of us have to work for a living."

"Oh really; I suppose you call playing with that little knife of yours work? I would be surprised if it could even chop through an onion," Zephyr jested.

"Let's find out." Novak rummaged through his pack and pulled out a large, red apple. Tossing the apple into the air, he pulled his sword from its sheath and swung just before the apple hit the ground. It landed in two perfect halves.

"Breakfast, anyone?" Novak smiled.

Zephyr and Cad clapped their approval as Novak wiped his blade clean and returned it to its place. "We still do not know if it will cut an onion, though," Zephyr said.

"And it cuts through bone just as easy," Novak bragged, ignoring her comment.

"In another few minutes we will have enough light to see what Reddland has up his sleeve." Cad returned to the business at hand.

The three friends sat enjoying each other's company and were eventually joined by Thadus. The sun crept above the horizon. In no time they could clearly make out Reddland's lines. The Royal troops seemed to be just climbing out of their bedrolls.

"Look, someone is over there." Zephyr pointed to a lone figure on the path to the oratory gate halfway between the Royal troops and the perimeter walls. The person was alone and didn't appear to be moving. As dawn turned brighter, it became clear the lone figure was tied to a stake and hanging limp. "It is a woman," Zephyr said. By now they could plainly see her disheveled hair and her head hanging down as if she were unconscious. Ropes bound her hands and feet behind her to a wooden post. She had been disrobed and, from the looks of her lacerated body, had been given a terrible beating.

Cad lowered the spyglass. "Bloody aye, what have they done to her?"

Novak had a look of disgust. "Why didn't they kill her and be done with it?"

"Do we know who she is?" Zephyr couldn't bear to look at the twisted figure in the distance.

"I don't, but she's still alive. She just moved slightly." Cad handed the spyglass to Thadus. "Do you recognize her?"

Thadus took the telescope and studied the abraded and lacerated body tied to the post. His lips parted in a slight gasp. "Yes. It's Iris."

"The woman who tried to defect to our side before the battle started? The one Scorpyus spied on?" Novak asked.

Thadus nodded and handed the glass back to Cad. "That's the one."

"Well, that explains a few things," Cad added. "Her change of heart wasn't well received by Reddland."

"What are we going to do about this? We cannot just leave her out there. I mean, she tried to join us." Zephyr made a passionate plea.

"I don't know about you, but I've had enough of these pigs." Novak started for the ladder that led down from the parapet. He was going to untie Iris from the post and get her to Doc. Maybe her life could still be saved.

Cad grabbed Novak's arm. "Wait! Riders are coming forward with a white flag."

Those on the parapet looked to see four riders break rank from the Royal lines and come forward. One rider carried a pole with a white flag. Cad recognized three of the riders. Reddland, Lexton, and the Tanuba cleric rode with an as yet unidentified man, to where Iris was staked.

"Are they surrendering?" Thadus was ever hopeful.

"They probably just want to call a momentary truce in order to talk. Reddland may even be daft enough to offer us another chance to surrender. I guess we'll find out soon enough." Cad grabbed his shield and prepared to meet Reddland. "Novak, why don't you ride out with me and Thadus this time? We might need help in case we run into a couple of apples." Novak rolled his eyes at Cad's remark. "Zephyr, keep us covered with your archers."

"Sure." Zephyr replied between giggles. "But be careful out there." Zephyr turned to busy herself with preparing her archers.

Three horses were rounded up from the few that remained. Cad, Novak, and Thadus mounted up and rode from the oratory gates. Thadus carried a piece of white cloth tied to a spear. Cad instructed the sentries to close the gates behind them but to remain alert in case they had to make a hurried retreat.

Cad, Novak, and Thadus saw exactly how badly Iris was beaten when they rode out to meet Reddland. She hung limp ten feet from the cobblestone path where the meeting took place. Her arms were cinched tight behind her; a rope coiled from armpits to wrists held her firmly to a wooden pole that had been driven into the ground and was all that kept her on her feet. Her ankles were lashed together at the bottom of the post. A limp piece of rope dangled in the dirt, the means, no doubt, by which she had been dragged there behind a horse. Her head hung down; her long dirty hair, matted with blood and straw, obscured her face. Iris was bruised, cut, scraped, scratched, and caked with dirt. It was hard to find one square inch of flesh that wasn't marred in some way. Soft moans told them she was still alive.

Reddland saw Cad, Novak, and Thadus surveying the pitiful sight. "Take a good look, gentleman. Take a good, hard look. Let it serve as a warning."

"A warning for what? For proof you can beat a defenseless woman? Any coward can do that. Taking on someone your own size, I'd venture to say, is a whole other matter," Novak said and stared unflinchingly into Reddland's eyes.

"Ahh, grrrr. The beast can talk." Reddland spat sarcastically. "And the beast better watch his tongue lest he should suffer the same fate." Malvagio cackled joyously at Reddland's remark; his jagged grin ever in its place.

"Is that a threat?" Novak's temper started to flare and he was eyeing Reddland like a starving wolf eyes a crippled sheep.

Cad interrupted. "So, what do you want, Reddland? I don't believe you came out here to cast blooming insults our way again."

Reddland eyed Cad with a strange look in his eyes. Cad didn't know what to make of it. He knew he had never seen Reddland before. Maybe Reddland was simply "sizing up the enemy."

"Cad, is it?" Reddland waited for Cad to nod, and then continued. "You are correct. I am not out here to waste my time. I am here to offer the rebellion one final chance to surrender. This time, however, with a condition. Those who fail to surrender now and are captured—and make no mistake, it will be one or the other—they will be treated to the same fate that Malvagio meted out to Iris."

Malvagio erupted into a laugh that sent chills down every spine. He clearly enjoyed his duty as the Royal implement of torture. Lexton glanced at Malvagio, who sat rubbing his hands together with eager anticipation.

Reddland continued. "On the other hand, if you surrender now, only the rebel leaders will be put to death, and quickly at that, without all the suffering. The others will be deported to

Kelterland." Reddland smiled broadly. "This is your chance to spare your men many days of needless suffering. Does not your "god" call for compassion? Now is your chance to show it. If you reject my offer now, I can assure you each and every man, woman, or child captured or wounded, will be put to death as slowly and painfully as possible. Surrender now and they will live." Reddland sat back smugly on his mount.

It was obvious to Cad that Reddland was not interested in negotiations. He was here to threaten, scare, or bully the rebellion into surrender and Cad counted on nothing else.

"You know, Reddland, I think of how many blokes there are in the world, and how so few of them I will actually meet in my lifetime. I have to admit, meeting you has been as pleasant as finding rat droppings in my porridge, and about as appetizing."

Novak was furious. At this moment nothing would give him more pleasure than to twist Reddland into impossible shapes.

Thadus looked sullen and morose. He had a sad countenance, like a parent whose child has gone irrevocably wayward and was now at the gallows hanging his head. Thadus was clearly disappointed with Reddland's offer.

Reddland was visibly angry with Cad's remark but held his temper. "I will give you three minutes to decide."

Drakar, the Tanuba cleric also had something to say. "Surrender now or I will place another Tanuba curse of death upon you. You cannot defeat us. Tanuba is with the Royal soldiers and we will be victorious. Her wrath will pour out on those who oppose her."

Novak grinned at Drakar. "I wouldn't be too sure about that. Tanuba lost her head the last time I saw her."

"Didn't we smell her down at the docks? Or was that just a barrel of fish heads?" .Cad asked.

Drakar's eyes bulged, and he started to speak. Reddland stopped him. "You now have two minutes."

"What do you think, Novak?" Cad whispered.

"I say we fight. If by some strange reason God wants Reddland to win, then so be it. It's worth the risk." Novak leaned toward Cad in his saddle.

Cad agreed and turned to Thadus. "What about you, Thadus? What is your opinion?"

Thadus let out a heavy, heartfelt sigh. "Reddland's offer to spare the troops might have been tempting if we had any reason to believe he would keep his word. Unfortunately, I fear he won't be satisfied until we are all dead. With that in mind, there is no point in surrendering. If we all must die, let us die fighting. It is better than by execution, which I am confident is our only other alternative."

Cad nodded approvingly. "You're right, mate. I also believe Reddland will stop at nothing to see us all dead. This is just a scheme. He has killed innocent people for far less than this; people he knew were not even involved in the rebellion."

"So, the fight is on then!" Novak was always ready for a battle.

"Well, the one thing I can't figure out," questioned Cad, "is why Reddland even bothered to offer us such a surrender. Does he think we are so ignorant as to trust him? Or is he that confident of his power of persuasion? I could tell by his men's faces that even they don't believe we will accept the deal. It just makes me wonder...." Cad stroked his goatee.

"Reddland is vain and unstable enough to be thinking any..." Thadus was cut short.

"Your time is up. What have you decided?" Reddland tapped a gloved hand on his saddle.

Cad resumed speaking in a normal tone. "We have decided you are nothing but a bloody liar and cannot be trusted. We don't believe you will deport the troops and just kill the leaders. Most importantly, we are winning, and you know it. It is we who should be offering you the chance to surrender." Cad enjoyed goading his opponent.

Reddland's face flushed and he looked to Lexton who carried the guidon with the white flag. Lexton lifted and changed the guidon from his left hand to his right hand. Drakar stared at Cad with the utmost hatred for one he held to be an enemy of Tanuba. Malvagio remained silently smiling.

"Seeing you die will be a pleasure," Reddland sneered at Cad; then he turned his gaze toward Novak and Thadus. "You will all pay dearly for this uprising against my authority."

Cad and Novak saw Lexton switch the guidon to a different hand and started looking all around. No movement could be detected from the Royal lines.

"Did he just signal someone?" Cad's eyes darted all around searching for the unusual.

"It looked like it." Novak didn't see anything to warrant alarm either.

All of a sudden, a loud roar came from the rebel lines. Cad and Novak jerked around. At the wall opposite the gate, the tiny figures of the rebels could be seen in a bustle of activity.

"The east wall is under attack!" Zephyr screamed to Cad.

Cad and Novak whipped back around to face Reddland. He gave them a large grin.

"Well, it looks as if you have other problems to worry about now." Malvagio cackled at Reddland's remark. Reddland heeled his horse hard, turned, and galloped toward his lines; Lexton, Malvagio and Drakar followed. The Royal archers retrieved arrows from their quivers and notched them.

"Quick, I'll cut Iris from that post and you take her back to the oratory." Cad rode to Iris and cut her ropes as Novak placed his cloak around her limp body and lifted her across his saddle. Novak hopped on behind Iris's draped body. Rebel arrows shot overhead on their way to the Royal troops.

Novak heeled his horse hard toward the main gate while crouched low over Iris draped in front of the saddle. Thadus was on his heels. Sentries at the wall were opening the battle-scarred gates. Zephyr had her archers in two groups that alternated their fire in order to send a constant barrage of arrows down range for cover. They were loosing arrows as fast as they could. Novak and the others could hear them "swoosh" by overhead.

Cad looked back over his shoulder. As soon as Reddland and his squad were in a safe position, the Royal archers loosed a tremendous barrage. Nearly two hundred arrows came hurtling toward the rebels, many at Cad's party.

"Arrows! Incoming!" Cad shouted and swung to the side of his horse. Novak immediately followed Cad's lead and grabbed Iris's arm. She started to slide off the other side of his horse and Novak had to drop the reigns. With one hand gripping the saddle and the other tight on Iris's arm, he had to count on his horse to continue in a straight path.

At first Thadus thought Novak had fallen from his mount. By the time he realized Novak was decreasing the target area his body provided, Royal arrows were already hitting their marks, three in the chest of a sentry helping to open the battered gates another arrow in the ground near the gateway. Thadus immediately swung to the side of his horse in the same manner he had seen Novak. His foot slipped from the stirrup and his body slammed against his mount's side, his feet dragging in the dirt. There was little he could do but let the animal drag him along to safety.

Novak held fast to his saddle. An arrow hit his horse's neck. Another struck him in the helmet. He pulled on Iris's arm to keep her from sliding off the other side. His grip was sure to be cutting off blood flow to her hand. When Novak was far enough inside the oratory grounds he swung back on top of his mount and halted it. Quickly, he dismounted, lowered Iris to the ground, and slapped his horse on the rump to get it out of the way. Waiting stretcher bearers rushed over and loaded Iris onto a litter. She was still wrapped in Novak's cloak.

Thadus lost his grip and fell from his horse just inside the gate. He tumbled and rolled before coming to rest in a heap. His horse continued on in a gallop. Dazed and battered, he slowly sat up cradling his left wrist. Blood trickled from his nose.

Cad entered last and reined his horse to a stop. Two arrows protruded from his saddle. He retrieved his battle-axe and sent his mount onward.

"They are starting to charge!" Zephyr yelled down to Cad from the parapet. Hundreds of infantrymen and cavalry charged toward the oratory gate yelling and shouting.

Cad ran to where Cyrus supervised the closing of the gate. "Cyrus, take fifty infantrymen to the south wall and hold it at all costs. I'll need Novak here. Reddland's throwing everything else he has at the north wall."

Novak ran toward the gate. While sentries frantically spiked the left gate closed with wooden stakes, others struggled desperately to close the badly damaged right door. Cad was busy setting up the infantry for defense.

The distinct sound of catapults snapping forward echoed from the tree line behind the Royal forces and projectiles hurtled toward the oratory gates. This had been Reddland's plan from the beginning. His offer of surrender had been a ruse to prepare an attack on the south wall. Novak pieced the strategy together quickly. Reddland would attack the south wall, forcing the rebels to dedicate some of their forces to its defense, get the gates open under a false offer of surrender, and then hit the main gate with everything. The catapults had been repositioned during the night.

Iris was beaten to add a sense of realism to the request for surrender.

"Take cover!" Novak dove for the front wall and got as close to it as he could. With every catapult aimed at the front gates, it would matter little if the sentries had the right half closed.

Rebel soldiers scattered and pressed themselves against the wall. Zephyr had her archers take cover on the parapet. Cad pulled a sentry out of the gateway and dove for cover. Thadus sprinted toward the wall, still holding his left wrist.

Boulders thudded all around, sending plumes of dirt skyward. The sounds of wood splintering, rocks slamming into the stone wall, and men shouting filled the air. Out of the corner of his eye Cad saw a sprinting infantryman crushed beneath a boulder. Huge stones soon littered the area. A part of the wall tore away and landed on an archer's foot. Near the gate, the barrage rumbled and shook the place like an earthquake.

It was over in a few seconds, and the badly weakened gate and surrounding wall were reduced to rubble. Cad sprang to his feet and peered through the breech. The Royal cavalry was charging. By the time the Royal forces had their catapults readied for a second assault, the horsemen would be at the gates. Reddland wouldn't order another barrage with his men in the strike zone.

"Infantry, listen! Form two lines, one on each side of the breech. Only a few of Reddland's men will be able to get in at a time. Let's make them run the gauntlet." Novak took command of a line on one side of the breech while Cad assumed command of the other. Both men placed themselves at the front of their lines with weapons drawn.

Zephyr repositioned her archers. Before the first of the Royal cavalry could breech the gate they would have to ride through a deluge of arrows.

A tidal wave of blue surcoats washed toward the oratory. Reddland's cavalry led the assault with the infantry close behind.

Novak and Cad faced each other on opposite sides of the shattered gate. In a few seconds, the first of the Royal troops would be at the breech. Each held their weapons in anticipation.

"Let's put a stumbling block in this opening and take out the first horse," Novak suggested. Cad gave a quick nod of agreement.

The first Royal cavalry soldier appeared in the doorway, and Novak brought his sword down hard just above the animal's knee severing the leg. Cad did the same with his axe to the leg on his side. The horse, which was at a full gallop, struck the ground with its chest and launched its rider over its head. The soldier flew twenty feet before crashing and skidding to a stop. Rebel troops made quick work of the dismounted and disoriented soldier. Cad put the wounded horse out of its misery.

Two more Royal troops came through the opening. Reddland's cavalrymen knew better than to stop at the entrance and tried to continue into the oratory grounds as far as they could to allow their comrades space to gain access. Being forced to slow and steer around the fallen horse made their task more difficult; riding through a barrage of flailing swords and axes made it nearly impossible.

Novak ducked the mace of a passing cavalryman, and then swung his sword against his back. With a clank, Novak's sword jarred with a terrible vibration as it met its target. Cad swung his axe against another, striking the soldier in the thigh. A flood of crimson indicated a direct hit.

The battle raged violently at the north wall and Cad and Novak were in the thick of it. Steel slammed against steel, metal tore open flesh, swords ground against bone, fists pounded out pain. Mayhem rose from the tangle of furious arms and weapons. Droplets of blood sprinkled the scene in a grotesque rain. A severed arm fell at Cad's feet. Two rebel soldiers lay dead to his right. A dismounted Royal cavalryman with an arrow in his neck ran screaming by, only to collapse after a few steps. Zephyr was busy on the parapet directing the best archers to make the most difficult shots.

But the Royal cavalry kept advancing despite the valiant efforts of the rebel infantry. Humans could not stop horses no matter how hard they tried. After the two hundred Royal cavalry breached the gate, then came the flood of Royal infantry. The battle grew so fierce that the stretcher bearers did not attempt to evacuate the wounded.

Reddland smiled as the flood of blue surcoats poured into the oratory grounds.

Both sides were mixed together in a chaos of death. Plans and organization gave way to the struggle to survive. If either side had a plan, it was now lost in confusion. The sentries left the parapets to join the pandemonium on the ground. Zephyr and the archers fired as fast as they could. Arrows whizzed all around, darting between the swords. The "gauntlet" the rebels had set on each side of the breech was nothing more than a swarm of bodies. For the moment the fight had nothing to do with right or wrong, or good versus evil, and everything to do with who got to go home when it was all over.

Emerald swung open the oratory door in response to the insistent pounding. Her father was on the other side. Draped around his neck was the arm of a wounded stretcher bearer he was helping to walk to the hospital.

"What happened?" Emerald's eyes registered the shock of seeing her father covered in the wounded man's blood.

"One of the Royal troops ran a sword through him, and we were unarmed! Here, help me get him to sick bay. I can't carry him much farther with my sprained wrist."

Emerald grabbed the wounded man's other arm and helped her father get the faltering man to aid. "What is happening out there? I've never heard so much yelling and noise in all my life. This sounds worse than the last battle."

"Oh, Emerald; I've never seen such vicious fighting; not in the last battle, not even during the war. It's a complete bloodbath. I think it's only a matter of time. We cannot hold out against such an onslaught. The Royal soldiers just keep advancing, and part of our strength is at the south wall. There were just too many horses for our men to stop. We cannot even get close enough to help the wounded. Reddland's men don't hesitate in attacking us."

"It sounds like we are being overrun."

Thadus placed his free hand on his daughter's shoulder and took a deep breath. "I don't see how they can force the enemy back out. I am certain Cad and Novak will have to retreat. Their only chance will be to get the men in here with us."

Emerald and her father entered the sick bay and put the wounded man onto a cot.

"Cad told me he expected to have to pull back here at some point. Everything will work out according to *His* will in the end." Thadus embraced his daughter in a warm hug.

"I pray you're right, Father."

Emerald released her embrace and smiled halfheartedly. She set to work tending to the wounded, forcing herself to carry on. War was worse than she remembered.

In the pitched frenzy of battle, Novak and Cad worked themselves into a position where they were back to back and fought to maintain a three hundred and sixty degree zone of coverage. They moved methodically through the swarm of arms and weapons while keeping watch on the status of the battle. Occasionally one of them would shout out an order to the troops.

"It looks like we'll have to pull back to the oratory sooner than expected. There are just too many and they keep coming." Novak brought his sword down hard onto the shoulder of a Royal soldier, sending him to the ground. He followed that with a kick to the chin.

Cad blocked a deadly blow from a flail with his shield, and then planted his battle axe in the offender's armpit.

"Yeah, we're going to have to split up. You get Zephyr and Cyrus to pull back first. When I see you going, I'll pull back the infantry." Cad slammed his shield into another soldier's chest and took another swing at the first soldier. This blow caught the man on the collarbone. The Royal soldier staggered backward, and then tripped to the floor. He didn't get back up.

Novak's opponent swung at him, hitting him in the greave. Quickly, Novak stepped on the soldier's blade with his other foot, pinning the sword to the ground. "All right, let's do it! I'll see you back at the oratory."

With a roar, Novak charged through the crowd heading for the parapet where he had last seen Zephyr. Those Royal soldiers who didn't move when they saw Novak's hulking figure looming toward them were knocked to the ground. With his buckler held tightly to his chest and his shoulders down, Novak looked like a bull trampling through a flowerbed.

Cad stayed behind and began notifying some of the rebel men of the upcoming retreat. They quickly relayed the message, relieved at the decision. The trumpeter was nowhere to be found.

Zephyr released an arrow and saw it appear in the back of the knee of a Royal cavalryman. He grabbed his leg in agony. The hit was enough of a distraction for a rebel fighter to pull him off his horse. The man was soon lost somewhere beneath a sea of legs. Zephyr notched another arrow when she saw Novak approaching her. He severed the head of a Royal soldier who was about to climb the ladder to the parapet. A dead sentry lay near its top.

"Pull the archers back into the oratory!" Novak yelled above the din. Another soldier squared off with Novak and brought his sword down hard. Novak blocked the blow with his head. Zephyr found her next volunteer. An arrow dug deep into a soldier's buttocks. His pain was short lived, as was the remainder of his life.

"I could use the break! See you back at the oratory." Zephyr immediately started pulling back her archers. Almost out of arrows, she would have no other choice but to pull the archers back anyway. She hoped the fletchers had been busy making new and repairing old arrows for the battle ahead.

Zephyr ran the length of the parapet sounding out her orders. "Pull back now! Everyone into the oratory!"

The archers scampered down the ladder at the far end of the wall to avoid the pitched battle. Zephyr made sure the few casualties the archers suffered were carried back by their retreating cohorts. She felt terrible for the wounded infantry. Their comrades had to fight all the way as they pulled back, taking the wounded with them.

"When you get to the oratory, take your positions on the roof. We will need to cover the infantry's retreat," Zephyr shouted to her troops as she ran, bringing up the rear.

Cad blocked several blows with his shield as he fought two Royal soldiers simultaneously. One of the soldiers took a spread-leg stance against Cad and raised his sword. In a flash, Cad swept the soldier's leg with his boot, sending the dazed man to the ground. Cad took advantage of the soldier's up-side-down turtle-like position. Cad spun his battle axe around, slammed it into the other soldier's breastplate. The spear-shaped point penetrated the soldier's armor.

"Whenever you are ready," Novak told Cad. "Zephyr's pulled her archers back into the oratory to cover us. Cyrus should have the sentries back soon." Novak continually shifted his gaze to the battle around him.

"All right, let's go!" Cad and Novak started the rebels on their free-for-all retreat. The pullback didn't go smoothly at all, and many of the wounded were left behind for the time being. It was either that or lose everyone. Maybe, if the retreat went well, Cad could negotiate a temporary truce so both sides could tend to their wounded. All would depend on whether the rebels could successfully fortify themselves in the oratory. Cad heard the trumpeter signal the retreat from the far end of the battlefield; he was glad someone found him. The pullback would move a little faster now.

Abrams watched the pullback from the oratory roof. Shortly after Cyrus brought the sentries back, the infantry started coming in a frantic stampede. A shout rose from the Royal soldiers when they realized the rebels were on the run. Cad and Novak, with two squads of men each, slowed the Royal advance so the others could retreat. One rebel soldier tried to drag his wounded friend.

"There's no time for that! We can't hold them back much longer! Move, soldier!" Cad ordered. His job now was to save as many men as he could. The rebel lines were collapsing rapidly and there was no time to waste.

Abrams, soaked with perspiration on this cool morning, could scarcely believe what he saw. He always thought of himself as tougher, less emotional than other men, but as of late he didn't know. There are certain things he expected to see, but this wasn't one of them. He fell to his knees, choked with emotion, and begged God for some sort of deliverance. His hands trembled as he wiped tears from his eyes.

On the battlefield below was the unthinkable. When the rebel army was pushed back to the oratory, they had been forced to leave many of their wounded strewn about the field. And there, running gleefully among the wounded and dying, was Malvagio, looking as if he had been loosed from the depths of hell. With a crazed look, his eyes rolling wildly, Malvagio ran from man to man, slaughtering the wounded that had been left behind. Horrendous screams rose from the men as they were mutilated while yet alive. He gouged out eyes, cut off appendages, and sliced flesh off his helpless victims. His bloodlust soon devolved into cannibalism, and like a spastic demon, Malvagio gyrated from person-to-person, blood dripping from his mouth, dagger in hand, carrying out his master's work. A few other depraved individuals followed suit completing Malvagio's goon squad.

Abrams fell face down prostrating himself.

"My God, please help my people. You said 'Blessed is the nation whose God is the Lord.' I pledge to you we would be that nation once again. Forgive us our past transgressions which caused us to fall to such a state as to allow a man like Reddland to come to power. Those gathered here today are sacrificing their lives to restore things to the way they were. But we need your help. The actions of the Royal soldiers are not hidden from you. They have mutilated your people to death, and driven the others back. Let not their actions go unpunished. Take up the battle with us. Let it not be your will that all of us should perish here. Restore us once again. Let the strong arm of the Lord be revealed against those who would blatantly commit abominations in your sight. Your will be done. Amen."

Abrams was numb and completely drained. He stayed face down in prayer pleading for the rebel army.

Unaware the wounded were being slaughtered, Novak and Cad fought intensely to stave off the Royal soldiers as the rebels retreated into the oratory. Zephyr and the archers fired arrows rapidly at the rushing onslaught. The tide of blue surcoats wasn't going to be stopped, but maybe it would be slowed long enough to allow most of the rebels to make it to safety. By now, the Royal archers were advancing into the oratory grounds.

"Move! Move! Move!" Cad shouted encouragement at the withdrawing rebels as he pummeled a Royal soldier with his battle-ax. He and Novak had formed a line with a squad of men at the base of the steps. In unison, they stepped backward slowly, step-by-step, bringing up the rear as the rebels funneled into the doorway. Zephyr was putting on the pressure. Every few seconds four dozen arrows plunged into the mass of Royal soldiers trying to ascend the oratory steps. The rebels would have the high ground as they retreated up the stairs. Novak took full advantage of the situation and kicked an advancing Royal soldier in the chest. The dazed soldier went sprawling backward down the stairs knocking several of his comrades down with him. The other rebel soldiers soon followed Novak's lead. The first rank of Royal troops was sent cascading down on the others. For a brief moment, the Royal troops became a tangle of legs at the bottom of the stone stairway. This gave Cad and Novak the needed time to get most of their squad inside.

Cad was the last one to enter the oratory and practically had to fight his way in. A mace came down on his helmet as hands, flails, and swords beat against the closing oratory doors. Inside, several rebel troops strained to close the doors. Others stood ready with an iron bar. Royal fingers and hands protruded through the crack trying to force the door open.

"Get a mallet and some spikes!" Novak shouted at a nearby infantryman; having said that, he retreated about fifty feet into the main auditorium. He grabbed a tattered pillow off the floor, held it like a shield, and barreled down on the door.

"A-A-A-R-R-R-G-G-G-G-H!" Novak roared, quickly reaching top speed. He slammed into the doors forcing them shut. The rebel soldiers erupted in a thunderous roar of approval.

The impact shook the room and dislodged a painting from the wall nearby. Two rebel soldiers were knocked to the floor when Novak charged between them. The door was quickly barred.

As a sentry started hammering spikes into the floor at the base of the door, Novak noticed two fingers twitching on the floor.

The battle raged so furiously that no one noticed the foreboding clouds gathering over Xylor. And the wind was kicking up. What started as a light rain soon became a torrential downpour. Lightning blazed across the sky.

On the roof, Zephyr could feel the thunder vibrate in her chest. She and her archers were soon soaked. The Royal soldiers regrouped on the oratory grounds, now a mud wallow. Rain streaked down her face. She had the archers hold their fire. The wind and rain made continuing to fire arrows a pointless waste.

Also on the roof, Abrams rose dripping wet from his prostrated position and headed for shelter. "Thank you." He smiled skyward as he descended the stairs.

For several hours the rain deluged the small island. Lightning struck several tall pines in the nearby forest. Thunder exploded in the air rattling the oratory shutters. Like a giant drum, the thunder resonated in everyone's ribcages. Powerful gusts of wind tore across Xylor, knocking down trees. It was the worst storm to hit the island in anyone's memory.

The Royal soldiers crouched miserably wet and cold on the oratory grounds waiting for their orders. Reddland had his tent moved onto the premises next to the wall for protection against the fierce wind. As long as the winds kept up, there would be few other tents erected.

Reddland was ecstatic with the recent Royal victory. "Excellent job, men; we will soon have the rebels crushed!" Reddland took a towel from his servant and dabbed his face. Another helped him out of his armor. Lexton and Marcus stood dripping, helmets in hand.

Lexton held a soggy piece of parchment. "Yes, Sire, but this victory came at great cost." His mood was somber.

"Yes, yes; what are the latest figures?" Reddland's joy in his victory was not to be dampened by a casualty count.

Lexton unfolded the parchment. "We have three hundred and eleven dead and forty-two wounded. The rebels have eighty-three dead and only a few wounded we know of."

Reddland was unimpressed. "Well, don't blame yourselves. This is war and soldiers die. We'll recruit more troops when we are done here." Reddland stepped behind a dressing curtain. Wet clothes soon plopped to the ground. His face popped up over the curtain. "Why so few rebels wounded?"

"Malvagio and a few other men killed the entire contingent of rebel wounded that remained on the battlefield." Lexton was blunt.

"Really?" Reddland contemplated that fact momentarily.

Marcus remained silent thus far, but now had to say something. "He did more than just kill them, Sire. He mutilated and ate them!" Marcus was clearly disgusted. He felt himself being pulled in a new direction. He was losing his taste for what he had been fighting for. In fact, he began to wonder just what exactly he was fighting for. Marcus had never been a religious man, and thought little of Tanuba. But lately, he had been thinking maybe there was a God; that maybe the rebels were more than very lucky—they were blessed.

"I take it you don't approve?"

"No, Sire. Malvagio is out of control. He needs to be reigned in." Marcus chose his words wisely. Lexton nodded his head in agreement with Marcus's conclusions about Malvagio.

"Did I not order all of the rebels to be put to death?" Reddland replied as he slipped into clean, dry clothes.

"Yes, Sire, you did. But mutilating them is unnecessary. Eating them is beyond comprehension." Marcus's words faded into a whisper as he spoke.

Reddland emerged from behind the dressing screen adjusting his shirt cuffs. "Granted, Malvagio became a bit overzealous, but that kind of loyalty to the cause is outstanding. I would take one man like Malvagio over ten others who would flee at the first instant the battle turns ugly. Don't let it bother you. Those he put out of their misery were nothing more than rabid dogs running lawless through society trying to overthrow it! It's not like they're orderly citizens."

Something clicked in Marcus's head. For the first time he saw the contradictions of the Royal policies for what they were. Reddland made a distinction between the rebels and the other citizens, but methods of dealing with the two groups were identical. The Royal Guard dealt as harshly with the "ordinary citizens" as with the rebels. In fact, accusing someone of insurrection had always been justification to put them to death. If Reddland perceived anyone as a threat, they were killed, regardless if a confession had been tortured out of them or not. Marcus was starting to wonder who the rabid dogs running lawless through society really were. It was a feeling he didn't like.

"So, are you saying Malvagio has your approval in this matter?" Marcus didn't even know why he bothered to ask.

Reddland nodded enthusiastically. "Malvagio not only has my approval, I've promoted him to the command team. He'll be just behind you and Lexton in rank."

Marcus kept a stone face as best he could. "Are you sure you want that, Sire? He lacks discipline. He was difficult for his sergeants and lieutenants to keep under control. Now I feel he will become unrestrainable."

"Marcus, I don't think I'm getting my point across." Reddland placed his fingertips together in thought. "As long as Malvagio follows orders to kill the rebels, who really cares if he takes a few liberties? As long as he gets the assigned task done, he will do just fine. I don't think we'll have a problem in that regard."

Marcus was too numb to respond. His whole world seemed to be turned upside down from where it had been only a week ago: ideas that used to make sense weren't making sense anymore; people he used to trust were suddenly untrustworthy; everything was changing—or was he himself changing?

"As you wish, Sire." There was no point for Marcus to argue.

Lexton thought it was a bad idea; Marcus could see it in his eyes. Lexton felt Malvagio had gone mad under the pressures of battle. Deep down he wanted to send Malvagio back to the compound for the duration of this battle. But Lexton bit off the truth and lied. "I think Malvagio was a good choice for promotion."

Marcus's heart sank and his face showed the shock of what he was hearing.

Lexton continued, all the while avoiding Marcus's gaze. "He is a self-motivator who gets the job done." Lexton didn't even sound close to convincing. But he had seen Reddland grow ever more suspicious of Marcus's loyalties, especially since Marcus had begun questioning Reddland's decisions. Lexton did not want to be put in that situation.

Reddland smiled at Lexton's support. Glancing in Marcus's direction, Reddland returned to the business at hand. "Good. That's settled. Now let's plan our next move. How do we go about sounding the death knell for the rebels? Are we moving the catapults forward yet? We'll raze the oratory if we have to."

"Well, Sire. That will be a problem. As you are well aware, it is raining tremendously. The ground is a muddy bog and we can't move the catapults. Those we've tried to move are buried up to their axles in the mire." Lexton gestured toward the tent walls, indicating the ferocity of the storm. Rain pelted the canvas in a stampede of droplets. Tent pegs strained against the wind to keep the structure upright.

"That's unfortunate, but, we can make do without them. We'll batter the door. The rebels can do little more than hole themselves up like trapped rabbits. Our only threat would be archers on the oratory roof." Reddland was certain of victory. The rebels were trapped under siege. What could they really do?

"Shall we wait until the storm clears before proceeding with our attack?" Lexton inquired.

"We may as well. The rebels aren't going anywhere." Reddland placed his foot on a stool so his servant could polish his mud caked boots. "Marcus, what is your opinion? You seem to be brimming with opinions as of late?" A sly grin curled Reddland's lips.

It just occurred to Marcus that even though Malvagio had been promoted, he was not going to be included in the decision-making process. It was still only Reddland, Lexton, and him making the plans. Reddland obviously knew the man was a poor choice or he would have Malvagio here to help formulate a strategy. Malvagio would be limited to carrying out Reddland's dirty work.

"I suggest we take the patient route. We should lay a siege and starve them out. They will be forced to surrender or starve to death, and I am confident the bulk of them would be killed should they try to escape. They are already trapped, and a siege will spare further loss of our men."

Reddland was unimpressed. "They could have a large stash of supplies. A siege could take a month or two. We don't have that kind of time."

"Why not?" Marcus knew of no time line imposed by Kelterland.

"Because, I say we don't! I want those rebels crushed now!" Reddland's face flushed with anger.

"As things stand now we've already won this war. The rebels are trapped; they cannot mount a successful counterattack. All we have to do is wait and we've won." Marcus tried to reason with Reddland. He didn't want any more of his men to die.

"How would it look to Kelterland if we took months to defeat a puny band of rebels?" Reddland asked.

"As long as we win and maintain control, I don't think they would care."

Reddland glared at Marcus. "You know, Marcus, I wanted to give you time to get over whatever it is that's been diverting your attentions lately. Don't let the few lucky breaks the rebels have had spook you."

Marcus was enraged. Had anyone else called him a coward they would have lost teeth. "Fine, we'll do it your way," Marcus concluded.

Once Reddland saw Marcus was through arguing, he continued with the battle plans. "Place sentries around the place, Lexton. I don't want anyone escaping."

Lexton did not want to be in Marcus's shoes. It was obvious Reddland lost patience with him. Lexton knew Marcus had the right idea but was not about to say anything now. The Royal army had won. Indeed, it would take nothing short of a miracle for the rebellion to succeed now.

"Sentries are already set up, Sire. No one will be leaving," Lexton reported.

"Very well; as soon as the storm breaks we will attack." Reddland was smug in his victory over Marcus.

"Cyrus, take two squads of men and make sure all of the windows and doors on the first floor are barred securely." Cad relaxed a bit after the main door was shut, but there was still work to do.

Cyrus looked puzzled. "We already have them sealed tight."

Cad nodded. "I know. But I'm going to need them double or triple-boarded. I want it to take at least half an hour for someone to get through. Also, get fires started in the fireplaces and be sure there is plenty of extra wood nearby." Cad pointed to the four large stone fireplaces that warmed the main auditorium. Cad was looking up at the balcony. It stretched across the entrance to the auditorium parting the two-story-high ceiling in half at the rear. The pews had long since been removed from the balcony. The damp, musty darkness of the ceiling and balcony area were covered with thick cobwebs.

"I never noticed how filthy it was up there," Novak remarked. He could see the wheels turning in Cad's head. "Are you thinking what I'm thinking?"

"Maybe. Does your idea involve that wooden beam over there and a balcony?" Cad pointed to a six-by-six-foot beam hewn from a log that had been used many years ago to assist with repairs.

Novak grinned. "Ya, it does. In fact, I was thinking of affixing some three-foot long spikes to the beam and tying it to the balcony. When the Royal troops breech the main door and enter the auditorium, they'll meet with a nasty welcome."

"Right you are, Novak! That should bloody well slow them down for my next plan." Cad's mind worked furiously to visualize the preparations needed to put his plan into effect.

"You'll have to fill me in later. I'll set to work on that beam." Novak slapped Cad on the shoulder and gathered several men to help him.

Cad surveyed the staircase to the far right of the altar. It was the only access to the second floor. As he was assessing his plan, he noticed two soldiers carrying a third on a stretcher. They moved toward the stairs. There was something odd about the wounded soldier that caught Cad's eye. He walked over for a closer look.

Cad's jaw dropped in horror. "What happened to this man?" Cad couldn't believe his eyes. He had never seen anything like this in his life. The soldier's lips had been cut off and his bloody teeth smiled out like a skeleton.

One of the stretcher bearers answered. "The Royal soldiers did this to him. He told us they mutilated all of the wounded before killing them. He managed to escape after they started cutting on him. He is the only one that made it back."

Cad would not have dared imagine this kind of viciousness, not even in the days of his youth. He filled with anguish: he blamed himself for what happened to this man and the others. Perhaps if he had conducted a slower retreat there would have been time to bring back the wounded—no; if he hesitated, the entire rebel army would have suffered the same fate. They barely made it back as it was.

I saved the lives of the others by retreating, Cad reminded himself. But he would not make the same mistake of underestimating the cruelty of Reddland and his men again. Cad pounded his fist into his hand. He choked back his emotions as the soldiers continued the task of delivering their friend to the hospital room. Noticing a side door, Cad quietly disappeared into a storage room. He was sickened at the thought that he failed so many good, brave men.

"What have I done?" Cad whispered. "Lord, forgive me for this. I didn't know. I didn't know." He buried his face in his hands.

Cad was so deep in thought he didn't notice Abrams walk into the little room. "It's not your fault, son." He witnessed the exchange between Cad and the stretcher bearers.

Surprised by the voice, Cad quickly regained his composure and turned to face Abrams.

"The leader is always to blame." His voice showed no emotion.

"I disagree." Abrams replied. "You had no way of foreseeing what Reddland's men were capable of. It is beyond the realms of sanity." After a few moments of silent contemplation, Abrams continued. "Every now and then, a man will come along who is so depraved, so utterly vile, that we are all reminded of the very depths of evil that surround us; forces of darkness exist that battle not only for the bodies of men but for their very souls. Reddland is such a man. There was no way to know how far he would go."

Cad pondered Abrams's statement. "Maybe you're right. But I should have known Reddland would kill those men."

"All of us were, and still are prepared to die. We knew the risks involved in this fight. The wounded men included. The majority of the injured were mortally wounded and would have died anyway. From the rooftop, I witnessed much of the horror and was as shocked as any. You did what you had to. Your quick thinking saved many more men than were lost. God will not hold you accountable for Reddland's deeds. Those men, if they can be called men, will be held accountable for every life taken. Judgment day will be their final defeat, and those brave soldiers' final victory."

Cad mulled the words over.

"Cad," Abrams continued, placing a hand on Cad's shoulder. "The outcome of this conflict is in God's hands; He alone is the final authority. He only asks us to do what is right and just. From what I have witnessed today, you did what was right."

Cad nodded his head. "I hope you're right, Abrams. I just wish there was something I could have done to prevent their suffering."

"Don't we all," Abrams agreed.

Taking a deep breath, Cad stood and faced Abrams. "Well, I've wasted enough time. I'd better get back and help Novak. The chap sure needs it." Cad smiled and slapped Abrams on the shoulder. "Keep praying. What happens next could very well decide the outcome of this whole conflict, one way or another." Abrams nodded silently.

"By the way," Cad whispered, "thank you."

"God speed, soldier." Abrams whispered back as Cad slipped out the door. "Godspeed."

Cad had scarcely walked into the auditorium when he saw Novak approaching at a brisk pace. Cad could tell by the look on his face that he was greatly upset.

"Did you hear what that…" Novak restrained himself from vulgarities. "Do you know what Reddland's men did to our wounded? And now he's stacking their corpses against the wall like a cord of wood."

A pained look came over Cad. "Yes, I am aware of their blooming atrocities; but there's nothing we can do now. We have to concentrate on getting out of this mess. What's our status?"

"Reddland better hope I don't get a hold on him." Novak shook his head in disgust. "As far as our status, it looks like the Royal army is going to wait for the storm to lift. They're bogged down in the mud. It's pouring buckets out there. All windows and doors are sealed so tight a gnat couldn't get through."

Novak turned and pointed toward the ceiling. "I have a spiked beam rigged on the balcony to greet the Royal Guard when they eventually breech the main door. Emerald and Thadus have evacuated all the wounded to the top floor. The cooks have moved their makeshift kitchen upstairs as well, and are preparing some grub. Zephyr is on the roof with her archers keeping us informed on Reddland's actions, and by now she has to be soaking wet." Novak grinned as he finished giving Cad a brief rundown on everyone's activities.

Cad was very relieved to see the rebel army was still running smoothly despite what it had been through. "Do you think Reddland can move his catapults forward?"

"Not a chance. It is too muddy out there. This is the worst storm I've seen in a long time, and it doesn't look to be letting up any time soon." Novak replied.

Cad smiled. "Fantastic! What an unexpected blessing that is. You know, if our numbers were equal with theirs, we would have already won this battle. We've been taking them out four or five to one. I'm starting to think the reason we only had five hundred troops was so God's power could be revealed. You know, like Gideon. It's becoming obvious this is more then mere coincidence. Now all of Reddland's catapults are useless."

Novak nodded in agreement. "I've always believed we would win."

"You always feel like we're going to win; even when we don't. You just live for the fight, Novak." Cad admired Novak's confidence. He never thought losing a possibility. This is what made his friend such a great fighter. And on the rare instances in the past when the Clandestine Knights lost a skirmish, Novak's confidence proved to be a steady rock.

Novak couldn't deny it. "Ya, you've got a point there."

Cad slapped his friend on the back. He had been through so much with Novak; it was a comfort to have the hulk around. "I have an idea. Collect all of the ropes we have and take them to the roof. Tie them off and have them ready to be used to rappel with."

"Uh, oh," Novak grinned broadly, "Reddland's in for it now, isn't he?"

Cad explained his newest plan to Novak. Novak liked the idea. He gathered together a squad of men and set to work on the ropes.

Zephyr was soaked. Rain ran down her neck and back making for an uncomfortable afternoon. At least Reddland's men were just as miserable. The Royal troops were huddled together, waiting for the storm to cease its fury. They were unable to start a fire for warmth and would be eating a cold meal tonight. The Royal wounded had been carted away and a few tents erected. Of course, Reddland was warm and dry in his tent.

Reddland's men were posted all around the oratory and Zephyr knew the rebels were trapped. She assumed Reddland would lay a siege and starve them out, but it looked like his troops were constructing a makeshift battering ram. Their other one burned. This one was smaller and lighter and could be carried. The ground was too muddy to roll a heavy ram into place. It didn't make much sense to Zephyr, but after seeing what happened to the rebel wounded, nothing much did.

Zephyr felt vulnerable on the roof during a lightning storm. She looked at the oratory's towering steeples. They would provide ample targets for lightning.

The rain droned on into the evening relentlessly, the storm devouring the rest of the daylight. The ground turned to slush with standing water on the oratory premises. At dusk, the storm started to ease, the wind blowing less severe, but it would be well into the night before Xylor would see total relief.

Reddland's troops were soaked through and miserable. Though they had just won a victory in pushing the rebels back into the oratory, a lot of their comrades died to achieve it. The fact the Royal Guard sacrificed four or five men to every one rebel was not lost on them. The unexplainable firestorm that consumed the battering ram added to their unease. Anyone could see the rebels, despite their current predicament, were enjoying a tremendous amount of good fortune. They had held out against superior forces for two days. It was a feat no other group could claim. The Royal army crushed other armies twice the size and had always done so quickly.

Many of the Royal soldiers were Tanuba worshippers. Even among those who were not, the general consensus was that even though Tanuba was goddess over the island of Xylor, the rebel's god must have authority over the oratory and its grounds. The Royal troops accepted there was a pantheon of gods, each with its own jurisdiction. Recent events led them to believe Tanuba's reign did not include the oratory grounds. The thought of fighting against a foreign god was unsettling. Murmurs of concern circulated through the Royal camp.

Marcus and Lexton mingled with their troops. The apprehensive looks they received told the story. Marcus's bloodied face didn't help matters. Marcus and Lexton found a clear spot to discuss this matter.

"The men are getting edgy. We can't afford another loss. I think superstition will get the best of them, and they could start to desert. There'll be no reasoning with them if their superstition mixes with terror." Marcus read the mood of his men well.

Lexton wiped rain from his face. "Yes, I believe you're right. I don't think we'll have to worry about another loss, though. I know we wouldn't if we just starved the rebels out like you wanted."

"Do you ever wonder, or have any doubts about this. I mean, about Malvagio, this storm, the rebels' good fortune? I know you don't believe what you told Reddland." Marcus wanted to know what conclusions Lexton had drawn about the unlikely occurrences.

"I don't think much of it. The rebels have some good leaders. They must be mercenaries with prior military experience. The rebels have some hired talent, nothing more. As for Malvagio, yes, I think he's a raving lunatic. But let me give you some advice, Marcus: you'd better change your attitude around Reddland. He's becoming suspicious of you. You won't be able to do any good if you are demoted. The last thing we need is for Malvagio to assume your position. I'm telling you this, friend to friend; you're wearing out Reddland's welcome." Lexton had no idea it was Reddland who brought the rebel leadership to Xylor.

"At what point do we say something?" Marcus inquired, slightly annoyed.

Lexton looked around quickly to make sure no one was listening. "Marcus, during a battle isn't the right time, that's for sure. Just relax. We've won this fight. It's only a matter of time now."

Marcus wasn't as sure of victory as his comrade, but he knew it was pointless to argue. Lexton convinced himself of victory rather than face the alternative. "The storm seems to be letting up. We may as well get to work preparing our attack. I'm sure we'll be starting again in the morning."

Lexton's tone softened. "Marcus, stay with me on this one. We'll win; you'll see."

Marcus forced a smile and headed out to hasten his battle preparations. How could Lexton think all was fine? Reddland was no longer listening to the advice of his top officials. Reddland had been blinded by vengeance, was making impulsive decisions, and was unable to evaluate the actions of his troops. Malvagio's promotion and Marcus's loss of favor were proof of that. The Royal army was losing its professionalism and legitimacy. They were becoming lawless mercenaries and he was getting tired of the whole thing. Surely Reddland's disease was affecting his mind.

But most of all, Marcus had a growing sense that there was something more to this rebel god.

--•◦•--

Emerald dried her hands on a bloody towel after finishing the stitches on her last patient. Doc redressed the leg of a soldier whose wound was severely inflamed. The prognosis wasn't good. On the other side of the cramped room, Abrams spoke with the mortally wounded. Several elderly women comforted the dying. The move to the second floor had been traumatic for the wounded, and Emerald was glad it was over. With every bump and jolt, the injured cried out in pain, and it wore on her nerves. Thadus took the dead to another room to await burial at some future date. Things were winding down in the makeshift hospital because few wounded survived the last battle. Emerald hung the towel from a chair and started sweeping up the littered floor. Pieces of bandages and torn and bloody articles of clothing lay everywhere. After sweeping, she would start mopping up the blood.

"How are *you* holding up, Emerald?"

Startled, Emerald turned to face Novak; his clothes were stained with blood. The rain streaked the blood like crimson tears down his arms, and his hands were purple with bruises. Novak looked tired and battle weary, but at least he didn't have any new wounds, though his armor had several new dents and his movements were slow and deliberate, betraying his pain.

"How are you holding up?" Emerald asked.

"I'm just a little sore." Novak played down his discomfort. Armor protected its bearer from being severely cut or impaled, but the blows left him battered and bruised. Novak blocked so many blows with his buckler that his left forearm was black and blue.

Emerald shook her head in amazement. "What you poor men go through. It's terrible. I mean, look at your arm. It's one big bruise." Emerald reached out but didn't touch his arm. She was becoming all too familiar with the effects of war. "Is there anything I can do for your arm, Novak?"

"Just seeing you is all the medicine I need." Novak gave Emerald a wry grin.

Emerald blushed. "Thank you. Seeing you alive has lifted my spirits a bit too. I just wish that was all it took to fix these wounded men."

Emerald cleaned two chairs so they could talk a while. Novak filled Emerald in on the latest details. She already knew about the atrocities committed against the wounded men. After a few minutes, Cad entered the room. He looked as bad a Novak did.

"What happened to your armor?" Novak noticed Cad was no longer wearing his cuirass.

"I'm having it repaired. That big soldier nearly drove his battle-axe clear through it. The crease was scraping against my back." Cad removed his gauntlets then slipped off the severed sleeve that hung loosely around his wrist. Since it was soaking wet from the rain, he used it to clean his face. When he was finished he flung it into the trash bucket Emerald had nearby.

"Let's get something to eat," Cad said and stretched.

Novak saw a flash of crimson. "Hey, Cad, turn around." He waited for Cad to oblige. "Lift up your shirt. You have a wound on your back."

"You're kidding." Cad turned around and pulled off his shirt, revealing a well-muscled back. His skin was red and irritated where his creased cuirass had been rubbing. There among the scrapes and bruises was a two-inch cut.

Novak raised his eyebrows. "You took a hard hit, friend. The axe must have penetrated your armor deep enough to give you that gash."

"The hit hurt pretty badly, but that's incredible. You're the only person I know who can hit that hard."

"Let me clean that up and put a dressing on it," Emerald offered, already gathering the materials.

"Cad, you look like you've been through a war," Novak joked as Emerald dressed the wound.

"Can you believe it? My good shirt is destroyed."

"Don't go to the same tailor you went to last time." Novak grinned.

Cad furrowed his brow, puzzled by Novak's statement. "Why's that?"

"Go to a tailor that makes men's clothes." Novak laughed heartily, clearly amused with himself. Cad and Emerald couldn't help but join in. A few of the nearby recovering soldiers looked over, annoyed by the outburst.

"Oops; it looks like we're waking some of the wounded men," Emerald whispered.

"That wasn't very nice mate; I owe you one." Cad pulled his shirt back down.

The three friends left in search of a quick meal. Most of the others already ate and now it was their turn; and they were hungry.

On the roof glistening green eyes peered out from wet eyelashes, squinting against the rain. The storm was letting up, but it was far from over. Zephyr pulled her short cape tight against her shoulders and huddled against the steeple. At least it blocked the wind. She was wet and miserable. Her only consolation was seeing Reddland's army ankle deep in the mud. She could see Reddland's troops intended to ride out the storm before they attacked, but someone had to stand watch. This task fell to the archers as Cyrus and his sentries were absorbed into the infantry. Now it was time to hurry up and wait.

XVII

THERE WAS LITTLE movement from Reddland's camp. The few trees on the oratory grounds had large groups of soldiers huddled under them. Horses milled about restless at their picket lines. An occasional soldier wandered off into the darkness. Lights flickered from within the few tents that had been erected.

High up on the roof, Zephyr looked into the shadows when lightning momentarily lit up the landscape. For a brief second she saw a horse with what looked like an injured rider. The rider seemed to be slumped forward in the saddle with his head hanging down. Zephyr thought it was odd. She stared intently at the place she had seen the horse and waited for the next flash of lightning. About a minute later the oratory grounds flickered like day again. This time the horse and rider were considerably closer than they were before. The rider seemed to teeter slightly. Either that or he was falling asleep astride his mount. His blue surcoat clearly identified him as the enemy. Zephyr wondered if maybe the man was just ill. At any rate, why was he coming toward the oratory?

Zephyr stood up to get a better look. *What is this soldier up to?* When lightening flashed again, the horse and rider were gone. Zephyr leaned out over the stone wall of the catwalk.

Where did he go? A horse and rider cannot just disappear. Zephyr darted her eyes all around, searching for the vanished rider. She had to be sure the soldier wasn't sneaking up to the oratory. It didn't make sense to send one man, but you never knew with Reddland.

Zephyr had to wait a long time for the next flicker of lightning. When it finally came, she spotted the horse, but the rider was missing. At least it looked like the same horse. It was dapple gray just like the one the soldier had been riding. This one was picketed by itself about thirty yards form a small group of huddled soldiers. Zephyr couldn't remember if that horse had been there before. Maybe the rider joined his friends who were passing a bottle around.

Zephyr watched the area intently for the next half hour. During the flashes of lightning, the horse stayed in place. She didn't see the soldier again. There was no other activity on that side of the oratory. Satisfied that it had been a soldier coming to join his friends, Zephyr relaxed. She crouched back down behind the steeple and pulled her cap down tight. At least the incident caused an otherwise dull night to slip by a little faster.

—•◦•—

Exhausted, he plopped his head down in the mud. The left side of his face sank into the cold, wet mire, weeds scratching against his face. His breathing was labored, white puffs of vapor rose from his mouth and nostrils. Tilting his head slightly, he saw Zephyr on the oratory wall through the knee-high weeds. The rebel soldier next to her paced nervously, occasionally throwing glances out toward the darkened grounds.

The man in the mud felt fortunate to have been able to slither this close to the oratory undetected. He had taken a full two-and-a-half hours to crawl the three hundred feet from where he staked his horse to the wall. It wasn't easy, to say the least. The trek left him drained and mud caked. He rested before continuing.

———•·•·•———

From the top of the wall, Zephyr could tell the Royal forces were settling in for the night. Sentries stood watch, hunkered down behind their shields. It finally stopped raining and the Royal soldiers were able to build a campfire and prepare food for the rest of the men. They ate in shifts, and a few more tents had been pitched.

Zephyr rubbed her eyes. She was tired and ready to be relieved shortly. She could hardly wait. A few more minutes and she could dry off and get some much needed sleep. Maybe when she awoke she would be someplace else.

Suddenly, Zephyr heard a clanking sound followed by a brief scrape. At first she thought someone had dropped a sword. But then she saw it; a grappling hook was latched onto the catwalk walls, its taut tope draped over the side. Zephyr ran the few feet to the hook and looked over. A lone Royal soldier was scaling the oratory wall. For a brief moment Zephyr stood frozen in disbelief. This had to be the one she had seen! Where had he been all this time? It was inconceivable that one soldier would muster an attack, yet here he was. There were no others. In fact, there was nary a sound from Reddland's camp. This had to be some sort of a ploy.

Zephyr pulled out her dagger and called for a few of the nearby archers. They had finally seen the lone intruder and were already hurrying over. In seconds, the oratory roof was bustling with excitement.

"Alert the others downstairs and let us secure the wall! This soldier cannot be acting alone." Zephyr directed the nearest archers

Zephyr and two others waited patiently for the Royal soldier to climb the four stories to the roof. He was taking an unusually long time to climb the rope. Zephyr thought about cutting the rope, but decided to capture the intruder instead. Was he a defector? After what the Royal soldiers had been through it was a distinct possibility.

The sudden bustle of activity on the oratory roof drew the attention of the nearby Royal sentries. They soon spotted the Royal Guardsman scaling the rebel stronghold and a runner was dispatched to alert Marcus and Lexton. The troops were taken aback by the boldness of their comrade and thought perhaps a secret plan was in the process of being carried out. They relayed the news up the chain of command for verification.

"Do not kill him unless we have to. I would like to find out what he is up to," Zephyr told her archers. Soon they heard the heavy breathing of the climber. A hand gripped the top of the catwalk wall, followed by a grunt and the appearance of a head and a blue surcoat. The Royal soldier was caked with mud, his black hair plastered to his scalp. Zephyr found his complete exhaustion at climbing the wall odd. *Why would someone that out of shape attempt such a feat?* Zephyr took another quick look around to confirm he was the only attacker.

The tired intruder provided little resistance when the rebel archers jerked him over the wall and slammed him to the ground. Zephyr stepped on the intruder's neck. "Quick, tie his hands behind his back."

The man was quickly swarmed by rebel soldiers, many of whom gave him a kick or a jab as they secured his hands. Some of their friends had recently been mutilated and this Royal soldier would pay for that. Zephyr didn't partake in the abuse of the prisoner, but did nothing to stop it either.

The archers lifted the prisoner to his feet, dealing him blows to the ribs and abdomen in the process. The prisoner's head hung to his chest and his feet were limp under his body. He had to be held upright by his captors. Zephyr realized the man had been in poor health even before the beating he received just now. He scarcely had the strength to grunt from the pain of the blows he was getting. His right leg was soaked with blood and he trembled all over like he had the chills. It wasn't that cold tonight. Zephyr thought perhaps he was scared until she grabbed the prisoner by the hair to lift his head. Then she realized he was burning with a fever.

"Zephyr?" A feeble whisper came from the bleeding mouth of the prisoner.

Zephyr let out a deep gasp. Her dagger clattered to the floor. Her eyes grew wide and tears welled in her eyes. She spoke in a quivering voice.

"Scorpyus, you are alive?" Zephyr embraced the battered frame of her friend. Through tears and great sobs she managed to order the rebels to untie him and find a stretcher so he could be taken to see Doc.

Zephyr gently lowered Scorpyus to the ground. "We thought you were dead. I cannot believe you are here. Oh, Scorpyus, forgive me, I did not know it was you." She rattled on, shocked that her friend was alive. How could it be? They had all seen him die a few days earlier.

—•◦•—

"We came as soon as we heard. Where's the attack coming from?" Cad hustled along the catwalk, ready for action, Novak at his side. He was sure he would find an all-out assault in progress by the time he made it to the roof.

"There's just one soldier, sir. Zephyr has him over here," A very young archer informed Cad of the recent activity.

Cad didn't know what was more confusing, that the archers had apparently killed the prisoner, or that Zephyr was so upset about it. She was in tears and holding up the Royal soldier in a seated position.

"What happened? Did you kill…" Cad stopped mid sentence, a look of bewildered shock on his face. Novak turned pale.

"It is Scorpyus! Somehow, he is alive!" Zephyr laughed through her tears.

Cad's body was visibly jolted by the news. There beneath the caked mud was a familiar although battered face. Novak stood speechless, staring at his friend back from the dead.

Bit by bit, the reality of the situation began to set in. Scorpyus was in fact alive. The "what" and "how" would have to be answered later. Getting him to Doc was their first priority.

An archer returned with a stretcher. Doc and Thadus were in tow. Cad and Novak loaded Scorpyus onto the stretcher. Their friend was in pain and burning hot. Even on this cool night Scorpyus was sweating enough to wash some of the mud off of his brow.

"Let's get him downstairs in the light where I can get a good look at this wound." Doc ordered urgently.

"You heard the man, clear a path." Novak picked up one end of the stretcher, Cad took the other. Both plowed a path through the gathered archers and headed straight for the hospital. Doc and Thadus followed.

"The rest of you get back to your posts. Your relief will be on the way," Zephyr gave last minute instructions before disappearing down the stairs to the lower level.

Reddland walked briskly toward the commotion where a man had been seen scaling the wall. He was tucking in his shirt as he went. "What is going on?" Marcus and Lexton hurried along behind him.

"Our sentries spotted one of our men scaling the oratory. It looked like the rebels took him prisoner once he made it to the top." A soldier reported.

"You fool! It was obviously someone defecting to the enemy; probably not even a soldier." Reddland was enraged.

"We thought that maybe you ordered a secret attack or…" The soldier was cut short by a backhand to the cheek.

Reddland struck the soldier again. "That's ludicrous! You should know we wouldn't send one man alone. You should have recognized a defection when you saw it. It's your fault that traitor made it that far in the first place. Who knows how many others you've let slip in to assist the rebels?" Reddland struck the Royal soldier several more times, sending him rocking back on his heels.

Reddland was beyond mere rage. After knocking the bewildered soldier to the ground, Reddland began kicking and stomping the downed man. Dazed from the blows, the soldier curled up into a ball and tried to protect his head with his arms. It was no use. Reddland kicked and flailed away like a mad man. He shouted obscenities and cursed the fallen soldier as he pummeled him. The ruckus woke the whole camp and drew the attention of the rebel archers several yards away. Something was happening, but it was too dark to tell what exactly. Reddland's anger over the rebellion, his frustration with the poorer-than-expected showing his army had displayed in battle, and now his fear of losing this conflict weighed on him tremendously. The rebels' unbelievable luck rattled his every fiber. Combine that with the knowledge his illness was getting worse, and Reddland was a man gone mad. The unfortunate soldier cowering before him would now pay for circumstances beyond his control.

Lexton and the other soldiers stood by frozen. None dared lift a hand against Reddland. It could mean their lives. Reddland kicked and stomped the soldier while screaming obscenities in a demonic, shrill voice. Saliva foamed on his lips. The soldier bled profusely from the mouth and nose. His jaw hung toothless to the side of his face.

Marcus reached his limit also. He grabbed Reddland by the shoulders and spun him around. "You raging lunatic! You're killing your own man!"

Reddland raised a hand to strike Marcus, but was too much of a coward to follow through. Marcus was a large, muscular man. Instead, Reddland called upon a god in whom he didn't believe to curse Marcus.

"Marcus that is the last time you will question me! You are hereby demoted. Malvagio is your new commander!" Reddland's face flushed beet red and his eyes glowed with the rage he felt.

"Fine. I'm still not going to let you kill that man!" Marcus was fed up with Reddland and all that had happened in the last week. He now felt he had wasted his whole life fighting for the wrong side.

"If you try to stop me I will have you arrested. This soldier will pay for his crime! He let a defector through the lines. His death will serve as a lesson to all the need for vigilance!" Reddland drew his sword and started hacking away at the beaten soldier like he was beating down a fire. Reddland used every ounce of energy, raising his body off the ground with each blow. In seconds the soldier was cut to ribbons.

"No!" Marcus yelled and lurched toward Reddland, but was held back by Lexton and a squad of Royal soldiers. The shock and terror of the situation could not overcome their will to survive. Disloyalty would earn them a place next to their dead comrade.

Reddland finally stopped. He was breathing heavily and splattered with blood. "That should be a lesson to all. No one falls asleep on duty in the Royal army and expects to live."

Marcus was repulsed. The dozen armed men holding him back were the only reason Reddland was still breathing. "You're a fool, Reddland; worse yet, a poor leader. Had you not lacked the ability to control your temper you would have discovered that the man you just murdered was not even on duty at the time of the defection. He was just the squad leader of the soldier who was. You murdered an innocent man." Marcus spoke calmly, already resigned to his fate.

Reddland's face registered a hint of disbelief. He was for a moment speechless. The gathering grew so quiet that the rustling of the weeds could be heard. The soldiers were horrified by what they had just witnessed. The men were afraid to even breathe.

Finally, Reddland broke the silence. "Well, as a leader he was responsible for the actions of his men. He should have made certain his men were vigilant."

"Using that logic, Sire," Marcus stated flatly, "as the leader of this entire army, aren't you responsible for the sentry's crime?"

Reddland's mouth fell agape, as if he would speak but no sound could come out. Marcus continued on, well aware of the danger he now placed himself in.

"I advise all of you to quit this fight." Marcus pleaded with his fellow soldiers, hoping to make them understand before more of them had to die.

"I know the rebels will win. For the first time in my life I can see this whole thing for what it really is; and I think you are starting to see more clearly also."

"We have been the perpetuators of evil. The rebels have been victimized brutally by us." Marcus's tone shifted. He now seemed to be thinking out loud. "All this time I've heard about the rebels' god and their religion. For all these years I've rejected their beliefs as mere superstition, their god as a crutch for the weak minded. But now, after all I've witnessed, after this," he pointed to their dead friend. "I realize that their God is Lord." Marcus was sincere in his words. No one doubted that. No one moved a muscle. The silence was deafening and weighed heavily upon each man present. Everyone waited for something to happen.

"I have been a wretched worker for this evil regime and that I regret. How could I, could we, have been so deceived?" Marcus fell to his knees, his face turned toward the sky, for the first time attempting to pray. He knew he didn't have much time left.

Marcus cried out, "I know I've never talked to you before, but I don't want to end up like that poor stable hand. Please forgive me all the wickedness I've done. I know it's a lot to ask. I've know you are with the rebels, and I claim you as my Lord also."

Marcus turned toward his comrades. "All those years I ignored Isaac, but he was right. I advise you to do the same. Stop living this nightmare we've created."

Marcus's head fell in shame and he wept before his commander, before his men, before his God. Suddenly, the short sermon Isaac had given him as a younger man made sense. He wanted what he knew the rebels had and what he had only just began to believe. Isaac had planted the seed; people and events had watered it; now, after a long, parched drought, a green sprout sprang forth. Such was the miracle of Marcus's salvation.

The Royal soldiers listened to Marcus, many torn between their loyalty to their commander and their fear of Reddland. Some believed what he had been saying and their torn loyalties showed on their faces. It was no secret that the troops had doubts as to their success in this battle. To hear the commander they had come to trust with their lives confirm those doubts frayed their nerves even further. Reddland's recent behavior did little to endear him to the men.

Reddland knew he had to act fast. Rallying together what mental facilities he had left, he made his move.

"Don't listen to Marcus. He is a traitor. He knows he stands condemned to death and would love nothing more than to deceive you all as well. If he had your interests at heart, why would he sway you toward treason?" Reddland spoke sternly while jabbing his finger at Marcus.

"Don't listen to Reddland. He's mad! You have witnessed with your own eyes the strange occurrences of these past few days. It's not coincidence. God acts on the rebels' behalf." Marcus couldn't move. Lexton had hold of his arm and held the blade of a sword to his throat. A dozen or so guards had weapons drawn on him as well.

The soldiers swallowed hard and looked apprehensively from Marcus to Reddland.

Lexton placed his bet with Reddland. He felt bad about it, but Marcus was a dead man without hope of resolving the predicament he was now in.

Reddland continued. "Marcus would have you believe that some god is helping the rebels? Don't be superstitious, men. No power from the sky is going to come down and help the rebels. Don't be naïve. All that went on these last few days has an easy explanation. We just had a few bad days and made some mistakes." Reddland paced slowly up and down the line of men, pausing every now and then to look a soldier in the eye.

"Their skill didn't bring them victory," he continued. "The rebels are trapped in our death grip. It is a testimony to our own great skill and courage that we recovered so easily." He did not mention the high cost in Royal blood it had taken to recover that victory.

"And this storm…let it trouble you not. It was long overdue. It has been a long time since a storm of that magnitude has hit Xylor. Storms like that have come before, and I can assure you that someday one will hit again." Reddland smiled as he noticed some of the men nodding their heads. "We mustn't let Marcus convince us there is more to this storm than there is. It was a storm and nothing more."

Marcus shook his head. "Reddland is beguiling you with wicked deceptions, just as he always has. He doesn't really care about you. He is a sick, vile man who only wants to use you for his own gain. His actions have proven that!"

"Lies!" Reddland burst out. "It is the rebellion that is wicked and evil. They are trying to overthrow the legitimate government put into place by the goddess of this island, Tanuba! Remember the fire display that greeted us when we first attacked the oratory? The flames shot out and killed many loyal and brave men. It is common knowledge that only evil sorcerers can produce such works! The rebels have hired warlocks from a strange land to come here and destroy our way of life. They hate Tanuba and blaspheme her with their wicked ideology." Reddland waved his arms and gestured frantically to incite the soldiers. "And now they have deceived Marcus that he should betray us all. He betrayed Tanuba! He spits in the face of all that is sacred!"

The Royal soldiers wavered in their thoughts. Deep down they felt that maybe Marcus was right, but they wanted so desperately to obey their lusts that Tanuba placed no restrictions on. From what they knew of this rebel God, there were standards of conduct that spoke out against their way of life. Still, they knew deep down that the rebels were honorable people.

Reddland offered the final ingredient to sway the soldiers his way. "I offer five hundred shillings and a barrel of ale to any soldier who kills that traitor Marcus now!"

Like a pack of starving dogs pouncing on a scrap of meat, the greedy soldiers attacked Marcus in a vicious betrayal of their commander. Swords tore their way through flesh and clothing in their quest for blood.

Reddland smirked as his former general fell in pieces to the cold ground. Lexton, who did not participate in the massacre, couldn't even bring himself to look at his fallen comrade. They had been friends for the better part of ten years, had worked their way up through the ranks together, and had been confidants in the planning of all operations conducted by the Royal military.

Reddland had successfully reestablished his authority, at least for the moment. "Good work, men. See the Royal treasurer when we return to the command post for your reward. In the meantime, sever Marcus's head and put his corpse on display at the outskirts of camp. I want this to be a lesson to all who would dare to commit treason. Let it show that no man is above the law here in Xylor."

Some of the soldiers were having second thoughts already. This act of loyalty to Reddland could not overcome their sense of betrayal to Marcus. Others showed no remorse, thinking only about the never-ending supply of ale and prostitutes their newfound wealth would bring. Lexton stood by numbly as the squad carried out their orders. Perhaps Marcus had been right: the only power Reddland had was what everyone allowed him to have.

One man cannot stay in authority without the consent of many others.

"Lexton, I want you to meet with Malvagio. Prepare for our attack on the rebels in the morning." Reddland had spent enough time relishing the death of his accuser.

Lexton scoffed within himself. What good would it do to get with Malvagio? He would be better off planning a battle with a donkey. At least a donkey could be trusted to perform its assigned task. In the realm of intellect, Malvagio would meet his equal in the donkey as far as Lexton was concerned.

"Yes, Sire." Lexton would carry out his duties professionally. This would be more out of habit than anything else at this point. He didn't know what else to do. Training would have to suffice for now.

———————

Cad and Novak placed Scorpyus on a wooden plank atop stacked crates that served as Doc's examining table. Thadus, Emerald, Zephyr, and a few others gathered around.

"I need a few of you to bring over some lamps so I can see better. Emerald, please get my bag. Thadus, could you draw a basin of hot water from the stove?" Doc set about his examination. Novak and three others held lamps to illuminate the area. Zephyr dabbed a cool rag on Scorpyus' feverish forehead. Emerald quickly returned with Doc's bag.

Doc pulled off Scorpyus's right boot and then cut off his right pant leg with scissors and tossed it into a nearby trash barrel. When Thadus returned with the basin of hot water, Doc dipped a rag into it and thoroughly cleaned Scorpyus' leg. The wound was red and inflamed and extremely tender. Scorpyus grimaced throughout the cleaning.

"I see you tried to stitch this up yourself," Doc noted as he removed the crude stitch work. Scorpyus nodded, gritting his teeth as Doc checked the wound. It still oozed blood.

Doc looked up with a serious expression. Scorpyus leg smelled like rotting meat. "I may have to remove the leg to save your life."

Scorpyus tried to sit up but was too dizzy. "No. Just put some of my medicine on it. My friends know which one," Scorpyus said, adamantly. He turned to Cad. "Cad, if the doctor takes a saw out of his bag, hit him."

Cad shook his head and grinned. "He won't be cutting anything bigger than a steak while I'm here."

Doc was puzzled. "I have never heard of a medicine capable of helping this condition. Once decay sets in, nothing can be done."

"Well then, Doc, you have something to learn from my Gypsy grandmother." Scorpyus stated, a hint of pride in his words.

"It's the same medicine I gave you to use on the other wounded. Unless they were too badly mangled, you didn't cut any of their limbs off. Scorpyus just has a gash," Novak added.

"The other wounded didn't have rotting flesh."

Zephyr piped in. "Trust us, Doc. The four of us have seen it work."

"Alright, it's your leg and your life if you're wrong. If this works, will you tell me how to make it?"

Scorpyus managed a smile. "I'd be glad to show you."

Doc applied the medicine to Scorpyus's wound and stitched it up. The pain was tremendous. By the time Doc was finished with the thirty-seventh stitch, Scorpyus was faint with pain and completely exhausted. Doc bandaged the leg and Scorpyus immediately drifted off to sleep.

"Here, let's make him more comfortable." Thadus took off the other boot. "And Cad, why don't you help me get this muddy surcoat off of him. I'll have one of the nurses come in to clean him up and tend to him." Doc finished up and headed off to make his rounds with the other patients.

Cad motioned to Novak. "Help me move him to a cot." Novak grabbed Scorpyus' feet and he and Cad carried him to the cot. When they placed Scorpyus on the cot, they jostled him awake. Scorpyus looked up to see Cad.

"There's one more thing I have to tell you," Scorpyus said and grabbed Cad's surcoat and pulled him close.

"What'd he say?" Scorpyus had spoken so softly that Zephyr hadn't heard him. Novak shrugged.

Cad bolted upright, anger clearly written on his face. "What? Are you absolutely sure?"

Scorpyus nodded. "I found a signet ring in his drawer. It was one of the Ravenshire Knights' rings. Exactly like the ones our fathers had."

"Who had a Ravenshire Knights' ring? Reddland?" Novak's brow furrowed.

Cad ignored Novak's question. "That's highly suspicious, but it's not proof."

Everyone hung on Scorpyus's reply. "When I found the ring I knew. It suddenly all made perfect sense. But later, when I was hiding in the attic, I found something else."

"What?"

Scorpyus continued. "I found an official document concerning Luther Raistlin. It bore the seal of the king of Kelterland. He…"

Zephyr cut Scorpyus off. "Luther Raistlin? Was not he a Ravenshire Knight?"

"I thought they were all killed," Cad added.

"Ya, but nobody could say for sure. There were seventy-three knights and seventy-three corpses hung skinned in the trees. The bodies were unrecognizable." Novak remembered the incident all to well.

"I cannot believe what I am hearing!" Zephyr exclaimed.

"That bloody traitor!" Cad roared and turned back to Scorpyus. Emerald and Thadus listened with fascination. "What did the letter say?"

"It gave Sir Raistlin the Countship in Xylor for services to the crown. It gave him total authority on this island as the king's representative." Scorpyus laid out the bitter truth for the others.

"Then Raistlin *is* Reddland? He is responsible for our fathers' deaths." Novak pieced it all together and was flush with anger.

Cad shook his head. "Sir Raistlin betrayed the Ravenshire Knights in exchange for the Countship of Xylor. He changed his name to Reddland so no one would find out."

Thadus went pale. The news seemed to drain him. Emerald stood frozen in shock with the discovery.

"If there is any doubt that God meant for us to be here, let it now be dispelled. How fitting an end to Reddland; the children of those he betrayed are now the ones who will bring about his downfall. His past has returned to haunt him," Emerald noted the irony of the situation.

Novak turned his grief to anger. "I saw what happened to our fathers. Now that we know Reddland is the one responsible, he will pay."

"By the way, how did you escape? We thought you were dead." Cad asked Scorpyus.

"Ya, I checked your pulse. You didn't have one," Novak added.

Scorpyus managed a faint smile and a groggy reply. "I had to fake my death. It was a gamble, but I had no choice. I knew you three would try to break me out of the compound, and didn't want you to die trying. Once I realized Reddland had his men prepared I had to do something."

Cad remembered seeing blood on the wagon near the compound wall. "You jumped from the wall into the wagon?" Scorpyus nodded and Cad pictured the scene again in his mind. Scorpyus lay sprawled on the ground, blood oozing from his thigh.

"You tricked us!" Zephyr's attempt at being miffed couldn't mask her joy at seeing her friend alive.

Scorpyus shifted his weary body on the cot. "I knew you wouldn't leave unless you felt the situation was hopeless. The only way I could see you thinking that was by being dead. Thank God it worked. When Reddland sent his troops after you it freed me up to do one more job while everyone was distracted by the manhunt."

"What job?" Zephyr pulled up a chair.

"I wanted to break into the Royal Records Office," Scorpyus said.

"What did you find?"

"Reddland was installed as count of Xylor by Kelterland's governing regent in a private meeting at the compound. Drakar performed an anointing ceremony later that same day." Scorpyus took a deep breath. "And this happened three days after the death of the Ravenshire Knights. So there is no doubt. I had to be absolutely sure."

Zephyr finished the puzzle. "Which is about how long it would take to arrive here from Kelterland and organize the transfer of power."

"But what about your pulse? You didn't have a pulse." Novak wanted an explanation.

"I tied leather cords around my upper arm to cut off circulation. I had to convince Reddland I was dead. If you were convinced, and he saw that you were upset, he would have no doubts. I put blood from my leg in my ears, mouth and nose. I didn't need a worried and vigilant Royal army around when I went to the records office. I needed relaxed security. With me dead and you on the run it worked; though not exactly as planned. Besides it was the only way we all could have got out of there alive. I'm sorry I put you guys through that. It was all I could think of at such short notice." Scorpyus yawned and rubbed his eyes. He was exhausted and battered and starting to fade.

Cad thought back to that dreaded day. "That's it! I knew something was bloody well strange. I can still see it in my mind. Blood was still oozing from your leg as you lay on the ground. The dead don't bleed. I wonder why I didn't see that till now. Maybe I somehow knew and that's why I was able to keep my head and get us all out of there."

"It sounds like a miracle." Thadus interjected. The group mulled over the possibility briefly.

Zephyr noticed a nasty scratch on Scorpyus's face. "How did you get that?"

Scorpyus forced his eyes open. "I got that when you dragged me. It made it hard to play dead as my face scraped across the rocks."

Zephyr shrugged her shoulders. "It serves you right for putting us through that. Now we are even."

Scorpyus was sympathetic. "If there was any other way…" By now he was closing his eyes in long blinks.

"Well, we'll let you get some sleep. We could use some ourselves."

Moments later Cad led the others from the room. They hadn't gone far when a soldier ran up to Cad.

"I thought you should know that after you left the roof a fight of some sort erupted from among the Royal troops. There was a lot of yelling and they killed one of their own men." The soldier reported.

Cad's eyes widened. "Really? That's good. It shows the Royal army is getting tense and starting to turn on each other."

"They are having some doubts about winning," Novak added.

"Do you think they are starting to fall apart, getting a little spooked?" Zephyr asked.

"We can only pray they are starting to falter in their dedication to their cause." Cad replied.

———◦•◦•◦———

Sometime in the middle of the night Scorpyus awoke and barely opened his sleepy eyes. In the dim light a shadowy figure reached for his face. Instinctively he flinched.

"Easy now, I'm not going to hurt you." A woman's voice came from the dark blur. She placed a cool, wet, rag on Scorpyus's forehead. It felt good.

He rubbed his eyes and squinted. One of the most beautiful women he had ever seen came slowly into focus. Her dark locks were pulled back to reveal exotic features and sad eyes. White teeth sparkled behind smiling lips. "I'm dreaming or in heaven."

"No, you're awake," She replied with a laugh.

Scorpyus forced his eyes open wider. The woman wore a drab brown tattered dress under a bloodstained apron. Despite her attire she exuded a radiant beauty.

"I'm Natasha, one of the nurses," the woman explained. "Do you always flinch when someone touches you?"

"Hands that touch me usually have a big set of knuckles attached." Scorpyus lifted his head off the pillow. "How did I get my clothes on?"

"Your friend brought them in. We had to clean you up. You were caked with mud. You were so tired you slept through the whole thing."

Scorpyus's eyes widened and his speech became flustered. "Ahh, you mean, you?..."

Natasha laughed. "No, I didn't. That woman over there cleaned you up." She pointed to an elderly woman who was tending to another soldier.

Scorpyus let out a breath and plopped his head down on the pillow, clearly relieved.

"What's that supposed to mean? You don't trust me?" Natasha wasn't smiling anymore.

"Nothing! It's um…it could have been a little…well you know, I wouldn't want to be…immodest…you being so young and um…beautiful." Scorpyus was tongue-tied. How could he explain without saying more than he wanted?

Natasha found her smile again. "Well I guess I can forgive you." She didn't want to make her patient squirm too much.

Scorpyus breathed a sigh of relief as Natasha dabbed his face with the cool, damp cloth. The soft touch of a gentle hand was a rarity for a Clandestine Knight. He tried to keep his eyes open, wishing he wouldn't fall asleep too fast to enjoy it.

"Go ahead and sleep," Natasha whispered. "I'll be here when you wake up."

Scorpyus managed a faint smile. "I hope so."

XVIII

DAWN BROKE TO reveal a dreary, overcast, damp, morning. Creeping fog kept visibility down to a few hundred feet. From her perch on the catwalk, Zephyr looked down on the amassing Royal soldiers. Reddland's men looked tired and apprehensive as they trod through the mud, reluctantly preparing for the day's battle. It had been a cold, wet, restless night for the men and it showed on their sluggish, early morning movements. Once pristine, blue surcoats were now speckled with mud; polished boots and greaves were also mud caked. The Royal army looked every bit the battle weary veterans they were. It would take a while for them to become a fluid unit.

Zephyr made certain her archers were on the alert and sent a runner downstairs to bring Cad. Zephyr pulled her cap down tight, and bundled up in her short cape against the morning chill.

"Is Reddland going to attack us this fine morning?" Cad asked, his breath visible in the cold air.

Zephyr nodded in the affirmative. "I would say that is a certainty. I think if they were planning a siege there would not be all the activity."

Cad agreed with Zephyr's assessment. "Good. We'll be getting this over with rather than dragging it out." Cad scanned the scene below as he made a circuit of the roof on the catwalk. Coming full circle, he stopped again by Zephyr.

"His archers are forming up on this side, here, below us." Cad pointed directly below where they stood. "There's not much activity on the other side. The attack will more than likely be against the oratory's main doors. If there's one thing I can say about Reddland, it's he's very predictable."

"He does not take us seriously. That is why he uses conventional tactics," Zephyr concluded.

Cad continued to study the scene below. "He should take us seriously by now. But Reddland's an impatient man. The need for instant gratification runs strong in his veins. He probably feels pressure from the King of Kelterland; after all, how would it look if it took him a month to crush a little rebellion?"

— • ◆ • —

Down below in a Royal tent, Reddland prepared for the day's battle. Unlike his men, Luther wore polished boots and armor, and the rest of his lavish attire had been cleaned and pressed to match. He sat in his tent as a servant groomed his beard. The strain of the situation weighed heavily upon him. The chilly morning could not prevent beads of sweat from forming on his brow; his servant had to continually dab them with a cloth.

If the truth were known, Reddland was downright frightened. He wanted nothing more than to end this nonsense and put it all behind him. If he failed to win this battle, he feared his men would desert him. If he failed to end the rebellion, he feared the king of Kelterland would remove him from his position as count of Xylor.

Reddland knew he hadn't been himself lately. He blamed everyone and everything for his violent outbursts, and convinced himself all would return to normal if he could only be rid of this rebel menace. Reddland had also lately noticed the marked decrease in his stamina, and he had greater difficulty concentrating. In just the last few days he had noticed numbness in his left arm. His illness was growing worse and it terrified him.

Reddland was ever the more fearful of his looming death. Deep down he felt he didn't have much time left. He wouldn't have time to hire another team of skilled mercenaries to find the Hyacinth Blue. Cad told him he found the recipe. If for no other reason than to get his hands on that medicine, he had to crush the rebels. No one else, now that Marcus was dead, knew how desperate he was for that medicine. Little did anyone know the power one little vial of Hyacinth Blue held over Reddland, and how it had been shaping recent events. Reddland had literally bet his life that Cad was telling the truth about having the medicine.

He dismissed his servant and tried to massage feeling back into his left hand. He could still move it, but the numbness had now spread up to his elbow. He rubbed his eyes and took a deep breath, then placed his helmet on his head. The idea of going into battle without Marcus made him uneasy. He had been a highly skilled general. But what choice did Reddland have? Marcus had started sympathizing with the rebellion. Worst of all, was his insistence on laying siege on the oratory. It could take months to starve out the rebels and Reddland didn't have that kind of time. The men respected Marcus. He would have convinced Lexton and the rest that a siege was in order, and Reddland couldn't allow that. Reddland had to stop Marcus. All this nonsense about the rebel god and Marcus's defection from Tanuba made it all easier to justify to the men. Still, it didn't help Reddland's nerves any.

After a sleepless night, Reddland stepped from his tent with only one objective: to do whatever it took to end this rebellion and thereby obtain the Hyacinth Blue.

Reddland gave the order to Lexton to proceed with the attack. After the victory, Reddland himself would lead a search of the oratory. Until then he would oversee the battle preparations from atop his mount.

Cad and Zephyr saw a squad of Royal soldiers materialize out of the fog carrying a hewn log to be used as a battering ram. They headed for the main doors just as Cad predicted. The Royal archers notched their arrows.

"I'd better get downstairs," Cad said as he took in the latest development. "And, Zephyr, I'm going to need your archers to take an undo risk."

Zephyr furrowed her brow. "What do you mean?"

"The Royal archers are going to be concentrating on you and your archers. They'll be firing heavily on your position in order to protect their battering ram. Go ahead and take cover for this first part, but I predict that after their infantry breeches our doors they'll make a hasty retreat. At that moment, while you're being fired upon as the Royal army is retreating; I need your archers to hit them with everything they have: fire fast and fire often." Cad explained.

"If you say you need it, the archers will be ready." Zephyr trusted Cad's judgment. "But how do you know they are going to breech our doors so quickly?"

Cad turned to Zephyr and smiled. "Because I'm going to let them mate."

Zephyr watched Cad head down the stairs, wondering what he had in mind. She then briefed her archers on Cad's plan and had them gather on the west side of the oratory above the main door.

As the soldiers with the battering ram neared the oratory doors, the Royal archers drew back on their bows.

"Get down!" Zephyr and her archers lay flat on the catwalk as arrows streamed toward their position. She could hear them strike the catwalk ledge and ricochet off the slope of the roof. Several splintered off the steeple above Zephyr. Once the Royal archers had the rebels pinned down on the roof, the arrows became sporadic with shots taken only to keep them down.

Zephyr stayed below the catwalk ledge, sneaking an occasional look at the activity below. Soon she heard the rhythmic thud of the log crashing into the door.

"It shouldn't take them long to break through the doors with the locking cross beam removed," Novak said as he lay the heavy beam aside. "I'll be in the auditorium preparing our counterattack."

Cad let out a heavy sigh. "Alright…this is it."

Thadus, Abrams, and the other stretcher bearers were upstairs with the wounded. All non-essential personnel were upstairs as well. Cad remained in the foyer with two squads of soldiers. Novak and Cyrus waited with the main force inside the main auditorium. Timing would play a big part in the next minutes.

Cad looked everything over one last time. The oratory's double wooden doors opened up into a sixty-by-thirty-foot foyer. Directly above the foyer was the balcony. Once you walked the thirty feet to the end of the foyer, the ceiling rose from ten to forty feet as you entered the main auditorium. Cad chose to set his men at this point where the balcony and foyer ended, just before entering the auditorium. They maintained a defensive line. Cad knew that once the Royal soldiers breeched the doors they would funnel into the foyer rapidly and he intended to hold them there for a time. Reddland's forces would have to ascend a set of ornate stone steps before they could gain access to the oratory. It would take a few minutes before they could fill the foyer, and then fight their way into the auditorium.

Cad was as ready as he would ever be. His men remained silent. The only sound was methodic pounding against the doors.

With a loud snap the door latch gave way, and the doors flew open, slamming into the wall. Amid whoops a flood of blue surcoats washed into the oratory. Cad and his men braced for the onslaught.

Reddland's face lit up when he saw his men breech the oratory. He was surprised that it happened so soon. He watched Lexton direct his troops up the stairs and into the building. Reddland gloated, warmed by his thoughts on this cold foggy morning. It wouldn't be long now before the rebels were beaten.

Cad made quick work of the first soldier to meet him. The man seemed surprised to be in the oratory. It had always been off limits. He took a quick look around at his surroundings. His curiosity cost him his life. The next soldier didn't make the same mistake and was able to land a blow on Cad's shield.

The Royal troops slammed into Cad and his men with a violent explosion of metal that echoed throughout the main auditorium. Cad blocked a blow with his sword and slammed his shield into a second attacker while kicking the man in the groin. After knocking his first attacker's sword to the side, Cad dealt him a mortal blow. A quick thrust to the man holding his groin freed Cad up for whomever was next.

A rebel soldier to Cad's right was felled by a burly, hairy soldier, whose body stench stung Cad's nostrils. Cad locked swords with this smelly opponent. The two pushed against each other's swords, each trying to shove the other off balance. Face-to-face, inches away, the burly man's breath brought tears to Cad's eyes.

Cad shoved the flea-ridden man back with enough force that he tripped over a fallen comrade and was lost in the press.

Novak watched the fight from his perch with great restraint. The foyer was nearly full with the influx of Royal troops, and Cad's defensive line was starting to crumble. They had already been pushed back into the main auditorium. Novak saw that it was time to implement Cad's plan.

"Now!" Novak roared above the din. The rest of the rebel troops readied themselves for a charge.

Cad's men instantly dove to the ground, Cad himself landing on his back. A Royal soldier moved in on Cad for what would be an easy kill. The putrid odor left no doubt as to his identity.

From the balcony, several rebel soldiers shoved the heavy beam off the rail. Cad pressed himself flat as the beam swung from the balcony suspended by several ropes. Protruding from the beam at all angles were dozens upon dozens of razor sharp spikes, each three feet long. The prickling beam swung from the balcony into the front ranks of the advancing Royal troops. The weight and force of the beam easily sent the spikes through the Royal armor. In a brief few seconds nearly forty Royal soldiers were impaled on the beam; in some places two deep. One unfortunate rebel who forgot to get down fell victim to the device.

The auditorium echoed with cries of pain that mixed with the shouts of the charging, Novak-led infantry. Pandemonium broke out in the Royal advance. Panicked by yet another trap; this one claiming so many of their comrades in an instant, the Royal troops fled in terror, a retreat so sudden and so forceful that other Royal soldiers were stampeded. Ducking below the dangling spiked beam, Novak and his men soon had the Royal army pushed back out of the oratory.

Outside Reddland basked in the glory of what he believed would be a quick end to this uprising. His men had effortlessly breeched the oratory, and several squads entered the rebel stronghold. His archers had effectively neutralized the rebel archers, keeping them pinned down on the catwalk. Finally things were making a little sense. The rebels would soon crumble and he would be rid of a nagging problem. And at last the recipe for Hyacinth Blue would be his.

Reddland rode his mount to the base of the oratory steps next to Lexton. Men had been filing up the stairs at a steady rate. "It looks like this shall be put behind us once and for all."

"Yes, Sire; we breeched rather quickly, and our advance seems to be going smoothly." Lexton was pleasantly surprised.

Reddland's pleasure was short-lived. His smug grin melted away when the influx of Royal soldiers came to an abrupt halt and shouts of terror erupted from within the oratory. For a brief moment soldiers at the doorway shuffled about and tried to shove their way in. Soon those who didn't step aside were trampled or washed away by a retreating, screaming mob. Reddland looked bewildered for a moment as he absorbed the fact Royal soldiers were in a full retreat, were stampeding like crazed cattle.

"They're dead! They've all been killed!" a terrorized young soldier bellowed as he bounded from the oratory. The Royal troops couldn't distance themselves from the oratory fast enough. Discipline and military bearing were gone.

"Halt! You cowards! Halt!" Reddland was irate at this display of fear. "Lexton, stop them! Get the officers on line to stop this madness!"

Lexton had already given the order and was trying to regroup the men. He grabbed one by the arm forcing him to stop. "What happened in there?"

The soldier could barely be restrained. "I don't know! They're all dead, I tell you! Let me go, they're coming after us!"

Lexton backhanded the young man and shook him by the shoulders. "Control yourself! How did this happen?"

"I don't know! Spears came out of nowhere! The first few ranks were impaled all at once." The soldier started to sob uncontrollably.

A sick dawning came over Lexton. His men had rushed into a trap. Curse those rebels! Spears didn't come out of nowhere. But judging from the retreating soldier's reaction, something drastic had occurred, something incredible enough to frighten the men witless.

"You stay here." Lexton ordered. The soldier nodded his trembling head. Lexton's officers were struggling to regain control of the troops. Malvagio beat those who refused to end their flight. Reddland was in a rage and rode around ranting at his men. Before the Royal leadership could stem the tide of the retreat, arrows began raining down on the mass exodus.

Arrows flew everywhere. Zephyr and her troops were braving a massive launching of arrows from the Royal archers in order to fire upon the fleeing soldiers. They were sacrificing themselves in order to carry out their attack, and Lexton had never seen anything like it. Though it bordered on suicide, the tactic was proving to be quite effective. Much to Lexton's dismay, Royal soldiers were going down all around. As if that weren't bad enough, rebels stormed out of the oratory and attacked the fleeing Royal army from the rear.

Lexton had to act fast. He grabbed the trembling soldier. "Go find the commander of the cavalry. Tell him to charge the rebels."

The young soldier sprinted off, relieved to be getting away from the chaos.

Royal arrows peppered the rebel archers, yet the rebels ignored the danger. To Lexton's left Reddland was still pacing back and forth on his mount, berating his men, and shouting profanities. Lexton just shook his head. Maybe now Reddland would see that Marcus had been right. Lexton needed no further convincing.

Zephyr took careful aim and loosed an arrow. An instant later it appeared protruding from the back of a Royal soldier's knee. Despite the distraction of projectiles whizzing all around and splintering near her on the catwalk rail, she hit her mark more often than not. After she saw the soldier go down groping his knee, Zephyr notched her next arrow. The bowstring snapped near her wrist and another soldier went down. This one tumbled down the oratory steps taking two others with him. His retreating comrades didn't break stride to help the fallen soldier.

Two rebel archers fell next to Zephyr, and she felt a sharp tugging at her short cape. A hole appeared in the velveteen material about an inch from her side. She crouched to one knee, took aim, and loosed her next arrow in one fluid motion. A Royal arrow shot past her head splintering against the steeple. The barrage from the Royal archers was tremendous and Zephyr didn't know how much longer her troops could withstand such punishing fire. At least her archers were inflicting heavy damage on the Royal troops who were bunched up in a chaotic, unorganized retreat.

"Concentrate your fire on the rebels nearest the doorway!" Lexton shouted to his archers as he watched his men dropping all around him. This was turning into a slaughter. He had to regroup his men before it was too late.

Lexton started grabbing retreating soldiers and spinning them around to face the oratory. "Start forming into squads right here!" Get your shields up and crouch down behind them! We'll need to meet their attack. Retreating is only leaving you vulnerable; you're exposed too much. Did you men forget your training? Take cover now!"

The men responded to Lexton's calm during the storm of battle. He seemed confident, like he knew what he was talking about. It didn't take long to see that crouching behind a shield was better than taking rebel arrows in the back. If Lexton could get his men on a defensive line they would be able to defend against the coming rebel charge. He was confident the rebel archers would stop shooting arrows once their own soldiers were close to his.

As Lexton scanned the field he saw an arrow appear in the face of one of his men. Almost simultaneously he felt a sharp pain in his left arm. The soldier with the arrow in his face tumbled over dead.

"Ahhh!" Lexton looked to see that an arrow had entered on the inside of his forearm near the wrist, and traveled just below the skin the length of his arm, lodging against his elbow. Lexton could no longer make a fist with his hand, his fingers contorted in all directions. He couldn't straighten his arm, so he held it close to his side. He turned toward a tremendous shout from the top of the oratory stairs and saw a rag-tag horde of rebels burst through the doors at a run. Immediately they were upon the retreating Royal army.

Reddland pacing his mount was still trying to reverse his men's retreat. He cursed them continually, unable to control his rage, looking and sounding more like a madman than a leader. His men stepped around him goggle-eyed on their retreat. Reddland did more to unsettle his men than he did to stem the retreat.

Cad and a squad of rebels erupted from the oratory with a raucous yell in hot pursuit of their fleeing foes. Cad bore down on a Royal soldier and swung hard with his battleaxe, catching the man square between the shoulder blades. The Royal guard's cuirass may have spared him from a mortal wound, but the force of the blow sent him to his knees and headfirst down the stairs.

Novak led the rest of the rebels into the battle; excitement coursed through his veins and his senses sharpened. He hammered down a Royal soldier as he bounded down the stairs on the heels of Cad's squad. Raw power surged through Novak and he transferred it through his two-handed sword and onto the Royal soldiers with devastating effect. It felt good to be on the offensive. He knew this was his calling, that God made him a brute force to be reckoned with; a muscled weapon for the cause of good, and he intended to fulfill his purpose to the utmost of his ability. If there were to be any negotiations, Cad would have to handle them. Novak was not in a negotiating mood. He was too busy tearing a swath through the Royal soldiers like a tornado through a wheat field. Exhilarated by the sight of Novak, the rebel troops attacked with a vengeance.

Zephyr saw Cad, Novak, and the rest of the infantry bound down the stairs. She loosed the arrow she had notched and saw it appear in the wrist of a Royal soldier. "Rats!" she exclaimed as the arrow missed its intended mark: the man's neck. "I guess I was lucky to have hit him at all considering these circumstances." Zephyr mused. Within a second an arrow was fired at her. It stung where it grazed her neck. She quickly ducked behind the catwalk railing. Holding a hand to her bleeding neck she saw another one of her archers fall, quills protruding from her abdomen.

"Cease fire! Cease fire and get down!" Zephyr called off her archers. To continue would not only place the men below in jeopardy as they were now in the projectile zone, but it would be certain suicide for her archers. Royal arrows continued to slam into the rail and roof overhead. Zephyr rolled onto her stomach and looked down the length of the catwalk. Her heart immediately sank. Several archers were sprawled out in macabre poses, arrow shafts sticking out from all sorts of places. It looked like she had lost one-third of her archers in less than five minutes. The sight brought tears to her eyes. Though she knew she inflicted heavy losses on the retreating

Royal troops in that same time span, she wondered if it had been worth it. "I hope Cad knows what he is doing," Zephyr prayed quietly.

"Let us start moving the wounded downstairs," she said, then crawled to the door to the stairwell and opened it. Slowly, the wounded were passed down the line, from one able-bodied archer to the next.

Reddland stood slack jawed in shock at the sudden burst of rebels from the oratory. He stared as if in a trance at the frightful sight of his men being routed. It was too much. He couldn't speak, couldn't even muster up a curse against his men for allowing this to happen. Jerking his head from side to side he desperately searched for a hint of good news but found none. Beads of sweat trickled from his brow and through his beard. Many of his men lay wounded, crying out in anguish. Those who were engaging the rebels were visibly shaken. Reddland could do nothing but stare; his blood-drained, ashen face cool and clammy. Never before had so many things gone so wrong.

A mix of anger and shock filled him. Why couldn't the Royal army perform as they had so many times in the past? How could this pathetic patchwork of rebels gain the upper hand? It was as if the Royal army had been cursed.

Reddland saw one of his soldiers beheaded less than ten yards away. "Stop! I said stop it!" Reddland's shrill scream availed him nothing.

Lexton drew his sword, his left arm throbbing with pain. The bulk of his men were in unorganized disarray, but at least he had two squads on line. Ignoring the pain, Lexton led the twenty-four men in the only organized resistance the Royal army could muster at the time. Once the men were engaged like a trained team, Lexton relinquished command to a sergeant and set about the task of rounding up another squad.

Lexton avoided combat as he made his way through the chaos. He had to get more men working as units if the Royal army was to hold out until the cavalry arrived. Malvagio was of no use. He looked out only for himself and was, in fact, nowhere to be seen. Lexton spotted Reddland sitting motionless atop his mount, apparently in shock.

Malvagio was on his own program. If he wasn't springing from behind someone or something to attack a rebel who had his back turned, he was busy looting bodies, and the bodies he looted were not always those of the enemy.

Thadus came out of the oratory with several stretcher bearers. He wasted no time in helping the wounded inside. He wanted to leave as few wounded behind as possible should the rebels need to hurriedly retreat again. Abrams lent a hand to this task as well, and recommended for expediency's sake to only carry the wounded into the main auditorium. From there, Emerald, Doc, and the other nurses could take over. Abrams did not want to cease his prayers for the rebel army, but could not bear to witness the needless mutilating slaughter again. He knew God would understand his decision.

The Royal archers held fire when their targets took cover. Seeing the last of her wounded being carted downstairs, Zephyr decided to take a peek at the action below. A lopsided battle was underway. The Royal soldiers were preoccupied with retreat. A few were putting up real resistance, but most were reluctant combatants, fighting only until they could get away. But escape was not easy.

Cad chopped away at what little Royal resistance formed. Stopping reorganization was a priority. He brought his battle-axe down hard against a soldier with a scraggly beard. The man was able to get his shield up in time to save his life. Cad's second swing was from down low up towards his opponent's groin. The scraggly soldier instinctively stepped back and lowered his shield to block. When he did, Cad's metal-gauntleted fist smashed him in the mouth. The man tumbled back onto his hindquarters. The fallen soldier blocked Cad's next blow with his hand. It was a move that cost him four fingers and half of his palm. Cad finished off the man and quickly found another.

As he engaged another blue surcoat, Cyrus appeared at his side. Together they threw themselves at the two squads of soldiers

Lexton had organized into a fighting force. Other rebels soon fell in with them. Cad was glad to see the men follow his lead without him having to shout orders. His had to keep the enemy retreating as long as possible. Breaking this pocket of resistance was a priority.

On the other side of the oratory steps Novak had just beheaded an opponent when he heard a shrill, piercing scream so odd and out of place from the cries normally associated with war that he couldn't help but look towards the source. Much to his surprise the shrill voice belonged to a mounted Reddland, and he was a mere twenty yards away. Novak shoved a wispy thin soldier out of his way and stalked toward the man who betrayed his father.

"Stop! Stop it!" Reddland pressed his hands hard over his ears and bellowed in a loud ear-splitting cry, spittle on his lips. Royal troops shot their leader bewildered looks as they fled past him.

Reddland lurched up and out of his saddle and tumbled to the muddy ground. He felt as if he had been rammed by a charging bull. Novak slapped the rump of Reddland's horse with a broad hand and sent it scurrying away. With the horse out of the way, Reddland had a clear view of Novak about to bring a two-handed sword down on the top of his skull. Although Reddland suffered some numbness and loss of strength, his reflexes were still intact. He rolled to the side, narrowly avoiding the blade that slammed into the ground, cleanly severing the back of Reddland's ornate robe. Novak kicked Reddland in the thigh then pried his sword from the earth. Reddland limped to his feet with sword drawn in a flash.

"You betrayed my father, Reddland. For that you will pay." Novak held his sword up and maneuvered around his foe, looking for an opening to strike. They looked like two dogs circling each other.

Reddland wiped mud from his face and jabbed at his opponent. Novak answered with a blow to Reddland's shield. Reddland had been a Ravenshire Knight, and even in his late forties he was still faster than Novak. His agility and added years of experience gave him a slight edge. Novak on the other hand, definitely had more power and was able to deal punishing blows. The two dodged, swung and clashed against each other in a virtual stalemate. Although

Reddland was a very worthy adversary, Novak felt confident his youthful stamina would eventually wear the older man down.

Novak's intuition proved correct. After only a few minutes he could tell his powerful blows were starting to tire his opponent. Reddland's face confirmed that he knew this as well. His breathing grew labored; recovering his sense of balance and direction also became more difficult. As Reddland's strength waned, the approaching victory seemed to feed Novak's own vigor.

In a series of lightning strikes, Novak slammed his sword against Reddland, driving him back thirty feet. Blows glanced off his shield, sword, and helmet. To Reddland's credit, he was skilled enough to block most of strikes. He lashed out with an impressive series of feints and slashes, trying to retake some lost ground. His blade caught Novak across the bicep. Blood sprang from the superficial wound. Reddland couldn't help but smile at the sight of his opponent's blood. Novak took advantage of Reddland's split-second of pleasure and feigned a blow to Reddland's legs. When Reddland lowered his shield to block, Novak brought down his two-handed sword with all the force he could muster. The blow drove the rim of Reddland's helmet into his forehead. Blood trickled from Reddland's brow as he dizzily fell back onto his haunches. He strained, trying desperately to see Novak through his blurred and watery eyes. Reddland knew he was in trouble. His balance was impaired and he fumbled, temporarily incapacitated, trying to stand. Pain pulsed through his head, keeping time with his staccato heartbeat.

Novak raised his sword and brought it down with enough force to cut a man in half. Reddland flinched at the looming shadow that stepped up to him.

"No! Don't do it!" Thadus, who had been watching the events unfold, grappled at Novak's arm with both hands and tried to pull him back. Thadus released his body's weight, jerking Novak off balance.

Novak spun around, trying to free his arm. Thadus clung to Novak's arm as tightly as he could and wrapped his legs around his waist.

"What's wrong with you, Thadus?" Novak was irate. He spun and shook trying to dislodge his burden. Finally, after a fist to the gut, Thadus collapsed to the ground. "What are you trying to do…" but before he could finish his sentence, Novak's eyes opened wide and he gasped. He sank to his knees.

Reddland pulled his sword from Novak's side. Thadus's distraction had given him ample time to find the seam in Novak's cuirass. Reddland shot Thadus a gloating smile. Then seeing Cyrus and other rebels coming, he slithered away on shaky legs into the mass of fleeing soldiers confident he had mortally wounded his imposing adversary.

Reddland reached the oratory's perimeter wall and stopped. He leaned heavily against the shattered gate and fought to catch his breath. The swelling excitement over his slim victory soon washed away his fear. A new version of the fight began to evolve in his mind as he quickly convinced himself the victory was attributed to his superior skills. Catching his breath, he strutted like a proud rooster and relished the thought of telling his version of the events to whomever would listen.

Reddland wiped blood from his forehead as his cavalry entered the oratory gates. He didn't expect to see them. He was glad someone was thinking besides him. "Beat the rebels into the ground! I've just neutralized one of their leaders for you!"

The cavalry charged toward the chaos near the stone staircase that ascended into the oratory. Seeing the mounted soldiers bolstered the confidence of the retreating infantrymen. Many slowed and turned to follow the cavalry back towards the enemy. Reddland smiled smugly at this turning of the tide in his favor. Before long he would convince himself he was also responsible for the cavalry's timely deployment.

As he reveled in the sight of his men again on the offensive, a bitter smell rose to his nostrils: urine. Surely some of the men had been careless, as was expected during the heat of battle. But a quick check revealed the vulgar truth, that his own trousers were darker along the inseam. The memory of his terrible fear during the preceding battle with Novak flashed through his mind. Reddland rushed to his tent to change clothes.

Thadus could scarcely believe what just happened, what he had caused. Cyrus rushed to Novak's aid and helped him to his feet. Novak glared at Thadus with a look that burned holes through his soul.

"Why?" Novak gasped. The look of betrayal on Novak's face nearly brought Thadus to tears. It would have been easier to suffer Novak's wrath.

Cyrus wasted no time in helping Novak to the oratory. Another rebel carried Novak's sword.

"What have I done?" Thadus could barely speak. Tears washed his cheeks, his stomach churned, and he began to vomit violently.

With the aid of Cyrus, Novak ascended the steps to the oratory. From the roof, Zephyr saw her friend and her heart sank. He was obviously in great pain and cradled his left side. Zephyr bounded down the stairs two and three at a time.

"Get a stretcher!" Cyrus shouted to a nearby soldier. Zephyr appeared from the stairwell to find Novak collapsed in the main auditorium. His helmet clattered to the ground as Cyrus propped his head off the hard stone floor.

"How bad is he?" Zephyr asked and rushed to her friend's side.

"I can't say for sure. He's bleeding a lot. We won't know how bad the wound is until we get him upstairs to Doc." Novak's side was soaked with blood. A small pool had already formed beneath him on the floor. A soldier rushed over with a stretcher and they loaded Novak onto it.

Cyrus took one end of the litter. Another soldier took the other. Zephyr followed the procession up the stairs. Novak winced with each jarring step.

"You'll be alright," Zephyr tried to comfort him. Novak managed a nod.

Thadus slipped into the main auditorium. As she took the stairs, Zephyr saw the somber Thadus enter a side office. *That is odd,* she thought, but had more pressing matters to tend to.

Down on the battlefield, Cad just subdued another attacker when he noticed the Royal cavalry form up for a charge. It was time for the next stage of the plan.

"Fall back to the oratory!" Cad issued his orders and had two nearby rebels spread the word. He expected the Royal cavalry to arrive eventually. Their mere presence already started to slow the retreat of the Royal infantry.

Word spread quickly through the rebel ranks and they fell back. Cad and two squads of soldiers brought up the rear of the retreat. Things had gone well so far; now if the next stage went as planned…

By the time the Royal infantry was out of the way of the cavalry, the rebels were well into their retreat. Other than a few minor skirmishes along the way, the rebels were able to retreat into the oratory unmolested.

Lexton studied the scene. He was disappointed that he was unable to unleash the wrath of his cavalry on the rebel troops. Had the Royals been quicker to respond, it could have ended the war then and there. At least the retreat and the slaughter of his men had stopped. Now he would recommend a siege to starve out the rebels.

Cad and a few others who were the last ones inside the oratory barred the doors shut. Soon, the loud report from Royal soldiers slamming into the door echoed through the foyer and main auditorium.

"Spike the door shut!" Cad ordered as he placed another brace against the door.

Once Reddland's men realized they would need a battering ram to breech the doorway, they pulled back. The rebel archers started firing on them again which gave them yet another reason to retreat. Reddland's army regrouped a safe distance from the oratory and awaited word from their superiors.

Once the door was secured, Cad directed his attention elsewhere. "You, there," Cad said, pointing to a man near the fireplace. "Throw some more wood on that fire. The rest of you get upstairs. One squad stays behind." Soldiers hurried in every direction. No one knew how much time they had before Reddland would make his next move.

Cad pulled a young soldier aside. "I need you to make sure the barrel of caltrops is at the top of the stairs."

"The what, sir?"

"A young chap like you has never heard of caltrops? They're little, pronged metal objects shaped like pyramids. No matter how you set them down, they'll always have a point sticking up. There should be a barrel of them at the top of the stairs. I need you to make certain they are there."

A look of understanding crossed the young fellow's face. "Yes, sir!"

Cad watched the young rebel rush up the stairs, then surveyed the room again. His plan was unfolding as expected. Few things felt better than the success of a well-executed plan. Cad couldn't help but smile as the wheels turned in his head.

———•◦•———

"Clear the table!" Zephyr shouted to Doc from across the room. Cyrus and another soldier were right behind her with Novak. The strain of climbing the stairs with him was evident on their faces. Doc toweled off his hands and gathered his surgical implements from the table. Cyrus guided Novak's stretcher into place on the table.

"How bad is it, Doc?" Novak's voice was labored.

"We'll know in just a second, son." Doc removed Novak's cuirass, then cut his shirt open on his left side, pulling it away from the wound. Grabbing another towel, Doc wiped away the blood so he could get a better look. Novak's wound was ghastly. A portion of his intestines protruded from the four-inch gash on his side. Doc didn't have to say a word; the gravity of his expression spoke volumes.

"Um. I'm going to need some space. I need to stop the bleeding."

"You heard the man, everyone out of the room." Cyrus ushered everyone away except Zephyr, who refused to leave.

"It's that bad huh, Doc?" Novak knew the wound was mortal. The expressions on everyone's faces followed by a sickly silence told him that much.

"I'll do what I can, Novak; but you're in God's hands now," Doc replied somberly.

"Then I've got the best there is," Novak whispered.

Tears streamed down Zephyr's cheeks as she clutched her friend's limp hand. "You will make it. You will be alright, Novak." She was trying to convince herself.

Novak managed a faint smile. Loss of blood was already making him drowsy. "Do me a favor."

"Anything." Zephyr choked back the tears.

"Watch Cad's back for me. With Scorpyus wounded, and me…" Novak paused to gasp for air. "You're the only one he can trust. Make sure he gets the rest of you out of here alive." He swallowed hard.

Doc gently placed a hand on Zephyr's back. "You may stay if you want, but Novak needs to save his strength. Talking won't help him."

Zephyr nodded through teary eyes. As she pulled a chair close, she thought to herself, *what did he mean, I am the only one Cad can trust?*

Doc went about his arduous task. He would try his best, though the only thing that could save Novak now would be a miracle.

XIX

---·•◆•·---

T HE PANICKED CHAOS of retreat slowly faded from the
Royal army and they began to regain a military bearing.
Sergeants and junior officers took charge and regrouped their
men. The galloping herd again became a regimented formation.
Having carried out their duty without error, the cavalry now
moved to their place behind the ranks. The Royal archers readied
themselves to defend against the unlikely event of a rebel assault.

On the field around the oratory steps, lay hundreds of dead
and dying Royal soldiers. Lexton surveyed the carnage with
trepidation and embarrassment. There had to be around five
hundred casualties. Had the Royal army not fled like frightened
jackrabbits, the losses would have been less than a-third of that.
Had Reddland taken Marcus's advice for a siege, there would have
been no casualties. Lexton felt a slap on the back.

"We've got those jackals on the run now!" Reddland was giddy
with excitement.

Lexton gave his superior a look of disbelief. "Sire, we suffered
tremendous losses. I'd hardly call that a victory."

"Oh, Lexton, leave it to you to look at the gloomy side,"
Reddland chided. "We had them running scared. They couldn't
slither back into their hole fast enough."

"Sire, they merely withdrew so as not to engage our cavalry. If we had deployed the cavalry sooner, we could have averted many of our casualties. We should have foreseen the possibility of our men making a panicked and haphazard retreat and had the cavalry prepared. What took place here was a disaster." Lexton was beside himself. How could Reddland not see the Royal army had been dealt a serious blow? Never in the last ten years since the war had the army suffered so many losses on a single day.

Reddland's smile shrank to a smirk. "Lexton, the rebels retreated shortly after they lost one of their leaders because they were demoralized by the blow. Cut off the head and the body becomes useless. And I might add that I was the one who single-handedly vanquished the traitorous mercenary who dared assist the rebellion. Which brings up another point—where were *you* when I was saving the day?"

Lexton's jaw dropped. "Sire, we've lost nearly half of our army. Let's not compound today's disaster by acting prematurely again. I suggest we lay siege and send word to Kelterland for reinforcements." Lexton knew Reddland was full of himself due to some perceived battlefield victory. Had his superior not had a gash on his forehead, he wouldn't have believed he had seen any combat. Lexton wanted nothing more than to talk sense to his boss.

"Lexton, you're starting to sound a lot like Marcus. This is war. Casualties are expected. We move on…" Suddenly Reddland noticed Lexton's arm. "My, my, whatever happened to you?"

Lexton moved his left arm from his side to inspect the wound, wincing in pain as he did so. "I took an arrow. I fear it's pretty bad."

"I should say so. No doubt you'll lose the use of the arm." Reddland's total lack of concern was chilling. Not even now, at a time like this, could Reddland muster up any feeling for anyone else. Hundreds of his men were either dead or wounded or being carried off the battlefield before his very eyes. And Reddland couldn't have cared less.

"See that you have the Royal physician tend to your arm, then meet me in my tent with Malvagio. We have to plan our next attack. I want the troops ready within two hours. We must strike while the iron is hot." Reddland gave his order then stamped off to find Malvagio. He was intent on another attack, unwilling to heed any advice.

If there had been any doubt in Lexton's mind it was gone now. Reddland had indeed lost his mind. Reddland would sacrifice every last man to achieve his ends. Why was he in such a rush? A siege would eventually force the rebels to surrender. Their only alternative would be to attack. And if the rebels waited for a few weeks, reinforcements from Kelterland would be in Xylor to ensure their defeat.

Lexton decided to resign once this was over. He would have resigned immediately had it not meant handing the rest of his men over to a madman and his patsy. Even though it meant risking his life, he had to do what he could for those that remained.

Reddland's arm was completely numb. He tried to massage some feeling into it as he ate a meal in his tent. The muscles in his forearm twitched uncontrollably. His shield arm had taken a terrible beating at the hands of Novak, but Reddland knew better than to think that was the cause of his current problem. His disease was advancing rapidly. It had become a constant reminder of impending doom and vulnerability. Reddland hated that feeling. Not being in total control drove him mad. He had to get that medicine. It infuriated him to think that the adventurers he hired had betrayed him. At least two of them were dead. The others would soon follow. Maybe he would even take his pleasure with the female before killing her. She was attractive.

Reddland wrung his hands, unable to stop the insistent twitching in his forearm. He changed into a long-sleeve shirt. It wouldn't look good if the others found out about his illness.

Reddland wanted to attack the rebels again before they had the chance to set up another trap. He had to admit, the rebels were good. But they also suffered losses. It was only a matter of time before they were defeated.

Sweat trickled from his brow. No matter how hard he tried, his thoughts always veered back to his dreaded illness. His twitching arm wouldn't let him forget.

"Those stinking mercenaries!" Reddland slammed his fist on the table. They stood between him and Hyacinth Blue. He no longer thought about restoring order to Xylor. As far as he was concerned that would be no more than a fringe benefit of killing the rebels. They had his medicine. No price was too great to get it. Not even the lives of a thousand more of his men. He still had five hundred elite troops back at the compound should he need them.

———•◦•———

"You men did well! The Royal army took a beating." Cad congratulated the troops who were nearby. The battle was far from over yet there was cause for some celebration. The rebels had inflicted heavy loses on Reddland. Feeling good about the achievement, he congratulated the men with slaps on their backs and vigorous handshakes, praising their bravery and determination. The troops filed upstairs in a jovial mood.

Cad's mood was suddenly shattered at the appearance of Cyrus descending the stairs. By the look on his face, Cad knew something was wrong.

"What is it, Cyrus?"

"You better go see Doc. It's Novak."

Cad's stomach lurched up into his throat. Not waiting for an explanation, he shoved his way upstairs. Cad entered the treatment room to a familiar scene. Doc had Zephyr pulled aside and was speaking quietly to her as he wiped blood from his hands. By now they were stained a purplish hue and no amount of vigorous rubbing could get them clean. Cad caught the tail end of the conversation.

"I stopped the bleeding and closed the wound. Novak has lost a lot of blood and lost consciousness. He could very well have internal injuries to his intestines, but I don't know. I've done all I can with my limited experience with humans."

"Will he live?" Zephyr sniffed and wiped her eyes.

Doc looked at the floor unable to make eye contact with the grieving woman. "I'm afraid his wound is mortal. I'm sorry."

Zephyr held her hands over her face and sobbed. She slowly sank into a chair. She doubled over and heaved violently.

Cad walked over and placed a hand on her back. One minute he had been fighting side by side with Novak. The next minute it was all over. Rage tore through him.

Novak lay on a table, his abdomen heavily bandaged. He was pale but his chest still rose with each shallow breath.

"Novak's not dead yet?" Cad inquired.

Doc shook his head. "No, but it's just a matter of time."

Cad seized upon that statement as a glimmer of hope. "If he's still alive then we still have a chance."

Zephyr looked up curiously at Cad. What could possibly be done?

Cad continued. "In Scorpyus's pack is the vial of Hyacinth Blue. Give Novak a dose." By Cad's tone he made it clear there was no room for discussion.

"It won't help," Doc said, trying to sound reasonable.

"We won't know until we try."

"The medicine could kill him instantly. We don't even know if we made it right. The whole idea is based on legend. The ingredients of the recipe could be lethal for all we know. I know mistletoe is."

Cad was insistent. "Novak will be a test case. What does he have to lose?"

"I suppose you're right. I'll give him a dose. I have Scorpyus's pack right here. I've been using his medicines."

Cad and Zephyr watched Doc measure out a dose of the blue liquid and pour it into Novak's mouth. He coughed as he swallowed. Everyone watched for a few minutes to see if anything happened. Novak displayed no change.

"Oh let it work." Zephyr sobbed.

"I have to check on other patients." Doc gathered up his tools and placed them in his medical bag.

On Doc's way out the door Cad remarked, "You did what you could." Doc nodded as he closed the door behind him.

Cad turned to Zephyr. "Thadus bloody well better hope Novak makes it; because if Novak dies, Thadus will follow."

"Why would you say that?"

"Thadus betrayed us." Cad stated with more than a hint of anger. Zephyr's eyes grew wide.

Cad explained. "Cyrus saw the whole thing. Novak was one swing away from ending this war. Reddland was finished. Thadus appeared out of nowhere and stopped him from killing Reddland. He jumped on Novak's back and held his arm while Reddland ran him through with a sword."

The news hit Zephyr like a charging horse. "I do not understand. Why would Thadus do such a thing? The rebels are his friends. Why would he want to jeopardize them or get us killed?"

"I don't care what his bloody explanation is," Cad stated firmly. "Does Scorpyus know about Novak?"

"No, he is sound asleep. He needs his rest. I was going to tell him after he wakes."

"That sounds good, Zephyr. Why don't you get Novak moved next to Scorpyus. We may need them both where we can find them if things get worse." Cad walked to the door then turned to Zephyr briefly before departing. "I wish I had never heard of Xylor."

"There you are," Cad hissed when he found Thadus in a side room that had once been an office. Isaac's desk was there along with several chairs stacked along a wall. Cad stormed across the room. Thadus stood in front of the desk and raised his hands, gesturing for Cad to stop.

"Now wait a second, Cad, I can explain."

"Shut your bloody mouth!" Cad backhanded Thadus and sent him sprawling over the desk.

Thadus scrambled to his feet and held a hand to his throbbing cheek. "I didn't want this to happen. Let me explain!"

Cad's fist slammed into Thadus jaw, knocking him into the stack of chairs. With a crash they came tumbling down all around, Thadus lost in the mix. "I said, shut your mouth! You betrayed us! And if Novak dies, I'll cut you to pieces and feed you to the blooming dogs. Now get on your feet!"

Thadus staggered to his feet and wiped his bleeding lips with the back of his sleeve. They were already starting to swell. There was a gap in his smile where a tooth had once been. "I swear, I didn't mean for Novak to get hurt."

"No, you were arranging for Reddland to give him a massage," Cad spat sarcastically. He advanced toward Thadus who scampered to the other side of the room.

Thadus pleaded, "If you'll just listen…."

"No! You listen!" Cad jabbed a finger forcefully at Thadus. "You lied! And we were helping you!"

Cad's fist slammed into Thadus and sent him reeling across the floor where he fell and lay dazed, cradling his mid section with his sprained wrist. Cad waited patiently for Thadus to shake the haze and get to his feet. He was in no hurry to dispense justice.

"We trusted you." Cad shook his head. "And you were working for Reddland the whole time. What's he promising you? Money? Women? A bloody title? I hope it was worth it."

"You don't understand," Thadus panted.

"Novak had beaten Reddland. In all likelihood this battle would have been over. But you rescued Reddland; it's pretty blooming simple to understand. You're a traitor, and now more people will die before this is over. Get on your feet or are you going to take your beating lying there like a snake?"

Zephyr appeared in the doorway, her eyes red from crying.

Thadus was relieved to see her. "Zephyr, thank God you're here. Talk some sense into Cad. Let me explain," he pleaded with Zephyr, hoping her influence with Cad would buy him the time to explain himself. His heart sank when she responded by closing and locking the door. She stood and glared at him.

"I had no choice…" Thadus' words were cut short by Cad's boot in his ribs.

Cad reached down and jerked the man to his feet. Thadus gritted his teeth in agony, his ribs on fire. Cad shoved him against the wall and drew back an arm.

With tear-streaked eyes Thadus shouted his final plea through bloody lips. "He's my brother!" Immediately a flood of tears and heaving sobs erupted from the broken man, his darkest secret now revealed.

The revelation froze Cad while he digested the information. Thadus stayed pinned to the wall, Cad's fist drawn back on the verge. Thadus sobbed, unable and unwilling to resist any further. He expected to feel knuckles crash into his face at any second. And he didn't care anymore.

Cad slowly turned toward Zephyr in disbelief. She too was in shock. Since their arrival in Xylor it had been one oddity after another.

Cad lowered his fist and released Thadus's cloak. "Reddland is your brother?"

"Yes, he's Bartus' and my older brother." Thadus started to regain some composure, and was visibly relieved to not have a fist aimed at him anymore.

"Why didn't you tell us before?" Cad asked insistently. Zephyr walked up.

"Where do I begin? In what seems like fifty lifetimes ago when I was a child, there were the three of us Raistlin brothers: myself, Bartus who is a year younger, and Luther who is two years older. We also had an older sister who died in the plague before the war." Thadus shook his head as if to clear his memory.

"Anyway, Luther was a rebellious teenager, cocky and disrespectful. He rebelled against our parents and started stealing. His poor attitude was only fueled by the fact that he was an extremely gifted swordsman and charismatic leader. He was good looking and had a way of making people believe in his dreams. The women loved him. Men flocked to him wanting to be part of his grand schemes. Even at the young age of sixteen, Luther commanded a small band of miscreants and was up to no good."

"Our parents were humiliated. We all had a very moral and godly upbringing. No one expected any of the Raistlin boys to turn bad. Still, our parents always tried to steer Luther right and prayed for him constantly. Isaac even talked to him, but it was futile. Luther wanted no part of a god that frowned upon his greed and thirst for more power. The final blow came one night when Luther hit my mother, busted her lip wide open. Father kicked him out of our home, and Luther set off on his own. He broke all contact with our family."

"Later we heard he joined an elite band of soldiers."

"He became a Ravenshire Knight," Zephyr injected.

Thadus nodded somberly. "Yes. I was as shocked as you were when Scorpyus told us that bit of news. I'm sorry for what Luther did to your fathers. You have every right to hate him. It looks like he stayed pretty true to his character."

"So then what happened?" Cad inquired.

"Then about ten years ago, he turned up in Xylor as our new count. He'd changed his name to Reddland. Luther was also more ruthless and full of hate than he had ever been. Clearly he was sinking deeper and deeper into wickedness. Bartus confronted him about it. Luther responded by seizing Bartus's farm and having his family killed, all on a false charge of not paying his taxes. Bartus was never the same after that." Thadus shook his head. "I thank God my parents weren't alive to witness what happened." Thadus lowered his head in shame. He wasn't sure what hurt him the most, the pain in his body or the pain in his heart.

Cad and Zephyr were dumbfounded at Thadus' story. They took several minutes to absorb the information fully. Cad's anger softened the more he thought about it. If there ever was such a thing as a demon seed, Reddland was it. Not only was he capable of killing strangers for as little as a wrong look, he had killed members of his own family.

Thadus could bare the silence no more. "So you see, even though I'm sorry and deeply regret what happened to Novak, I felt compelled to help my brother in some faint hope for him. I wanted to give him one more chance to repent. I thought Luther would be moved that someone still cares about his soul. Instead, he selfishly took advantage of my gesture by attacking Novak. I now realize my hope for Luther's redemption was vainly misplaced. He will never change. My only regret is what happened to Novak. I would gladly change places with him if it were possible."

There was another long moment of silence. Reddland was unrepentant and hell bound. The thought of a stranger in that lost state was a heavy burden; seeing one's own brother bound for hell had to be heart wrenching. As much as he didn't want to admit it, Cad thought he may have done the same thing had he been in Thadus' shoes. Those who knew the reality of hell were compelled to extend hope and prayers for those bound for it; and Reddland had to be the first in line. Thadus knew this.

Cad cleared his dry throat. "Well, I understand why you did what you did. If a man won't try to help a brother…" Cad left the sentence unfinished. He saw no use in reinforcing Thadus's conclusions about his own brother. Thadus wore that pain on his face like a mask.

Zephyr placed a hand on Thadus's shoulder. "You did what you could Monsieur. The Luther Raistlin you knew long ago was killed as a child. He was killed by this monster, Luther Reddland. Your brother was his first victim."

Thadus nodded somberly.

"And, Thadus," Cad waited until he looked up. "If I meet up with Reddland, and he insists on a fight, I'm going to do my bloody well best to kill him. I don't expect any less from the rest of the troops either. I want your promise that you won't interfere. If you don't think you can guarantee me this, we'll lock you away for your own safety. I can excuse you this once. But if you interfere again, it could cost you your life."

Thadus nodded. "Do what you must. Whatever happens to Luther now is his own choosing. I guess it always was. You won't have any trouble from me."

Stifled sobs echoed in the otherwise dreary quiet of the storeroom that had been converted into a hospital. Here, the rebel wounded were gathered on cots, beds, and tables, to either recover or pass on. Occasionally, a groan escaped one of the many injured soldiers. Novak had been placed on a table in a far corner next to Scorpyus. Scorpyus lay fast asleep on a rickety, old cot, a basin of water and a rag on the floor next to him.

Emerald sat by Novak's side praying and crying. There had been no change in his condition since taking the Hyacinth Blue.

Emerald was startled by Doc, whose foot scraped against the ground as he walked up to a soldier two beds away form Novak. She hadn't heard him enter the room. Doc paused at the foot of a soldier's bed as he walked by. Something about the soldier caught his eye. Doc went to the man and bent down, placing his ear by the wounded man's mouth. He placed his hand on the man's chest. After a few seconds he felt for a pulse on the side of the soldier's neck. Doc pulled the soldier's blanket up and over his face.

"I'll send someone in to get him," he told Emerald.

Emerald nodded, her stomach knotting. It was the second time Doc had done that in the past thirty minutes. Emerald looked at Novak and wondered if he would be next. She yearned to talk to him. Faced with the possibility of losing Novak, she realized she was in love with this knight.

Emerald sobbed and clutched Novak's hand and pressed her lips to the scarred knuckles. Why hadn't she told Novak how she felt when she had the chance? She coyly avoided the subject not wanting to get too close too fast. Along with the attraction came a fear that this too would be taken from her as so many other dreams had been. Emerald believed Novak shared her feelings. Now, he lay cool, pale, and motionless, his hand registering nothing of her grasp, or her kiss.

Perhaps the war, with its threat of imminent death, had brought them together so strongly so fast. Perhaps the times compelled people to cling to the few good things among a world full of death and horror. Emerald didn't know the reasons why, only that it had happened. And it had happened so unexpectedly.

Doc returned with two soldiers. They carried off the corpse of their dead comrade. Doc walked over to Emerald.

"Take your time here." Doc spoke in a soft and sympathetic voice. "But Reddland is forming up his men for another attack. I'm going to need your help to prepare for the next group of wounded."

Emerald nodded and released Novak's hand. "I'll be right there."

Doc smiled uncomfortably and left to give Emerald a last moment of privacy.

Emerald leaned down and whispered in Novak's ear, "I love you." After taking a few moments to regain her composure, Emerald left for the operating room.

Had Emerald stayed a moment longer, she would have seen the single, solitary tear slowly streak toward Novak's ear from the corner of his eye.

———— ·•·• ————

Downstairs, as soon as Thadus left the room, Cad began the next stage of his plan. "Zephyr, I need you to keep an eye on Thadus. He may have lost his resolve now that he's torn in his loyalties. He's got a lot on his mind right now and that makes him unstable. Who knows if he'll try something again? I know this is Scorpyus's forte, but he's wounded and you're the only one I know I can trust beyond a shadow of a doubt. Let's hope no one else has a relative with the Royal army."

"I will get the archers in place and brief them on what comes next. I was thinking of putting Rutger in charge. I know he is barely twenty but he has good instincts and he is a skilled archer. Anyway, my first two choices were killed in the last fight."

"I trust your judgment." Cad thought a moment wanting to be sure he covered all the possibilities. "Is Bartus still incapacitated?"

Zephyr nodded. "He is still with the other wounded. Reddland's men tortured him something terrible. He will not be going anywhere for a long while."

"I want to make sure. Reddland is his brother as well."

As Cad and Zephyr left the room, Cyrus came up to them. "Reddland is forming up his men for an attack. He's hewn another log to be used as a battering ram. Our archers are pinned down under a heavy barrage from the Royal archers!"

A loud thud shook the oratory door and echoed through the auditorium in confirmation of Cyrus's report.

"Alright, listen! Get all the men upstairs to the roof to the back side of the oratory. I've already got ropes in place. At my signal you know what to do."

"I'm ready," Cyrus said. "The fires are burning in the fireplaces. A barrel of oil is at the top of the stairs next to the caltrops. And I have a pile of oil soaked rags in a corner at the side of the stairs."

"Did you double check all the doors and windows?"

"Several times now; everything is ready."

"Good!" Cad released a sigh of relief. "Leave me a squad here… the oldest people we have. I have the women who were cooking helping me too. Leave me four or five swords for them to use. Did you get that spiked beam cut from the balcony and moved out of the way?"

"It's been taken care of, but I have one question. If you are only keeping one squad with you, wouldn't you rather have our younger and more adept soldiers? Our oldest sentries are in their sixties, and the cooks have no training or experience." Cyrus was puzzled.

Cad couldn't help but laughing. "Don't worry, mate. They won't actually fight if I have anything to say about it." Cad held up a hand. "Now don't take this wrong. I have nothing but respect for these people who are willing to risk their lives in defense of their fellow Xylorians. I just want the Royal soldiers who break through that door to think we are in a dire predicament and down to the last little bit of resistance we can muster. I want them to think we're scraping the bottom of the barrel."

XX

THE BROOMSTICKS CAD bound together to bar the oratory doors gave way to the battering in a matter of minutes, and Royal soldiers streamed into the oratory with swords drawn, ready to hack the rebels to pieces. When they saw Cad and his meager squad of defenders on the stairs it filled them with a surge of confidence. If this was the best the rebels had to offer, the battle was already won.

"They're retreating upstairs!" A Royal soldier exclaimed as he made his way through the obstacles of broken furniture.

"You men spread out and search the side rooms. The rest of you follow me! These old men and housemaids shouldn't take long!" Malvagio cackled and licked his lips in anticipation. He was right. The cooks were terrified and ran screaming up the stairs, one dropping her sword. Seeing they were vastly outnumbered, the older men weren't far behind.

Cad gave a signal, and a sentry at the top on the stairs departed on a predetermined mission. Cad backed up the stairs as Royal soldiers cautiously ascended after him and his retreating band of defenders. Other soldiers spilled into the oratory entrance while others searched the side rooms.

Cad bolted to the top of the stairs close behind his squad. He couldn't have planned it better. The cooks' genuine terror at the sight of advancing troops did the trick. There was no doubt as to their extreme fear. As predicted, their reaction bolstered the attacker's confidence. Cad regretted having to use the cooks in such a manner, but he needed to put on a convincing show. The cooks' expressions—bulging eyes with tongue-fluttering, wide-mouth screams was priceless. The cooks' total and abject fright was contagious. The elder rebel soldiers were sent into a panicked flight. It was more than Cad had hoped for.

He reached the top of the stairs. After he cleared the last step, he dumped over the barrel of caltrops, sending them tinkling down the steps. The first few pursuing soldiers impaled their feet on the small iron spikes of the caltrops. The ascent of the Royal army came to an abrupt halt while their wounded, hopping comrades got out of the way. The others would now have to carefully negotiate their way up the stairs as they pursued Cad.

"Those cowardly rebels!" Malvagio loosed a slew of curses for his predicament. With a howl of pain he pulled the sharp prong of a caltrop from the arch of his foot.

In order to add further to the confusion, Cad dropped a lit torch onto the pile of rags at the side of the stairwell. The oil-soaked cloth ignited. Royal troops continued to pour into the oratory as Cad closed the door at the top of the stairs. Immediately, he and the elder men braced the door shut with two-by-fours and pushed crates, furniture, anything they could get their hands on in front of the door to barricade it.

"Get the steps cleared!" Malvagio ordered and then watched as two soldiers swept the caltrops off the side of the staircase one step at a time. They tinkled to the stone floor below. Several unsuspecting soldiers at the side of the stairs stepped on the caltrops, not knowing they were in danger.

"Watch out along the side of the staircase! Caltrops are being swept down!" Malvagio responded to their shrieks of pain a little late. He limped to the banister and leaned on it, his foot burning with the pain of a deep puncture wound.

Lexton sprinted toward the oratory. The Royal physician had made a small incision near his elbow to cut the arrowhead from its shaft and remove it. He then pulled the shaft from the path it tore just under the skin of Lexton's forearm. The pain from the procedure left Lexton faint and bathed in perspiration. Halfway through his operation he heard the trumpeter sound the attack. He instantly put his bleeding arm in a sling, grabbed his helmet, and headed for the battle. What was Reddland doing launching an attack without him?

When Lexton arrived at the oratory steps all seemed to be going well. His archers had the rebel archers effectively pinned down on the catwalks. Infantry troops swarmed into the oratory unhindered.

"Nice of you to show up. I was about to have you arrested for cowardice," Reddland spat venomously at his senior officer.

Lexton was about to reply when Reddland's countenance turned from livid rage to wide-eyed disbelief. He turned to see scores of rebels running along the catwalks. Many others rappelled down ropes. They threw themselves at the surprised Royal soldiers, putting them on the defensive.

Panic shot through Lexton like lightning. A team of rebels led by Cad cleared the steps of Royal soldiers. Others closed the doors and roped the handles shut. They drove metal spikes into the crack between the doors to further wedge them shut. More spikes were driven into the doorjamb, and planks were nailed in place across both doors.

What are they doing? Lexton wondered to himself. When he saw the rebel archers stuff blankets into the chimneys, it became all too apparent.

"No!" Lexton yelled, feeling helpless.

"Don't just stand there, do something!" Reddland ordered and hit Lexton, desperation in his voice.

"Ahh!" Lexton bellowed and grabbed his limp blood-soaked arm after Reddland manhandled it.

"My arm, you idiot!" Lexton didn't stop there, but confronted Reddland for the first time in his career.

"Look what you've done now! You more than likely have just finished off your army! You couldn't wait! Your stupidity has cost you it all!" Spittle flew from Lexton's mouth and the veins in his neck bulged as he raged against Reddland.

Fear resurfaced on Reddland's face. "What, who, what do you mean?" he sputtered.

"Look!" Lexton pointed out the archers clogging the chimneys with blankets. Smoke was billowing out of the small cracks along the boarded up windows and door. Screams erupted from the oratory. The trapped Royal troops pounded on the door frantically trying to get out before they were overcome with smoke. Lexton threw his hand up in disgust at Reddland's paralysis at this time of crisis. His superior could only stare in disbelief.

Lexton ran toward the oratory steps and shouted orders to his troops. "We have to fight our way to the top of the stairs! Follow me!" He had to get that door open before his men were suffocated.

Lexton pulled his sword and with one arm led the charge against the rebels. Cad had placed his best men on the steps with orders to hold the line at all costs until the yells from the trapped Royal soldiers ended. After that they could abandon the doors.

A muffled whimper escaped Reddland's mouth as he saw black smoke billow from small crevices in the doors and windows. The screams from hundreds of frantic men echoed through the cool air.

Inside, the men turned on each other in a delirious panic, fighting for access to a window or door. Malvagio stabbed a few men with his dagger in his quest for breathable air. He was in the area with the thickest smoke. It didn't matter how many men he stabbed, the soldiers couldn't get out of his way fast enough.

Others followed Malvagio's lead as a sense of doom enveloped the trapped men searching for an escape that could not be found.

Reddland watched paralyzed as his hopes of a cure for his illness literally went up in smoke. His men were lost. Slowly their screams and pleas faded into the sickly silence of death. Several hundred of his men suffocated as he stood powerless.

His heart pounded in his ears and filled with a high pitched ringing, and his tongue clung to the roof of his mouth, dry and numb. What could he do now?

When the cries stopped within the oratory, the remainder of the Royal army knew the battle was lost. Surely the gods were angry with them. Many called upon Tanuba for deliverance. She never answered.

The rebels were emboldened at this shift in the atmosphere. They charged the Royal soldiers. Lexton rallied his men together. He could see they were wavering on retreat. In a grind of metal against metal the two armies clashed in a fierce battle, the rebels sensing victory, and the Royal army searching for survival. Sparks, dust, and blood flew in all directions.

In the twinkling of an eye a strange glow from overhead bathed the combatants on the oratory field, and a loud sizzling, hissing came from the sky. All the soldiers were shocked and paused to look skyward. An otherworldly sight stunned all who beheld it. A ball of fire streaked across the sky pulling a plume of flaming smoke behind it. It looked as if the moon caught fire and was shooting across the heavens. It started near the horizon and flew directly overhead, growing larger and louder by the second.

Horror filled the faces of the Royal troops. The remnant of the Royal army turned tail and ran like a herd of wild hogs. They couldn't get away from the flaming fireball fast enough.

For the rebels, the fireball signaled God's deliverance. He would finish the battle in glorious fashion.

Rebel archers fired parting volleys at the scattering Royal troops. The infantry were hot on their heels. On the oratory roof

Abrams tearfully dropped to his knees in thanksgiving. Victory had come at long last.

Lexton threw down his sword and raised his good hand in surrender. For him, the fight had been over since Reddland killed Marcus. He would now accept his fate like the true warrior he was.

Reddland refused to concede. He grabbed the reins of the horse of one of his fleeing men. "I'll take that!"

Reddland slashed his sword across the neck of the youthful soldier, and then shoved him from the saddle. He hoisted himself atop the mount, leaving the young soldier to bleed to death on the battlefield. Spurring on the stolen mount, Reddland trampled a few of his men in his desperation to flee.

Cad surveyed the scene with great satisfaction. All around the Royal troops were on the run. Many had surrendered. Other more stubborn ones were being dispatched in combat. Once word of the loss reached Reddland's compound, Cad was sure the Elite Guard would desert their posts and also flee.

Cad watched the fireball cross the sky and eventually disappear over the horizon. It was a moving experience. Then out of the corner of his eye he saw Reddland whipping his horse frantically, heading for the gate.

"Cyrus, take over here. I'm going after Reddland." Cad wasn't about to let Reddland escape. He jerked the nearest Royal soldier from his horse and set out after the man who had been the cause of all of this.

———•◦•———

A surge of terror sent a jolt through Reddland as if he had been gored by a bull. He didn't expect to see another rebel pursuing him, and so close at that. Until now he thought he had made an unnoticed departure from the chaotic battle. His armor-clad pursuer hunched low on his mount and heeled it onward with determination.

Reddland dug his spurs deep into his mount's side and whipped it with the reins. With a painful whinny the horse charged on, running frantically to escape the stabbing pain in its ribs. Reddland answered his mount's increased effort with more lashes. He steered his mount down a trail out of town, the water skin draped across his shoulder flopping vigorously. His pursuer followed.

Reddland jettisoned his saddlebags to lighten his horse's burden. He threw off his helmet. He tried frantically to reach the straps to loose his mount's armor, but couldn't reach them.

Cad was not going to lose Reddland. He had waited for this moment for as long as he could remember, waited to settle the score on his father's behalf. It was time to pay the piper, and Reddland had accumulated a large debt. Cad was bound and determined to collect.

Reddland turned down a small and slightly overgrown trail, beating his horse mercilessly. The gently-sloped path zigzagged around several large trees. Cad had not been on that trail before but surmised that it would eventually lead to the ocean if it continued in its present direction.

Reddland turned around in the saddle only to find his pursuer had closed some of the distance. Now Cad was close enough to be identified. Reddland's heart jumped into his throat.

Reddland kicked and beat his horse. The sweaty beast was frothing at the mouth and nostrils, nearing its limits of endurance.

The trail left the woods and emptied into a clearing a hundred yards from rocky bluffs overlooking the sea. Reddland heard the surf and smelled the salt air. The cool air felt good. He led his faltering steed along the shoreline looking for an escape. Cad was now a mere ten yards behind him.

Reddland reined his horse to a halt and dismounted.

Cad followed suit, eager for this moment. He had dreamed of this moment since he was a child.

Cad drew his sword as Reddland spat curses at his exhausted mount. He cast a few profanities at Cad as well. Dried blood was smeared on his forehead.

"You should have given up the chase earlier. Now your persistence shall cost you your life." Reddland's arrogance was still intact as he drew his weapon.

Cad threw his helmet to the side and squared off against his opponent. "No, Reddland, or should I say Raistlin; I think it is time for you to pay for betraying the Ravenshire Knights. They were your friends. You fought and bled alongside of them, then betrayed them."

"Whatever are you talking about?" Reddland circled Cad looking for an opening.

"Enough with the daft lies! We know you're responsible for our fathers' deaths. Scorpyus found a Ravenshire Knight signet ring in your room."

A mild look of surprise flashed in Reddland's eyes. "So you found out, did you? I anticipated you might. At any rate, you shall meet your end in the same manner as your father, squealing like a slaughtered pig."

Cad controlled his burst of anger. Reddland wanted him to lose control and lash out in a blind rage. Cad was determined to keep his wits about him.

"Now let's see if Basil Van Kirke's boy is as good as he was." Reddland laughed and left no doubt as to whether or not he knew who Cad was. With a jolt he swung at Cad.

Cad deflected the blow with his shield. "You recognize me then?" It was Cad's turn to be surprised.

Reddland smiled arrogantly. "I recognized you that first day before the battle. You're the spitting image of your father." Reddland swung again, and Cad deflected the blow with his sword.

"And if I had to guess, I'd say that big friend of yours was Oskar Reinhardt's son. Of course, he's already reunited with his father now isn't he?" Reddland cackled clearly amused with himself.

Cad released a flurry of blows, driving his opponent back. Reddland was slightly startled but blocked and deflected them all. He smiled at Cad, proud he had struck a raw nerve.

Cad quickly regained his composure, realizing he was playing right into Reddland's hands. Cad was going to need to keep his temper in check if he were to win this confrontation. Blind rage would be terminal.

Like a cobra and a mongoose, the two rivals maneuvered against each other, lashing out with their swords. Cad blocked a blow with his shield, and then brought his sword down hard on Reddland's clavicle. Even though he wore a cuirass, pain registered in Reddland's face. It was a fortunate shot. Cad seized the moment and brought his blade down again and again in rapid succession into his foe. The bone jarring vibration in his hilt told him he was striking metal, but nonetheless he had Reddland on the retreat. Reddland kicked up dust as he frantically backpedaled toward the cliff. Cad thrust his sword, catching Reddland just under the arm near the armpit. The tip was red when he pulled it back.

Reddland was worried but not panicked. He felt a bolt of pain through his clavicle, but the slash to his underarm caused no pain. He had lost all feeling in that appendage earlier. Assuming it was a scratch, he fought on.

Reddland blocked the follow-up blows he anticipated Cad to deliver. Years of experience had its rewards. His adversary was bolstered by drawing first blood and was showing no signs of letting up. Their swords slammed into each other in a clangor of sparks. Each could feel their ribs bruising under the blows to their cuirasses, especially Cad, who had been battered in the previous day's battles. Both groaned under the punishment they were dealt by the other.

Cad hammered away at Reddland but could not get a decent opening. The two scurried around the bluff, kicking up dust as they relentlessly attacked each other. Cad was amazed. He knew he wasn't leading his blows, and yet Reddland was staying half a second ahead of him. For nearly fifty, Reddland was still a formidable foe. His hard-learned lessons in swordsmanship and training with the Ravenshire Knights were showing. Cad would have to exhaust his opponent into making a mistake.

Cad feigned a blow, and then struck from the opposite side. Reddland judged him to be a better fighter than his father was, and his father was exceptional. Finally with much relief, Reddland saw the break he was looking for. He noticed that before Cad thrust to the chest, he feinted to the shield arm to draw that arm away from the torso. The move was fast and fluid, and hard to counter.

The next time Cad feigned a swing to the side, Reddland sidestepped in preparation for the inevitable thrust, and when Cad thrust for the chest, Reddland swung hard at his younger opponent's back and followed it with a blow to the front of the ankles. Cad tumbled to the ground, his sword clattering out of reach, caught off guard by the maneuver.

Before he hit the ground Cad knew where he had gone wrong and what he had to do to correct the situation. As soon as he landed, he tucked his shield in tight and rolled to the side. Reddland's sword slashed deep into the dirt where Cad had just been. Again Cad rolled, and again Reddland's sword slashed into the ground. Three more times Cad ate dirt as he threw himself to one side and then the other while dodging Reddland's blows. Attempts to retrieve his sword were futile. Reddland hacked away as fast as he could at his disarmed but elusive opponent.

Reddland anticipated Cad's next roll and brought his sword down onto his rival's cuirass. The force of the blow resonated through Cad's chest and momentarily dazed him. Reddland stood straddling his fallen foe. His next blow caught Cad on the arm. Cad gripped his bicep in agony, a two-inch gash throbbing in his limb. Through a grimacing squint, Cad saw Reddland raise his sword with both hands to drive it into Cad's neck above the cuirass.

When Reddland started to bring the sword down, Cad gripped his straddling opponent's ankles, and in one jerk pulled himself under Reddland, practically bringing his armpits onto Reddland's feet. The sword stabbed deep into the dirt where Cad's neck had once been. Quickly he grabbed the blade of Reddland's sword to keep him from taking another stab at him.

"Where's your god to save you now?" Reddland grinned sarcastically and jerked up on his weapon. Immediately Cad felt a stinging sensation on his right hand through the leather palm of his gauntlet. Warm droplets trickled down his wrist and arm.

Cad didn't reply but sat up and reached out with his wounded hand and grabbed the hilt of Reddland's sword. That blade was staying in the dirt if he had anything to say about it. Reddland tried to jerk his sword out of the ground and free of Cad's grip. Cad pulled down hard. Reddland started to smash down on his knuckles, but Cad's mail gauntlet protected the back of his hand from the attack.

"Do you think your stupid game is going to save your life?" Reddland spat vehemently. Keeping his right hand on the hilt of his sword, he pulled a dagger with his left.

Cad brought his foot up into the back of his straddling opponent and hit Reddland hard on the tailbone. Reddland lurched forward, surprised by the blow from the rear. He mistakenly turned to see who had struck him.

Cad seized his fleeting opportunity and curled his leg up bringing his knee to his chest. With all his might his kicked upward and struck Reddland hard in the crotch. Reddland flew backward, dropping both sword and dagger, his face crimson. A guttural groan escaped his contorted lips as his hands reflexively guarded his crotch from another hit.

Cad sprang to his feet, and sent a crushing uppercut to Reddland's chin. Reddland's head snapped back. Cad threw blow after blow, metal gauntlets crashing against flesh as he drove Reddland backward and downward. Each time Reddland got up, pain and punishment were there to meet him. He pummeled Reddland until his face was a bloody mess. Finally, Reddland collapsed to his hands and knees panting violently. Bloody froth drooled out of his mouth. Cad picked up his sword.

"Judas," Cad hissed, grabbing Reddland by the hair. With the tender jugular now exposed, Cad had every intention of sending this demon to the very pits of Hades where he belonged; but something held him back.

Vengeance is mine, saith the Lord. The familiar scripture echoed in Cad's mind. He had to remember and obey this many times before, that the Lord would avenge the wrongs committed against him and those he loved. It is what separated him from barbarians like Reddland. This time it proved to be much more difficult to obey than ever before. For a long few seconds, Cad held his sword to Reddland's neck just waiting for an excuse.

With a deep, regretful sigh, Cad reluctantly submitted again to the One who was really in control, and released Reddland's hair. "Get on your feet! You'll stand trial for all the murder and mayhem you visited upon the people."

Oh how Cad regretted not being able to kill Reddland in combat. What a miserable way for the fight to end. Reddland was clearly beaten and deserved to die more than any other man Cad had ever known. But by killing a beaten man, Cad would become like Reddland.

Reddland looked up through swollen eyes amazed at what he heard. "Thank you. You're a good man," he said through split and bleeding lips.

"Now hurry up before I change my mind." Cad knew the compliment about being a good man was nothing more than pretense. Reddland was a man who knew no true gratitude. He said, and did nothing, unless he felt he could somehow personally benefit from it.

Reddland remained on his hands and knees a moment to catch his breath. Cad patiently allowed him to wipe the blood from his nose and mouth with his surcoat. His nose was tender when he touched it, and slightly bent toward the left. At least Reddland got a broken nose out of the confrontation.

Reddland went on to wipe the sweat from his forehead, and take a long drink from the water skin he had slung over one shoulder. He poured some on his head, slicked back his thinning hair, and then got up on one knee. Again he paused and looked down, one hand rubbing his brow, still panting significantly. Reddland was taking his sweet time regaining his composure.

Cad's patience with the man was gone. "Get up!" He tapped Reddland's leg with his foot and held his sword at the ready.

Reddland nodded. Instantly he sprang to his feet and lunged at Cad. There was a flash of metal and Cad felt a pain in his abdomen just below his cuirass. Reddland, ever a deceiver, decided he wasn't going to cooperate with Cad's demand. With his illness, what did he have to lose?

Cad reeled backward clutching his lower abdomen. He saw Reddland with another dagger in his hand.

"You worthless piece…" The time for talk was over. If Reddland wanted to pit a dagger against a sword, that was fine with Cad.

Reddland grinned although he knew he didn't stand a chance of defeating Cad with a dagger. "Either way, you're dead too." He motioned to Cad's abdomen. "It looks mortal to me." Reddland smiled with deep satisfaction.

Cad flew into a fury. He swung his sword like a madman at the epitome of evil that stood before him. It was as if by Reddland's death the whole world could be made right. Reddland answered the barrage, feebly holding up his dagger in defense.

Reddland's dagger fell to the ground along with most of his right arm. Reddland stared horrified at his severed appendage, and then met his opponent's gaze. Cad briefly stared the devil of a man in the eye. And without hesitation, he swung his sword with every ounce of strength he could muster. Cad felt his blade sink into Reddland's neck, jerk slightly as it severed the spine, and then slash out the other side. Reddland's head thudded to the ground, a look of horror frozen on his lifeless face. His body slumped to the dirt in a heap.

For a second Cad could only stare, numb with disbelief that it was finally over. He had dreamed about this moment since he was a child. He thought that killing the man responsible for so much pain in his and his friends' lives would be a more joyous occasion. Instead Cad felt sick to his stomach. Even though Reddland left him no choice, it didn't make him feel any better. He was sick of the killing, sick of the death, and sick of the world.

Cad slowly sank to his knees. Now he knew what Scorpyus meant when he said how he wished he had been born in a better time.

With a groan, Cad removed his cuirass and lifted up his shirt. He had a deep slash across his left side. Upon closer inspection, he realized that it didn't penetrate below the flesh. Reddland had thrust the dagger in hard enough that the force caused Cad to step back to keep his balance. Then Cad saw his cuirass. About one inch from the bottom was a puncture in the metal.

A wave of emotion flushed over Cad. He had been through too much in the last week; in fact, far too much in his young life. Once again he survived the impossible. If there was any doubt in his mind that God was looking out for him, it was dispelled today.

Cad slowly gathered up his things and mounted his horse. He didn't have the strength to bury Reddland, and quite frankly didn't care if the vultures got him. If someone else did, he would let them know where to find Reddland.

Cad rode back to the oratory. He came to the conclusion that revenge was far from sweet.

XXI

BY THE TIME Cad, Zephyr, and Cyrus finished with the battle, Lieutenant Tiberious had set sail for Kelterland, taking the Elite Guard and many loyalists with him.

The first order of action was to find a place to hold the prisoners left over from the battle. They were placed in the dungeon at Reddland's compound along with Drakar and Tanuba's council of clerics until their fate could be decided. Tanuba worship was speedily outlawed.

Patrols were established to keep the peace. Rebel soldiers now guarded against the rash of pilfering that resulted from the chaos after the sudden change in government. Within the first week citizens came forward to volunteer their assistance. Scores of people who were once too afraid to join the rebels were now inspired to lend a hand. No comment was made about why they waited till now to come forward. Abrams felt it was better late then never.

The lifting of the dark veil of Reddland's regime breathed new life into the tiny island. People returned to their normal routines, albeit with the addition of a strange new feeling of joy. For the younger citizens it was a fresh new sensation readily welcomed. For the older ones it was reminiscent of days gone by, a fond memory of their youth.

Even the staunch Tanuba sect held their peace. Food was plentiful, good will abounded, and they were being left alone. Though they were greatly displeased with the closing of the Tanuba temple, and the removal of all references to and statuary of Tanuba from town, they couldn't argue that life was better. Still, some Tanuba followers left the island. No one tried to stop them. Others looked upon the rebels with a simmering hatred. Cad and the others could see the animosity in their eyes when they walked by. The rebel leadership would have to keep an eye on the potential for trouble brewing among the Tanuba loyalists. Every effort was made to treat them with respect and kindness. Angry about the removal of their stone idols, it would be a long road fraught with much political struggle.

Abrams reinstituted services in the open air of the compound until the oratory could be repaired. Many came out of curiosity to see the "new" religion. Some who came listened, believed, and accepted what they heard. Others returned repenting their departure. The congregation began to grow. Abrams welcomed all who came.

Thadus was named the new regent of Xylor by popular demand. He rejected the title of count on the grounds that Reddland had tarnished it.

The week following the rebel victory had been a time of welcome change met with enthusiasm. It culminated in the establishment of an eight-day celebration called the March Octave, a time of thanks for past deliverance and prayer for future guidance and protection. The feast commemorated the return of Xylor to God. It would also be a time to remember heroes and those who sacrificed their lives for their friends.

"They certainly aren't sparing any expense for this, are they?" Scorpyus was impressed but also embarrassed by the fuss being made over him and his friends. As far as the island was concerned, the Clandestine Knights were their deliverers sent to restore their land. No matter how many times Scorpyus or the others tried to credit God or the citizens who chose to fight for their land, the people insisted on giving them a place of honor. The Xylorians were grateful for all who helped, but held a special fondness for the knights who they believed were the key ingredient to their newfound liberty.

Scorpyus hobbled on crutches to the banquet table and was seated near the head between Cad and Zephyr. The discoloration around his eye looked much better. Novak, a tad pale, sat across from Emerald with Cyrus and Bartus. Thadus was at the head of the table. A server helped Scorpyus to his chair and took his crutches.

"It's about time you joined us, mate." Cad smiled and motioned to the huge crowd gathered in what had been Reddland's compound. Tables were placed end-to-end, making several eighty-foot rows of tables. Citizens were seated everywhere, and even crates were used as makeshift tables to accommodate all who came. With the beautifully hedged gardens in the background, the scene was majestic.

The celebration extended to every inn and restaurant in town. Citizens from Sage and the other small villages came for the festivities. During the eight-day celebration almost everyone made the trek to the compound, if for no other reason than curiosity. For ten years harsh justice had been dispensed from the premises. Many had seen their loved ones taken to the dungeons on the grounds never to return. Thadus didn't want his new government to be shrouded in secrecy. His first directive was to allow the people to have access to the grounds. All trials and hearings would be open to the public. Thadus had nothing to hide and wanted the people to know it. It went a long way to relieve the distrust and fear Xylorians previously held about such matters.

The Clandestine Knights were served first, a privilege of sitting with Thadus at the head of the table. The meal consisted of smoked pheasant and a lentil soup with fresh bread. The four couldn't remember the last time they feasted so well or had so much.

"Eat up, Novak; I tell you this; you need to regain your strength," Zephyr coaxed her friend to seconds.

"Don't worry about me. You're the one nibbling a hummingbird portion," Novak teased. Emerald sat beaming by his side.

Zephyr feigned vexation. "I see you are feeling better. You sure sound like your old self."

Novak couldn't help but laugh. When he did he held his side gingerly. "Ahh, don't make me laugh."

"Still a bit tender, I see," Cad noticed. "You scared me, Novak. For a while there I thought the reaper was coming."

Novak nodded appreciatively. "His sickle was drawn back. It's a miracle I'm here."

"I think Scorpyus blocked the sickle for you with his leg," Cyrus chimed in. A burst of laughter erupted from the table. Novak cradled his side again.

Scorpyus shook his head. "Only if the reaper looks like a forty five year old stable hand."

Cad had a bandage on his arm and his side still hurt, but it didn't impede his appetite. He cut himself another piece of bread and served up some more pheasant.

"Cad can still eat I see," Zephyr observed and received a round of laughter.

"Quit making me laugh," Novak teased while looking stern.

Zephyr eyed her three friends, noticing their various bandages and bruises. "If it wasn't for that panther, I think I would have fared the best." A red line on her neck marked where she had been grazed by an arrow. She had been fortunate. Three-fourths of her archers were wounded or killed.

"One thing I find unbelievable," Cyrus puzzled over, "is that Hyacinth Blue actually works. I didn't think Novak was going to make it."

Novak furrowed his brow. "You gave me Hyacinth Blue?"

Everyone paused to greet Abrams who was late to arrive. He helped himself to some food and silently said grace. When he finished, the others continued with their conversation.

"Yes we did. You were barely awake when Doc gave you a dose at Cad's request," Emerald beamed with relief that Novak would be alright.

"Not only that, but the others who were given Hyacinth Blue recovered also," Cyrus noted.

Novak didn't know what to say. He stilled had doubts about the existence of unicorns.

"The only problem," Scorpyus added, "Is that Hyacinth Blue should have little to no effect on wounds. It is for diseases. Aside from some pain relieving quality, there is nothing in the medicine for someone in Novak's condition."

"Maybe it was the tears of the unicorn?" Emerald pondered.

There was a moment of silence as the idea was pondered. No one knew what the effects of unicorn tears were on the medicine. Some still couldn't believe Zephyr's incredible story. She had, after all, been attacked by a panther and hit her head on a rock. Unicorn tears represented a faith in something not seen.

"I have an explanation." Abrams waited until all eyes were on him. "Novak recovered because God answers prayers."

"Amen to that!" Cad retorted. The others nodded in unison.

One of the servers had been listening intently to the conversation. A look of revelation came over the young man's face. "Is that your secret? I know your god is more powerful than Tanuba was." The server meant no ill will by his remark. He was just without understanding on the matter.

Abrams tried to explain, "You see, there is a big difference between us and Tanuba worshipers, as there is between us and all other religions. They have to perform acts or deeds to court the favor of their gods in order to earn a place in their heaven or get prayers answered. We, on the other hand, believe God gave His son as a gift and payment for our sins and shortcomings because, left to our own merits, we would fall short of earning any favor or meriting a place in heaven. Heaven is obtained by accepting the free gift. We perform good works out of gratitude for being forgiven, not to earn anything."

The server furrowed his brow. "It sounds too easy to be true." He turned to Cad. "Do you believe that?"

"Absolutely mate," Cad put down his fork. "If we didn't believe that we wouldn't have stayed to help the rebellion. This may not be our land, but anywhere there is a Reddland persecuting other believers, it becomes our fight."

"Let's have a toast to that!" Novak raised his tankard.

All seated at the table raised their cups in a toast. Even the server joined in.

The March Octave continued on with scores of citizens coming to the table to meet those responsible for their new freedom.

"They're making too much out of this," Scorpyus said, self conscious of the attention. He was uncomfortable in the crowd of well-wishers.

"I tell you this, the real heroes are those who never gave up hope and worked for the last ten years to bring about this day," Zephyr told the citizens.

"We couldn't have done it without your help," Thadus interjected and turned to Cad. "And I want to apologize for the incident the other day."

Cad made a stopping motion with his hand. "Now don't worry about that mate. I understand. It's all in the past now. I'm sorry for your brother." Cad knew Reddland's death was hard on Thadus. Knowing Reddland's final state would be hard on anyone.

"My brother chose his path willingly." Thadus's voice was breaking. "My conscience is clear. Luther knew I tried to help him till the end. And now he knows he was wrong. He'll have regrets forever. I try not to think about it."

Novak changed the subject. "Now you can build a better Xylor, Thadus. And we'll stay around to make sure you get off to a good start. The four already discussed staying in Xylor for a time. Kelterland would have a reprisal planned, and the Clandestine Knights couldn't leave the job half finished. They would make sure the new government was off to a good start so all that had been done not be in vain.

"And we can't thank you enough for your sacrifice. Lesser men would have left us on our own. That's why one of my first proclamations as regent of Xylor was to establish the March Octave. Each March, the people of Xylor will celebrate for eight days, commemorating this time, thanking God for His miraculous deliverance from oppression and remembering the four knights he sent to assist us. This year you are rightfully the guests of honor."

""Monsieur, you did not have to. We were glad to help," Zephyr added modestly.

"But if you must, we'd hate to disappoint the people." Cad feigned an air of importance that brought the table to near tears with laughter. It had been a long time since Xylor could laugh. And it felt good.

Epilogue

CINDERS POPPED IN the fireplace; flames hungrily consumed the logs amidst a sea of glowing ash. Embers pulsed with a throbbing orange glow casting nervous shadows about the small room. The huge stone fireplace had been blackened by years of use. A sheathed sword hung from hooks on the stone wall above the mantle, its handle bearing the signs and scratches of a long history of combat. A colorful but worn rug stretched across the wood plank floor in the center of the room.

The fireplace nestled in the center of the wall in a room that appeared to be a library. It was a twenty-by-twenty-foot room, modestly decorated with a few tapestries, and with a few books on a shelf along one wall. The books were of all sizes and shapes, many well worn from repeated readings.

A large table and four wooden chairs were centered in the room. There was a large black book with a pheasant feather bookmark sitting neatly on the table in front of one of the chairs. The leather cover of the book was worn. If the book once held a label with a title, it had long since worn off. The letters "ER" on the bottom of the front cover were all that remained of the original markings. An extinguished candle stood nearby in its holder.

In front of the fireplace an elderly woman swayed gently in a rocking chair, a quilt draped over her legs. She was thin with long gray hair pulled back in a ponytail. Her eyes sparkled with obvious contentment, and she looked to be at peace with this stage of her life. Her gently-wrinkled face indicated a life full of happy expressions. Though aged, she still had an air about her that gave one the impression she turned the heads of more than one man in her younger days.

Tiny weather-beaten hands poked out from lace cuffs on her burgundy cotton dress and clasped the ends of the chair's armrests. The wood had been worn smooth. She spoke in a soft reminiscing voice, a warm smile on her lips. Seated on the rug at the old woman's feet were three children, two girls and a boy. The girls were in their middle teens, one with long blonde locks, the other with curly brown hair. They both would keep parents frazzled during their courting years. The boy, the youngest, had short-cropped brown hair and was full of boyish charm. He was tall for his age and lanky, and fancied himself an avid hunter. All were enthralled by what the old woman was saying.

"So you see children, that's how the March Octave started a long, long time ago. It commemorates the first victory of the war. You children are coming of age and need to learn about our history, especially before all of my generation passes on. You'll carry on the tradition, and your children after you. We must never forget what happened before lest we repeat it." The old woman had come to the end of her story.

One of the girls spoke, clearly having enjoyed what she just heard. "That's incredible, Grandma. I never knew you met the Clandestine Knights."

The other children were equally impressed. They had come to visit their grandmother as they did each year during the March Octave. They always loved to hear the stories about the olden days when their grandmother was a young lady. But this was the first time she told them she had actually known the Clandestine Knights themselves. Everyone told stories, but few could tell them from first hand experience. Their rapt faces left little doubt as to their keen interest in this matter. The thought that their grandmother had actually known the legendary heroes was exciting.

"Where are they now, Grandma?" The boy asked enthusiastically.

The old woman paused a moment to reflect on the question. A certain somberness came over her as she looked toward the fireplace in reflection. Her eldest granddaughter thought she saw a tear well up in the eye of her grandmother. Before the elder woman could answer, the door to the library swung open. In walked a burly man in his mid-forties.

"Dad! Dad! Guess what? Grandma actually met the Clandestine Knights!" The young boy was eager to report his grandmother's claim to fame.

The burly man shot a knowing grin to the old woman. "Oh? Yes, your grandmother knew them quite well. She's been telling you stories, I see. That's good. She has a lot of them to tell. Your grandmother was right there with the Clandestine Knights during the war. She's a hero herself."

"Really, Grandma? You were in the war with the Clandestine Knights?"

The thought was so very exciting that the children could hardly keep still. All their lives they had heard the legends behind this momentous celebration, the March Octave. Each year they, as well as all the territories including Ravenshire and Xylor, took eight days each spring to reflect upon and celebrate their deliverance from a repressive, brutal, and Godless regime. One-fourth of the population died at the hands of that regime; many more died while fighting to regain their freedom. Overthrowing the tyranny was a huge victory that the people were never going to forget. The Clandestine Knights were looked upon as the catalyst that started the long road to freedom. They were beyond legends; they were looked upon as a miraculous band of deliverers sent by God to lead his people toward freedom in their time of need. The celebration was held on the date commemorating the rebellion's first victory in Xylor nearly fifty years earlier. It was an occasion that was worth remembering, and held dear in the hearts of all citizens of Ravenshire and Xylor.

The celebration also served as a tool to teach and warn the next generation about the dangers of apostasy. Turning from God to seek one's own ways held a terrible price. The reason the territories needed deliverance in the first place was a direct result of the previous generation's apostasy. Not everyone turned from God. All it took was a few, and silence on the matter of the rest. Now the citizens take the time to thank God for their blessings, and to teach the next generation how to sustain them. Those heroes who stepped forward and risked their lives to help make it all possible were remembered. Realizing their grandma played a part in the effort was the most exciting thing the children ever heard.

"Now, children, I do believe your father is exaggerating just a wee bit there. Granted, I was present at that first battle that began the road to restoration of the land; and there were more than a few setbacks, mind you. But to say I was a hero..." The elder lady chuckled modestly. "To say that is stretching the imagination."

The children's father burst in. "Now hold it right there. Children, don't let your grandmother tell you otherwise; she's being far too modest. She was right there in the thick of the revolution with the Clandestine Knights, Abrams, Thadus, and the others who answered the call to fight for the freedom we enjoy today. In fact, here's something we've never told you children yet. We've been waiting until you'd grown so you could have as normal of a childhood as possible. But not only did your grandmother know the Clandestine Knights, she was..."

The elder woman boldly interrupted. "Now hold on, Jakob! I thought we agreed not to tell the children until they were older. We wanted them to wait until they had grown before we let them in on the secret. We didn't want them to face the 'difficulties' that you and your siblings had when you were youngsters. Your daughter is two years shy of eighteen, and your son has eight to go."

The burly man winked at his mother with a sly smile on his face. "I think it will be all right. Enough years have passed now."

The children took their cue from their father. "Tell us! Please tell us, Grandma! Tell us oh, please tell us! We won't tell anybody else, we promise!" The children begged for the information like puppies.

The elder woman smiled lovingly at her grandchildren. "Well, I suppose I'll have to now that your father has let the cat out of the bag. I don't think we'll get a minute of peace otherwise."

An excited squeal erupted from to children. Their eyes lit up with anticipation like it was Christmas morning.

"Gather around and listen. I'm not inclined to repeat myself, so you'll want to listen closely." The older woman motioned for the children to gather around her. "Now what I'm going to tell you I don't want you to go around repeating to just anybody. It has the potential to bring trouble. This is something you'll want to only tell your closest friends and your spouses."

A seriousness graced the children's countenances as they listened with rapt attention to their grandmother's every word.

Jacob crossed his arms and leaned against the wall.

The old lady brought the children in real close to her, looking each in the eye one by one, and whispered to them in a soft and soothing voice

Jakob watched the excitement register on his children's faces as his mother revealed a family secret.

The old woman's grandson voiced his excitement. "Oh boy!"

"What happened next?" The girls chimed in.

The old woman grew silent for a moment and looked toward the floor lost in thought. Jakob knew his mother was reflecting on the many memories she held about her youth. Even though she had many fond recollections, there were painful ones as well. Her youth had been spent in a time of war.

After a somber silence the elderly woman looked again to her grandchildren, a warm smile now on her face and a misty look in her eye. The children still registered the excitement of the news and wanted to hear more. She was pleased to see her grandchildren so happy and proud. She couldn't help but think of how proud her husband would have been to see this moment had he been living.

"Tell us more, Grandma. What happened next?" Her eldest granddaughter respectfully asked.

"It's getting late." The old woman looked lovingly at the three eager faces. "We'll save that for another time."

About the Author

A FTER SERVING IN the U.S. Air Force, Tony Nunes graduated from California State University, Chico. He resides in northern California with his family and is currently employed as an officer in the California Highway Patrol. This is his first book in the Chronicles of the Clandestine Knights series. Also available is book two in the series *Curse of the Valkyrie.*

COMING IN THE FUTURE

---◆•◆•◆---

**Look for the third book in the Chronicles of the
Clandestine Knight series:** *Hellbourne Manor*

This book finds the knights venturing to the dreaded Ethereal
Region; a land shrouded with mystery and legend. Little is known
of the Ethereal Region, but what is known is to be avoided. It is a
land where some say the very wind groans out a warning, where
mysterious noises and wailing screeches can be heard in the
distance. It is a land filled with strange tales; tales of a barbaric
people called Trepanites, and a misty dead forest. It is a place
where most dare not go.

   The long lost heir to the throne of The Dales disappeared,
and with it the hopes of the rebellion. The Clandestine Knights
are called upon to find the heir. It is a task by which the very
balance of the war hinges. Once again Cad, Novak, Scorpyus, and
Zephyr find themselves in harms way. In order to track down the
missing heir, they must travel to the Ethereal Region and find
the lair of an evil warlord. But doing so will require unwavering
bravery, and the utmost intelligence. The knights must overcome
many perils and sift through many myths. They must confront
one of the oldest legends known to the world; that of the Holy
Grail.

   Join the knights on their next adventure…if you dare!